Praise for the Author…

Historic Novel Society:

"…Haviaras handles it all with smooth skill. The world of third-century Rome—both the city and its African outposts—is colourfully vivid here, and Haviaras manages to invest even his secondary and tertiary characters with believable, three-dimensional humanity."

Amazon Readers:

"Graphic, uncompromising and honest… A novel of heroic men and the truth of the uncompromising horror of close combat total war…"

"Raw and unswerving in war and peace… New author to me but ranks along side Ben Kane and Simon Scarrow. The attention to detail and all the gory details are inspiring and the author doesn't invite you into the book he drags you by the nasal hairs into the world of Roman life sweat, tears, blood, guts and sheer heroism. Well worth a night's reading because once started it's hard to put down."

"Historical fiction at its best! … if you like your historical fiction to be an education as well as a fun read, this is the book for you!"

"Loved this book! I'm an avid fan of Ancient Rome and this story is, perhaps, one of the best I've ever read."

"An outstanding and compelling novel!"

"I would add this author to some of the great historical writers such as Conn Iggulden, Simon Scarrow and David Gemmell. The characters were described in such a way that it was easy to picture them as if they were real and have lived in the past, the book flowed with an ease that any reader, novice to advanced can enjoy and become fully immersed…"

"One in a series of tales which would rank them alongside Bernard Cornwell, Simon Scarrow, Robert Ludlum, James Boschert and others of their ilk. The story and character development and the pacing of the exciting military actions frankly are superb and edge of your seat! The historical environment and settings have been well researched to make the story lines so very believable!! I can hardly wait for what I hope will be many sequels! If you enjoy Roman historical fiction, you do not want to miss this series!"

Goodreads:
"… a very entertaining read; Haviaras has both a fluid writing style, and a good eye for historical detail, and explores in far more detail the faith of the average Roman than do most authors."

SINCERITY IS A GODDESS

A Dramatic and Romantic Comedy of Ancient Rome

THE ETRURIAN PLAYERS
BOOK I

ADAM ALEXANDER HAVIARAS

Sign-up for the Eagles and Dragons Publishing Newsletter and get a FREE BOOK today.

Subscribers get first access to new releases, special offers, and much more.

Go to:
www.eaglesanddragonspublishing.com

For Angelina,
My true love, and my best friend…

SINCERITY IS A GODDESS

A Dramatic and Romantic Comedy of Ancient Rome

DRAMATIS PERSONAE

Felix Modestus - popular actor, director, producer, and leader of The Etrurian Players. He is responsible for much of this.

Rufio Pagano - Felix's boyhood friend who is always out-of-sorts and has never left Etruria.

Clara Probita - Felix and Rufio's childhood friend. A young widow who never let go of her dreams, or her sense of guilt.

Electra - leading lady of The Etrurian Players, as well as Felix's concubine. Do not get in her way.

Silas - the parasite and financial manager of The Etrurian Players who is also obsessed with Felix.

Julius - the well-respected veteran actor of the company.

Fausto - the newest addition to The Etrurian Players. He is young, handsome and shows a lot of promise.

Castor and Pollux - two brothers who were tradesmen but decided they wanted to be actors. They like to drink.

Damon - a muscly mute who can play the flute. The strong, silent member of the company.

Beatrice - the company's seamstress and makeup artist. She also acts, and is easily embarrassed.

Sextus Annius Sabinus - the wealthy Roman official who is in charge of putting on the Games of Apollo in Rome. He loves theatre!

Leno - a loan shark who keeps company with goons. You do not want to get involved with this guy!

Numonius - one of the best offering sellers in Rome. He always seems to be in the wrong place at the wrong time. Or, maybe not.

Astarte - a rather large, scantily-clad street priestess, or beggar, depending on your point of view.

Longus - a famous poet and author who is in Rome for the Games of Apollo. He is also a friend of Felix Modestus.

Errol - Rufio's old, inherited servant and the only worker on the dilapidated farm.

Meretrix - a cheerful prostitute who helps steer Rufio in the right direction. She knows what is going on.

Emrys - one of the best sculptors in the empire. His workshop is next to Felix's base of theatrical operations.

Peli - a happy, but extremely naughty dog that attaches himself to Rufio. Maybe the Gods know something we do not?

Youth ages, immaturity is outgrown, ignorance can be educated, and drunkenness sobered, but stupid lasts forever.

— ARISTOPHANES

PROLOGUS

Mortals are amusing to the Gods, make no mistake. To think otherwise would be to miss out on one of the great mysteries of this world. True, the Gods toy with them, manipulate and encourage them. They guide them toward their destined paths and then leave them to their own devices.

However, just as a horse cannot be made to drink, so too the Gods cannot always force mortals to place one foot before the other upon a destined course of action.

Mortals also frustrate the Gods who watch from lofty Olympian heights. They dawdle and rove, piling error upon error, ignoring what is plain and obvious to immortal eyes. Dreams, omens, and portents are not always of use, for mortals have ears only for what they wish and what is most easy. They have eyes only for what is directly before them. Oh yes, they are an endless source of frustration and bewilderment.

And yet, like errant children who heap mistakes upon misfortune, having ignored divine grace and intent, they are often welcomed back anew.

They are often the creators of their own suffering, and the Gods are the arbiters of that great stage upon which humanity plays itself out.

However, heroes do rise up and, on occasion, even Olympus takes notice and applauds. Boldness among mortals does indeed earn Fortuna's favour.

It is a mad world that mortals inhabit, but when Love and Happiness burn brightly in hearts and minds, then those are moments to be cherished. Those moments are often missed, or ignored, but they are there, and repeatedly, for the Gods do have a weakness for their mortal children. They do not wish to see the death of any man, woman, or child's genius, though it often happens.

Thus, Sincerity is perhaps the most important of all, when it comes to mortals and their ways, for she is a beacon upon the dark road they tread upon the Earth.

What follows is the story of three friends who lost sight of Sincerity's beacon and of each other.

As has been stated, however, we welcome back our children, for love, for laughter, and not a little entertainment. And so, these three wanderers are brought back together for another chance at their destined lives…

ACT I

THEIR SHADOW LIVES

THE BRAGGART'S DREAM

2 03 CE

I T WAS A NEW YEAR. J ANUS' DOOR HAD ONLY JUST OPENED ONTO a fresh array of opportunities there for the taking. In the dim winter light of that new day, when marble was more grey than white, and the sky a paler blue than Thracian eyes, the streets of Ephesus were unusually quiet. The revels of the long night had only just recently faded, and masters and slaves alike dozed in wine-soaked slumber wherever - and with whomever - they had fallen.

In a richly-adorned domus on the hill above the great theatre, the scent of eastern incense and Gaulish wine still lingered in the air and pooled upon the mosaic floors of every room where bodies lay in tangled heaps, as if in the aftermath of a great battle. It was in one such room that the company of actors from the previous night's much-lauded performance lay scattered with other guests upon the couches and cushions of the long, gilded triclinium.

It would have been difficult to ascertain where one person ended and another began, for Bacchus had shown no mercy the previous night whilst Eros fired indiscriminately into their riotous ranks.

From beneath a particularly tangled pile of bodies surrounded by low-burning braziers, Felix Modestus, the owner and great captain of The Etrurian Players, as they were known, opened his eyes groggily from beneath the trellis of naked limbs under which he found himself. Without moving, he took stock of his surroundings. There were the twin flute girls who had played upon various pipes the whole evening. There was the Nubian acrobat, whose great skill had so bewitched them all, and the female slave of the rich merchant and his mistress whose domus it was. The hosts lay entwined with the others, not having been spared the effects of the excellent vintage.

Felix Modestus lay there, still, buried beneath the colourful array of his fellow celebrants, and it reminded him of how, as a youth, he would bury himself beneath the autumn leaves amongst the rolling hills of his home in Etruria.

That thought of home reminded him of something, and he began to panic as he sought to remember.

I had a dream!

Beside him, his concubine, Electra, groaned and wrapped her body about his.

Felix turned, looked at her and smiled, but the thought of his dream drew him back.

From his other side, a flatulent echo burst from the grey buttocks of Silas, Felix's slave who was also the company's account manager. He was good with numbers, but it never failed that Silas would sidle up to Felix mid-debauch, only to be pushed away.

With a thick arm, not easily freed, Felix reached up and pushed at the full moon so that it tumbled from atop the mound of bodies to roll beneath a nearby table.

His broad chest began to rise and fall more strongly then, and his eyes darted.

Such a dream! Etruria…a play… The threads of his reverie began to reveal themselves slowly, and the more his mind pulled at them, the more the whole of the plot unravelled.

Felix Modestus was not usually one to panic, but in that moment of remembrance, he did. He pushed up with his muscular arms to clear a path, his eyes locked on the soaring Corinthian columns of lapis and gold, and rose up from the fleshy mound like a naked Hercules.

All about him, people groaned at his action, but they fell back into their inebriated slumbers upon the floor and couches.

Sensing her missing dominus, Electra sat up, her long dark hair falling about her shoulders, and her sleepy, dark eyes seeking his. "Why are you so awake?" she whispered. "What is wrong?" she asked, seeing the wild look in his brown eyes.

Felix did not answer her, but took her extended hand and pulled, raising her up out of the fleshpot. Searching the couches, he found his red and gold tunica and marched over the celebration's detritus of bodies and broken crockery toward the flapping curtains that led onto a balustrade overlooking the city. There, he relieved himself over the edge, his mind swimming. When finished, he slid his tunica over his head and scratched at his thick beard in thought. He leaned on the railing, his eyes falling over the theatre of Ephesus where he had received the greatest of applause of his career; *Lysistrata* was always a crowd-pleaser and Electra, as usual, had outdone herself with her performance, despite her protestations that they should have performed a tragedy.

Felix shook his head and tore his eyes away from the theatre below. His head reeled from the vast amounts of wine he had drunk, the spinning, the dancing, the social intercourse he had upheld long into the night. His mind stretched into the fog of that winter morning to search for the dream. He gazed at the risen sun in the distance and there, then, he began to remember.

He felt Electra come up to him, her naked body pressed against his muscular bulk.

"What is it, Felix?" she asked.

"The Gods sent me a dream last night…or was it one god in particular? I don't know!" He did not look at her, but stared out over the Ephesian streets that had been so raucous the night before, but which were now supremely silent. It was eerie and discomfiting, and if Electra had not been by his side, he might have thought he was still dreaming. "I dreamed that… No… It can't be!"

"What?" Electra pressed, her voice growing impatient. "What did you dream? Are you still drunk?" Electra stepped back. "It was that flute girl, wasn't it? She kept pressing the cup to your lips and-"

"Stop it, woman!" Felix barked. "Let me think!" He paced along the balustrade a couple of times, then stopped and looked at Electra.

She smiled at him.

"There was a letter!" he said quickly. "Someone gave it to me after the performance last night!"

Her smile faded. "Yes," she confirmed. "The letter from Rome. From the…adu…lite… I think."

Felix shook his head. "From the *aedile!*" he over enunciated the word for her benefit. "I told you to leave Latin alone in the mornings. Stick with your Greek!"

"If you don't speak nicely to me, I will withhold my favours like Lysistrata!" she threatened.

"Whatever shall I do?" he said dramatically, sweeping his hand over the naked room behind them. "I need that letter!" he said before rushing back inside and searching for his belongings in a far corner beside an errant couch. "Gods, what a night!" he said as he spied his mute stagehand, Damon, sleeping bent over the edge of the couch with his own aulos protruding from his arse. Felix yanked the instrument out and tossed it onto cushions before rummaging through the satchels in the corner. There he found his own and pulled the papyrus scroll free. He unrolled it again and leaned in close to a nearby brazier the better to see. Felix mumbled as he read, his eyes scanning the words. When he finished, he felt his heart pounding within his ribcage.

"Did you find it?" Electra said as she approached, now wearing a long robe she had picked up from the floor. "Felix?"

He looked at her, his face white, his eyes wide as his massive shoulders rose and fell.

"Tell me of your dream," she said.

He wanted to. Electra always had a knack, a gift really, for deciphering the Gods' messages in dreams. This time, however, he was shaken. "The Gods have given me a warning."

"What warning?" she pressed, reaching out to place her long, lithe hands upon his chest to calm his raging heart. "Tell me," she whispered, kissing his cheek.

Felix Modestus stared out to the sky and, with the letter grasped in his hand, made his way across the New Year's battlefield. Once outside, he could breathe the fresh air and feel the emergent sun.

Electra followed and they both stood looking out once more.

"I think it was a goddess…or a god… I don't know!" He was frustrated and flustered, but he pressed on. "They told me I am to go to Rome. I must."

"The invitation in the letter from the…aedile?" she forced herself to say the word correctly, and that calmed him.

"Yes. I must accept. I must put on a specific play…a comedy-"

"Not another comedy!" she protested. "What play?"

"Shhh!" he put up his hand, trying to find the words. "I can't? It won't be possible!" he said to himself.

"You are the greatest actor in the empire, Felix. There is no play which you cannot successfully put on. Why are you so scared?"

"It's just… It will be very awkward in many ways. But the Gods have clearly shown me. This performance in Rome must be perfect in every way. Exactly as they have directed."

"They showed you the outcome?" she asked, her voice hesitant now as she touched the mati necklace about her neck, the eye that watched over her always.

"The Gods have told me exactly what I must do," he said. "If I don't…" He stopped speaking and looked into her eyes. "If I don't…then I will die."

They were both silent for a few moments, robbed thoroughly of speech.

Electra stood tall then, for she could see he needed her strength. She held his face in her hands. "I don't want to lose you. Whatever the Gods want from you, you must do it. You *can* do it!"

He nodded. "I must write letters at once!" Energized once again, he spun and went back into the triclinium where the household slaves were starting to clean around the prostrate bodies, trying not to laugh at the compromising positions in which the guests were found, or nibbling at the remnants of the feast, emptying the leftover cups of their residuals.

Felix found their host, the rich merchant, and bent down to speak to him. "I need to use your tablinum to write some letters urgently," he said, trying to shake the man awake.

When the merchant did not move, Felix erupted. "Your tablinum, man! Where is it?" Several people jolted awake, including the merchant who turned over and vomited.

Wiping his mouth, the merchant looked up at the man

standing over him. "It was a wondrous performance last night," he said.

"Of course, it was!" Felix bellowed. "Now, your tablinum. Where is it? I must write!"

The merchant snapped his fingers at one of his nearby slaves. "Show Felix Modestus to the tablinum and give him whatever he needs."

"Yes, Dominus." The slave boy bowed unnoticed by his master who fell back to the ground. He then turned to Felix and Electra. "I will show you the way."

They followed the slave out of the triclinium and down a corridor to the peristylium garden where more party-goers slept upon the grass or leaned against the citrus trees. One man splashed his face in the fountain whilst a likeness of Cupid urinated onto his bald head. On the other side of the gardens they crossed the atrium and came to a large, bronze door which the slave opened for Felix.

"There are papyrus sheets, styli and ink upon the table," the slave said.

"Good," Felix replied. "Now, summon a courier for me and gather some coin to pay the man."

"Of course," the slave said before running out. He knew his master would do anything requested by Felix Modestus now, for in receiving The Etrurian Players in his own home, he would be the talk of Ephesus.

Felix sat down at the table while Electra poured water and wine from a silver pitcher into golden cups that sat upon the broad surface of the yellow marble table.

Felix spun his seal ring with the masks around his finger a couple of times. He dipped the stylus into the ink pot and, for a moment, his shaking hand hovered above the page. Then, he began a furious scribbling and did not stop for some time.

As Electra watched, she wondered what god or goddess

had spoken to him in such a way as to set so blazing a fire alight beneath him.

SOME TIME LATER, AFTER THE LETTERS, AND NO SMALL AMOUNT of the merchant's coin, had been given into the hands of a courier, Felix and Electra entered the triclinium once again to find their company still lying about.

"Gods, what a motley bunch," he muttered. "Apollo hide your eyes from such poor players as these." Felix waded into the middle of the room. "Wake up!" he shouted, his deep, bellowing voice echoing off of the columns and painted cedar ceiling. "Get up, all of you! Now!"

Felix went about, slapping faces, and kicking bodies he recognized. "Julius, Beatrice…" he called to the old veteran and his seamstress who were already dressed and eating at one of the tables. "Help us get everyone up."

"Yes, Dominus!" Beatrice said, helping the aged Julius up from his stool.

"Castor, Pollux!" Felix threw an orange at the two brothers who were tangled up with several women. "Fausto!" he called to the youngest member of the company. "Rouse Damon for me!"

"Yes, Dominus," Fausto groaned, brushing back his long hair from his face and searching for his tunica among the previous night's companions.

"Silas!" Felix shouted at the actor and account manager. "Get up, Silas!"

Silas turned his jaundiced face and bulging eyes to look up at Felix and smiled. "What a night," he groaned. "A great victory, Felix."

"Of course it was. But now, we are for another battle!" Felix roared.

"Can we not sleep a bit longer?" Castor said.

"No! You may not!" Felix bellowed, supremely impatient now. "Get up or I will sell the lot of you!"

More quickly now, the company rose and dressed, and wiped the sleep from their eyes as the other guests rolled over and went back to sleep, or slinked off to the latrines, anything to save their aching heads from the angry man in their midst.

Once the company were all on their feet, swaying where they stood before Felix and Electra, Silas spoke up. "What's amiss, Dominus?"

"Yes, tell us," Pollux added, confusedly pulling long strands of blonde hair from his dark beard.

Felix, his arms crossed, looked over his group of gathered players and shook his head. "Look at you..."

The group looked at each other, their dishevelled hair, the stibium-streaked faces, and the strong but slow Damon who had not yet found his tunica.

"You look like you just came out of a tavern brawl, the lot of you..."

The cast lowered their heads, all of them but Silas who furrowed his grey brow.

Then, Felix smiled. "You look like you brawled...and WON!" He began to laugh, his thick shoulders rising and falling as he looked upon his hearty crew. "You all performed excellently last night. Congratulations!"

There were a few sighs of relief, smiles all around, nudges and nods.

"But," Felix continued, "it will not be enough for our next production."

"What do you mean?" Julius said, brushing back his grey and blond hair and pinching the bridge of his thin, aquiline nose. "As the veteran here, I thought we did supremely well, especially Electra," he smiled at her, but Felix held up his hand.

"It was fine, but not perfect. Not nearly enough for what comes next."

"What is next?" Silas asked, his big eyes more alert now.

"The Etrurian Players have been invited to perform in Rome during this year's Ludi Apollinares!"

The company gasped, their aches and spinning heads quite forgotten.

"We're going to Rome?" Fausto said, hugging Beatrice beside him.

"That's right!" Felix said. "And it will be the performance of our lives!"

The company burst out in excited chatter, for it was something they had all wanted and dreamed of as they travelled to, and performed in, the cities of the Middle Sea.

"So," Felix said above their hubbub. "Gather your things, and get to the baths to wash last night's wine and celebration from your bodies! We leave for Rome on the first ship available! Quickly, there's no time to waste!"

"IO! IO!" they all shouted, as Damon jumped about naked, his flute in hand, ready to play them a tune for dancing.

"Damon!" Felix called out to the mute. "You may want to wash your reed!"

II

A WIDOW'S HOPE

It had been a mild winter on the plains and hills outside of Syracusae that year. The tang of the sea could be tasted on one's lips. It mingled with the bitter smell of the olive presses that dotted the land between that ancient bastion of Hellenism all the way to the slopes of angry Etna far to the North.

Not a few merchants had found enormous success in Sicilia, with easy access to the sea, but enough distance from Rome to more easily avoid certain political figures eager to tax others' success. Sicilia was a world unto itself, and Syracusae more so. It was beautiful, and ancient, and very proud. Those who called it home rarely thought of leaving.

But Syracusae had never truly been home to Clara Probita. People whispered in agora and upon the temple steps of Syracusae that she was the youngest widow they had ever seen. Some believed she had worked her much older husband to death in the cubiculum of their vast villa near the sea, and others wagged their tongues in saying that she had poisoned his olives.

None of the rumours were true, of course, but during the Winter in Syracusae, people needed to entertain themselves, and that entertainment, more often than not, took the form of cruel gossip.

Clara Probita, however, paid them no mind. She had never been a local, and never felt welcome.

On that temperate day in Februarius, she sat upon the terrace of her large, lonely villa gazing out to the cold blue sea, retracing the steps of her life, and finally allowing herself to indulge in the remembrances she had for so long tucked away. Wrapped in a long woollen cloak, she sat upon a cushioned couch, sipping golden wine from Samos from a silver cup, dipping wedges of apple into the sweet nectar. The wind played with the strands of her slightly-curled, golden hair which she occasionally brushed aside. Her wide, inquisitive, grey eyes took in the details of her surroundings, but what they truly sought in that moment were the green and gold hills of Etruria and the once-happy memories that she had previously exorcised from her mind.

Clara had been the only daughter of an Etrurian trader who was, and always had been, supremely disappointed in having been given a sole daughter, and losing his wife in the birthing of that same daughter. He had made it known to her throughout her youth, and so, after an escapade in Rome in which she had run off with her two best friends - the worst sort of people, according to her father - he had sold her off to an older trading partner of his in Syracusae.

There had been a time when Clara would have fought that. She was never one to give way in an argument. But things had happened in Rome during her brief escapade that encouraged her to accept her father's commands. She had surrendered, and never been comfortable with it, no matter how much she felt she deserved it.

The Gods, however, had been kind to Clara in that the man she had been fobbed off on turned out to be kind of heart and gentle of speech. Much more so than her own father. Her new husband, a successful Syracusan olive merchant by the name of Aeson, had met her in Pisae one year when she happened to be there with her father for his dealings. Aeson, a childless widower himself, saw how cruel Clodius Probito was with his lovely daughter and so, after that encounter, put forth a proposal to marry the young girl without the need for a dowry.

Clara's father jumped at the offer and was at last rid of the unwanted girl who did nothing but remind him of his dead wife.

What Probito did not know, however, was that although officially Aeson had married Clara, what he really had gained was the daughter he had never had but always wanted. He explained as much to Clara on their journey from Pisae to Syracusae and she, somewhat relieved, acquiesced to the arrangement he proposed. In public, they would act as husband and wife, but at home, she would be his daughter, learning all that she could from him about the trading and farming operations that had made him a very rich man.

After three years, Aeson died peacefully in his bed as Clara held his hand. Despite what the locals said, no lustful acrobatics had taken his life, nor the tang of poisoned olives. It had been old age. Nothing more. But Clara took comfort in the fact they had made each other happy for a time, in a familial sort of way, and she had been there to hold his hand as he passed gently into Elysium.

At first, Clara had only felt shock and sadness. She believed the Gods were punishing her for past actions and betrayals which she rarely visited in the confines of her mind. After a period of mourning, however, she took it upon herself to honour Aeson's kindness and ensure that his legacy thrived, for he had left everything to her - the business, the land, the villa, the ships, servants - everything. He had made her a very wealthy woman, and yet, she was never comfortable with the idea. She had never wanted to be a trader, though she made a success of it, emboldened by the fact that under Roman law she could keep the lands, business and money bequeathed to her.

After another three years, Clara was as lonely as ever, and in her loneliness she began to revisit long lost memories from when she and her very best of friends had roamed in Etrurian idyll.

It was the eruption of mount Etna to the North that made her sit up and take notice of her situation and the incessant dissatisfaction in which she found herself. She took the eruption as a sign that she needed to wake up and begin living again.

It was that realization that had caused her to sell everything - the business, the ships, the land, and the villa - to the highest bidder, so that she could return to Etruria to build a new life on her own.

A new life.

It was a strange concept and an even scarier prospect. That very morning, Clara Probita had put her seal to the final documents which the steward of her latifundium had brought her. She had three more days in the place that had been her home for six years, and then she would take ship for Pisae.

The slaves and farm workers were sad to see their domina leave, for they had loved her for her kindness and generosity. As a final gesture, Clara had freed them and given them the option of leaving or staying on with the new dominus whom, she assured them, was also kind and fair. She had seen to that.

Many were undecided on that account, but they did stay to see her off.

It was a strange thing to be sitting there upon the terrace, looking out to sea, waiting to leave, waiting to begin anew. The servants wept at the prospect of her departure and, though she too was saddened to leave them, she also felt great comfort in the certainty of her decision. She had made offerings to her departed Aeson and knew that his spirit was content with the length of time that she had remained after he died.

Taking another sip of her wine, Clara picked up a scroll she had been wanting to read entitled *Daphnis and Chloe*. It was written by a new, upcoming writer named Longus, and had something to do with youths who fall in love but who are separated by gruelling circumstance before being reunited. Clara unrolled the scroll and began to read aloud…

"When I was hunting in Lesbos, I saw in the grove of the Nymphs a spectacle the most beauteous and pleasing of any that ever yet I cast my eyes upon." *Oh, I'm going to enjoy this!* she thought, taking pleasure in the utterance of such smooth and lovely words. "It was a painted picture, reporting a history love. The grove indeed was very-"

"Domina! Domina!"

Clara Probita sighed as the sweet words were stopped at the edge of her tongue by one of the servants rushing up from within the domus behind her, his feet padding quickly along the marble floor. "Yes, Dematos," she said. "What is it?"

The slave boy arrived panting, waving a round leather case. He bowed and handed it to her, his dark curls sweaty about his brow from his running.

"Catch your breath and tell me what this is," Clara said, sitting up now.

The boy stood up. "A courier just brought this… He said he has been sent from Ephesus in all urgency."

"Does he require an answer?" Clara asked.

The boy shook his head. "He did not say as much, Domina. Only that it was urgent."

"Is he still here? Does he know who sent it?"

"He is gone, Domina. I did not ask who sent it."

"Very well," Clara said, smiling. "You have done well, Dematos. But now I wish for you to relax. Calm yourself. You are the newest addition to this household, and you have yet to learn the ways. But remember, when you bring your new dominus something like this, be quick, but do not make him nervous. Be quick, efficient, and most of all, calm."

"Yes, Domina. I am sorry."

She shook her head and smiled. "Do not be sorry. All is well." She looked at the leather tube in her hands. "I will read this alone. You may go."

The boy bowed and left at a run.

Clara Probita chuckled to herself but her smile quickly faded as she looked down at the courier's tube. "Who could this be from?"

It was a good question. The only people she was acquainted with were some of the citizens of Syracusae, who rarely deigned to write to her, and then other merchants, some of which were based in Ephesus. But they had already written final missives to her in the wake of her sale of the business.

She pulled the cap off of the leather tube and tipped out the contents.

A rolled papyrus fell out into her lap. It was tied with a red, silk ribbon, and sealed with a deep blue waxen image of tragic and comic masks. She did not recognized the seal, but for some reason it gave her pause, a fluttering in her stomach.

She broke the seal and stretched out the papyrus to read to herself…

To Clara Probita,

From your admiring friend across the sea, Felix Modestus.

Love and Greetings.

Clara gasped at the words. "Felix?" she said aloud, her voice at once nervous and incredulous. Her heart pounded and the fluttering became a thrumming as she read on.

My dear… It has been many years since we last spoke. Even though much time has passed, I have thought of you daily in my travels. It is not without some jealously that I have wondered if married life has been kind to you, and if the man to whom you were sold as wife was fitting.

I know that much has been left unsaid between us since that day in Rome so long ago. It seems another lifetime, but I remember it as though it were yesterday. How the Gods play with us!

You may be wondering why, after all this time, I should write to you.

It is a long and complicated tale to tell, and one which I would rather relay to you in person. Suffice it to say that the Gods have sent me a sign, and I am taking it most seriously.

I need you, Clara. Desperately. In all honesty, it is a matter of life and death.

I do not know when this might reach you, though I have paid handsomely for a speedy delivery. But I hope it is in time for you to travel to Rome.

"Rome?" Clara said aloud when she read that. That one word conjured so many memories for her, and the fact that she read it as she was holding a missive written by Felix Modestus was, well, disquieting.

I pray that - and as the Gods command - that you will be able to come to Rome to meet me on the Kalends of Aprilis, on the first day of Veneralia.

"For the festival of Venus?" If Clara was nervous before, she was positively sweating now. "Why does he want me to meet him in Rome of all places? And at such a time!"

I know that perhaps after so much has happened, your inclination will be in the opposite direction of Rome, of all places. But please trust me, your old friend, when I say that you will not regret it. As you know, I am rarely afraid of anything in this world, but for what the Gods have shown me this time, I need your help.

If you decide to come - and I pray that you do - meet me in the evening at the Taberna Macedonica near the theatre of Marcellus, on the Kalends of Aprilis. I will explain everything to you at that time.

I look forward to seeing you again, my dear.

With all my love and affection.

Felix

Clara's hands fell into her lap gripping the papyrus. Her

head spun with what she had just read - so urgent, so forthright, so worrying.

"What has he got himself into?" she wondered, suddenly very fearful for her old friend.

The mixture of feelings that letter brought about threatened to unravel all of the certainty she had only just felt that morning. Her new life had not even begun and yet, here was an obstacle. There was a part of her that wanted to decline, to leave the past in the past. There was a lot of pain there, but Clara also remembered much joy, the only happiness in her depressing youth.

Felix had always dominated the space about them. He had been her protector, her confidante, and then…in Rome…

She shook her head and stood to look out over the fields toward the dazzling blue of the sea. The wind played about her unblemished face, toying with the strands of her hair as she considered the letter, as she realized that her heart had already decided, despite the more reluctant pace of her mind in coming to the same conclusion.

"Perhaps the Gods have set this scroll in my hands at exactly this moment for a reason?" she wondered aloud, biting her lip. She remembered Felix fondly, but also with a measure of guilt that had never fully gone away. She picked up her cup of wine, took a deep sip, and set it back upon the pedestal table beside her couch.

"If he is in danger, I must help him," she decided, immediately feeling some weight lifted. "I can then apologize to him, and let him down gently."

She tried to remember that foggy night in Rome, so long ago, and realized that it had been gnawing at her heart over the years.

"Now the Gods are giving me a chance to set things right…with Felix, anyway." She rolled up the letter and put it back in the leather tube. "Etruria will have to wait."

Leaning upon the marble railing overlooking the fields and sea, Clara Probita turned to look upon the vast villa where she had spent the last six years. She had happy memories in that place, but she was content with leaving it behind. It was time.

"Aristaeus!" she called to the estate steward whom she knew was not far off, completing the documents for the transfer of property with the new owners.

The older man emerged from the corridor to the right, and she could see that he had been weeping silently, for he too had appreciated her kindness over the years, and the care with which Aeson had nurtured her. "Yes, Domina?" he said, straightening his long white tunica and belt.

"May I ask one last favour of you, Aristaeus?"

He looked aghast that she should even ask. "Anything, Domina! Anything at all!"

She smiled sadly at his bowed head. "Please go into Syracusae and change my passage. I am not going to Pisae."

"Where are you heading, Domina?" he asked.

"Ostia, Aristaeus. I'm going to Rome."

The steward backed away, bowing before going to take care of it.

Clara Probita turned to lean upon the railing again, the leather tube clutched tightly in her long, pale fingers.

III

A FARMER OF LONELINESS

I t was a cool morning in Etruria, but the month of Martius had arrived with its usual stomp to awaken the living from their winter slumbers. Birds flit and sang in the still-naked branches of the trees, and boar ranged over the hills and through the forests. Farmers began to prepare their fields, ploughing the loamy depths of their lands for the Spring planting, seeking the blessings of Mars and Ceres by placing offerings upon their hidden altars wherever men lived by the land.

Men and servants tended to the dormant olive groves, fields, and vineyards from the moment the sun's chariot broke over the horizon to the moment it fell over the far edge of the world. It was a busy time in that idyllic Etrurian world, from the smallest holding to the largest latifundium, but on one farm in particular, the altars to the Gods were cold, the soil untilled, the trees unclipped, the vines tangled and wild.

At the base of the northern slope of a tree-topped hill, a small farm and its owner had slept in after the Winter pause, though the cock crowed at all hours to rouse its distracted owner.

If one was close enough to that ramshackle plot of land in the hilly wilds between Florentia and Saena Iulia, one would have heard the harsh sound of digging at the edge of the owner's property, accented by the muttered grumblings of one

Rufio Pagano who, in that very moment, was digging a grave for his recently departed father beside the long, weedy pathway that led from the main road.

Rufio Pagano was not a large man. He was quite average and lean for a farmer, if you could call him that. Whilst his neighbours had armies of slaves to labour upon the land, Rufio endeavoured to do it all himself, especially since his father's mind had quit the world before his body, leaving a cantankerous old man behind to torture and tease his only son.

"Come-on, Ginger boy! Work faster! Everything will rot at this rate!" his father would say, clapping wildly as he did so.

There was no end to the insults and berating of this paternal lunatic who shouted incessantly from beneath the loggia of their run-down domus where mice were more in charge. Still, Rufio knew that he could not shame his father into lifting a gnarled finger to help in any capacity, for he was more likely to use a plough to cut a loaf of bread than to till the soil beside the spindly trees in the olive grove.

"The senator on the other side of the hill is a better farmer than you!" Rufio's father would say.

"Yes, Father," he would answer and then, under his breath, "The senator is also a wealthy cunnus and has an army of slaves to help."

"Don't you talk to me in that way!" his father would shout having, for some inexplicable reason, heard the muttered words from a great distance.

"Yes, Father," Rufio would answer.

It was strange then to be digging so resolutely that morning whilst the fire of his father's pyre still burned and consumed his remains. But dig Rufio did, beside the long-overgrown grave of his mother who had passed away close to seven years before.

Rufio stopped digging for a moment and wiped his forehead of the cold sweat that had gathered beneath the fringe of his receding red hair. He shook his dirty tunica off and rubbed the dirt from his short beard. The sun broke through the clouds then and he closed his eyes for a moment, trying to imagine that he was not doing what he was doing, but sitting indoors by a warm hearth fire reading one of his favourite plays. He had set out his treasured scrolls that very morning upon the pigeon hole shelf in what was now his tablinum.

Rufio, despite growing up in the Etrurian hills, had never wanted to be a farmer, but he was always told that it was his destiny to do so. Of course he had. No, what Rufio had always wanted as a child was to be a player, to act alongside his two childhood friends. Together, they had performed their own mimes upon a makeshift stage hidden away on the wooded slopes nearby, and on warm, bright summer days, one could hear their excited proclamations and dialogues echo to the blue sky above.

When he had got older, Rufio and his friends had attempted to make good on their dream by leaving Etruria behind and heading to Rome to seek employment and opportunity. It was a heady time for them, two lads and a girl, to wade into the sweaty press of flesh and colour of the empire's capital.

It had all, however, come to naught for Rufio, for his mother had passed suddenly and he was forced to abandon that naive and childish dream of performing and writing for the masses in the streets of Rome.

When he returned to Etruria, walking up the drive to the small domus, he remembered his father standing in the path clapping wildly as he approached. "There you go!" his father had said. "You have your applause! Now bury your mother!"

It was from that moment that Pagano Pater began to clap whenever Rufio came or went from his presence. "Now, you are an actor!" he would scoff. "You should read Cato! Not Terence or those despicable Greeks!"

He never heard from his old friends again and became

comfortable with his anonymous excellence, waiting for a time when he would show his father. But he never did. Eventually, it got to the point where no-one but his father and Errol, the servant, remembered him. He did not bother with others, for he had too much responsibility, and not a little regret.

Rufio Pagano wiped his face again and looked at the fire that now consumed his father's remains and, for some strange reason, he began to clap at it.

"Master Rufio!" his old servant, Errol, chided from beside the fire where he had been tossing more oil and wood upon it to feed the flames' intensity. "Why do you clap so?"

Rufio looked at the balding dotard he had inherited and felt a little shame. "Sorry, Errol! Sorry. I thought Father might appreciate the applause," he added sarcastically.

Errol shook his head and wiped his tears away, the wind playing with the grey whips of his long, grey hair at the back of his head. "Such disrespect."

Rufio wondered why Errol should weep so, for his father had never really been nice to him, especially since the death of his mother. She had always been the source of jollity in their small familia, but since her passing they were but a chorus in a tragedy.

Rufio looked askance at his mother's tombstone and saw that it was spattered with dirt from his digging. He went over to it, bent, and wiped it clean with his hand before taking the jug of wine he had been drinking from and pouring a libation over the grave. "Maybe you can cheer him up in the Afterlife, Mother." He smiled sadly for a moment, then felt something nudge his thigh. He turned to find his loyal donkey, Stella, leaning into him and he pat her furry grey head and long ears. "It's all right, girl," he told the animal. "From now on, I'll do better at this."

Rufio had tried to take over the farming operation after his mother passed, but even he had to admit that he was hopeless at it. It was dark on the northern slope of the hill, there was blight in one of the fields, and no matter how much he encouraged them, the olive trees and grape vines refused to grow more than a little every season. His days were spent going over the list of problems he had to solve rather than harvesting the fruits of his half-hearted labour. They had eggs aplenty, and a preponderance of mushrooms in the dark wood up the hill, but that was about it. He had become more adept at catching rabbits, however, and the occasional boar, so there was meat often enough.

Much of his time was also spent putting off the aggressive approaches of the equestrian senator on the other side of the hill who wanted to buy their land. If anything, his father had been good at turning back their rich neighbour's advances. "Thinks he can suck up all the land around here for himself because his dead ancestors lord it over us from the tomb at the top of the hill!" his father had said after every interaction with the senator. "He's got another thing coming!"

"I'll have to deal with that now too," Rufio muttered as he turned to take up the shovel again and get back to digging. He could hear Errol weeping aloud. His father's death seemed to have caused chaos on the land, for not only was the servant weeping for his departed jailer, but their old horse had escaped that very morning, and two of the cows had fallen in the stream and found it extremely difficult to right themselves. They were all drunk with grief, all except Rufio who, in that moment, would have welcomed a bit of Bacchic inebriation.

Still, a part of him was relieved that the Gods had decided it was his father's time. He knew it to be a horrible sentiment, but when the guilt would start to eat at him, he had only to remember his father laughing at him and clapping, shouting "Only whores are actors!" and "Nobody pays for a ginger whore!" Remembering such paternal encouragements usually assuaged his guilt speedily.

"Right!" Rufio said to Stella the donkey. "Let's get this done!" He took up the shovel again, and jumped into the hole to dig the last few bits of dirt. As soon as he was finished, a scream ripped through the air and Rufio jumped out of the hole.

"Master Rufio!" Errol shouted. "The hog has broken loose again!"

Rufio emerged onto the surrounding grass in time to see their one large sow charging across the field toward the lane for yet another escape attempt. "Oh no you don't!" Rufio yelled, bursting into a run parallel to the portly pig. Ravens seemed to guffaw in the surrounding trees as they watched the scene below, but this did not distract Rufio from his attack.

Their course turned as the sow avoided him, and they headed back toward Stella and Errol who stood near the newly dug hole.

When Rufio was alongside the speeding sow, he lunged onto her back and held on for dear life. "I've got you!"

The animal carried her master a short distance before her short legs buckled and they both went down in the mound of dirt which Rufio had only recently laboured at. Amid a cacophony of squeals, grunts and screams, Rufio, in a surprisingly-deft act of athleticism, quickly unbuckled the cingulum from his waist and strapped it around the hog's legs.

The sow ceased her wriggling and looked up at him with her accusing eyes as Rufio stroked her head to calm her.

"It's all right, girl," he said, his breathing heavy and ragged. "All I ever wanted to do was leave this place."

For a moment, she was calm and Rufio saw the quizzical looks upon his servant and donkey's faces. The moment he looked away, however, the hog bucked, flexing like a singular giant muscle, and swept Rufio's legs from beneath him so that he fell backwards into the dark depths of his father's waiting grave!

For a moment, Rufio Pagano lay upon his back looking up at the cold blue sky above. He groaned and wondered why he had dug such a large whole for so small an urn, and in that moment, he thought he could hear his father clapping at him. "I'll just lie here then," he said to himself. "Go to sleep and not get up. And so the curtain falls on the last of the Pagano family!"

For a few minutes, he listened to the crackling of the funeral pyre which, he assumed Errol was tending to rather than helping him remove himself from the earth. Then, another sound broke into his nightmare. The sound of galloping.

The hoofbeats which Rufio heard were of a younger, more swift animal than that which had escaped that morning. There was a loud neighing as the rider pulled on the reins, and muted voices when Errol approached the newcomer.

"I have a message for Rufio Pagano!" the rider said, panting.

"He's napping!" Rufio heard Errol reply. A moment later, Errol's tear-stained and wrinkled face appeared over the edge of the grave to look down at Rufio, then Stella's - the donkey had a more worried look than Errol - and then the courier who held out a leather tube.

"Are you Rufio Pagano?" the man said, pushing back his woollen cloak.

"Unfortunately, yes. I am," Rufio said, not making a move to stand.

"Well what are you doing in that hole?" the man asked.

"Resting," Rufio replied. "And it's a grave."

"Rather large, isn't it?" the courier looked over Rufio's handiwork. He waited a moment for a reply, but when he received none, he cleared his throat. "Is it for you?"

"The letter?" Rufio asked.

"Yes. No!" The courier scratched his head. "Yes. The letter is for you, if you are Rufio Pagano."

"I already told you I am," Rufio said, feeling quite damp and uncomfortable now.

"I meant the grave. Is it for you for future use? You seem to be testing its comfort," the man said.

"No!" Rufio barked. "It's not for me. It's for my father."

"Where is he then?" the man asked.

"In the fire."

Errol cried out loud at that and began to weep anew.

Stella looked sidelong at the servant, her ears back at the howling that emanated from his shaking lips.

The courier looked at the fire and made a sign against evil before turning back to Rufio. "Do you want this letter or no? I've come all the way from Ephesus with it."

"Ephesus?" Rufio sat up at that, suddenly very curious, for he did not know anyone in Ephesus. He did not think so anyway. "Can you help me out?" he asked the courier.

The man set down the leather tube and leaned forward to give Rufio his hands. He pulled with a grunt and extricated the son from his father's grave.

"Careful of the pig," Rufio said as the sow began to buck again. "She's relentless."

The courier stepped back and took up the leather tube which he handed to Rufio.

"Do you need a reply?" Rufio asked.

The man shook his head as he brushed the dirt from his bracae and cloak. "No. Just to deliver it."

"Do you want water and food before you go?" Rufio asked, seeing as the man had obviously come a very long way.

The courier looked down the lane at the ramshackle domus just as a clay tegula slid from the roof and broke into pieces on the ground. "Na. Must be going," he said, moving toward his horse. "I'll eat at the tavern."

Rufio shrugged. "Suit yourself," he said as the man mounted up and sped away. "Ephesus?" he queried himself. He was about to break open the container and read when Errol addressed him.

"Master Rufio. The fire has done its work."

Rufio looked at the smoking, ashy mass of remains. He felt his heart tighten, despite all that had happened, and looked back at his mother's grave. "I'll read this later," he said to Stella who stood beside him. "I'll get the urn from the domus, Errol. You rake the ashes so that they can cool. Then we can shovel father into his new home."

Errol burst into a new chorus of weeping at that, and Rufio walked up the lane to the domus to get the clay urn which he had purchased from a neighbouring potter only the day before.

Stella followed him.

LATER THAT AFTERNOON, RUFIO, ERROL AND STELLA INTERRED Pagano Pater after sprinkling his ashes with wine. Rufio was feeling more solemn by then, the bitterness of the past having leeched away. After having placed the urn in the grave, Rufio placed his father's favourite clothing in with him so as not to walk naked through the Afterlife, a pair of sandals, and the ring that was the twin to that of Rufio's mother. Therein, he also set a small jug of olive oil - the last from their meagre harvest - and a small jug of wine, this last somewhat reluctantly, but dutifully.

When all was set within the dark hole, Rufio and Errol both began replacing the dirt that had been removed. When they were done, Rufio stood over his father's grave and sprinkled wine, milk, and honey upon it. "Rest easy, Father. Go find Mother now. Be happy again."

In that moment, Rufio Pagano did weep for his father. Not for the loss of his tormentor, but rather for the wasted years and fractured family they had been. "Goddess Ceres," Rufio said as Errol lit a chunk of incense in a bowl upon the mound of dirt, "Keeper of Elysium's door, open it wide for my departed father that he may rejoin my mother and feel joyous once more." Rufio then knelt and placed his hand upon the soft mound of earth. "Goodbye, Father."

In that moment, Errol began to clap loudly, and when Rufio turned to look up at him, he saw that the horse had returned, and was now standing between Stella and the delirious old clapper, all of them looking down at him.

When the clapping stopped, as abruptly as it had begun, Rufio sighed, stood up, and began to walk toward the domus. "Errol, please put the horse back in her stall."

"Yes, Master Rufio!" Errol replied, taking the horse by the harness and leading it away.

"Come on, Stella," Rufio called to the donkey. "Let's see who's written us from Ephesus."

THE DOMUS IN WHICH RUFIO HAD BEEN RAISED WAS NOT SO small as a hovel, but it had been allowed to run down so much over the years since his mother's death that it was clothed as one. In truth, it had once been rather clean and sprawling, cool in summer and warm in winter. There were four cubicula for sleeping, a triclinium - now used as storage - a small kitchen with a single charcoal oven and a few bronze pots and pans, and a tablinum with a hearth, large wooden table, and pigeon hole shelves, where Rufio spent most of his time.

After the rites for his father were completed, Rufio retreated to this sanctuary to continue the work he had begun previously, removing his long-hidden scrolls from their locked chest and setting them in the shelves. He dusted and swept away the cobwebs his father had allowed to gather, finding some distraction in the act of cleaning. When he finished, and was sitting beside the hearth with a clay cup of wine, he slid the papyrus roll out of the leather tube the courier had delivered and held it up to the light.

"Two theatre masks?" he remarked to himself as he looked upon the seal. "Strange." He broke the seal then, unrolled the letter, and began to read…

To Rufio Pagano,

From Felix Modestus.

Greetings old friend!

"Felix?" Rufio said aloud to himself, sitting up straighter, his eyes wide in shock.

It has been many years, Rufio. Too many! The last time we met, we were in Rome about to make our great dream a reality…

And then, you left.

I have often wondered why you did not stay, to tread the path of adventure with your childhood friends. We had dreamed so greatly then, sworn before the Gods that we would make a go of it. I do hope you have been happy these many years with the choice you made. I know that I have.

Rufio, I did make our dream come true. I've travelled the world and walked the stages of the greatest cities in the empire. I've entertained kings and queens, senators and consuls, and I've made more coin than we ever dreamed of performing the plays we used to re-enact in the forest back home. The Gods themselves have been entertained!

"There he is," Rufio slumped back in the moth-eaten couch on which he sat. "As humble as ever!" He shook his head. Felix never had taken to humility but then, Rufio knew, that was why he was so successful.

Despite all of this success, Rufio, or perhaps because of it, the Gods have threatened to throw me down from the great stage on which I stand.

I am in trouble, my friend, and only you can help.

I know that I have no business coming to you for help after so many years of silence. I never did write to you. Then again, I did not think you wished to be written to.

The Gods have a way of throwing people together, however.

If you are willing and able, I need for you to come to Rome, where we last saw each other.

"Rome?" Rufio shouted out loud.

"Master Rufio?" Errol suddenly said, poking his head around the doorway of the tablinum where he held a clay lamp out before his squinting eyes. "Did you call me?"

"No, Errol. I said 'Rome', not 'Errol'. You can go back to sleep."

"Why did you say 'Rome'? You don't like Rome," Errol said, pointing his finger at Rufio as if accusing him of something.

"Yes, I know. But I did say 'Rome'. It's in the letter!"

"What letter?"

"The one the rider brought earlier today," Rufio said, only wanting to get back to reading.

"Very well," Errol said, yawning and turning to leave. "Such shouting. Don't know what rider he's talking about," he muttered from the corridor, making Rufio wonder if he could even find his way back to his cubiculum.

Rufio turned back to the letter, squinting in the firelight to find his place again.

Come to Rome on the first day of Veneralia, on the Kalends of Aprilis. Meet me in the evening at the Taberna Macedonica, near the theatre of Marcellus. I will tell you more then. And don't worry about expenses. I will take care of everything.

I hope you do come, Rufio. I do need your help, and you know that I never ask lightly for aid. But this, for me, is a matter of life and death.

May Janus guide you safely on your journey.

Your friend,

Felix Modestus

Rufio was silent as he laid the letter upon a nearby table and stared into the fire. He felt like his world, and his head, were spinning out of control. Before that letter, he had known with certainty that his only task was to put all he had into the farm to get it running properly again now that his father was not there to impede him.

"And now this letter," he grumbled as he stood and paced around the room. "Rome is too dirty," he said, trying to ignore the irony when he looked at the condition of his own domus, "and crowded! I hate crowds." He shook his head. "And he assumes I'm poor. Bastard! I'll take care of everything!" he mocked, as if he were the sole performer in a pantomime.

Then, Rufio Pagano stopped his flailing arms and looked around his tablinum, poked his head into the dirty corridor outside, decorated with scattered dead leaves and cracked amphorae. If there had ever been joy in that place, his home, the memory of it had been snuffed out long ago.

"But...it would be good to see Felix..." he mused, smiling to himself as he remembered how big and vibrant his childhood friend had been. Then he remembered something else, someone else. He rushed to the table and re-read the letter to make sure. "I can't face her...not after what I did," he said to himself, sighing with relief when he saw that Felix only mentioned himself. "Maybe it won't be so bad? Two friends, catching up. Me helping out an old friend?"

...a matter of life and death.

He re-read the words and felt a chill.

"Gods, why do you mock me?" he asked, his eyes straying to the darkness outside the window to the freshly heaped mound of his father's grave.

Rufio sat back in his chair and looked up at the pigeon hole shelf in which his scrolls lay, and the mere sight of them rekindled past dreams, even though to look upon them was akin to looking upon the friends he had betrayed, so humiliating and embarrassing.

"But Felix has come to me! He's asking *me* for *my* help!" Rufio told himself. "But Rome? I can't!" he shook his head.

"I've just buried my father and my farm is going to shit. I need to make things right here!"

Rufio tossed the letter onto the broad wooden table, determined to go to sleep and try to forget that mad business and Felix's proposition. Besides, when he thought of Felix, he thought of others, and that was far too painful a thing to ponder. He stormed out of the tablinum and made for his cubiculum.

THREE HOURS LATER, RUFIO STILL LAY ABED, STARING UP AT the cobwebbed ceiling of his cubiculum with the moonlight angling its way onto his face.

"Felix is as likely to wallop me as welcome me for what I did to him all those years ago," he whispered to himself. "I would. And then…"

Rufio's habit of working things out by speaking aloud to himself was something his father had hated, but which now he was able to do without fear of retribution.

"Quiet in there!" Errol suddenly yelled, as if Pagano Pater's genius had spirited itself into the confines of the old servant to continue to haunt his son's life.

"Sorry, Errol!" Rufio called out, shaking his head.

Truthfully, Rufio knew that there was a part of him that longed to go to Rome, to make amends for what he had done to Felix. "To both of them," he said, feeling the sting of guilt and great embarrassment. "Perhaps it won't take long? A few days at most?" He pursed his lips and rubbed his thin beard. "But I have to be responsible and mind the farm. It's all up to me now." He shook his head. "Who am I kidding? My domus is run down and my crops are dying. I annoy my only servant, and even my animals are trying to flee. Stella will miss me though," he reasoned. "It'll break her heart if I leave."

By the time Rufio decided he should get some sleep, the

sun was rising over the ruined fields of his lands, and lighting up the orbs of his blood-shot eyes.

"A matter of life and death," he repeated, closing his eyes for a moment before they shot wide open. "Futuo!" he said through gritted teeth as he threw his legs over the edge of the bed and stuck his head out into the corridor. "Errol! I'm going to Rome!" he yelled.

"But you hate Rome!" the answer came.

Rufio hung his head and tried to ignore the clapping he thought he could also hear echoing throughout the domus in that moment.

ACT II

ETRURIA WILL HAVE TO WAIT

IV

VENUS IN ROME

Veneralia, the festival of Venus Verticordia, the Changer of Hearts, had arrived in Rome, and with it came the hopes and dreams of many a man, woman, and longing lover. This was indeed a propitious time of year in this beating heart of the world. Spring's fresh face was now fully visible, and the scent of new growth and splash of coloured blooms was everywhere.

The people of Rome were truly content, especially as the great wars that had raged were now at an end, and waves of Roman troops had already returned home to their families, friends, and sweethearts.

After a long and brutal civil war, in which Emperor Severus had come out the victor, the legions had almost immediately marched East to combat the Parthian Empire. It had been a long and bloody conflict, but Rome had been victorious once again. And what better way to have celebrated than with a grand triumph and games in the city of Rome itself.

By the time Veneralia arrived, the people had exhausted themselves in a great fit of ecstasy and drunken celebration and were now ready to welcome the goddess into their midst and adhere to the traditional moralities and proprieties of the married and unmarried which were pleasing to the goddess.

More or less, at any rate.

That very day, the beauteous and pale statue of Venus had been removed from her vast temple and carried to the baths where she was washed by her priestesses with warm water, before being dressed in myrtle garlands, and returned to her seat in the temple where she would be honoured and adored by many thousands who had come from across the empire.

Altars throughout Rome burned with the scent of sweet incense dedicated to the goddess and were laden with herbs and flowers, and sweets drenched in milk and honey.

In the midst of this celebratory atmosphere, Felix Modestus was being carried through the streets of Rome upon a perfumed litter which he had hired. He reclined as the litter bearers grunted and heaved, manoeuvring their way through the crowds, however slowly, with the yellow and crimson curtains open so that he could see and be seen.

Electra, dressed in a shimmering stola of red silk, which Felix had bought for her that very morning, curled up beside him in the litter. Her long dark hair, scented with rose water, cascaded down his shoulders as she leaned against him, her fingers tracing the line of his chest beneath his indigo and gold tunica. As many eyes gazed upon the reclined goddess in the litter as they did upon the muscled hero who seemed to possess her, his broad smile and confident air a sign that Venus had certainly blessed them with untold pleasures.

Felix and the company had been in Rome for just over a week by then, and had taken up residence in a rented warehouse along the Tiber, south of the Forum Boarium, in which they could build their sets and rehearse in a space large enough for the performance which Felix secretly envisioned. Since they had arrived, however, he had allowed his troupe to enjoy the delights of the city before the real work began in earnest.

That morning, Electra had expressed her wish to visit the temple of Venus and Rome so that she could make offerings to the goddess upon Veneralia.

Felix had agreed, but insisted that they be carried in style through the Forum Romanum on the way there, much to the disgruntled looks of the litter bearers who knew that it would be an arduous trek through the crowds at that time.

"We're actors in Rome now!" Felix bellowed. "We must put on a show everywhere we go!"

Electra would gladly have walked by his side, but she did not say as much, for she could see Felix had grander plans. So long as she arrived where she wished, she was content. Once they were being carried from the warehouse to the Forum, they could just about hear the whispered expressions of love between young men and women in corners and against walls, and upon the steps of temples. Flower petals twirled on the breeze and seemed to fall from the very skies in the Forum Romanum, as if the Gods themselves tipped baskets from Olympus' heights upon them.

"It feels like new beginnings everywhere," Electra said to Felix as they passed the round temple of Vesta, sighing as she felt a ray of sunlight angle its way upon her face.

Felix turned to her with a quizzical look. "I didn't think you enjoyed Rome. You always complain about how dirty it is, how crowded and uncultured compared to Athenae or Alexandria."

Electra shrugged. "It seems different this time, more hopeful. Certainly cleaner."

"That's all well and good, but we need to focus on the great task at hand, and you need to help me."

"Does it always have to turn to business?" Electra leaned away from him and looked out the opposite side of the litter. "Can we not simply enjoy some time alone, away from Silas and the others?"

"We are a familia, Electra. And one cannot escape one's familia. Besides, we are in Rome for the greatest production of my career, and that is serious business."

"And what of your friends? You hang much of your hopes,

as well as your life, upon them," she turned back to him, her arms crossed. "What if they do not show?"

"We'll find out later," Felix said, stroking his beard and shaking his head as if to wheedle his way out of worry's grasp. "For now, we need to focus on our meeting with the aedile. We need his support."

"He's already invited you here to perform. What more do you need from him?"

"We need him to fill the seats with the best of people."

It was Electra's turn to shake her head. "I would think your name would be enough to fill a theatre."

"Not here. Not in Rome," Felix admitted.

The litter came to a stop at the bottom of the steps of the temple of Venus and Rome, and was set down by the litter bearers.

"Now we set business aside for a moment," Electra said as she slid from the litter to stand upon the cobbles, straightening her stola and looking up at the temple. "The goddess requires our attention."

She walked around to join Felix who held out his arm to her, taking in the admiring looks from those citizens who stood about the temple.

Together, Felix and Electra walked up the broad marble steps.

"Ohhh!" cried a rather large woman who was seated at the bottom of the steps with a wide clay bowl filled with coins. "Now there's a couple whom Venus has blessed!" she said when she spied Felix and Electra.

The woman smiled broadly, her yellow-gold hair tickling the tops of her thick shoulders, and the strands of beads that hung thickly about her neck doing little to cover her large exposed breasts. "Venus' blessing upon you!" she cried to the radiant couple as they passed.

Electra turned to look at the woman but Felix pulled her along.

"There are several street priestesses in Rome, and they crawl out at this time of year to prophesy for the masses."

"Perhaps we should offer her some coin for her blessing?" Electra said. "She has blue eyes, and will curse us if we don't."

"Will you stop that?" Felix barked. "Not everyone with blue eyes is capable of cursing."

"You keep telling yourself that," Electra said, pulling away from him to peruse the items on a nearby offering seller's table at the top of the temple steps.

"Good morning, my lady!" said the friendly seller who had just finished with another customer before moving down the table to speak with Electra. "The blessings of Venus be with you both!" he added affably when Felix approached, still distracted by the admiring looks from a group of women along the temple steps. "My name is Numonius, and I have an offering for every god, goddess, and occasion. Can I help you find something in particular to offer Venus on the occasion of her great festival?"

The offering seller was tall and thin, with short-cropped dark hair and a smile that made one feel comfortable in parting with any amount of coin, knowing that he would not gouge on price or quality. It never did to rob the Gods of quality offerings, nor to cheat hard-working people of a sestertius or two.

"Does anything catch your eye, lady?" Numonius said. "If you like, I can make suggestions. I do pride myself on knowing what is appropriate for which god or goddess."

Electra looked back at Felix and frowned before turning back to the offering seller. "Preferably something to make this one take notice of me more."

"I'm sure there is no need for that, my lady," Numonius said.

"Relax," Felix said. "It's all part of the act, Electra." He turned to Numonius. "We've been invited to perform at the Ludi Apollinares in a couple of months. We just arrived in Rome."

"Ah, a company of players?" Numonius asked.

"The Etrurian Players, to be specific," Felix clarified. "We're out of Ephesus, but have performed everywhere from Antioch and Alexandria, to Athenae and Nova Carthago. Rome will never be the same after we entertain her!"

"I cannot wait!" Numonius said, bowing dramatically.

"Now, buy something from this good man so that we can offer it to the goddess. We can't keep the aedile waiting!" He turned to the offering seller. "Something pleasing to the goddess will be sufficient. I couldn't ignore this one if I wanted to." He nodded to Electra who shot him a stormy look.

"Erm," Numonius began, his eyes quickly glancing over the laden table. "I might suggest this crown of spring flowers and laurel," he pointed at the delicate piece, "or this bundle of scented herbs bound with a golden ribbon that has been washed in the sea from whence Venus herself emerged."

Electra looked from one to the other of the items, trying to divine which of them the goddess would prefer. She then reached out to take up one of the bundles of herbs and put it to her nose to inhale the sweet scent of rosemarinus, thymus, and salvia. "I'll take this," she said, before looking to Felix for approval.

Felix smiled at her and looked to Numonius. "We'll take both."

Electra's dark eyes widened.

Felix shrugged. "We need the goddess to be kind to us."

She looped her arm through his and leaned in.

"If my plan is to succeed, that is," Felix added, opening the soft leather scrip that was attached to his cingulum.

Electra removed her arm at once and took both items from Numonius.

"This should cover it," Felix said, handing the offering seller a silver denarius.

"Oh, that's too much," Numonius said. "Four asses will be enough."

"Nonsense! Add to it your ongoing promise to spread the word about The Etrurian Players, and that will be sufficient."

Numonius bowed again. "I will certainly do so," he said, allowing Felix to drop the coin into his hand.

"Good man!" Felix bellowed, before turning to go into the temple. "I'll take that," he said to Electra as he took the flower and laurel crown. "I need a victory from the goddess. You may offer her the herbs."

Electra breathed deeply before smiling once more at Numonius and pushing past Felix to go into the temple on her own, clutching the bundled herbs to her breast.

A short time later, after some rushed and very different prayers to the goddess on both their parts, Felix and Electra emerged from the high temple. They descended the steps through the thickening crowd toward the waiting litter bearers who stood when they saw them.

Electra stormed past Felix, reaching deftly into his scrip to pull out a coin as she passed and went directly to the street priestess at the bottom of the stairs.

Felix stopped, ready to yell, but caught himself, aware of the eyes upon him.

"Erm," Numonius cleared his throat to try and get Felix's attention.

Felix turned back to the offering seller, shaking his head. "She'll never learn. Always a sucker for these scamsters!"

Numonius watched Electra speaking with the street priestess and turned back to Felix. "Oh, I wouldn't worry about Astarte. She's quite adept at what she does. She has the true sight."

"She's naked in the street," Felix replied, knowing full well he might not be so sour were she more beauteous.

"As naked as the Goddess Venus herself when she emerged from the sea foam," Numonius added. "You are here for a while, it seems, but might I also suggest that you consider giving your lady something nice…a jewelled token of your love for her?" He waved a hand over that section of his table which displayed intricately carved bangles of gold, rings, and a few other items of beauty and workmanship.

Felix shook his head. "She's my slave. There's no need," he said.

"Forgive me," Numonius added. "It does not appear so, the way you look together. "You look more like Venus and Mars to my humble eyes."

Felix flipped Numonius a bronze assarius and went to collect Electra without another word. "We need to go!" he bellowed at her.

"All will be well, dear," the street priestess said, smiling at Electra and holding her hands. "The goddess sees you…and so will he," she whispered.

"Thank you," Electra said, dropping the coin she had taken into Astarte's bowl.

"Get in, woman!" Felix said. "We're late! To the Esquiline Hill," he called to the litter bearers. "Quickly!"

As the litter bobbed along again, Electra closed the curtains on her side, crossed her arms and closed her eyes. She was silent, and Felix realized that it might not make the best impression upon their patron if he did not mend things immediately.

"What is wrong?" he asked her, closing the curtains on his side now.

For a few moments, Electra refused to speak, enjoying the tension she could tell was building in Felix beside her. "I heard you tell Numonius I am your slave."

"It's true, is it not?" Felix defended.

"Is that all I am to you?"

"You're a headache is what you are!" he barked, too stressed about his meeting to take the time to soothe her. He knew they needed to make a good impression on the aedile. He also knew, however much it frustrated him to admit it, that he did not like to see her unhappy. "Electra, you know you are more to me than a slave. I honour you above all the others."

"I should hope so!" she said, feeling his strong hand upon her waist.

"I'll make it up to you. I promise," Felix whispered in her ear. "For now, help me get through this meeting with our patron whose support we need. Then, we can focus on the pleasures of Venus."

She relaxed then. "Until your friends arrive, that is," she added.

"*If* they arrive," Felix said, his voice low and riddled with unaccustomed doubt.

Electra placed her hand upon his chest and felt his beating heart as she leaned in to kiss him. "They will come. No one can resist you," she said as she straddled him.

The curtains remained closed for the rest of the climb up to the Esquiline Hill.

A SHORT WHILE LATER, AFTER SKIRTING THE SMELLY EDGES OF the Suburra, the poorer, more crowded of Rome's neighbourhoods, the litter came to a halt in a place where the bustling sounds of the streets were left behind and the air smelled of lemon and jasmine as opposed to the stink of the sewers.

"We're here, Dominus!" the head litter bearer said, as they set down their burden, breathing heavily after the climb and the jarring motion caused by their passengers along the way.

"Just a minute," Felix said to them from within the curtained world of cushions and perfume.

"What is an aedile's job again?" Electra asked as she straightened her stola and adjusted the pins in her hair.

"He's a patrician nobleman on his way to becoming a senator. He's been put in charge of the ludi by the emperor himself, and so, he needs us as much as we need him. We can use that to our advantage to get everything we need."

"Is he paying for everything?" Electra asked.

"He is paying for the games, but he cannot bankroll our entire production. Not the way I want to do it. Of course, he should give us a set amount, but we will need funds from elsewhere to bring my vision to life."

Electra frowned at that.

"Don't worry," Felix put up his hand. "I've taken care of it."

"How?" she asked.

"Never you mind. For now, just look beautiful and smile at the aedile. I'll do the rest."

"I hope you know what you're doing," she said before quickly sliding the curtains open and stepping out.

They were on a long, cobbled street with high walls covered by cascading greenery on either side. The sun shone, it seemed, more brightly in that part of Rome, and from no place in particular, the sound of trickling water and cawing peacocks could be heard as faint echoes.

"It's beautiful here," Electra commented as she turned around.

"You haven't seen anything yet," Felix said. "This area was home to some of the richest men in Rome. It still is. If I remember correctly, the gardens of Maecenas are over there." He pointed down the street. "Right now, we're in the Horti Lamiani."

"Who lives here?" Electra asked.

"Politicians and rich merchants, I suspect." Felix got down

from the litter and fixed his tunica and cingulum. "Come," he held out his hand to her. "Let's meet the aedile."

Together, they walked up to a large, thick oak door with a bronze knocker upon it in the shape of a she-wolf. Felix raised the knocker, and slammed it down three times. He did not step back, but filled the doorframe as he waited for someone to answer.

When the door slave opened a moment later, the young man looked up, his mouth open as he gazed upon the enormous man before him.

"Felix Modestus. I am here to meet with your dominus."

"Ye...ye...yes, sir," the slave stuttered before gathering himself. "The master and mistress are in the gardens. I will take you to them. Please follow me."

They followed the slave through the doorway and an entire new world opened up before their eyes. It was as if they had left Rome far behind, for all about them were elaborate gardens dotted with cypress trees that pierced the sky, and umbrella pines from which birdsong emanated against the blue backdrop of the heavens. Statues of gods and goddess peered at them from behind geometrically-shaped shrubs while peacocks, with their great tails fanned out, roamed slowly and assuredly along the manicured pathways. Some distance ahead was the sprawling, tiled roof of a vast domus where smoke rose up from the kitchens and the private baths somewhere deep within.

However, the slave turned down another path that led away from the domus and headed for a spot deeper within the gardens. They passed more statuary and mosaics open to the sky, fish ponds and hidden places which, Felix felt sure, saw many an intimate encounter during what must have been magnificent parties.

Electra watched Felix transform as they walked, for he seemed to get bigger, more vibrant and commanding. She had seen him try to impress rich patrons before, but this time it felt different. There was a nervousness about him constantly, and so he tried even harder to mask it. But she knew him and his manner. There was definitely something worrying about all of it.

At last they came to a smaller building supported by ionic columns and topped by a tiled roof. It was open on one side, more like a loggia than a domus, and before it was a broad, mosaic pool with a fountain in the middle portraying Cupid with his bow drawn.

Suddenly the slave stopped and, trembling a little, addressed Felix and Electra. "Please wait while I announce you," he said before going directly to a young man and woman who were reclined upon two couches beside the pool.

When the slave whispered to his master, the man stood at once and waved to Felix and Electra to come and join them. Rather than sit back down, he came around the pool himself to greet them, a broad, relieved smile upon his face. He wore a finely made toga, the folds of which held their position perfectly, as if he had been trained for years in how to comport himself. He was younger than Felix had anticipated, clean-shaven and youthful, if not a little heavier than most men, which suited him quite well. His dark hair was short and neatly cut, and were it not for the slightly protruding ears, he might have resembled an affable, portly Caesar.

Behind him, just rising from her own couch, a woman with an elaborate hairstyle and a shimmering, floor-length stola in pale blue approached as well. She smiled also, and when she did so, the golden necklace about her long neck shivered upon her collar bone.

Felix observed their smiling host quickly and from the corner of his mouth, whispered to Electra. "Oh, I can handle this one easily."

"Felix Modestus, Captain of The Etrurian Players!" the aedile greeted them aloud. "Welcome to Rome!"

Felix set his hand upon his heart and inclined his head dramatically.

"I am Sextus Annius Sabinus," the aedile said, "and this is my wife, Martia Annia. We're so pleased you accepted our invitation to come to Rome."

"Your invitation honours me and my company, Sextus Annius Sabinus…lady…" Felix bowed to the aedile's wife and kissed her hand.

Martia Annia blushed, but composed herself quickly.

"And this," the aedile turned to Electra and took her hand, "this is the famous Electra. You are most welcome, lady. I still shudder from your performance in Ephesus, and I've seen many a production in my time, being somewhat of a theatrical enthusiast."

"Erm," Felix intervened. "Yes, well. Electra does, on occasion draw the audience in, especially when it comes to the tragedies of her Hellenic homeland." Felix could feel her stiffen beside him, feel her eyes burn into the side of his head, but he ignored it.

"Oh, she does more than just draw in the audience!" The aedile turned to Electra. "Lady, you are simply bewitching upon the stage!"

Felix was just about to interrupt this high praise when the aedile turned to him. "And you, Felix Modestus! Every person in the great odeon of Ephesus could not rip their attention from your commanding presence. It was as if Apollo himself stood there to address us. I've never seen anything quite like it! That is why I invited you to Rome!"

"Sextus," his wife said softly beside him, her hand upon his shoulder. "We should sit with out guests."

Just then, a couple of slaves came across the garden with a

fourth couch which they set with the other three that had already been set up beside the pool.

"Of course!" the aedile said. "Please, sit with us. The servants are bringing food and drink for us." He looked upon them and smiled again, positively sweating with his enthusiasm as he took a deep breath. "What a beautiful spring day," he said, cocking his head to listen to the birdsong in the trees above. "Come. Sit with us," he repeated.

"Thank you, Sextus Annius Sabinus," Felix said.

"Please, call me Sextus!" the aedile said quickly. "I don't go in much for titles. At least not with friends, which I hope you consider me to be. After all, we are launching a great campaign together!"

Electra could not help but feel at ease with these nobles, which was never the case for her. She could tell that Felix enjoyed the attention too, but that he was taken a bit unawares. She secretly relished his discomfort.

They were shown to the four gilded couches which were set out in a crescent before the pool and the image of Eros hovering above the water. Watered wine was poured for all of them by the four attendant slaves who had also laid out platters of fruit, bread, and cheeses.

"Martia and I often come out here to eat at midday. To be alone and away from the bustle of the domus." Sextus nodded toward the distant expanse of his home.

"As a freedwoman, such lavish surroundings sometimes make me uncomfortable," Martia suddenly said, "but Sextus always makes me feel like an empress."

The aedile took his wife's hand and leaned across his couch to kiss it, smiling lovingly at her. "I see you are shocked, Felix Modestus! But as one knowledgeable in the ways of love and drama, you must surely know that Venus cannot be held at bay against her will. Martia was my family's freedwoman, but we fell in love and there was no turning away from it."

"Surely, as you come from an ancient family, your father would have been against such a union. The law forbids it, no?" Felix asked, sipping from his golden wine cup.

"Thank the Gods, I'm a sixth son!" Sextus said. "For my older brothers, especially the first three, you are quite right, it would never have been permitted. But by the time one gets to the sixth, no one much cares or notices!" he laughed. "I used to think it a curse to be born so late, so high upon the family tree, but then I never would have been able to follow my heart as I did."

"You are a poet, Aedile," Electra said.

He smiled. "I do dabble, that is true," he replied. "But please, lady. Call me Sextus."

"I'm surprised you did not take up a career as an artist," Felix said, a hint of disdain in his voice that went unnoticed except by Electra.

"Oh no," Sextus answered. "I wouldn't presume. I am more of a hobbyist with a great appreciation of art, especially the theatre. Though a sixth son who was able to marry the woman of his dreams, I am still expected to follow the Cursus Honorum and enter into politics. Many hands secure the family's position."

"Hence the importance of the Ludi Apollinares," Felix added.

"Precisely!" Sextus agreed. "When my father put forward my name, and our family's money, to run these games, Emperor Severus was most enthusiastic, as was Empress Julia Domna. She is a great lover of art! I've been invited on occasion to her intellectual symposia, and let me tell you, she is no slouch. A formidable woman!" Sextus slowed himself, took another sip and sighed.

There! Felix thought. *There is the stress!*

"But not only do I see these games as a necessary step in helping my family. I also see them as a way to enrich the lives of the people of Rome. To help them heal after the long wars."

"My husband is very noble in his intent," Martia said proudly.

Electra could not help but smile at both of them, but also feel a little envious.

"That is why you are here, Felix Modestus," the aedile said. "To help me help the people of Rome. If the Ludi Apollinares, which I have been commanded to put on, are a success, then I will be able to secure my own political future and that will allow me to become a great patron of the arts and artists which I so admire."

"It has always been his dream to do so," Martia said.

Sextus winked at his wife. "You understand me perfectly."

"Such noble ambition!" Felix said loudly, making the aedile grin proudly. "You honour me with your invitation, Sextus, and I promise you that our performance will not disappoint."

Sextus sat up and looked directly at Felix. "Oh, I have no doubt, Felix Modestus. That is why, when I saw your performance, I knew the Gods had led me there that night, that you were the one who would help me make these games the success they are destined to be." Another sigh. "I am afraid, however, that I may have overshot the budget. Do you know how expensive it is to bring in thousands of exotic animals from as far as Africa Proconsularis and Britannia? And then there are the gladiators...so costly!"

"I'm sure," Felix added, sympathetically, though secretly disgusted at the thought of competing with games in the amphitheatre. "And how many theatre troupes have you brought in?"

"Well, there I am excited. I've hired upwards of a thousand different companies - tragedians, mimes, pantomimes, acrobatic and musical groups and more from all corners of the empire. I want the cheers from the theatres to reverberate throughout Rome and drown out the blood-curdling cries of the amphitheatre and hippodrome crowds."

"A thousand different groups?" Even Felix could not hide his surprise.

"Yes, but you Felix Modestus…The Etrurian Players…will be the centrepiece performance of these ludi. I know how things work. If things play out as I hope and imagine, then there is no city in the Empire where you will not be welcome. The name of your company will be legendary."

Felix leaned back on his couch, his chest rising and falling as he imagined such a thing. The Etrurian Players were already famous in the East, but if he could take Rome by storm, then the West would open up to them like an eager virgin on her wedding night. "Sextus," Felix began, staring in earnest at the young politician, "I can tell you now that the Gods have given me signs that this production will be the greatest of my career. I promise you that."

The aedile let out a breath of air and smiled nervously. "You have no idea how relieved I am to hear you say that. Truly, this was meant to be!"

"Yes," Felix agreed. "But I was wondering if it is at all possible to secure more funding." He saw Sextus' face drop slightly, but pressed on. "You see, for this production to be of the caliber we need, only the very best of materials must be used in every aspect of its creation."

"I hear you, Felix Modestus, but I'm afraid that my coffers are nearly empty. To be honest, you have been given the largest allotment of funds. I can try and secure more from some of the other nobles, but they are not such lovers of theatre as I am."

"No, no!" Felix cut in, his hand up graciously. "Say no more. We are a successful company and quite capable of putting on this performance. I have other patrons who will be glad to help in this endeavour."

"Really?" Electra asked. "Who?"

Felix shot her a dark look as he swept back his thick hair. "You do not know them."

Electra let it go, despite the twinge in her stomach, and sipped at her wine, watching Felix closely.

"I'm glad to hear it," Sextus said. "If I can get more funding, I will though. I want to help."

"I appreciate that, Sextus," Felix smiled again.

"For now, is the warehouse I secured for you sufficient for your needs? You said you needed a large space, and that was the best I could find. Rome is so crowded now."

"It is perfect. We have everything we need there."

"Excellent!" Sextus stood then and walked to the edge of the pool to look at the three others upon their couches. "And now…for the good news!" He stood like an orator, his toga draped over one arm, standing as tall as his thick frame would allow. He smiled at his wife, and then looked at Felix and Electra both. "Yours will be the climactic performance of the Ludi Apollinares, and as such, you require a fitting stage."

"Yes?" Felix sat up at this.

"No temple steps performance for you, my friend. Not for The Etrurian Players!" Sextus was brimming with excitement now, matters of money set aside.

"Which theatre?" Felix asked.

"You will be performing in the great Theatre of Pompey!"

"You jest, Aedile!" Felix said.

"I do not!" Sextus clapped his hands loudly, making the slaves in the loggia nearby jump to attention. "The theatre is yours!"

Felix was on his feet instantly, his thick hands grasping the aedile by the shoulders and laughing joyously. "It's perfect!"

Rather than pull away, Sextus hugged Felix tightly, and it was as if a pact was made between brothers-in-arms.

"When can we move into the theatre?" Felix asked when they had all calmed down.

"Ah...well... There is that," Sextus said more soberly. "Because of all the performances throughout the city, you will only be able to rehearse in the theatre for one week before you take the stage in front of the audience."

"One week?" Felix asked, trying to hide the panic in his voice. "That is all?"

"I'm afraid so."

Felix recovered quickly. "It's fine. We shall rehearse in the warehouse. It certainly is large enough."

"I'm relieved to hear you say so," Sextus said. "But now, the main question I have…"

"Yes?"

"What play will you be performing? I assume you have decided. Is it a tragedy this time?"

"I wish," Electra grumbled under her breath.

Felix could feel her staring accusingly at him from the side. "No. It is not. We will be performing a comedy."

"Really?" Sextus' voice sounded doubtful and disappointed. "Which one?"

"Plautus' *Menaechmi*," Felix said.

"Really?" Sextus' voice was hesitant but he remain composed. "And how did you decide upon this?"

Felix wondered if he should tell the aedile about the dream he had had the night his letter had been delivered to him, that the Gods had demanded he perform *that* play, but he decided against it. "I know that the tragedies have a great impact upon the audience, Sextus, but comedy, when done correctly, can pierce the heart just as much, perhaps more so. Sometimes it is more impactful to send spectators away with tears of laughter in their eyes rather than tears from weeping. I strongly believe that. And what better way to win over Rome than with the greatest work of one of Her favoured sons?"

"I suppose," Sextus said, rubbing his chin as he tried to comprehend Felix's decision. Then, he began to nod, more and more convinced. "Yes. Yes, absolutely! The *Menaechmi* is very funny!"

"My thinking is that Rome needs to laugh after the long civil war, and then the bloodbath in Parthia," Felix added. "I've only just heard of more trouble in Africa Proconsularis and Numidia too!"

"Yes," Sextus agreed. "Something about a large-scale attack by the Garamantians or some such tribal group. A bloody mess." The aedile slapped his thick thigh. "You're right! Rome needs to laugh again. It *must* laugh! And you are just the man to make that happen, praise Apollo and the Muses!"

"They will laugh so hard, they'll piss themselves in their seats!" Felix added with a flair.

"Hahaha!" Sextus howled. "Quite! But perhaps not in front of the emperor!"

Felix paused at that. When he spoke again, his voice was serious. "Do you think you could manage to get the imperial family to attend?" He knew that if that happened, the production would be a resounding success. *If all the other pieces fall into place,* he reminded himself.

"I can make no guarantees," Sextus said, wiping the tears from his eyes. "But I will try."

"You are a man after my own heart, Sextus Annius Sabinus!"

The aedile smiled and motioned to one of the slaves to refill their golden wine cups. "A toast!" he said, looking from his wife to Electra, and then to Felix. "To making Rome laugh again!"

They tipped some wine onto the ground, and then drank together.

The conversation slowed after that, for Felix's mind now turned to the long list of things he must do, but more importantly the people he hoped he would be meeting that very night. So, once the wine cups were empty and the sun tipped fully into the afternoon, he and Electra took their leave of the friendly host and patron and departed the quiet world of his private gardens.

Sextus and Martia walked with them for some distance and paused in the path to wave them off as the slave led them back out into the street and their awaiting litter bearers.

When their guests were gone, Martia turned to her husband and grasped his hands. "You put a lot of faith in that man, friendly as he is."

"Yes, I do." Sextus sighed. "His idea is brilliant, but the play is a risk."

"Do you think they will be able to pull it off? Can they be relied upon?" she asked.

"He's a professional, and she a wonder upon the stage," Sextus said, holding his head up high, still watching the door in the wall through which their guests had departed. "I just hope the rest of their company is up for the task."

"As you say, my love, they are professionals. Pray the Gods help them to make Rome laugh."

Sextus smiled at his wife and leaned in to kiss her where they stood, alone in the middle of their idyllic surroundings, away from the cries of the crowded streets without.

"I'M STARTING TO GET NERVOUS ABOUT THIS IDEA OF YOURS," Electra said to Felix as the litter made its way back down the slope of the Esquiline Hill into the city streets. "Are you sure you interpreted your dream correctly? You know how you get after a long night of wine and debauchery!"

Felix waved off her accusatory tone.

"Why were you putting on such airs with the aedile? He and his wife were quite nice, sincere even. They were not like any patricians we've ever met before."

"They can afford to be," Felix said. "But yes, you're

correct. He is nice, but I wonder if he is strong enough to do what I need him to do. I need to make the man feel confident. He is hiring me for my performance, and that is what he will get. If that means putting on airs, then so be it."

Electra smiled. "He hired our company for me too."

Felix turned to look at her. "You enjoyed that, did you?"

"I enjoyed the look on your face when he said it!"

Felix laughed and kissed her. He tried to make light of it, but she could tell that he was nervous.

He was trying to think, but he found it extremely difficult to navigate the pathways of his mind when the one thing on which the Gods' plan hinged was in fact the greatest uncertainty. He would know by the end of that night if success would be within his grasp or not.

"There is time before this evening," Electra said, running her hand down his heaving chest. "Let's honour Venus for a while."

Felix reached up to touch her face and brush back her lustrous hair. "If only it were that easy."

Electra leaned back against her cushions, threw the curtains open, and watched the world of Rome's streets pass by without uttering another word.

V

A PROPOSITION AND THE PAST

The day was brilliant and sunlit when Clara Probita arrived in Rome on the barge from Ostia. It was a relief, for Rome was not the same in the rain, and she always remembered it in sunlight. She was not sure why she found that she could not enter Rome prior to the appointed day, but the thought of it made her nervous, and so she had rented an apartment for several days in Ostia, as if preparing herself for the coming encounter.

Rome held many memories for her, some warm and comforting, some painful, and some just plain awkward. After so many years, the letter from Felix Modestus had jarred her usually calm demeanour. She had thought of nothing else since her final days in Sicilia. However, when she boarded the ship for Ostia, she felt no regrets about her sojourn there, for she had been treated kindly by her husband. With him gone, she had the permission she needed to get on with her life.

"Oh, Roma…" she said to herself as she stood in the sunlight looking down on the Forum Romanum from the edge of the Arx of the Capitoline Hill. It was as if she were looking down on her past life again, waiting to see those same scenes of joy and pain play out amidst the crowded press of flesh below. "What do you have in store for me this day?" she wondered aloud. She sighed with great relief, however, for she had at least made the depositum of her entire fortune with one of the most reliable argentarii in Rome.

When Clara had arrived at the kiosk outside the temple of Juno Moneta to make her deposit, the man had, at first, looked on her with disdain. She wore only a simple, blue, gap-sleeved tunica and cloak, and no jewellery, for a woman walking alone in Rome did not want to attract too much attention. The argentarii of the Capitoline handled only the wealthiest of patrons, but when the man saw the amount upon the depositum note from the argentarius in Syracusae, he became quite friendly indeed.

While the argentarius noted the details of the depositum in his tabulae, Clara was offered a seat and refreshment at a small table beside the kiosk. It took some time, for the man was thorough in his scribblings, but Clara was in no rush to leave. Every step she had taken since arriving on the shores of the Tiber in Rome was hesitant, every thought weighted. There were memories around every corner, of laughter, of love, and of loss.

But she had walked on, determined not to be a silent Cassandra in the crowded world, but rather an armed Penthesilea wading into the thick of it. With her funds safely deposited on the Capitoline, and her single trunk of possessions held there for her, she descended into the Forum Romanum to walk onto the via Sacra before the Curia building and the newest triumphal arch which was, as she understood, only recently unveiled by Emperor Severus.

Flower petals still coloured the cracks between the great cobblestones of the forum, creating a vast colour mosaic at the foot of the soaring columns of the temples of Mars Ultor, Saturn, and of the Basilica Julia.

Clara could have hired a litter for the day, but she had opted to walk, and the more she walked, the more she fell in love with Rome once more. Of course, men's eyes followed her, despite her plain appearance, for it was the start of Veneralia, and most were feeling amorous. Yet she ignored them and walked on, enjoying the tangible air of joy and love that permeated the air. Flower petals rained down on her, catching in her blonde hair as she walked. But her steps halted abruptly when she stood before the Temple of Antoninus and Faustina.

She stood there staring up at the steps and remembered the performance that had almost happened, the image of her fleeing friend, and the shouts of the angry crowd that had gathered to be entertained and left only disappointed. Clara shook her head and refused to look upon the steps. She walked on toward the end of the via Sacra and turned right onto the via Appia, ignoring the roars emanating from the Colosseum and continuing on along the edge of the Palatine Hill until she arrived at a crowd of people standing before the recently unveiled Septizodium.

The play of water and marvelling cries of the crowd filled Clara's ears as she approached this new wonder of Rome. She joined the throng and looked up with the rest to gaze upon the enormous nymphaeum dedicated to the seven planetary deities, foremost among them, the Sun. The structure rose up three stories into the sky, each level supported by thick, colourful and polished columns of marble from around the Empire, including the emperor's homeland of Africa Proconsularis. Water cascaded from the upper levels to the lower ones in a graceful choreography about the feet of the statues of the Gods that adorned the niches set within. It was soothing to look upon, and was a welcoming sight for those entering the city from the South.

Clara Probita watched as children played about the base of the nymphaeum, their nursemaids or parents smiling as they tilted their heads to the sky to feel the gentle spray of water upon their joyous faces. When the breeze picked up, and the sunlight kissed the spray of sparkling water, the crowd was treated to a display of rainbow streaks arcing over their heads. Clara laughed in spite of herself, and perceived the structure as a theatre of water that could bring joy to any who stood before it.

It's good to be back! she thought to herself as she turned reluctantly away from the Septizodium, yielding her position in the crowd to the next onlooker.

Clara turned back onto the via Appia and followed the flow of traffic north. She passed beneath the soaring arches of the Aqua Claudia which brought fresh water to the Caelian Hill and the imperial palaces on the Palatine Hill and other districts of the city. The crowd thickened in the plaza surrounding the Colosseum then, and Clara began to feel the discomfort of many a wolf's eye staring at the form of her lonesome self in the crowd.

Veneralia was a time of love and joy in the city, but still, one had to go forward with caution. When she spied the peak of the temple of Venus and Rome, she made for the grand staircase before it and the sanctuary the goddess could provide.

The wind picked up and tussled the tresses of her blonde hair as she approached and paused at the bottom of the stairs.

"Why are you reluctant to go in?" A woman asked from the bottom right of the stairs.

Clara turned to her and felt a twinge of embarrassment for a moment as the woman's large breasts were open to the world. She had quite forgotten the colourful world of Rome's streets. The woman, however, emanated joy for some strange reason and Clara approached. "Are you not cold?"

The woman laughed, and the layers of her belly shivered. "No, dear. I am not. The goddess keeps me warm. Her temple is a great fire beside which I sit everyday."

"Are you a priestess?" Clara asked.

"Of a sort. I speak when there is a need. Some come to me for guidance, and I give it if I can honestly do so. Others, the

Gods throw into my lap. Those sorts are usually stubborn as mules!"

Clara chuckled and the act made the priestess smile widely where she sat in the sunlight. "The Gods have a way of setting people upon the right path."

"They certainly do." The woman observed Clara closely for a moment and then turned her thick neck to look up the stairs at the temple. "You should go in, dear. Make an offering to Venus and Rome, for they may change your life."

"They changed my life a long time ago," Clara countered, her smile fading before she looked up the stairs again. "But I will go in, and offer my prayers to the goddess."

"Astarte agrees," the priestess said.

"Astarte?"

"I was named for that goddess of war and love," she said. "And so, what better place to sit than between the bloody sands of the Colosseum, and the temple of Love herself."

"Well, Astarte…" Clara began, reaching into the scrip that hung hidden beneath the folds of her cloak. "I thank you for urging me up the stairs. I shall go and offer to Venus this day. Here." She bent down and dropped a brass dupondius into Astarte's bowl.

"May Venus' blessings be upon you, lady!" Astarte beamed.

Clara smiled and turned to go up the stairs, a little slowly and uncertainly. She had been there once before in the past, in the week before the almost-performance, praying that things should work out. But everything had fallen apart then, her dreams, her world, her heart. She had then tumbled embarrassingly down the wrong path. "This time, I will make things right."

"Are you all right, lady?" a man asked from nearby.

Clara did not respond for a moment, for her eyes were burning as she looked upon the temple.

"My lady?" the man said again.

Clara was about to turn away when she saw that it was a kindly man selling offerings who spoke to her. He was tall and thin, with short dark hair and a friendly smile. "Oh, uhm, yes… I need to purchase an offering for the goddess," she said, gathering her wits as she walked up to the table.

"Do you require something to win over the heart of some fortunate young man…or indeed a woman? Venus passes no judgement when true feelings of love are involved."

"No," Clara answered. "Not to win over someone, but to make amends for hurt feelings."

"I see…" The offering seller rubbed his smooth chin and cast his eye over his wares. The woman did not look wealthy, and he had seen her act kindly toward Astarte at the bottom of the stairs. "I have just the thing," he said, reaching down to pick up a small, blue glass phial of sea water. "Here. This water comes from the shores of Kythera where Venus herself emerged from the sea foam to bless the world."

"Are you sure that isn't just plain water?" Clara asked, immediately regretting her words when his smile faded.

"I assure you lady, Numonius takes his offerings to the Gods very seriously. This is sea water from that same island I spoke of. On my life. If you offer this to the goddess and utter your water-tight prayers and promises, the goddess will indeed listen."

Clara knew that water-tight promises to the Gods were a serious matter, but she also knew that she needed to make things right again with Felix in order to carry on with the new life she now envisioned for herself. "I will take it, Numonius. And I apologize for doubting your integrity. I have not been back to Rome for many years, and the last time did not go as planned."

Numonius smiled. "Things never do, lady. But the Gods can surprise us. I have seen much hope and expressions of love this day in Rome. How can things be wrong in the world when there is so much love? Do not worry."

"That is a lovely sentiment," Clara said. She nodded. "How much for the water?" Clara asked.

"A dupondius will do," he said.

"So little?"

"The Gods also reward generosity and kindness." Numonius glanced at Astarte down the stairs.

"Thank you," Clara said, most sincerely. She placed the coin in Numonius' hand and picked up the small glass phial before turning to go into the temple.

"May Venus bless you, lady!" Numonius called after her.

Clara walked slowly beneath the ten soaring Corinthian columns into the temple. She stopped to allow her eyes to adjust and, once they did, she gasped upon seeing the east-facing cella with the statue of Venus looking down on myriad people. Offerings were heaped about the goddess' feet - piles of flowers and herbs, coronae, and fruit. There was no victimarius at work, slaughtering animals to spray blood over the goddess' altar that day. It was not a time for blood-offerings.

Everywhere, men and women, girls and young men, stood gazing up at the high statue of the goddess whose head nearly reached into the domed rotunda of the temple. Garlands of flowers swayed from the beams of the cedar roof and clouds of sweet-smelling incense hovered among the colonnades on either side where smaller altars were also heaped with Veneralian gifts.

Clara gazed straight ahead, however, wishing to make her offering and prayers at the main altar. She pressed on through the crowd of worshippers, across the multi-coloured floor that resembled a beach of coloured pebbles, or a forest floor in autumn, until she arrived at the main altar.

The goddess stood there, one arm up above her shoulder, holding the folds of her peplos, while her other shoulder and one breast were bare. She held a golden orb in her left hand and gazed down lovingly.

Clara felt that the goddess looked upon her, but the guilt she felt threatened to spoil her prayers. For a moment, she thought of turning and running out, but then she took in the hope and love that surrounded her in that moment, listened to the whispered prayers upon others' lips, and knew that it was right she should be there. She raised her arms, palms up, and closed her eyes as she prayed.

Divine Venus, Goddess of Love… Guide me in this endeavour to make amends for the past so that I may move forward. I know that love is not meant for me, but let there be kindness in my future life, whatever form it may take. I let go of my illusions long ago, when last I was in Rome. Help me to cleanse my heart…

She could feel the frustrated tears gather upon her lids, and it surprised her that she should feel so strongly about it. It churned up the bitter and hurt feelings of the past in a way that she did not expect or want.

Clara opened her eyes then and unstoppered the phial before gently pouring the water onto the altar's crowded surface.

In that moment, the tang of sea water filled her nostrils and it was as if she could feel a strong, cool breeze upon the back of her neck.

"Guide me, oh Goddess," Clara whispered. "I will listen and follow." She then set the phial upon the altar as well, and made her way around the cella to go out the other, distant side of the temple which led back into the Forum Romanum.

Outside, the sun was dipping and she immediately felt her heart begin to race.

"Evening," she said to herself as she looked around to get her bearings.

Clara Probita breathed in and out slowly a few times and then descended the steps onto the via Sacra to make her way

through the forum and then on to find the Taberna
Macedonica.

To Rufio Pagano, Rome was a stinking cesspit. He had
always known that, but to be reminded of it was no pleasant
experience. Even before he entered the city, he had felt a sting
in his nostrils that made him stop to check the bottom of his
sandals and discreetly sniff his underarms in the midst of the
lines of carts and people going in and out of the city on the via
Flaminia.

"Rome," he said to himself through gritted teeth. "I can't
do this!" He turned suddenly to go back the other way, no
matter that he had travelled some days in a neighbouring
farmer's cart to get there. He had thought about riding his
horse the entire way, but when he had tried bridling her she
had kicked him and run off again. When he heard his neighbour was heading to the markets of Rome with a wagon load
of mushrooms, he tagged along reluctantly.

"What are you doing?" someone yelled at him and he tried
to go back against the traffic.

"Wrong way, dummy!" shouted another.

Rufio stumbled, twisted and turned to avoid a particularly
large wagon and tripped on the cobblestones so that he fell off
the side of the road into the drainage ditch with a great splash.

The parade of wagons, horsemen and pedestrians howled
with laughter at him as he spluttered around trying desperately
to extricate himself from the foul quagmire of mysterious dark
and lumpy liquid running alongside the road.

Rufio's gorge rose and he pulled himself onto the sunlit
grass and shook as if he were an angry cat. His satchel had
been spared the experience. He had thrown that over the ditch
as he fell. But the lumps of rubbish on his face made him sick,
and he began to wonder if the Gods were mocking him. *Is that*

clapping? he wondered angrily, looking about for the shade of his father.

"Here! Use this to wipe yourself!" someone from a passing wagon yelled, and tossed a piece of linen at him which stuck to his chest.

"Thank you!" Rufio said aloud, but as he lifted the cloth to his face he smelled the bowels of Hades there and realized it was a soiled baby's breeches. He tossed it quickly away from himself as a chorus of laughter exploded from the back of the wagon. "Cunnus!" Rufio cursed at them. He had an urge to vomit then, but refused to give another roadside performance to all of the people watching him as they passed. He gathered up his satchel, shook his tunica free of lumpy detritus, and rejoined the flow of traffic toward the city. "Felix…you better be dying."

A SHORT WHILE LATER, RUFIO HAD PASSED THROUGH THE CITY gates and the city of Rome enclosed him as if he had walked into the maw of some giant beast. Though he had already been reminded of the stench of the city, he had forgotten the feeling of buildings about to fall over onto him, the puddles of filth, the rudeness of the people, and the beggars and pickpockets who swarmed and hunted any outsider.

However, Rufio had no such problems in that moment as a halo of space formed around him, onlookers, including streetdwellers, covering their noses and turning from him with disdain.

The curtains of a passing litter opened wide then and a matron with bulging eyes tossed a bronze assarius at him. "Get thee to a bath, beggar!" she yelled before slamming the curtains shut again.

"I'm not a beggar!" Rufio yelled back. "I'm a farmer!"

Nevertheless, he bent to pick up the coin and continued down the street.

Rufio had no memory of Rome's warren of byways and thoroughfares. In truth, he had no idea where he was going. And though he had waited outside the city before approaching, he knew he had arrived too early in the day to meet Felix. Already, he longed for the quiet fields and forests of Etruria. He had forgotten how much he hated the crowds in Rome and his eyes sought danger around every corner as he went along like a paranoid and skittish mule, plodding along reluctantly into the heart of the city.

Finally, the looks and comments that were constantly thrown at him, like the contents of piss pots from upper storey windows, became too much and he realized he had better wash before meeting his friend. "They'll never let me into the taberna if I don't!" he said to himself.

Having wandered for a while, Rufio arrived quite by accident at the baths of Titus on the slope of the Oppian Hill. The quiet echo of water and splashing was a welcome sound to his ears, but not so much the sneering of the attendant slaves who ushered him through as quickly as possible.

"Wash quickly, man! In a few minutes it will be the hour for women and children."

"Yes, yes!" Rufio barked back at the man. "All right!" he said before going into the apodyterium and placing his satchel in a lone cubicle at the end of the row. He turned to the slave on the other side of the changing room. "Can you wash my tunica while I bathe?"

"No!" the slave retorted. "I can burn it though!"

Rufio looked down at his soiled travel tunica. "Cacare," he muttered, nodding to himself. "Yes. Please burn it," he said to the slave. "I have an extra in my satchel."

"Good for you!" the attendant bit back.

Rufio glared at the slave, removed the stained and stinking tunica, and tossed it at him. "Off you go!"

The attendant squealed in disgust and recoiled as the garment fell in a heap at his feet.

Rufio tossed him the assarius his non-begging had garnered him.

The man ran away, pinching his nose with one hand and holding out the soiled tunica with the other.

Having stripped down, Rufio entered the baths to soak and scrub himself, having paid a quadrans for scented oil and a strigil, not having any of his own. The tepidarium was warm and welcoming and not too crowded. It allowed Rufio to calm his shattered nerves as he washed the filth from his body, hair, and short beard. He watched the filth run away from him toward the drain and sighed as he imagined what he must have looked like going through the streets.

"I should have made more money," he said to himself, his voice echoing to the domed ceiling above.

Once he was finished in the warm room, he proceeded to the caldarium to begin his sweating, apply oil, and use the strigil to scrape away the remnant filth that felt as though it were seeping out of his pores. It felt good to bathe in this way, he had to admit, for back on the farm, he had only a single tub into which he poured water heated over the fire.

He sat himself upon one of the benches in the hot room, letting the sweat bead on his forehead when someone sat down. For a moment, he tried not to look at the naked man beside him, however, he could sense the bare white buttocks sidling toward him on the bench.

"How are you today?" the man asked in a croaky, hushed voice that made Rufio's skin crawl, not unlike it felt after falling in the ditch.

Rufio stood quickly and began to walk away. "I'm quite fine thank you. Just want to be alone."

"You don't have to be, you know!" the man called after him from the room's steamy cloak.

"Oh, yes I do!" Rufio said as he rushed through to the frigidarium and threw himself into the cold pool. "Rome!" he growled.

After a few sputtering minutes in the cold plunge to revive himself, Rufio climbed out and went back to the apodyterium to dry himself off and dress in the only tunica he possessed that was without holes or stains. He unrolled the dark blue garment and slid it over his head before buckling his cingulum around his waist. Once he had tied up his sandals, he spied the bath slave watching him. He looked from the slave to his satchel and, immediately suspicious, opened his satchel and searched inside to make sure everything was still there where he had wrapped them in the folds of a rust-coloured cloak - the letter from Felix, his pouch of coin, still the same weight as when he had entered, and a couple of scrolls in case he had time to read.

Everything was accounted for, and he sighed to himself with relief. He then carefully removed the cloak and wrapped it about his shoulders before hoisting his satchel and making for the exit.

"Those colours don't match," the slave muttered as he passed.

Rufio paused, and turned to the slave. "Oh, I forgot to tell you, there's an older man in the caldarium. He asked me to send you in for help. I think he wants to give you a tip for your hard work."

"Really?" the slave said.

"Oh, yes. He seemed quite eager!" Rufio said over his shoulder as he left, smiling to himself before heading toward the towering mass of the Colosseum before him.

. . .

RUFIO FELT MUCH BETTER ABOUT HIMSELF AFTER HIS VISIT TO the baths, more hopeful for the day, due in no small part to the the brilliance of the sun that lit the cobblestones as he walked along. He was suddenly very hungry. He always was when his mood improved, and so he stopped at a vendor of honeyed pastries before one of the arches about the base of the Colosseum. Looking carefully about as he dipped a finger into his money pouch, he fished out a quadrans and paid for the cheese-filled delight.

The plaza about the amphitheatre was crowded, and this normally would have bothered him no end, but then he felt a strange optimism. He could not explain it to himself, the reason for his lightness of heart, but then he was where he was meant to be in that moment, despite the tang of the city still clinging to his nostrils.

Rufio even hummed as he walked, looking up at the arches of the Aqua Claudia as he passed beneath. A couple of running children bumped him as they passed on their way to join a larger crowd up ahead. He checked his satchel quickly, feeling his muscles tense at the brief encounter, but relaxed when he realized that he still carried all of his possessions. He shook his head at his momentary paranoia and carried on toward the crowd to see what was happening. "Maybe some street performers?" he wondered to himself.

He pushed his way to the front of the crowd the better to see, and when he reached the vanguard of the cheering mass, he found himself not in front of a group of tumblers or musicians, but rather a massive wall of brightly coloured marble where jets of water sprang and danced about the feet of the Gods.

"What is this?" he said with awe in his voice, for he had never seen such a thing.

"People are calling it the 'Septizodium'," said a man beside him. "Emperor Severus created it for the people of Rome…another beautiful addition to the city."

Rufio looked at the man and saw that he, and the crowd of massed faces behind him were adorned with joyous smiles as their heads tilted skyward as if to feel the sun itself. "What a marvel!" Rufio said, turning back to the watery performance.

He watched for at time, wondering how the creators had managed such a feat, for he had a passing interest in such things, though he was no engineer.

It was then that the watery jet at the bottom near him began to sputter and then stop, causing other jets to fade to nothing.

Rufio heard the crowd behind him moan with such sadness then that he turned to see clouds crossing their assembled visages. He looked back to the Septizodium, already longing for the feeling of peace and beauty the structure had lent him. He stepped forward and hoisted himself up on the marble edge of the pool at the base to peer inside. There, beside the stoppered jet of water, shimmering beneath the surface, Rufio spied a piece of linen blocking a water intake. He rolled up his sleeve and reached in to pull at the obstruction which was solidly lodged. His feet dangled in the air behind him and the people at the front of the crowd wondered at the buttocks of the man that had joined the constellations of the emperor's nymphaeum.

Finally, after pulling harder and harder, Rufio yanked out the blockage and immediately, a loud groan erupted from within the Septizodium. He looked down into the water just in time to feel the full force of the paused jet smash directly into his face.

Rufio felt himself throttled and tumbling backward from atop the pool's wall to land in a sputtering heap upon the cobbles at the base. He could not see as his head spun, but he could certainly hear the loud applause and howling laughter of the crowd as they took in his public misfortune. He had bumped his head and when he made to get to his feet, the world spun and his vision went black.

THERE WAS WATER EVERYWHERE IN RUFIO'S MIND, UNDER AND over him, smashing into him from every side, pounding into his face. His hearing, muted and not at all what it should be, came in and out in waves, and a great discomfort invaded the world of his brain. Then, he saw her, behind the curtain of his mind, and he remembered his last time in Rome.

"I'm sorry, my love… Forgive me…"

But the apparition leaned in to kiss him, her face one joyous, smiling light…

It was the great peals of laughter that made him stop and take note of the wet feeling all about him, especially the sloppy lashing of his face.

Rufio sputtered and opened his eyes to see the howling mass of people before him, jeering, pointing, buckled forward in the grips of a humorous rictus. He felt his face lashed again and turned to see the furry black and white visage of a dog licking him upon the lips.

"Ahh!" Rufio screamed and crabbed backward against the marble wall.

The hound followed and licked again, his pointy ears and mismatched eyes not a thing of terror but rather of city mischief and mocking.

"Get away!" Rufio shouted, pushing the animal away.

Without another lick, the dog spun, lifted its leg, and urinated upon the fallen bumpkin.

"What in Hades!"

The crowd roared again, quite forgetting the water dance of the Septizodium for the sputtering tourist at their feet.

The dog turned back to Rufio, seemingly proud of his aim

and accomplishment, and then eyed the satchel which lay a couple of feet away.

"Oh no you don't!" Rufio said.

But the dog did! The animal lunged for the satchel, took it up in his teeth, and made a quick retreat back toward the Colosseum.

"Come back here!" Rufio shouted, tearing after the animal, the mocking applause in his wake.

Rufio followed the black and white blur as quickly as he could, weaving his way in and out of milling groups of lovers and friends, past the aqueduct, and then toward the Colosseum, until the dog made a sharp left and headed straight for the large temple and its steps.

He felt his gut stinging with the effort, his clothes sodden and urine-spattered. *I hate Rome!* he wanted to shout, but then his eye caught sight of the dog at the bottom of the temple steps sitting beside a large, seated woman who was peering into the depths of his satchel.

"Hey! Stop that! That's mine!" Rufio yelled as he ran toward the woman.

She looked up at him with a beaming smile. "I wondered where Peli got this!"

Rufio did not wait for her to extend the satchel but snatched it quickly out of her hands only to reveal the broadness of her naked bosom behind. "Oh! Um… Sorry!" he turned away, his face an even darker shade of red than it had been. "This is my bag. The dog stole it from me."

The woman's smile never faded. "Not to worry, dear. Peli meant no harm. I'm sure he only wanted to rescue you from some embarrassment or other."

"More like add to it!" Rufio growled, looking at the dog whose tongue hung out such that it gave him a smiling air. Rufio wiped his mouth, the memory of the dog's embrace falling hard upon his mind then.

The woman pat the dog, and it nuzzled the side of her bare chest.

Rufio recoiled slightly.

"It seems that Venus…and Peli…have brought us together this day," the woman said. "I have helped many people until now, and the goddess is pleased with Astarte."

"Astarte?" Rufio repeated.

"I am Astarte!" she replied, leaning back against the stone wall and stretching her arms wide.

For a moment, Rufio could not help but gaze upon the twin moons beneath her beaming smile, but then he looked away and up the stairs to the temple.

"It is the start of Veneralia. Venus demands her offerings, does she not?" Astarte asked. "You look like you are in need, and I would help you."

Rufio looked down at his sodden, dirty tunica, and felt desperate at his newly-filthy state.

"Let us make love into the night and offer ourselves to Venus," Astarte said, her smile thinning as her green eyes brightened.

"Oh…ah…my thanks, lady…" Rufio began to back away toward the stairs. "I'm meeting a friend soon and I don't want to be late."

"She's a lucky woman," Astarte sighed.

"Oh, she's not a woman," Rufio added.

"Venus is pleased by all loves, not to worry, dear," she said, her palms turned to the sky.

"No, no, no!" Rufio said. "I'm just meeting a friend, is all."

"Go then," Astarte said, her smile returned. "And may the goddess bless you, and whomever your heart sets its sights upon."

"Thank you…Astarte…" Rufio said, bowing to her for no reason.

She chuckled as she watched him run up the stairs, and

turned to the dog at her side. "Stay with him, Peli. This one needs help." She kissed the dog upon the muzzle and he immediately went up the stairs after Rufio's retreating form.

At the top of the stairs, in the midst of the congregation of people going in and out of the temple of Venus and Rome, Rufio stopped and looked up at the sky which was now on the verge of evening pink. He focussed upon that sky, trying to ignore the mass of strangers about him as he clutched his satchel to his chest.

Breathe, Rufio, he told himself. *Breathe…*

He coughed, for the air was choked with the scent of sweat and perfume, incense wafting out of the temple, and a pungent hint of urine. He longed for the earthy smells of Etruria, to be away from the stench of the city. He sniffed the air again, like a boar coming into the open field at dusk, then sniffed closer until he realized that the smell of urine was coming from him. He felt something nuzzle his leg, and looked down to see the dog, Peli, looking up at him most quizzically.

"You," he said to the animal whose head tilted sideways. "You did this."

The dog sat, and sighed audibly.

"Yes. That's how I feel." Rufio waved his hand, hoping the dog would flee, but it rested upon its haunches most resolutely. "I'm not going to be your friend. You know that don't you? Friends don't piss on each other!"

The people around Rufio gave him a wide berth as they passed around him, and he was not quite sure where to go from there.

"Peli!" said a man from not far off. "Leave that man alone! Come here!"

Rufio turned to see the nearest offering seller waving at the dog which now ran to him and sat before him. He followed, having nothing better to do. "Is he yours?" Rufio asked.

"Oh, no," the offering seller said as he held out a piece of a biscuit for the animal to take out of his hand. "Peli belongs to no one. He kind of goes where he wishes. He's very protective of those whom he likes, especially Astarte down there." He pointed to the priestess at the bottom of the temple stairs. "The other day someone started shouting at her because he didn't like the fortune she gave him, so Peli bit the man. Nabbed him right in the figs!" The offering seller laughed, but Rufio instinctively covered himself. "You should have heard the man howl!"

"I'll wager he did," Rufio said, distracted by the smell wafting off of him.

"I'm Numonius," the seller said, trying to catch Rufio's eye.

"Rufio," he muttered in return.

"Tell me what's wrong, Rufio. Love troubles? I've seen it all today."

"Pfft!" Rufio scoffed. "Not likely. No."

"You can tell me," Numonius pressed. "Perhaps the goddess will bless you. I have many offerings. Not all is lost or unrequited love on this day. True, I've seen many a broken hearted man or woman at my table since the start of Veneralia, but I've also seen love in its full bloom. Look over there!"

Rufio turned to where he saw a man in a toga standing on the steps, looking out over the crowds for someone. He seemed nervous, but held his head high. "Why? Who's that?"

"That's what it means to be blessed by the Gods. He's a young tribune. He's made quite a name for himself in the legions and has come to the attention of the emperor."

"Good for him, I suppose," Rufio shrugged.

"You miss my meaning," Numonius added. "He's found great success, but what concerns him most today, in this moment, is the woman he's waiting for. From what I've heard from the tribune's sister, Venus herself has thrown them together, here in Rome, even among so many people. They have found each other. Look, there…" Numonius pointed as two women approached and the tribune went to meet them. "I see meetings every day in my work, but that is one of the most honest moments I've ever witnessed." Numonius looked up at the temple and then to the three people who headed down the stairs and onto the via Sacra into the Forum Romanum.

"What's your point?" Rufio asked.

"Just that there is love and hope for everyone. Veneralia reminds us of that. From what I hear, the tribune is a great warrior, but when it comes to love, even he worries."

"I stopped thinking of love a long time ago," Rufio said, trying not to look up at the temple which, he felt, was leaning more closely over him. The subject caused Rufio no end of discomfort, especially there, in that place, and so he turned to browse over the items on the table. "You have quite the array of fine, fresh herbs, I see. Rosemarinus for sepsis… Origanum for sickness… Do you grow them yourself?"

"My cousin has a farm near Albanum. I buy them from him." Numonius looked over Rufio again. "You're a farmer," he stated with certainty.

"Yes!" Rufio said, looking up from the table. "How did you know?"

"Just a hunch." Numonius smiled.

"I have a small farm in Etruria. Not far from Saena Iulia."

"What do you grow?" Numonius asked.

"Grow? Oh, well… I suppose I try and grow olives…some grapes…" Rufio shook his head. "Enough to survive on anyway. I have a small domus, a horse, Stella my donkey, some chickens… In truth, I'm not much of a farmer, but I do love it in the countryside. It's not like Rome. It smells good. There is colour everywhere, even in winter. I can think to myself when I come out of my domus in the morning and look upon a tract of land that is all my own… At least I can now that my father is gone."

"My condolences," Numonius said, feeling for the man before him. "How long has he been gone?"

"A few days," Rufio said suddenly.

"May he find his way to Elysium then," Numonius said kindly.

"Oh, he'll clap and shout until the Gods themselves open the gates for him. Of that I have no doubt!"

Numonius chuckled but put his hand to his nose as he caught a whiff of Rufio. "So…erm…what are you in Rome for?"

"I'm here to meet a friend I haven't seen in many years. He needs my help. It's a matter of life and death, apparently. I arrived from Etruria just today."

"When are you meeting your friend?"

Rufio looked at the sky. "Soon, but I…ah…"

Numonius nodded. "You want to go to the baths first?"

Rufio pursed his lips and looked down at Peli who still sat upon the ground between them, looking from one to the other. "That's just it! I did go, but then, I was knocked unconscious by that wall of water down the road there, and then this one…" he glared at the dog, "…he decided to urinate on my only tunica."

Numonius felt for the man. It was not a warm welcome to Rome, especially on a day when so many felt joy. "Listen…ah…"

"Rufio Pagano."

"Rufio," Numonius repeated and touched him on the shoulder. "I don't need to sell you anything, but I am going to give you something to help. Here." He reached down and picked up a tiny phial of oil off the table. "This is clove oil. Sprinkle it on your tunica and it will cover up the smell enough to enter your friend's domus."

"I'm meeting him at the taberna Macedonica, wherever that is."

"I see." Numonius knew the place. It was crowded and boisterous. "Use the whole phial then."

"All right…" Rufio said as he took the phial and removed the cork. He smelled it and found that, though it was strong, it was much better than what he already stank of. He then poured droplets on the sleeves of his tunica, and into his hands to dab beneath his arms and behind his neck.

Numonius smiled courteously at passers by who observed the strange man at his table, seemingly doing a mime of washing before the temple of Venus. He looked back at Rufio. "That's a much better odour than what Peli gave to you!"

Rufio sighed. "Yes. Thank you. How much do I owe you."

Numonius put up his hand. "It is a gift from me to you this day. May it help you in meeting your friend, and perhaps lead to a lusty encounter with one of Rome's lupae, of which there are many."

"What happened to true love?" Rufio asked.

It was Numonius' turn to shrug. "Love comes in many forms, my friend."

"I'm fine," Rufio held up his hand. "I just want to see my friend, and then get out of this place."

"I understand," Numonius said. "But you are good to leave the beauty of Etruria behind to come and help your friend. You must be close."

"We were," Rufio said. He felt sadness wash over him then. "I let him down before…and another good, dear friend. I didn't want to repeat that mistake. If I can help save his life, I will."

"As I said, you're a good friend."

Rufio looked about a little awkwardly, aware that it was a natural end to the conversation. "Can you tell me which way to go to the taberna Macedonica? Apparently, it's near the theatre of Marcellus."

"Just follow the via Sacra through the forum, then round the base of the Capitoline Hill. Then turn left. Once you are in that neighbourhood, just ask anyone and they will point you in the right direction. The theatre crowds gravitate to that taberna in particular."

"Thank you for your help, Numonius," Rufio said, growing quite nervous about wading into the crowds once more, worried about what else might befall him on route to his destination.

"Think nothing of it. If you need anything else, I'm usually around here or at the temple of Apollo on the Palatine Hill."

"Thank you. But I'll likely be back in Etruria in a couple of days, if all goes well," Rufio said as he began to leave, eyeing the dog to make sure he did not follow.

"Wait!" Numonius said quickly. "Don't you want to make an offering to the goddess? It is Veneralia after all!"

"No thanks! Venus doesn't care for this one!" Rufio indicated himself, turned, and carried on his way. "I'll be happy just to make it to the taberna without getting pissed on!"

"Good luck, Rufio Pagano!" Numonius called after him as he watched the farmer head down the steps and into the Forum Romanum. He looked down at Peli who remained with him. "Another biscuit?"

The dog licked his chops.

"Oh, all right," Numonius said. He handed Peli a biscuit which was quickly gobbled up. "Go on then. Follow him. Keep him out of trouble."

Peli quickly charged down the temple steps, rounded the corner and then went after Rufio who had already disappeared somewhere in the forum crowd.

.   .   .

IT WAS DUSK, AND THE SKY ABOVE ROME WAS BURSTING WITH pink and red that lent loving shades to the facades of the temples and colonnades about the city.

Clara Probita had been walking for some time before she had worked up the courage to head for the theatre of Marcellus and look for the Taberna Macedonica where Felix had asked to meet.

After searching for a time, she finally found it on a narrow street, along the cliff base of the Capitoline Hill. It was a smaller establishment at the end of a row of a dozen or so tabernae, all of them busy, all of them smelling of wine. Some were louder than others.

Once she found it, Clara stood before the double wooden doors. They were flanked by Ionic columns covered with grape vines. On either side, two torches flickered in the gathering dark.

Clara found she could not make her feet go forward, and noted that her heart raced as if in a strange, forgotten rhythm from her youth.

Don't be ridiculous! she chided herself. *It's Felix! One of your best friends in the world.* She knew it was true, but there was that part of her that could not relinquish the embarrassing circumstances of the last time they had met in Rome. *Stop it, Clara! It's time to put the past behind you!*

She reached out, took hold of the door handle, and marched into the taberna.

The place was warm and brightly-lit, not full of patrons yet, but busy enough to make it hard to find Felix.

Clara wondered if she would even recognize him and searched the many faces gazing in her direction.

"There she is!" a great, booming voice swept from the back of the taberna toward her, like a warm, gusty sirocco out of the South.

Clara turned to look and spotted him, standing alone above

a table laden with food, his arms spread wide, and a great smile spanning his bearded face. Clara felt an easiness wash over her that only Felix could bring about, and she cut a weaving path through the scattered tables toward him.

"A round of applause for my dearest friend!" Felix bellowed, and the patrons hooted and obliged with gusto.

"You haven't changed!" Clara said as she walked up to him, stopping short before his bulky outline.

Before she could say anything else, Felix took her up in a great bear hug. "It's been too long!" he said, finally releasing her and standing back to look at her. "I'm so grateful you've come, Clara. I had begun to wonder."

"What? That I wouldn't come to help an old friend in need?" she said.

He grew quiet, his eyes softening as he took her hands. "I had hoped, and the Gods have delivered. Thank you."

"Felix," she said, taken unawares by the swirling emotions she was beginning to feel, and the strangeness of being alone with him. "What is wrong?"

"All in good time," he said, patting her hands. "For now, let's sit and eat and talk." He turned to the tavern keeper. "Philemon! A crater of wine!"

"Right away, Felix Modestus!" the burly Greek said from behind his bar.

"People still know you here?" Clara laughed as she removed her cloak and sat down with her back to the rest of the tavern.

"In some places, yes. This is my world, and though I haven't been back to Rome since…well…for a while…the name of 'Felix Modestus' is still known among those of discerning tastes."

Clara eyed him. *Same old Felix.* His grandeur still made her smile, even though she had known him from a time before his muscles had bulged into formation upon his body. "Speaking of Rome, and the last time we were here. I need to say something-"

Felix put his hand up. "We can discuss that later. For now, let us drink and eat while you tell me about your life since then. I've missed you, Clara!"

She sat back, resigned as ever to his direction.

"Here we go!" the tavern keeper, Philemon, arrived with a crater decorated with theatre masks, filled to the brim with carefully watered wine. He set it down and smiled at Clara, while one of the serving girls also set down two clay cups. "You'll find, my lady, that I have the very *best* of everything here, especially the wine, and especially for Felix Modestus!"

"You're too kind," Felix said as he ladled some wine into the cups. "This is one of my oldest and dearest friends, Philemon. Whenever you see her, treat her well and kindly, and give her whatever she wishes…on my tab!"

"Oh, really. There's no need for that!" Clara said, but Felix brushed it off.

"Very good, Felix Modestus!" Philemon said before leaning down to speak with Clara. "You know… I saw him perform the Tragedy of Herakles in Athenae once. He had me in tears."

Felix bowed his head. "It was a good show," Felix said.

"Will the rest of your company be joining you this evening?" Philemon asked.

"Not today. They are back at our theatrical base of operations, preparing for the start of the campaign. Tonight is just for Caesar and his lady."

"Right." Philemon nodded, touching the side of his nose.

"Please have the girl bring a third cup when you have a chance," Felix said quickly. "Things are better in threes."

"Right away." Philemon left them alone then to talk. Shortly after, the girl set another cup on the table, which Felix promptly pushed aside. He leaned to look Clara in the eyes.

"Please, let's eat, and drink and talk, Clara. I've missed you so much these many years."

"I…I've missed you too. So much has happened," she said nervously as she took up a piece of flat bread, cheese, and a fig, all of which she placed on the small plate before her.

Felix helped himself to the platter of food as well, filling his plate with strips of grilled meat, bread, beans, and figs. "Try the grilled meat. Best in the city, and not made of stray cat."

Clara took more food and then nibbled distractedly on the bread. "So, you have a company of actors?" she asked finally, trying to get the conversation going so as not to have to endure his stare for too long, as warm as it made her feel.

Felix leaned back, his chest and arms out. "Yes! 'The Etrurian Players', we're called."

"You've had a lot of success then?"

"We've performed in every major theatre and city across the Middle Sea, from Carthago Nova to Antiochia, from Alexandria to Athenae. We're based in Ephesus."

"And Rome?" Clara asked. "You must have performed here many a time?"

Felix lowered his arms. "No, actually. Rome has eluded me."

She was quiet, staring at her plate of food, but he pulled her attention back when he reached across the table to take her hand.

"What have you been doing, Clara? How have you been? I heard you had married…a man from near Syracusae." He looked guilty then as he let go of her hand, his eyes on hers again. "I thought about contacting you when I was performing there several years ago, but I didn't want to intrude. It felt strange."

Clara sat back. "I was married, yes."

"Did your bastard father arrange it?" Felix growled, remembering how cruel Clara's father had been to her.

"He did, and it was the only good thing he ever did for me."

"Oh?"

Clara smiled. "The man I was married to, Aeson, was much older than I and lonely in life. He did not want a wife so much as a daughter to care for, and who could care for him."

"Where is your husband now?"

"He passed away some three years ago." For a moment, Clara remembered the older man, his smile, his gentle, fatherly demeanour.

"I am sorry." Felix rubbed his beard. "Was he kind to you?" Felix asked, his voice dark, almost as if he dreaded the answer.

"Most kind."

"Thank the Gods! I thought I might have to inscribe a curse tablet and send it to him in Hades."

"Nothing of the sort is required. Aeson was a good man, better to me than ever my father had been."

"I'm relieved to hear it. And life in Syracusae?"

"I never really fit in, especially after Aeson died. The locals thought I killed him."

"That's absurd!" Felix bellowed. "You? Not a chance!"

"I know. But I couldn't stay there anymore. I stayed for a few years after he passed, and now I've sold everything."

"Was he…was he very wealthy?" Felix asked.

For some reason, Clara did not want to talk about money. She did not know why exactly, but that she wanted Felix to see her as she once was, not as the wealthy widow she had become. It was not a role she relished. "I had all that I needed. But I did bring everything I have with me."

"You've left Syracusae for good?" Felix asked.

Clara nodded. "Yes. I'm going back to Etruria."

"Really? Back home?"

"Exactly."

"Back to olives, and pigs, and cattle, and grapes? Back to your parents?"

"Not to my parents, but yes, back to Etruria. I've missed it and want to make a new start."

Felix took up his cup and held it out to her. "Well…to the Gods and to new beginnings!" He tipped some wine onto the floor and she followed suit before they both drank.

There was an awkward silence then as Felix seemed to be lost in thought as he stared into his cup.

"Felix," she said, seeing her opportunity to broach the subject that had been haranguing her mind ever since she received his letter. "We need to talk about the last time we met here in Rome."

Felix looked up quickly at that but his wide eyes stared past her and he was on his feet before she could speak. "THERE HE IS!"

Clara turned slowly in her seat to see who Felix was talking about. *Probably one of his actors,* she thought, but when she followed Felix's gaze a great lump caught in her throat. *Rufio?*

Felix was practically walking over the tables to get to the dishevelled, rough-looking man who stood at the entrance to the taberna looking like a gazelle in the middle of the amphitheatre.

All around him, people eating covered their noses and paused in their conversations to catch their breath.

Felix, however, did not care, and took up his old friend a great embrace. "Rufio Pagano!" he cried, laughing. "You came! And you smell of clove!"

"Felix!" Rufio laughed in spite of himself. He felt his bones crack as Felix hugged him, and air filled his lungs once more as he was released. "It's good to see you, old friend!"

"My brother!" Felix said, looking over Rufio. "The Gods bless us, you came! I had my doubts, I must admit." Felix, his arm around Rufio, turned him to walk him back to the table.

Rufio, who had been staring at the floor, trying not to meet the eyes of the people about who most certainly smelled him, raised his head as they began to walk and then stopped in his tracks.

What? He screamed inside, his heart suddenly pounding wildly, his eyes taking in the dirty sight of his tunica and cloak. *It's Clara!* He began to turn away for the shear panic he felt in that moment, but Felix's grip on his shoulder was unyielding.

"Clara!" Felix called across the taberna. "Look who it is!"

Clara stood, her grey eyes wide in disbelief. She looked down at her blue tunica and straightened it before looking at the missing person in their former triad.

Rufio's eyes looked in every direction except at Clara. In that moment, he felt a resurgence of myriad joyous and painful emotions, all of them tainted with a guilt that made him want to turn and run for the doorway. Finally, he could no longer avoid looking at her as Felix took him and Clara by the shoulders as though forcing the greeting. Rufio looked into his childhood friend's eyes without smiling. "Hello Cl…Clara."

"Rufio," she said. The sound of the name upon her lips felt strange after so many years.

Felix looked from one to the other of them. He had, of course, been nervous about the deception, but he wondered if either of them would have come if they had known the other would be present. "Together again!" he said loudly and as joyously as he could manage.

Rufio and Clara both turned to look up at him, their eyes both terrified and accusing at once.

"What?" Felix said in an unusually sheepish way for his greatness.

"You said you needed my *help*!" Clara stood back a little from them.

"I do!" Felix nodded.

"You said it was a matter of *life and death*!"

"It is!" Felix protested. He looked from Clara to Rufio and then back to Clara.

But he did not see Rufio backing away, his eyes still fixed on Clara. Rufio felt dizzy, and would have vomited there and then were his stomach not empty once more. No matter how much food was heaped upon Felix's table, he could not bear to be manipulated in that way, forced to look upon Clara in his current state. He could hear Felix and Clara talking, but had no inkling about the subject of their conversation.

"Rufio?" Clara's voice came into his hearing as if from behind a curtain. "Rufio? Say something!"

Rufio shook his head and looked at both of them. "I...I...I have to go." He turned and began to flee the situation with his eye set on the far door of the taberna, like his own horse making for the open gate of the paddock.

But the second he turned, his first step took him straight into the passing form of the tavern girl who was carrying a tray of wine-filled cups to a table of men nearby.

A second later a great crash erupted about the place and wine rained down like a shower from the heights of Olympus upon every patron in the vicinity.

Rufio and the tavern girl flailed around on the floor trying to extricate themselves from each other and the net of embarrassment that had been cast over them.

"Be careful you cunnus!" one man shouted at Rufio.

"My fullo just cleaned this tunica!" cried another.

"All right, ginger knob!" a man with great sausage fingers reached down and pulled Rufio to his feet. "I'm taking you outside to teach you some manners!"

Rufio looked up at the Colossus, his eyes stinging from the wine, pulled back a fist and slammed it into his gut.

"Oh, you want to dance, do ya?" the man said, his own clubby hand reaching back, only to be grabbed in the vice of another hand.

"That's my friend, citizen." Felix's calm, deep voice reached out to Rufio's aggressor like a soothing bit of music to calm a beast. "It was an accident. Let me buy you and your friends a round of drinks. On me!"

The man relinquished Rufio, stared at him for a moment, and then acquiesced to Felix's offer. "Sounds good," he said to Felix.

"Of course it does!" Felix smiled. "In fact," he turned to the rest of the taberna. "A round of drinks for everyone, on Felix Modestus!"

A great cheer went up and everyone went back to their conversations.

Meanwhile, Rufio bent down to help the tavern girl clean up the broken crockery. "I'm so sorry!" he said to her, but when she looked up it was with fire in her brown eyes.

"Leave me alone, peasant!" she said, and slapped him across the cheek.

"Come, Rufio!" Felix said, pulling him to his feet. "Let her do her job, and let us sit and talk. You're not getting away that easily!" he laughed.

They found Clara sitting at the table, her eyes wide, her arms crossed as she took in the sight of her two oldest and best friends. She shook her head. "Two minutes together and you've already been in a tavern brawl!"

Felix sat Rufio down forcibly against the wall where he had been sitting, and then fixed himself across from both of them. Before speaking, he sniffed and looked at Rufio. "You look like you've had a rough journey, my friend, like you crawled out of a ditch along the via Appia!" Felix fixed him with a gaze.

Rufio could not figure out if he was being facetious or displaying genuine concern. He grumbled. "It was the via Flaminia."

Both Felix and Clara burst out laughing, but Rufio, his face burning and red, made to get up from his seat again.

"Oh, no you don't!" Felix's arm reached out and pressed Rufio back down.

"Stop it!" Rufio shouted briefly, shaking his head. "This is not a comedy! I don't like being lied to, Felix. Since I've been in Rome, I've been knocked off the road-"

"The via Flaminia!" Felix added, unable to help himself.

"Yes!" Rufio shouted again. "I've been accosted by some old goat in the baths, insulted by slaves, knocked unconscious by the emperor's nymphaeum, and pissed on by a stray dog."

Felix snapped his fingers. "That's the other smell! I knew there was something behind the clove!"

"I hate Rome!" Rufio said rather too loudly.

"Keep your voice down," Felix hissed, reaching out to grip Rufio's hand to try and calm him. "Relax, my friend. You smell of wine now anyway."

"Ah, will you stop joking for once!" Rufio said.

It was then that Clara reached out a lithe hand and set it upon Rufio's shoulder.

He stopped himself and took a breath. He had often thought of what he would say when he saw her again - if he saw her! - And now, it was all ruined. He stared at the table and shook his head. "I can't do this."

"What exactly are you referring to, Rufio?" Felix asked. "I'm the one who asked you to come here. Both of you."

"Yes, you did!" Clara said, taking her hand back and staring at Felix. "You still haven't told us why? You don't look ill to me."

"Thank you, dear!" Felix said, sitting straight. "I will get into that, but first, let's catch up. It feels like old times again, no?"

The two across from him seemed distinctly uncomfortable with the thought of 'old times', but they remained seated.

"Rufio," Felix said. "Please eat something. This is for all of us. And do have some wine - to drink, I mean!"

Rufio shot him a look but could not help but reach out and fill the third plate with chunks of cheese, bread, and some salted meat. He then accepted the cup of wine which Felix had served him before refilling his and Clara's cups.

"To the Gods, and to being together again!" Felix said, holding out his cup, pouring a little and then touching the cups of the others.

They all drank and relaxed at last.

"Clara, why don't you bring Rufio up-to-date on your life? I'm sure he would like to know what you've been up to these many years."

Clara looked uncomfortable. "I just relayed it all to you, Felix. I don't want to go over it all again. I don't want to bore him. He's not interested."

Rufio looked at her and felt his heart catch. "But I am."

"I'll tell it for you then," Felix said. "Clara's father sold her to a merchant in Syracusae, but he was a kindly old man who was in search of a daughter and not a wife. They were married, but nothing untoward happened. He's dead these past three years, and Clara has sold the domus and lands in order to move back to Etruria and start a new life for herself."

"Well, that's one way to put it," Clara said, a little sadly. "My entire adult life rolled up into three sentences."

Rufio turned to her. "You were married?"

"Yes," Clara said. "But Felix was correct. I was a daughter to the man. He was kinder to me than ever my father was."

"What was his name?" Rufio asked.

"Aeson."

"I'm sorry for your loss."

Clara did not reply but nodded and turned back to Felix. "And Felix's theatre company, The Etrurian Players, is apparently quite successful and has performed all across the Middle Sea."

Felix inclined his head. "And there's my adult life, summed

up in a single sentence. Well done, Clara!" he laughed, before turning to Rufio. "Now, Rufio! Tell us what you've been doing with yourself. Despite what you might think, we have missed you."

Rufio looked at Felix keenly. He always did say much less than what he meant, always managed to get Rufio to say more than he wanted to. "Very well," Rufio began. "I've been living in Etruria on the same patch of land since childhood. I'm a crap farmer whose only friend is a donkey named Stella. My domus is falling down about my head, and my only farm hand is older than my father."

"How is the old goat, Pagano Pater?" Felix asked.

Without looking up from his food, Rufio answered. "He died. I buried him a little over a week ago."

"A week ago?" Clara said. "I'm so sorry, Rufio."

He felt her hand upon his shoulder again, but could not help shrugging. He regretted it instantly when she pulled back.

"Oh, come now! We all know how cruel a man he was," Felix said.

"No. You don't," Rufio said. "He got worse over time."

"And your mother?" Clara asked.

Rufio turned to look at her. He was not ready to go there. He shook his head.

"Rufio?" Felix prodded.

But Rufio turned to him. "What?"

"Have you been acting, rehearsing as you used to in the wood by the domus?"

"Every day is an act, Felix. You should know that."

"That's not what I meant," Felix retorted.

"I know." Rufio sighed. "I'm a crap farmer, and I was a crap actor too. No, I haven't been *rehearsing*, Felix."

"You were not crap, Rufio!" Clara said. "But you did prefer writing! Have you been doing that?"

Rufio laughed at her and she reddened. "Pfft! Not a

chance. If I had written anything, my father would have cast it into the hearth. No, I have not been writing at all. As it was, I had to hide all of my scrolls in a locked chest so that my father wouldn't destroy them all." He finished chewing a piece of meat and leaned back with the wine cup in his hand. "No. You both were always far better at acting than I ever was. It was all a child's dream."

"Not for me!" Felix said. "It is life to me, acting is. If I had not followed our dream, then I would have ended up in the legions, dead on some Parthian battlefield, never having heard applause or the adulation of the crowd."

"I heard applause all the time," Rufio added.

That threw Felix off, and he was about to press Rufio, but decided not to for the dark and faraway look in his old friend's eyes.

The three of them sat silently for a few minutes, processing the magnitude of what was happening. Something in each of them had been rekindled, and now burned like a country fire wherein, among the flames, were myriad impossible emotions and regrets, childhood remembrances of joy and friendship that now seemed unthinkably distant. It was strange beyond comprehension to be together again, each of them battle-hardened and scarred by life in various ways.

And yet, the familiar affection and understanding was still there, and they each took hold of that tiny thread in their labyrinthine hearts.

Finally, Felix spoke, a great smile spanning his bearded face as he looked at Rufio and Clara. "I can't believe you both came."

"You still haven't told us why we're here, Felix," Clara said.

"Very well," Felix refilled his wine cup once more, as well as theirs, and sat back to relate to them the purpose for his letters. "As you know, I have a theatre company - The Etrurian Players. We've been quite successful these past years. A few months ago, in Ephesus, a Roman aedile happened to see our performance. He loved it, of course!"

Rufio rolled his eyes, but Felix ignored it and pressed on.

"This aedile, one Sextus Annius Sabinus, has been tasked by Emperor Severus with putting on the Ludi Apollinares this year. And he has hired me and my company to perform in the theatre of Pompey!"

"Felix! That's wonderful!" Clara clapped, making Rufio shudder beside her. "What an honour!"

"Thank you!" Felix said.

"Yes, congratulations," Rufio added. "But what, by Apollo, has that got to do with us?"

Clara and Rufio both looked at him keenly, for the question had been hanging in the air ever since they arrived at the surprise reunion.

"Here, we come to it," Felix said. "For this to be a success, I need both of you to be in the production!"

Almost immediately, Rufio choked on an olive he had just popped in his mouth, coughed, and spat the savoury orb so that it ricocheted off of Felix's chest into Clara's wine cup, splashing her face with droplets.

Felix's smile faded, and they all stared at each other in dumb silence.

VI

CHEATING DEATH

"Why are you laughing?" Felix demanded, staring across the table at Rufio like Agamemnon at the walls of Troy.

Rufio shook his head. "I'm not!" Rufio answered.

"Oh really? Your cheeks are puffed out and your face is reddening by the second like an excited satyr."

Now it was Clara's turn to laugh out loud as she wiped her face with a cloth napkin from the table before her.

Rufio joined her and, for a brief moment, he felt freed of the constraints he had fastened upon himself.

The gaiety did not last long however, for Felix slumped back in his chair to look upon them with supreme disappointment. *This is going to be more difficult than I thought.* "You think I'm joking?"

Rufio nodded, his eyes watering from the exercise which his tightly-shut eyes underwent.

"I'm in deadly earnest," Felix said to Clara, ignoring Rufio for a moment.

Clara looked at Felix directly and her laughter died upon her lips, before she turned to Rufio and laid her hand upon his arm again. "Rufio, stop."

"Why? It's so funny!"

"My possible death is funny to you? I thought you were my

friend!" Felix said, smashing his hand upon the table so that their food danced upon the platters.

Rufio stopped, and he stared back at Felix. "Friends? Surely not! How many years has it been? How many times did you write to me or Clara over the past, what, seven years or so? Surely you performed in Syracusae, Felix! Did you contact Clara then? How many times did we write to *you*? There is only air between us now, nothing more."

"All right, Rufio," Clara chided. "That's enough!"

"Is it though?" Rufio bit back, immediately regretting his outburst for the shadow it cast over her face. "Life and death!" he scoffed. "Your idea is not funny, it's absurd! Friends?"

Felix leaned over the table, fighting the urge to grab Rufio by the hem of his foul-smelling tunica. "You are the one who left us hanging, remember?"

"Oh, I remember! And I've been living in Hades ever since while you've been travelling the Middle Sea, *acting!*" he said with a mock flourish.

Felix poured himself more wine, deigning to fill the others' cups, and drank it down in one gulp before leaning back again. He could have lectured Rufio on his betrayal, mocked him for not having followed his dream, for hiding in Etruria. But he decided against it.

Clara felt her heart tighten at the sudden anger between them, an anger, she had to admit, she did not share. If anything, she was intrigued by Felix's offer.

"Felix," Clara said softly, her voice like water dousing the angry fire between him and Rufio. "You said in your letter that it was a matter of life and death. What did you mean?"

"I will tell you both if *Gnatho* here will let me!" Felix growled, referring to the scheming parasite in Terence's *Eunuch*.

"Take that back, or my ill-tempered horse will piss up your nose and drown you!" Rufio said.

"Now I know what you've been doing on the farm!" Felix retorted.

"By the Gods! Will you two stop?" It was Clara's turn to shout. She turned. "Rufio, let's hear what he has to say."

Rufio crossed his arms and the two of them turned to stare at Felix again. "Go on then! Tell us."

Felix took a deep breath to gather himself. He had had his explanation all planned out, such fervent words as would convince them to join him in what he envisioned as a wondrous production. Now, however, the sea was still, and his sails limp upon the mast. He sighed deeply then, refilled his cup, and took a sip. "Look," he began, holding each of their gazes. "I'm sorry I did not contact either of you over the years. I regret how much time we have been robbed of…but I won't regret the life that I have lived during our mutual absences. I thought of you both every time I took the stage. Every time! And it pained me!"

"Felix…" Clara began.

But Felix held up his hand. "Please, let me finish." He took another drink. "I had a dream when I was in Ephesus, the very night of our great performance when the aedile sent me the letter inviting our company to Rome. It was more clear and real than any other dream I've ever had, so much so that I knew that the Gods had sent it to me."

"Which god?" Rufio asked. "Venus? Is that why we're here on Veneralia?"

"No. I don't know." Felix shook his head, trying to hold onto his train of thought. "It was a goddess, yes. But not Venus. Just listen… In the dream, she showed me a great production in Rome. I saw the whole thing, every detail from the costumes to the faces of the players themselves."

"Your Etrurian Players?" Clara asked.

"Yes," Felix replied, calmer now. "But not just them. We three were in the main roles."

"The three of us?" Rufio repeated.

"Yes. The goddess was most specific."

"This still doesn't explain the 'life and death' part of your letter, Felix," Rufio said, daring to take more food from the table.

Felix looked around to see if anyone was listening to their conversation, but the other patrons were too busy polishing off the round which he had purchased for them. He turned back to Rufio and Clara. "In my dream, the goddess said that in order for this production to be a success, in order for me to be free, you must *both* be a part of it. If you are not, if this is not a titanic success, I will lose everything, including my life."

"Your life?" Rufio asked.

"That's what I said."

"How is that?" Rufio pressed.

"I don't know, Rufio!" Felix's irritability began to return. "I'm not an oracle. I don't claim to know the will of the Gods. Do you?"

"I know my own will," Rufio added, but then eased up. "I understand you believe this, believe that we can pull this off for you, Felix. But-"

"Rufio," Clara suddenly said, wishing to stopper the flow of any more vitriol. "Felix is quite sincere here, and wasn't this our dream when we three were young in Etruria? Maybe this is a second chance?"

Rufio looked at her beside him. He wanted to believe her, to be near her, to once again feel the joy that being with her and Felix proffered him, but it was all too terrifying and ridiculous. "It was a childish dream, Clara," he said, shaking his head and rubbing his beard.

"No dream is childish, Rufio," Felix said. "That's your father talking."

"Well, maybe he was right!" Rufio said.

"You can't believe that!" Clara now added.

Rufio nodded. "I do!" he burst out, not for the proposal that had been made to him, but for the ghost of his father's clapping in his brain.

"There you are, Felix!" a deep, sultry voice wafted in at the door of the taberna and all heads turned to see Electra enter, a deus ex machina come to Felix's aid. She seemed to glide across the floor toward their table, a vision in indigo and gold, uncaring of the eyes upon her as she passed.

Rufio and Clara looked up from their seats in awe at the imposing beauty, but quickly rallied when Felix stood to kiss her upon the cheek and pull up a another chair for her.

"Are these your friends?" Electra asked as she stood, her hand possessively upon Felix's chest as she stared first at Clara and then at the open-mouthed Rufio.

"Yes," Felix responded. "These are Clara Probita and Rufio Pagano," he said. "They are my oldest and dearest...*friends*."

The last word stung, Rufio, for he knew that he had been unfeeling and biting, even as Felix had opened up to him about his dream.

"I am Electra," she said as she looked upon them as if she were Hera and Felix were Zeus, gazing down on two mere mortals from the heights of Olympus.

"Yes, you are," Rufio muttered.

"Close you mouth, Rufio," Felix said.

"It is a pleasure to meet you...Electra?" Clara said, standing up, suddenly feeling quite plain. Her hand strayed to her hair and she put back a strand of it behind her ear. "Are you also in The Etrurian Players?"

Electra smiled and laughed, only slightly amused as she looked upon the woman that had so often occupied Felix's thoughts over the years. "I am," she said grandly. "I am the only one who can steal the audience's attention away from this great man," she said, patting Felix's chest.

"I'm sure!" Rufio said.

"I am also his lover."

"Concubine," Felix corrected.

Rufio began to sputter as he sipped his wine, and both Felix and Clara stood back instinctively. He managed, however, not to spit up this time.

Electra looked at Rufio as if he were a tiny street urchin, groping at the hem of her stola for scraps of food.

Rufio sat back, silenced by her look.

"Let's sit," Felix said, and he held the chair for Electra before turning to Clara and Rufio. "Electra is the female lead in our company. You should see her Lysistrata, or the role for which she was named. Magnificent!" he stated.

Clara observed Electra beside Felix and could not help but see them as a magnificent pair. She was surprised by the sudden jealously that sprang up, and was grateful that Rufio was beside her in that moment, for his presence soothed her, despite the argument which had so recently sullied their reunion.

"So?" Electra said, her dark, outlined eyes staring from Clara to Rufio. "Are you going to help Felix cheat Death as the Gods demand?"

Felix did not speak this time, but looked expectantly at both Clara and Rufio. His expression was devoid of arrogance or even confidence. He was a man desperately in need of help from people he trusted, and he sat there across from them, fully exposed, his heart bared.

"Why do they not answer?" Electra asked Felix.

It was strange, as if the Gods were there discussing two mortals, waiting expectantly for an answer.

Clara knew that part of what Rufio had said was true. They had not cared enough, or perhaps dared enough, to contact each other over the years. But, to her, their shared dream had not been childish. It had been hopeful. And now, she was in search of a new beginning, a second life. *This is it,* she told herself. "Count me in!" Clara said suddenly.

Relief spread across Felix's face, as colour returns to one who sits by the fire after a long walk in the winter cold. "Thank you, my friend," he said, reaching across the table to grip Clara's hand, ignoring the stormy look Electra shot him.

Rufio turned to Clara. "But people will think you're a whore for acting!" he said.

"Rufio!" Felix said angrily.

Clara knew that was often the perception, for in Rome at least, actors were no higher on the social scale than slaves, gladiators, or prostitutes. She turned to Rufio. "That may be true, Rufio, but I don't care what people might say. I've lived in the shadow of other people's judgment for the last six years. I have my own money now, and I don't need anyone to approve."

Felix smiled. "You are Hippolyta incarnate, my dear!" he said proudly.

They all turned to Rufio then, waiting for him to answer.

He squirmed in his seat, shaking his head. "I can't afford to stay in Rome for this. I need to get back to the farm and get to work."

"You said you were a crap farmer!" Felix said. "Listen, Rufio. I will pay for all expenses for you both while we are here. I have rented a warehouse down by the docks along the Tiber, beside a sculptor's studio. I've fixed it up nicely so that it has living quarters for all of us. It's enormous with plenty of room and privacy, in addition to a rehearsal space. I will pay for your food and some new clothes."

"There's no need for that, Felix," Clara said, but Felix put up his hand.

"I'll hear nothing more! I'm happy to do it," he bellowed. He turned back to Rufio. "You'll incur no expenses."

"It's not about that," Rufio said, feeling the sweat bead on his forehead and beneath his tunica. "I'm not an actor, Felix. I never have been!"

"Of course you are!" Electra declared. "You are a perfect fool or parasite! I can see you would be quite ridiculous!"

"Hush, woman!" Felix said to her. "You're not helping!"

Rufio was already on his feet, shaking his head as he took up his satchel.

"Don't leave, Rufio," Clara said, holding onto his hand to try and pull him back down.

Rufio looked at her and felt the pang in his chest that had so often kept him awake in the night as he looked out the dirty window of his cubiculum at home to see the silvery moon above.

"At least stay the night in the warehouse," Felix said. "Give it some thought!"

"No, Felix," Rufio said, taking up his cup and downing the rest of the wine. He then grabbed another piece of bread from the table and made to leave, unable to look at Clara another second.

Felix grabbed him by the arm as he made to pass. "Rufio, please! I need your help!"

"I can't!" Rufio said. "I'm sorry!" He pulled away from Felix and stumbled through the taberna out into the night, leaving the others to stare after him in silence.

The night air was cool when Rufio found himself in the street outside the Taberna Macedonica, looking up at the moon and the fog his breath created as he gulped the fresh air.

He heard a strange sort of sigh and looked down to see the dog, Peli, sitting in the middle of the street staring at him, his head titled slightly.

It was Rufio's turn to sigh. "Why don't you leave me alone?" he asked the mischievous canine. Rufio's head tottered on his shoulders as the effects of the wine now began to seep deeper into his mind. Combined with the cold night air, he began to feel dizzy and tired. He had not drunk so much in a while, but found he could not help it, especially with Clara there.

"I can't believe this," he said to himself, though the dog might have thought he was addressing him, for it stood up from his haunches.

Clara's face hovered in Rufio's mind still. Seeing her had unnerved him, shocked him, given him a heavy dose of nostalgia and remembrance that he had not been prepared for. He began to turn for a flickering moment, as if some unseen force were willing him back inside, to reconnect with the two people in the world who had ever meant anything to him, but then he recalled what Felix had wanted of him, how he had been manipulated to get there.

"A matter of life and death," he growled, shaking his head before turning away from the taberna and heading in the direction opposite to the Forum Romanum and the Capitoline Hill.

He did not know where he was headed, but he was acutely aware of the danger of sleeping rough in the streets of Rome alone. Shadowy figures watched him from alleys and darkened doorways as he passed. He wished he had not drunk so much.

Rufio wandered for some time, past the temple of the divine Trajan, down a street that led toward the base of the Quirinal Hill, though to him, it could have been anywhere.

Peli padded along beside him, his ears perked up as he stared into each darkened space, more acutely aware of the surroundings than Rufio was.

"Who's this then, Peli?" said a plucky voice from a red doorway at the bottom of a small tenement.

Rufio looked up quickly, stumbling to a stop to find Peli sitting before a woman with long, dishevelled, henna-dyed hair and a smile that seemed to light up the street about her. Her friendly face immediately put Rufio at ease, for he had been both distracted and nervous about his surroundings in the city ever since his arrival, let alone after the unexpected encounter at the taberna. "Oh, hello."

The woman stood back, her hand upon her bosom in mock-surprise, the street filled with the jingle of the many bangles about her wrists as her green eyes widened. "Hello to you, citizen!" she said, smiling when she saw the confused look of the messy-looking person before her.

"Uhm…you know this one, do you?" Rufio said for lack of anything else, nodding toward the dog.

"Of course I do. Everyone knows Peli!" she said, crouching down to rub the dog's neck and make kissing sounds to him. "He's a good boy!"

"Is he?" Rufio said, quite unsure about the praise she heaped upon his four-legged companion. "He tried to rob me, and pissed on me earlier."

"Oh, he just likes you!" she answered with a chuckle.

"Is that what it is?" Rufio was not convinced.

"Yes! If he didn't like you, then he would have bitten you." Her eyes strayed to Rufio's crotch and he shifted nervously under her gaze. She leaned back against the doorway. "You're not from Rome, are you?"

"What makes you say that?" Rufio asked.

"You're clinging to that satchel like your entire life is in it, and you are wandering the streets of the city with your eyes darting every which way. Since you've been talking to me, you've looked back ten times. Why are you so nervous?" she asked, taking a step closer.

Rufio tried not to look at her, but she was quite alluring in a way with the jingle of her jewellery, her smile, and the long, bright tunica she wore which was fastened with a belt high above her waist.

She saw him looking and smiled. "You need a place to spend the night?"

"I suppose I do, but I have no idea where to go," Rufio said.

"I can help you," she said. "I live right here, and I have space."

"I don't have a lot of money, I'm afraid."

She put up her hand. "It is Veneralia, and the goddess Venus favours those who help others in a time of…need." She smiled again, and the act put him at ease.

Rufio looked up to see the dimly lit window above, and then looked back at her. "Are you sure?"

"I wouldn't have offered if I wasn't! Besides, Peli seems to trust you, and so should I." She looked down at the dog. "Right, Peli?"

The dog barked once and sat.

Rufio looked about the dark streets and shuddered to think what he would do or where he would go if he didn't take her up on her offer.

"I only want to help," she said most sincerely. "I live alone, so you need not worry about an errant husband stumbling back into the domus after you are asleep. Please," she said, standing aside and opening the door behind her, above which was a carved, erect phallus.

"Well, I suppose I can," Rufio answered, feeling exhausted. "Thank you."

"Think nothing of it," she said going in first. "Peli, stay outside here."

The dog sat down beside the doorway, looking up at Rufio as he entered and closed the door behind him.

"My name is Meretrix," she said as they went up the wooden staircase.

"Mine is Rufio. Rufio Pagano."

"What brings you to Rome, Rufio?" she asked as they

reached the top and she opened another door that led into a large, single room that was lit by a few clay lamps upon tables.

"Trickery is what brought me to Rome," he said a little bitterly. "A friend's false invitation."

"Really?" She stopped and turned to face him and he was struck by her beauty in the lamplight.

Then, he was struck more by the fact that he found himself in a room with red silks hanging from the rafters and surrounding a broad bed that lay against a wall painted in red and white. On another table there was a pitcher and an array of cups, the erotic reliefs of which were illuminated by the small lamp beside them.

"Oh, ah..." Rufio stiffened, obviously uncomfortable. "I thought you had a spare room?" he asked.

"Spare? No," she answered. "But I have the space," she said, going to the table and pouring some watered wine into the cups. "Here. Drink some posca. It will clear your head." She handed him a cup. "To Venus Verticordia," she said before drinking from her own.

"Oh, ah, yes..." he muttered. "To Venus." Rufio drank, keenly aware of her staring at him over the rim of her cup, amused by his discomfort. His face contorted at the sour, herb-infused liquid, and she chuckled. Rufio looked around the room more closely and spied images of Venus and Eros everywhere, their expressions at once interested and urging. But the more he looked upon them, the more they seemed to be mocking him. Rufio's eyes widened and he looked back at Meretrix. "Oh! Are you a...a lupa?" he said.

She frowned at him. "If that is what you wish to call me, but I am a woman first, and I have offered you a place to stay this night."

He put the cup back on the table and stepped back from her. "I'm sorry... I didn't want to-" He found he could not speak for the embarrassment he felt burning his neck. "I don't have much money and-"

"Stop," she said softly, reaching out to take his hands, her long fingers caressing his palms without him noticing. "I don't want coin, Rufio Pagano. I only want to help you, and to spend this first night of Veneralia with you. That is all. The Gods have brought us together for a reason, don't you think?"

They also had Peli piss on me! he thought, but did not say as much. "I should be going now," he said, backing away toward the door.

"You could," she added, "but you will be much safer in here with me than out in the streets at night. You don't want to wander Rome alone at night. In the very least, if you're not clubbed over the head by the gangs and left for dead, you'll end up with the priests of Cybele or some such, screaming and drunk on Bactrian poppy juice before waking up in the morning with your manhood cut off, only to find it burning on the altar before your very eyes. Now, you don't want that, do you?"

Rufio gulped.

"It would be a shame if that were to happen," Meretrix said, her face a plain smile.

"All right. I'll stay," Rufio said.

"It is right," she said, putting her cup down and going to blow out two of the lamps farther from the broad bed. "Make yourself comfortable for a moment, while I freshen up."

Meretrix went behind one of the many silk hangings while Rufio sat uncomfortably on the edge of the bed and laid his satchel down upon the floor. He looked around, then up at the sound of a delicate glass stopper, before the strong scent of rose water reached his nostrils.

"Lay yourself down, Rufio. Rest and make yourself comfortable. I'll be right with you. You can tell me about yourself a bit more…about your friend who tricked you into coming to Rome."

"Oh, uhm…all right…" he said, resigned to the adventure that awaited him, so overwhelmed with exhaustion that he did not care any longer what befell him. *This is it then!* he thought. *I'll forget the past in a whirlwind of wanton pleasures with this friendly lupa!* He leaned back on the bed and stared at the wood beams of the ceiling, his head spinning, his eyes so very heavy.

Felix you shit! he said to himself, before his thoughts turned tender. "Clara…" he muttered as his eyes closed.

"You can trust me, Rufio," Meretrix's voice said as she approached from behind the curtains. "I will make your visit to Rome worthwhile, but first I'll-" Meretrix stopped suddenly at the edge of the bed to see her hapless guest sprawled out upon the silks and pillows, snoring louder than a legionary's cornu. "What a pity," she muttered, smiling to herself. "At least I won't be alone tonight," she sighed before crawling onto the bed and curling up beside Rufio, gently turning him onto his side and pressing against him to sleep as his snoring faded away.

VII

PAST FONDNESSES

It was well into the night when Felix and Electra separated their sweaty selves to lay side-by-side upon the bed of their makeshift palace within the warehouse along the Tiber. They had, of course, worshipped Venus with gusto that evening in the dim light behind the layers of diaphanous hangings that surrounded them like trees in a private wood. However, the moment their passions paused to recuperate, Felix's mind tumbled down the bittersweet pathways of youthful nostalgia.

He stared at the high ceiling of cloth that masked the bones of that draughty warehouse, trying to decipher the evening, determined to hide the unfamiliar anxiety he felt over his failed mission to reunite with his dearest friends.

"It was good to be together again," he said as he lay there, one muscled arm above his head, the other resting upon his stomach.

"You were magnificent, as ever," Electra purred next to him. "But I'm not finished with you, Felix Modestus."

Felix frowned, distracted. "I meant to be with Clara and Rufio. The three of us together again."

Electra tutted and pulled away to wrap herself in the layers of covers. "You have been nothing but distracted today, especially since seeing those two. Leave the past in the past, Felix."

"Hush, woman!" he growled, not wanting Clara to hear,

though she was on the other side of the warehouse. "They are my friends! Besides, the Gods demanded that I bring us all together. And that has not happened."

"The production is doomed before it even begins," she said, knowing it would aggravate him. In truth, she had been jealous ever since seeing Clara, for she knew Felix's appetites, knew how close he had been with the woman in the past. She had hoped her pleasured cries just then, with added volume for Clara's benefit, would have the desired effect, but she doubted it very much. She needed to preserve her voice anyway.

"I don't want you speaking of failure at all. The others cannot know of this. It will kill morale."

"Your friend Rufio is a coward, not a man," she said, remembering the thin, smelly man she had found sitting at the table with Felix. "How could you think he would help you after so many years?"

Felix exhaled loudly, as if he had been holding his breath for a long time. "Rufio has changed a lot. I don't think it's the fact that he just buried his father though. They hated each other." He turned to look at Electra but she refused to meet his eye. He shook his head, annoyed, and looked back to the ceiling. "Rufio used to be quite good at acting. He also had an exceptional knowledge of plays and playwrights."

"I don't believe you," she said. "He is too nervous and uptight for any of it."

"It's true! He would pick the plays we would try and perform. He knew what the audience would want."

"What audience? The squirrels and pigs in your Etrurian wood?"

"Well…granted, there weren't many opportunities to perform in front of a proper audience. In fact, there was only the one and-"

"And he left you and your Clara upon the stage. He abandoned you."

"Yes," Felix said, feeling that painful sting of yesterday. "He did."

"Like I said. A coward."

"Go to sleep," Felix growled. It was true that he had not seen either Clara or Rufio in many years, but they had ever been there, in the back of his mind, whenever he took the stage. He knew that a part of him had been performing for all of them, and that made Rufio's dismissal of his proposition all the more painful.

Electra turned to look at him. "Rufio is gone, but the company can do this. Put Silas in the role. He's the best you've got, after me, that is."

"Silas?" Felix gritted his teeth. "I'll be damned before I let him press his lips to Clara's."

"I knew it! You have had her!"

"Do you hear yourself, woman? I think the wine and pleasure have clouded your mind!"

"What pleasure?" she retorted. "I tolerate a lot from you, but to know that she is sleeping nearby…" Electra shook her head and her dark hair fell about her face. "You push me aside."

"I'm lying here with you, am I not?" Felix said.

"Do not shame me, Felix Modestus. You will regret it!"

"Are you threatening me, my concubine? Maybe I should return you to the market where I found you in Alexandria?"

She punched him in the arm and then pinched his bearded cheeks. "It is better to tie up your donkey than go looking for it."

"What? Spare me your Peloponnesian gibberish, and mind your own business! Besides, you never worried about me with other women before."

"With the occasional lupa, no. But your Clara is one a man could fall in love with. And you look at her and speak to her differently."

"What a vivid imagination you have, my beauty!" It was Felix's turn to pinch her cheeks, but she pulled away, her face red with anger.

"Lysistrata had the right idea!" Electra muttered, her back to him.

Felix could only shake his head and go back to staring at the ceiling. He wanted to go and speak with Clara in that moment, to talk as they once did, but he knew that if he did so, Electra was likely to set the entire warehouse aflame, and that would pose more of a threat to the production.

ON THE FAR SIDE OF THE WAREHOUSE, CLARA LAY WIDE AWAKE in the private chamber which Felix had constructed for her. It was, perhaps, one of the strangest accommodations she had ever been in, for it was extremely luxurious with pedestal tables holding aloft three-headed bronze lamps to light the space, a tripod with a copper basin of water for washing, towels for drying, two chairs and a small table on which a broad bowl of fruit rested. There was even a couch where she could rest and read, and an ornate dressing table with a marble top, complete with a polished bronze mirror, camel hair brushes, and pots of kohl, stibium and other cosmetics if she so desired. In one corner, a tall, cedar wardrobe had been filled with various stolae, tunicae, belts, and silk cloaks. *Cleopatra might have felt at home in such a place,* Clara had thought when she first walked in, shocked by all that Felix had done.

The walls of her chamber were also solid, constructed of wood and plaster so as to allow her more privacy, compared with the sheer hangings of Felix's space. It did not end there, however, for Felix had, it seemed, instructed one of his crew to paint the walls with frescoes of a gentle forest scene, complete with silver-leaved olive trees, vibrant poppies, birds, boar, cypresses and vineyards. He had laid out Etruria before her.

Clara wondered at Felix's confidence that he had gone to such expense even before he knew she would accept his offer to take part. The space he had constructed for her was so luxurious that it was as if an empress had been given rooms in the midst of the Suburra itself. It was easy to forget that they were actually in the middle of a vast warehouse filled with building materials, carts, wagons, and tools.

She had not seen the rest of the company when she, Felix and Electra had finally returned from the Taberna Macedonica, for they were all out enjoying the delights of Rome. She had heard them return, though, singing drunkenly, cursing, and stumbling over the debris in the warehouse until Felix had shouted to silence them.

All was quiet now and Clara found it easier to gather her thoughts and feelings about that very confusing and confounding day.

Felix had indeed tricked them, but she wondered if he was right not to tell each of them that the other was going to be there. So many memories and feelings had been churned up by her return to Rome, like the silt at the bottom of the river they used to wade in as barefoot children so long ago. The watery memories were still cloudy when she laid down for the night, and she was staring at them, waiting for things to clear and the sunlight to pierce the darkness about her feet.

Clara had been prepared for her meeting with Felix. She had had ample time to do so. She had known the feelings that would meet her, of fondness and friendship, of some guilt, and not a little embarrassment. But she had not been prepared to see Rufio.

When the third part of their childhood triad had walked into the taberna, she had felt winded, as if a gladiator had punched her in the gut and left her unable to speak. She had felt numb, and struggled to push down the feelings that assailed her, forced herself not to unleash the accusatory words she had bottled up for so many years. As she lay in her plush bed in the warehouse, the thought of him, even then, after seeing how sad a man he had become, made her heart ache, and she rubbed her chest in an effort to ease the pain it caused.

After her anger had subsided, she had felt pity for him, for what he had evidently gone through, and for his 'failed life' as he described it.

When one gives up on one's dreams, the outcome is not a happy one, she thought as she remembered the three of them talking in summer fields about how they would take the theatres of Rome by storm. She remembered and felt that dream acutely, how she had wanted to be an actor, no matter her family's disinterest and disgust with the idea. She remembered the love and excitement she had felt even when putting on scenes in the forest near their homes.

After the shock of Rufio's appearance, once they were sitting, Clara had, for a moment, enjoyed the three of them being together again, the banter, the smiles over wine, or at least the potential of it all. It had been more awkward than anything, she had to admit, and that had been due to Rufio's appearance.

It made her deeply sad to think of Rufio, how things might have been different had he not left Rome, had he not deserted them on the day of their first big performance. But he had, and with a single act of cowardice, their united dream had shattered like blue glass upon a white marble floor. She remembered loving him prior to that, having encouraged dreams of another kind in her heart. But then he had ripped that heart out.

Too much had happened that last time in Rome.

Clara was sad that Rufio would not be in the play, whatever play it was, but she was glad of the chance to at least set things straight with Felix before starting a new life for herself.

After turning over these thoughts again and again in her

mind, Clara finally dozed off to sleep as the lamplight flickered and her eyes rested upon the painted scene of that Etrurian forest surrounding her.

RUFIO AWOKE IN THE MIDDLE OF THE NIGHT, THE SPINNING IN his head slightly subsided, only to find the lupa's arm across his chest and her breasts pressed against his shoulder. For a brief moment of panic, he could not remember a thing, but then the realization crashed over his head like a wave on a winter beach, quite sobering him up.

Clara, he remembered the last thought before he had succumbed to his inebriation. The lamps in the gaudy-coloured room of vermillion and ochre where he found himself were still lit, revealing the statues of Venus and Eros nearby. The musty smell of perfume, incense and sweat were tangled in the hairs of his nose and he tried not to sneeze and wake the woman beside him.

Many a man would have relished the opportunity laid out before him in that moment, free of charge, but Rufio could not rally himself for it. There were only two people who had domi-nated his mind and dreams since that evening, and he had left them behind…again.

Felix, you shit! he thought for the twentieth time that night, angered at how his supposed friend had tricked them into meeting. *He always did exaggerate!*

Meretrix began to shift then, and Rufio froze. Her eyes still closed, she began to nuzzle him, her hair tickling his neck and nose until he could not help but sneeze, making her jump back suddenly.

"Ahh!" she gasped in surprise, realizing immediately what had happened. "You startled me, Rufio," she said, her smile returning as she propped herself on her elbow to look at him. "Did you rest a little?"

"Yes. Thank you," he replied awkwardly, trying to avoid her lustful gaze. "Whatever herbs you put in your posca, they worked."

"Just some chamomile and valerian to help you relax," she said. She looked down his body and reached out to touch his manhood. She shook her head wistfully. "Looks like they worked too well!"

"I…um…"

"Don't fret, Rufio. I've seen it many a time with men whose minds are crushed by a world of worries." She sat up and leaned against the pillows beside him. "So tell me…who is Clara?"

"How did you know that name?" Rufio said.

"You only mentioned her several times in your sleep. Tell me, what happened last night that got you so worked up and drunk?"

Rufio frowned.

"Don't worry," she said, a gentle hand on his shoulder. "I'm a good listener and, some say, give great advice to those in need."

Rufio dared to look at Meretrix more closely then and had to admit to himself that what he saw was a happy woman, jolly even, whose smile was a challenge not to emulate. He relented.

"I met with two friends from my childhood last night whom I had not seen in many years."

"Yes," she nodded. "Clara and…"

"Felix. Felix Modestus."

"The great actor?"

Rufio sighed. "Yes, I suppose he is, from what I'm hearing."

"I heard he was in Rome!" Meretrix said. "By Bacchus! You know him?"

"Yes! Anyway… Felix, Clara and I grew up together, but had not seen each other in a long time…"

Rufio proceeded to tell Meretrix, without embellishment or

omission, about their past dreams of acting and how they had come to Rome, how he had deserted them. He relayed the matter of the letters Felix had sent in order to lure them to Rome, his supposed dream, and how much of a betrayal Rufio felt it all was.

"And would you have come if you knew Clara was going to be there too?"

"No. I don't know. It's complicated."

Meretrix laughed. "By Venus, it always is! And how long have you loved this Clara?"

The question hung in the air like storm clouds in the midst of a blue sky, threatening to change everything with the first rumble of thunder or strike of lightning.

"Love?" he replied, shaking his head. "I didn't say 'love'."

"You don't have to," Meretrix added. "It's obvious."

"I used to, perhaps, but not anymore. It's different now."

"You mean you are different."

"We're all different," he said curtly. "We were best friends."

"True love is born of friendship, I find," Meretrix said, smiling at her own secret memories of friends and loves gained and lost. She turned back to Rufio. "I think the Gods have presented you all with a second chance Rufio."

"How so?" he asked, though he knew the answer.

"You three shared a dream of being on the stage together, but that dream was put asunder by your decision to leave. That caused all of you a lot of hurt, correct?"

Rufio looked down. "I'm sure it did. Yes," he admitted.

"Your friend, Felix, then had this dream, or rather the Gods sent it to him to urge him to reunite all of you, despite years of no contact between you. You and Clara, the woman you *used to love* both accept the offer to come to Rome and help Felix, independently of the other."

"He lied!"

"Yes, he tricked you, but would you have come otherwise?

You obviously feel guilty about the past. Now you have a chance to make it right by joining them once again upon the stage!"

Rufio shook his head and pulled away from her as if the suggestion she put forth were supremely unpleasant. He swung his legs over the edge of the bed and turned his back to her. "Oh no! I'm not going to help him. I'm going home. I'm no actor!"

"But it's what you love!" Meretrix said, getting off the bed and going around to kneel before him. "You've told me as much."

"No. I haven't!" he protested.

She tilted her head, her eyes wide and knowing. "Yes, you have," she insisted. "And why not? They are your best friends - long lost friends - and now you are reunited! What if Felix really did have that dream? What if his life *is* in danger? And what about Clara? I see how you look every time her name passes your lips. Would you miss out on the opportunity to tell her how you feel?"

"I'm fine with that," he replied stubbornly. He was annoyed that she should speak so familiarly about his friends, as if she knew them better than he did.

"*Fine?* My breasts are *fine!*" she said, squeezing them with both hands.

Rufio found the emphasis unnerving.

"Rufio, you cannot afford to shun the Goddess' gifts!"

"It was a long time ago. Things have changed, Meretrix, but I appreciate your trying to help me."

"Well, you won't let me *help* you in other ways, so this is the least I can do. Besides, I've always been one for a happy ending."

"There's no happy ending for me, I can assure you."

"Sure there is. And listen to me," she said, taking his face in her jewel-bedecked hands. "When I used to work at the Grand Lupanar in Pompeii-"

"I'm sorry," Rufio cut her off, his eyes wide, for even he had heard of Pompeii's famous brothel. "You worked at the Grand Lupanar?"

"Why are you so surprised? I was one of the best, but the lena there thought I was too outspoken. I did, however, make a small fortune for myself, and so came to Rome to work for myself." She sat on the bed beside Rufio, her thigh pressed against his, as if they were two friends sitting on a log by a country stream, dipping their feet in the water. "When I was there, I used to help some of the younger girls out by having them send their mean clients to me. I would straighten them out." Meretrix proceeded to pull a knife from beneath the mattress, a cudgel from beneath the bed, and then a long pin from the layers of her dyed hair.

Rufio pulled back a little. *Am I now going to add 'clubbed by a lupa' to my list of Roman experiences today?*

"Don't worry," she said, setting the items aside. "These are not for you. I can see you are a good man, Rufio."

"Why would you put yourself in harm's way for the other girls then? That seems dangerous."

"It was," she answered. "The point is that when I was younger, I made a lot of the wrong decisions for myself…and I paid for it. But it did harden me to life. This is all I know and can do…and well, mind you." She stretched her arms out to display herself and the perfumed surroundings. "I figured that if I could sway the other girls away from this life, or at least keep them from cruel men, then I should." She shrugged.

The gesture was simple, her face content with the life she had led to that point. Rufio looked at her and saw that she was indeed beautiful, not even much older than he, though she had experienced a lot more in life than he had, hidden away in Etruria. He knew he was angry and afraid, but he also knew she had much more reason to be so. He took his cup from the table and drank again. "You were very brave," he said, relaxing again.

"I think you are a kind man, Rufio Pagano." Meretrix smiled and began to trace her fingers along the line of his beard.

"Hmm," he said distractedly. "Clara was always kind to me," he mumbled to himself."

Meretrix smiled a little sadly, and took the cup from his hand to set in back on the table.

Rufio's eyelids were heavy again, his mind spinning dazedly as he felt her lips upon his, ever so gently, before he leaned back. "I've missed you," he said before nodding off again.

Meretrix sighed. She would have liked to have lain with him, but she was content to have helped in some small way. She leaned close to him and whispered in his ear. "You should stay in Rome. Do what you were meant to do, and help your friends…"

She kissed him one more time before getting up and leaving him to doze the early morning away.

VIII

INTO THE FRAY

W hen morning broke on the second day of Veneralia, things felt different, strange even. Stretching upon her bed, Clara wondered if she was not back in Etruria, awoken as ever by birdsong. She opened her eyes slowly, only just able to make out the forest scenes upon the walls of her cubiculum in the dying light of the lamp she had left aflame.

She smiled briefly, for she had dreamed of the past, of happy memories before the complications of life had shredded her naive dreams. As fleeting as their reunion had been, it was good to see her friends again, despite the secrets and bitter resentment in their midst. But her smile faded as her mind awoke and she remembered Rufio's departure.

Clara's attention was then taken away by a chorus of snoring all around her, and she remembered that the entire company of Felix's players must be about. She thought she had heard muffled snippets of Catullus at one point in the night, but she had been so tired, she had fallen back asleep.

She lay beneath the covers of her bed for a time, staring at the walls and listening to the birds in the rafters of the warehouse serenading the Sun's chariot as it rose into the sky above Rome. She would have lain there and slept for a long while, but her mind busied itself more and more the longer she was awake and, before long, her eyes were wide and alert.

Clara sat up in the bed, lit a second lamp, and walked across the floor which had been covered with rugs from the East. She looked at her tunica and saw that it was still dirty from her travels. "I can't wear this," she said to herself, conscious that she did not want Felix to see her so filthy. She turned to the wardrobe and flipped through the hanging garments until she found a soft linen, gap-sleeved tunica of pale blue with golden knots on the sleeves, and a fine ribbon of gold to tie about the middle.

She removed it and held it up to the faint light. She began to regret having sold all of her other possessions in Syracusae, but she had been so determined to make a fresh start that she had not thought to keep much. With her trunk still at the temple of Juno, in the safekeeping of the argentarius with whom she had deposited her money, she was out of options.

She removed the thin shift she had worn beneath her tunica the previous day, readjusted her breast band, and then slid the pale blue tunica over her head until it fell all the way to the floor. It was warmer than she expected, which was welcome in the early morning chill. Having adjusted the garment, she then tied the golden band high above her waist, just below her breasts, and then sat to tie on her sandals.

In the past, her servants would have helped her with all of that. It felt strange to do it for herself again, but it was a welcome feeling of independence which she had missed. She then went to the small dressing table and picked up one of the bronze mirrors. She held it up and looked upon her reflection.

Clara shook her head as she observed her sad face. *Quite plain beside the exotic Electra,* she thought a little sadly. She looked at the table at the various cosmetics which lay there, and began to apply a little to her eyes, giving some life to her pale skin. She brushed out her hair so that it fell straight about her shoulders, and then tied it back with a simple golden thread that matched her belt. When she was finished, she stood in the middle of the makeshift cubiculum.

Something inside gave her pause, and she was suddenly filled with doubt. *I shouldn't stay. This is madness. Maybe Rufio is right?*

As soon as his name came to her, she became frustrated again. She would have liked to talk long into the night with him and Felix, but he had ruined that.

Maybe I should just call it off. I'm no longer an actress. I need to get on with my life, she thought. Ever since the death of her husband, she had taken to debating with herself, and it was not until that very moment that she thought how pathetic that really was. "I'll tell Felix what I have to tell him, and then get on my way to Etruria," she said, as if giving voice to the thoughts aloud were any less sad.

Clara opened the door of her cubiculum, and went out, determined to go to Felix and tell him of her decision to leave.

The warehouse was still dark when she stepped out, but for a small burning brazier in the middle and the distant light of the entrance which someone had opened to allow in the morning light.

It was like stepping from a world of luxury and peace into one of dirt and detritus, for all around her, Clara spied a wide array of boxes, carts, tools, piles of lumber and nails, work tables, and what appeared to be great bolts of fabric.

Amidst all of it were the sleeping forms of the people she assumed were Felix's company. She counted seven of them as she tip-toed among them, aiming for the distant, outdoor light, past another cubiculum and the thickly curtained area she had seen Felix and Electra disappear into the previous night.

"Good morning!" Felix's voice broke the silence as Clara passed.

In a small area beside his and Electra's cubiculum, surrounded by large pots of bitter laurels, was a small gathering of couches about a low table that seemed to serve as a sort of triclinium. A window in the side of the warehouse, above this area, allowed the morning light to fall upon it and Clara turned to see Felix reclined upon one of the couches, looking over a scroll which he had marked up.

"Sit with me. Eat something," Felix said, gesturing to the low table among the couches where there was a platter of fruit, nuts, bread and some honey. He poured her a cup of water and stood to kiss her on the cheek.

Clara held out her hand to stop him, merely accepting the water and nothing else.

His smile faded, only to be replaced by a look of concern. "What's wrong? Did you not sleep well? Were you uncomfortable?"

"I was very comfortable," she said quickly. "You've turned this warehouse into a palace!"

"I spared no expense," he said, stepping back, frowning a little. "I wanted you to be happy while here." He shook his head. "Did the others wake you up when they returned?" He stared beyond her to the darkness of the warehouse. "I knew it! Fausto gets loud when he is drunk, that I know. And Damon… well…he may be a mute, but his ass is anything but. Such flatulence!"

Clara put up her hands. "Felix, listen! They did not wake me. I slept well, my friend."

He relaxed his broad shoulders and nodded. "Sit then. Eat."

Clara did as he asked and looked across the table at him, reclined once more like an emperor in his triclinium in a deep crimson tunica bordered with acanthus leaves in gold, belted with a polished leather cingulum. The only thing that gave away his non-imperial role was the ink staining his fingers. She observed the scroll that he had set down beside him on which he had been making notes. "What were you reading?"

Felix looked at the scroll and he lit up, but the light in his eyes faded as he remembered something. "The play. I've had to make some changes since last night."

"What play?" Clara asked as she bit into a plum.

Felix put his finger to his lips. "All will be revealed. But not just yet. I want to make sure of some things first." He set the scroll aside and gave her his full attention. "You will have a magnificent role, however!"

Clara set down the pit of the plum she had been eating and looked at him. "Felix…there's something I need to tell you."

"Anything, my friend. Anything at all! I've missed our talks over the years. I've missed you so much, even though I did not write to you. It just felt awkward, I suppose, and for that I am truly sorry. We'll make up for the lost time now. Don't you worry."

"About that…about the last time we were together in Rome…" Clara took a deep breath and was about to say her piece when Electra emerged from the curtains behind Felix like a goddess from the mist.

"Good morning, my man," Electra said, bending down to kiss Felix from behind. She glanced at Clara who greeted her with a timid smile, and then reclined on the couch beside Felix. "You left our bed too soon."

Felix looked at her briefly before looking back expectantly at Clara. "There is too much to do and consider to be laying abed," he said to Electra. "Clara, what were you going to say? We should talk now while we can, before the others awake from their stupefied slumber. I'll introduce you to them at their worst, so that you aren't disappointed later on," he laughed.

Electra did not bat a long eyelash at this, but sipped water from her cup and dipped her finger in the honey that was there, before sucking it off. Her large, dark eyes then fixed themselves on Clara.

Clara met her gaze, but she knew the chance to speak to

Felix was now lost. She sighed. "It's nothing. Let's eat," Clara said resignedly. "Tell me of your favourite productions over the years."

Felix sat up, his face alight. "Oh, well! When we were in Halicarnassus…"

Clara did not hear most of what he began to say, for Felix's voice faded into the background behind the sound of her own inner voice, chiding herself to no end. She saw Electra gazing at her unnervingly whilst Felix spoke. *She knows!*

THE SUN'S CHARIOT HAD BEEN ARCING UP OVER THE EDGE OF the seven hills of Rome for some time when its light breached the window above Rufio's head to warm his sleeping face. On a rooftop somewhere, a lark sang as it flit from roof tile to roof tile. It was a lovely song of awakening before the sound of people milling in the streets outside and carts finishing their early morning deliveries prior to being banished from the by-ways of Rome for the rest of the day.

Rufio smiled to himself where he lay, for he had been dreaming of Clara, of the swimming pond where they had played as children, only now they were grown, and the smile upon her face as she looked upon him was brighter than any sun or nighttime constellation. His mind had begun to rouse, but he kept his eyes shut, not wanting the image of her to fade from his mind. "Clara," he said to himself.

"Oh, I'm not Clara, you naughty boy!" said a completely other voice.

Rufio's eyes shot wide awake and he turned his head to see Meretrix lying beside him, her breasts pointed to the ceiling, her face smiling where it was set in the tousled mountain of her dyed hair. "Ah!" he yelled.

She began to laugh. "Oh, calm yourself, Rufio," she said.

"I just wondered if I could try tempting you one more time." She winked and looked down. "Looks like I can!"

Rufio screwed up his face, and then looked down too at his morning glory before shouting again. "Ah!" he said, taking one of the pillows and covering himself.

There were tears in Meretrix's eyes now, for she laughed hard, her breasts joining in the jollity which only added to Rufio's discomfort. "It's a wonder anything fun at all happens in Etruria!" Meretrix finally said, sitting herself up and pulling her open robe closed for Rufio's benefit. "Good thing I'm a confident woman, or else you would put me out of business." She stood and walked over to a table. "Here. I've got some food for us. Eat, Rufio. I promise I won't try again." She sighed dramatically and sat down at the small table to eat bread and honey. "Join me."

Rufio looked down. "Allow me a minute."

She smiled. "I could have helped you with that, but I understand. You're saving yourself for your Clara. I do have to thank you though."

"For what?" Rufio said as he turned on the edge of the bed, his back to her as he dressed.

"For a lovely night. I haven't slept that well next to a man in a long while."

"Nothing happened," he said, more to himself.

"I wouldn't say that. Much happened. You told me much."

Rufio walked across the room and sat across from her to eat. "What are you talking about?"

"Your friends, of course. So," she said, setting her food down and leaning onto the table to stare straight at him. "Are you going to stay and help them?"

Rufio bit into a hunk of bread and took a piece of honeyed cheese, shaking his head as he mulled over the question.

"You can always stay with me, you know," Meretrix said, her voice softer but lacking any subtlety at all. She enjoyed teasing him. "I won't charge you. We'll have a wonderful time."

"Oh...ah..." Rufio dared to look at her. "I can't...I...I have to get back to Etruria. My donkey will be missing me."

"Well, that's one I haven't heard before!" Meretrix said, leaning back from the table.

"No, I mean-"

She nodded knowingly. "She must be a very special girl."

"She's been with me a long time. If I don't scratch behind her ears, she..."

"I don't know what you want to get up to with this Clara, but behind the ears is new to me!" she laughed.

"No, I meant my ass!"

"Well, I don't know. I have had a few men ask for that but...you surprise me, Rufio."

"My donkey!" he corrected. "She's special. A good girl."

"Poor thing!"

"What? No, I never!" Rufio protested.

"Not the donkey, silly man!" Meretrix said. "Clara must be very special, and you are the poorer for not going after her."

Rufio was silent, his head still spinning a bit after the wine-soaked night. "Ah."

"You are a definitely out of your depth here in Rome," she said, not unkindly.

He sighed. "Don't I know it."

They ate in silence then, he at odds with the racing thoughts in his whirling head, and she resigned to having to bid farewell to the kindest, strangest man she had almost lain with in a long while.

After a time, Rufio stood up. "It's getting late. I should be going."

"I suppose you should," Meretrix said, going across the room to take up his satchel and hang it over his shoulder for him. "I'll show you out."

Meretrix led him out of her own, private world to the door and then down the stairs to the street below.

Rufio followed her and stopped outside the door to look at the massive flow of the crowd going both ways on the street. He felt a sudden dread at seeing so many people again, then felt something nudging his leg. He looked down to see the dog, Peli, looking up at him and wagging his tail wildly.

"Peli!" Meretrix said, kneeling down to kiss his muzzle. "You waited for him? Good boy!"

"Not him again!" Rufio muttered. He looked at the dog without patting him. "You're not coming to Etruria with me, you know that, right?"

Meretrix stood up and looked at Rufio. "I will miss you," she said as she leaned in to kiss him on the lips. "Hmm. When you finally do kiss your Clara, you'll need to soften those up a little." She winked.

Rufio scratched his head and turned away awkwardly, about to wade into the crowd. He stopped, however, and turned back to Meretrix, shaking his head disconcertingly. "I... I don't suppose you can tell me the way to the via Flaminia? I never know where I am in Rome."

Meretrix looked at him for a moment and felt a deep pity for the man before her. *He deserves so much more than what he is allowing himself,* she thought. It was then that a glint of great certainty and purpose sparked in her bright eyes. *I'll help him on his way, by Venus, I will!*

"Of course, Rufio," she said. "Go down the street to the left here, and then straight ahead until you hit the Tiber. Then, go left again and follow the river."

"I thought it would be right at the river, no?" Rufio asked, still looking down the crowded street where she had pointed.

"Oh, no. It's definitely a left! Rome is confusing to outsiders."

"True enough," he muttered before turning to her and

looking her in the eyes for the first time that morning. "Thank you for helping me last night."

Meretrix smiled kindly. "You're welcome." She placed her hands upon his chest. "If you ever dare to come back to Rome, call on me."

"I will," he said.

Meretrix leaned in quickly one more time to embrace him. "Why not?" she whispered in his ear. "Why not?"

He shrugged. "All right! Why not?" he repeated.

"Exactly!" she said. "Why not?"

"What are you saying now?" he asked, thoroughly confused and wondering if the remains of the wine were still clouding his mind.

"Just repeat those words to yourself, Rufio, and you'll be all right. *Why not?*"

Meretrix turned, smiling to herself and went back inside to leave Rufio in the street with the dog looking up expectantly at him.

Rufio then turned and went down the street in the direction she had indicated. He looked at the dog following at his heels as he walked. "You piss on me again and I'll throw you into the river!" He picked a path through the crowd and waded in. "Why not?" he repeated Meretrix's words to himself. "What a strange and happy lupa!" He could not help but smile.

It was late in the morning as Rufio plied his way through the suffocating crowds of Rome, and it took no little effort not to gag as his senses were accosted by smells and sights he would be happy never to experience again. The streets were an odd and unpleasant mixture of human waste, perfume, and sweat that seemed to cling to the very stones of the buildings and to the people he passed. *This time, it's not me!* he thought. "Why not?" he muttered Meretrix's mantra to himself. "Why not?" with a little more gusto this time.

Rufio did not notice the people giving him a wide berth as

he strode along, for he was already thinking of the open countryside along the via Flaminia and the distant hills of Etruria. He looked down at the dog again. "You're not coming with me all the way home, you know?"

Peli looked up from his easy walk beside Rufio and carried on.

The crowd began to thicken and Rufio had to slow down in his progress. He began to feel his heartbeat speed up as people closed in around him, and he held his satchel close to his chest. He looked to the sky for some relief and breathed.

It was then, as the flow of pedestrian traffic slowed almost to a standstill, that Rufio heard the sound of loud voices, cheering, and applause. He paused to listen, and it was as if the entire crowd did so with a changed mood. Everyone about shuffled slowly with cocked heads as if straining to hear a prophecy from the Gods' mouths, or some such utterance. When Rufio too looked up and around, he realized that he was in the street between the theatres of Pompey and of Balbus.

Some raucous noise exploded from the circus Flaminius behind him, but this was as brutal as a barbarian's battle cry in the middle of the Forum Romanum compared with the melodic cadence rising from the theatres followed by the applause of the people so blessed with witnessing the performance in honour of Venus.

The walls of the theatres rose up to the heavens on either side, and it was as if the Gods applauded within.

"I can't hear!" Rufio protested as he strained to hear the actors' voices within above the laughter and music. He longed to go in and watch. "Why not?" he said once more, but in that moment he felt a hand upon his person and felt someone reaching into the mouth of his satchel while he was so distracted. "Get out of there!" he yelled at the scraggly, dirty-faced man who was trying to rob him.

"Give me your coin or I'll cut you!" the man growled as he pulled out a rusty-bladed onion knife.

Before Rufio could say anything, the man squealed louder than a castrati as Peli fastened his jaws on the thief's crotch, his knife falling to the ground with a clang among the feet of the others around them.

People turned their attention to the two men struggling, one with a dog attached to his genitals, and howls of laughter erupted, accompanied by more applause, as if they were two mimes putting on a gritty street performance.

"Peli, let go!" Rufio said.

The dog did so and before the thief could attack again, Rufio slapped him clumsily across the face, sending him sprawling backward onto the ground where some others began to kick him.

The sound of the theatre quite spoiled, Rufio pressed on through the laughing crowd toward the river which, he hoped, was directly ahead. As he went, the applause faded away, and he shook his head as it only reminded him of his father's violent clapping once more.

"Damn you!" he said, imagining his father's mean-spirited shade laughing in his wake as he pulled free of the crowded street and made for the retaining wall above the river directly ahead.

Rufio leaned on the wall, panting and gasping for fresher air which the Tiber was not eager to provide. Still it was a relief to stretch his eyes and see the midday sunlight sparkling on the water as it rushed by. Once he had gathered himself, he looked left to where Meretrix had told him he should go, and then to the right where he had thought he was supposed to go before her instruction.

"I feel like it's right," he said to the dog, finding some strange comfort in having an animal to speak to again. He looked left, doubtful about Meretrix's directions, but then she had only been helpful.

Why not? he remembered her voice, and shrugged to himself before going in the direction the lupa had told him, and heading along the river with the length of Tiber Island on his right and the rising arches of the theatre of Marcellus on his left.

Rome was much more pleasant from an open vantage point, but Rufio did wonder how people could live there, so confined, so stinking. As he walked, waiting occasionally for Peli to mark numerous points along the way, he began to reconnect with the memory of his last time in Rome, when he, Felix and Clara had walked along the river at that very point, each of them looking up at the theatres from a distance and imagining a day when they would perform within them.

Rufio shook his head. "So silly," he said to himself, stopping yet again to wait for Peli. "You're exaggerating now!" he said to the dog. "That's the twentieth time you've marked something, and I haven't even seen you drink a lick of water!"

Peli sat and barked once at him.

Rufio rolled his eyes. "Whatever. As long as you're not urinating on me, I don't care."

They walked on and soon, a pleasant and familiar smell reached Rufio's nose.

"Dung!" he said, just as the sound of lowing reached his ears. "Cattle!" Rufio walked more quickly, ignorant of the marbled heights of the Capitoline and Palatine hills above and to his left. He strode directly for the tholos of the Temple of Hercules, and then turned to see the expanse of the Forum Boarium where cattle were held in pens for sale by various livestock farmers.

Rufio took a moment to take it all in and sat on the steps of the temple to look the animals over. The smell was strong, pungent, but it did remind him of Etruria, of home. His enthusiasm, however, faded quickly and gave way to a wave of sadness. *What is there to go back to?* he wondered as he conjured the run-down domus, his decrepit farm hand, and the horse who hated him. Only Stella brightened the thought of returning.

The thought that came to him continuously though was of Clara, the touch of her hand upon his arm the previous night, and the feeling of being together again with her and Felix.

Being in Rome had awakened him to their dormant dreams once again, and it had made him think on the love-hate relationship he had with his farm. It was a place he loved for all the past remembrances it held, but he also hated it for the poisonous vitriol his father had injected into it after the death of his mother.

The smell of dung and lowing of cattle faded quickly then, unnoticed now as Rufio stood once more and descended the temple steps to go back to the riverside and carry on to find his way to the road. It still felt like the wrong direction, but he walked anyway, Peli at his side.

He did not get far, however, for the road narrowed and he found himself among sailors and labourers unloading barges and shifting crates along the docks to his right. On his left, a long expanse of warehouses stretched out, and he stopped. *Why not?* he wondered. "Meretrix!" he said, realizing what the lupa had done. He turned quickly to go back the other way, but it was too late.

"Rufio?" a deep voice shouted. "Rufio!"

Rufio turned to see Felix coming toward him between rows of unloaded amphorae.

The smile upon Felix's face was one of great joy and relief, and Rufio could not help but feel guilty at the sight. *Maybe he does need my help?*

"My friend!" Felix took Rufio up in a great, crushing hug.

"I knew you wouldn't let us down!" Felix released Rufio and sniffed, whispering to him. "You smell like a brothel!"

"Do I?" Rufio asked.

Felix smiled. "It's much better!" His laughter was contagious, and Rufio could not help but follow suit in it, that is, until he saw Clara emerge from behind Felix's bulk.

"Rufio?" Clara said, her voice unable to hide the surprise and shock of seeing him. She did not smile, however, but seemed deeply distraught, for she had just been about to tell Felix that she was not going to stay, when he had spotted Rufio and suddenly left her side.

"Cla…Clara," Rufio said, his voice caught in his throat for a moment.

"What are you doing here?" she asked, stepping closer to stand directly in front of him, sparing a look for the curious canine at their feet.

"I thought I was headed for the via Flaminia to go back home," he said.

"Oh." Felix's voice was immediately downcast. "You're going the completely wrong way then."

"I see that now," Rufio added. "I was misled by a lupa."

"A lupa?" Clara repeated.

Rufio shook his head. "No, no! I didn't… I was wandering the streets last night and she merely offered me a place to sleep. She was very kind, actually."

Felix laughed. "Sure she was!" He slapped Rufio on the back. "You know, for a farmer, you have a dismal read of the land."

"Rome is not the countryside!" Rufio protested.

Clara was looking at Rufio with a disapproval she realized she did not quite understand, and shook her head to relinquish the thought.

"I swear, nothing happened with her! We talked much of the night!" Rufio said.

Clara looked taken aback. "What you do is your own affair, Rufio. I didn't say anything."

"That's right, my friend," Felix added. "When in Rome… and so on!" He chuckled.

"It was that wine you gave me last night. I don't remember much!"

"I'll wager you don't!" Felix said, elbowing him. "Well, you no longer smell of piss, and you've picked up a friend along the way!" He bent down to pat the dog and Peli licked his hand. "I'd say you're better off than you were last night, and so are we for your return!"

There was an awkward silence as Felix and Clara both stared at Rufio, and then Clara at Felix as if there was something she wanted to say but could not.

After an uncomfortable minute, Felix stood back and looked at the two of them. "So, my friends? The Gods have brought you here. Will you both stay and help me to put on the greatest theatre performance Rome has ever seen?"

Rufio sighed. "Felix… The Gods did not bring me here today. A lupa did."

"Divinity takes many forms, Rufio!" Felix countered. "Besides, how can we not do this together?" He narrowed his eyes and stared at Rufio. "You walked out on us before. Please don't do it again, Rufio. By the Gods, I need your help." He turned to Clara. "Both of you."

Clara looked at the ground and felt not a little shame for wanting to leave, to do what Rufio had done to them all those years ago. She looked up and met Rufio's gaze as he was staring at her. She smiled slightly, but it was enough to have it reflected in his own face. "Yes, I'll stay." She looked questioningly at him.

Rufio stood there, his heart pounding as if he were about to leap from a cliff above the sea in summertime.

"Rufio?" Felix asked. "What say you?"

Rufio looked down at the dog, and then at both Felix and Clara. He remembered the brief sound of applause he had heard that morning when pressed between the theatres of Rome, and Meretrix's smiling face. "Why not?"

"Praise Apollo!" Felix roared, clapping loudly before embracing both Rufio and Clara.

Almost at once, Rufio regretted his answer, but he was caught up in a current now, and one out of which he could not swim, for almost immediately Felix was ushering him and Clara back toward the warehouse.

"Come! I'll show you the room I built for you! I spared no expense!" Felix said.

Rufio looked at Clara who simply smiled and raised a thin, blonde eyebrow. That look encouraged him no end as they both followed Felix inside while Peli lay down in the sun outside the door.

"I'll introduce you both to the company. They should be awake now!" Felix said as they plunged into the dark, gaping maw of the warehouse.

It took a moment for their eyes to adjust to the darkness, but once they had, the expanse of the warehouse stretched out before them to reveal the wagons, carts, supplies, building materials and myriad other theatrical furnishings. There were stations of tables everywhere, some laden with saws, hammers, nails, vices and an anvil, another with scissors, bolts of cloth, and an array of needles. Yet another table was covered in curled papyrus scrolls and wax tablets.

The smell of paint was strong in the air as well, for on the right side of the warehouse, opposite the cubicula Felix had built, there were great set piece facades being given colour and life.

There was even a small kitchen to the right of the entrance

where a young woman in a long tunica and apron was busy above pots and frying pans. She glanced at Felix and the two strangers standing there, before taking a platter of food to a long trestle table in the middle of the warehouse.

Beyond the table, in the most central position, a large makeshift stage was being built by three men, their hammering echoing off of the rafters above.

"You've been busy," Clara said to Felix, not having taken in all of the details of her surroundings before.

Felix smiled and nodded.

"Do you have a legion of actors now?" Rufio asked. "It's like you're on a military campaign!"

Felix slapped his back. "A great theatre production *is* a military campaign, my friend!"

Electra appeared beside Rufio and Clara in that moment, making the former jump a little as she did so without making a sound. She looked at him, sniffed and walked forward to join Felix who called out.

"Etrurian Players!" Felix bellowed like a centurion upon the parade ground. "Gather round!" He clapped loudly, and the hammering, sawing, cutting and painting stopped. The heads of various people moved about the warehouse toward the central location of the tables.

As one, the company lined up before Felix, Rufio and Clara, with Electra standing off to the side in long, flowing robes observing from her own vantage point.

Rufio and Clara felt the others' eyes upon them, some curious or friendly, others disdainful.

Clara was used to such scrutiny from the locals in Syracusae, and so she was not bothered, but Rufio felt distinctly ill at ease among the players.

Felix stepped in front of the company and opened his arms wide. "I present to you, my friends, The Etrurian Players! The best theatre company around the Middle Sea!" He bowed dramatically, and then started the introductions from left to right.

"These two bearded brothers are Castor and Pollux."

The two of them, dressed in identical grey tunica, smiled and focussed on Clara.

Rufio noted they were very similar looking and wondered if they were not twins but for the difference in size, one being lean and lanky, the other thickly muscled, though nowhere near the same as Felix.

"Castor and Pollux were tradesmen before, but they decided they wanted to be actors."

"That's right," Pollux, the larger one, said. "Now we build sets."

"You also act!" Felix countered.

"Bit parts, yes," Castor added.

"I'm easing you into things," Felix said, leaning to Clara and Rufio. "They are actually very good."

This made the brothers smile.

Felix continued. "Beside them is Damon." He presented a heavy, thick-armed young man who simply nodded without saying a word. "Damon is mute, but he understands everything in both Greek and Latin. He helps build the sets, and is an excellent flute player."

"Really?" Clara asked, smiling at the mute and making him blush.

"Yeah, from both ends!" the goggle-eyed man on the end blurted, making a few of the company chuckle.

"That's enough, Silas!" Felix said before continuing. "This young lady," he presented the girl in the middle who had been setting the food upon the table, "this is Beatrice."

"Pleased to meet you," the girl said, smiling such that her cheerful demeanour also made Rufio and Clara smile.

"Hello, Beatrice," Clara greeted.

"Beatrice acts in the smaller roles, and is also our seamstress," Felix added. "She's a wonder with a needle and thread, whether for fine fabrics or cuts after a tavern brawl!"

Castor and Pollux laughed at that and smacked Damon on the back, making him grunt in dismay as he leaned forward to show Rufio and Clara a faint scar above his left eye.

"Goodness," Clara said under her breath.

Felix's voice changed now to something more formal as he presented the oldest member of the company. "And this…*this*…is Julius."

The older man bowed in a distinguished manner, his pale, thin hair ruffled by the slight breeze blowing through the warehouse as he did so. He wore a fine, belted tunica that went to the floor.

Felix smiled. "Julius is the veteran among us, and was… is!…one of the greatest actors you will ever see."

"Apart from you, Felix Modestus," Julius added quickly and without an ounce of resentment.

"You are kind, Julius," Felix said, turning back to Rufio and Clara. "He lifts us all up."

Julius inclined his head most graciously before Felix moved on to the youngest member of the company, a youth with fine, unblemished skin and long, soft hair that tickled the tops of his shoulders.

"Fausto!" Felix said, most affectionately, like a father introducing a son with some pride.

The youth smiled as Felix pulled him forward from the lineup. "Fausto joined us not long ago, but he has shown great aptitude for the theatrical arts. And he can tumble like none of us across the stage!"

The man on the end frowned at this praise and without anyone seeing, jammed his thumb between Fausto's buttocks, making the youth squeal unpleasantly. "And he plays female roles most expertly!"

Felix turned on the man as Fausto rubbed his bottom, his

face red. Felix leaned in and growled so that only the man would hear. "Leave him alone. If you embarrass me, I'll have you crucified!"

The man met Felix's gaze, however, and merely nodded once.

"And this is Silas," Felix added as an aside. "In addition to being jealous of Fausto's youthful good looks, Silas can be an excellent actor when he wishes to be, especially in the role of the parasite." Felix shot him a deathly stare. "He is also our account manager and has an alchemical way of working with funds and squeezing every ounce out of our business dealings."

Silas crossed his arms and stared across the floor at Rufio and Clara, his bulging eyes unnervingly steady.

On the far side, Electra cleared her throat.

"Ah yes!" Felix said. "And you already know Electra, the goddess among us who can play both the heroine and the whore with great aptitude. Her singing voice can lull the audience into a deep state so that they do not hear my coming until I am upon them."

Electra pursed her lips, seemingly unhappy with her introduction, but she said nothing.

"Now," Felix said to the players, "I introduce to you my two oldest friends in the world, Clara Probita and Rufio Pagano."

Damon, the mute, laughed at the latter's name, but quickly shut his mouth.

"Damon…" Felix said, his voice low and deep, as if he were berating a hound. "Clara and Rufio are joining our company for this titanic production, for they are two of the best actors in the world!"

The praise Felix so easily heaped upon them quelled any other sound in the warehouse as the company looked on the two newcomers with no small amount of doubt.

Silas looked with great disdain upon them from the end, but Rufio and Clara paid him no mind.

"Felix exaggerates," Clara said, smiling at the group. "But we are thrilled to be here to help. It's lovely meeting all of you!"

Most of the others, besides Silas, smiled at the greeting.

"Now!" Felix bellowed. "All of you eat the meal which Beatrice has made for you, and we will get back to work. There is much to do!"

The players began to talk and turned to sit at the long table where Beatrice had set the food.

Felix turned to Rufio. "Now, I'll show you to your cubiculum. It's beside Clara's."

Rufio followed Felix while Clara stood still for an uncomfortable moment with Electra staring at her like a statue of Venus in the midst of the warehouse.

"Are you joining the company to eat?" Clara asked.

"No," Electra said, before turning away and going back beyond the curtains of hers and Felix's cubiculum.

Clara sighed and looked about the warehouse. *Gods, let this not be a mistake…*

ACT III

BEHIND THE SCAENAE

IX

A TITANIC PRODUCTION

Rufio Pagano awoke the following morning as if from a most strange dream devised by the Gods to confuse him, for he had dreamt that he was a youth again, blindfolded by his friends and being spun around on the spot. He could hear Felix and Clara's laughter as they spun him, feel the growing dizziness in his mind as his hands groped in the dark near the edge of the field. Birds squawked above, and the voices of his friends faded away as their hands released him. He bobbed this way and that, stumbling over the plough furrows in the field, tripping at every obstacle as he called out their names. Finally, he stopped, and tore the blindfold off.

When he could see, he found that he was not in a field, but rather in a feather-stuffed bed which was, by far, of greater comfort than any he had slept in before. Birds sang from somewhere beyond the ceiling of the cubiculum which, he now remembered, Felix had told him was built especially for him.

Rufio froze and looked around from the hem of the blanket under which he now hid. The walls were painted on two sides like a forest, complete with lurking animals, birds, and a few skulking satyrs and playful nymphs. A third wall represented the stage of a great theatre with ornate scaena frons and a pulpitum before a semi-circular orchestra, a stage on which he could let his imagination run riot.

The fourth wall was painted in a soothing blue and in the middle of it, behind a table with styli, wax tablets, and rolls of papyrus, was a pigeon hole shelf filled with scrolls for him to read. In the corner, to the left of the shelf, was a tripod with a basin of water and soft Egyptian towels. On the right, was a small brazier in which a fire had already been silently kindled. To the right of the brazier was a rack of leather cingula, bracae, tunicae, and cloaks of various colours. On the floor beneath the clothing were various pairs of sandals. It was a larger wardrobe than that which he had at home.

Rufio remembered then, and shut his eyes tight as if to return to the game in his dream. When he opened them again, he found himself back in the opulent quarters.

"Futuo!" Rufio rubbed his face brusquely, as if that would eradicate the predicament in which he found himself, but he was still abed in the warehouse. "What have I done?"

Very quickly, he remembered the previous day, leaving the lupa's home and then walking along the river to find himself standing before Felix and Clara. He remembered agreeing. "Why not?" he repeated to himself, pounding the bed with his fist. "You idiot!"

"Rufio? Are you all right?" The voice he had been dreaming of came in at the closed doorway. It was Clara.

"Uhm…yes!" He looked down on the ground and saw his clothes lying in a heap, realized that he was naked. "Don't come in!"

"I won't," she replied. "There is food!" she added. "No! Stay!"

"What?" he said confused. "I thought you wanted me to come out?" When Clara did not reply, he took down a pair of grey bracae and a blue tunica which he put on and belted with a cingulum. He looked over the sandals and shook his head, unbelieving that Felix had purchased a wardrobe for him when he did not even know for certain that Rufio would come to

Rome at all. "What is happening?" he said to himself as he slumped on the edge of the bed.

Rufio remembered clearly now the previous day. He had started to doubt his decision to stay almost immediately, but being around Clara had done something to him. Seeing her smile, and hearing her voice again after so many years had suddenly shackled him to Rome. He also had to admit that hearing Felix's joyous, booming laughter, and feeling the warm glow of their old friendship was more than he had enjoyed in a very long time. He could pick out their voices from the mass of banter beyond his room then. It made him smile briefly before he realized what it all meant. "Cacare!" he muttered as he took the door handle and pushed.

There was a loud squeal from the other side and Rufio, his heart jumping like a circus acrobat, pushed a little farther to stick his head out and see the dog, Peli, turned with his tail between his legs, looking up at him.

"What are you doing here?" he said to the dog.

It was Clara who answered. "Apparently he's been there all night waiting for you."

Rufio smiled and came out of the cubiculum. "Good morning!"

She smiled back, and that was all the sun he needed.

"Why did you ask me to stay inside?" he asked.

Clara shook her head after a moment. "Not you, silly! The dog!"

"Oh!" he said, feeling stupid. They stared at each other for an awkward moment before he spoke again. "Are we really doing this?"

"Seems that way," Clara answered pushing a strand of her golden hair back behind her ear. "Why? Have you changed your mind?"

Rufio noted the concern in her voice, the worried look in her eyes, and shook his head. "No, no!"

"Good…good," she said.

Rufio stared at her a moment longer, admiring the pale blue tunica she was wearing and how it clung to her. He coughed and tore his eyes away to look over the vast space of the warehouse. "Seems like everyone is busy already."

"You've slept late," she said. "Felix has had them all building, painting and sewing for some time. "He sent me to wake you so that he can tell all of us what the play will be."

"You mean, no one knows yet?" Rufio said, aghast that Felix should keep it such a secret.

Clara shook her head. "No. They've just been making the things he's asked for without any inkling of what they were going to put on."

"Why the secrecy?" Rufio asked as they began to walk slowly toward the table before the stage where the last of the food was awaiting Rufio.

Clara shrugged. "I don't know, but he is going to tell all of us now that you are awake."

"Ah! The great actor appears!" the man named Silas said from the edge of the stage before the table where he was going over the company's accounts.

Rufio looked around, confused, and realized those bulging eyes were fixed on him.

Silas shook his head and craned his neck. "Felix! Now can you tell us what exactly we are going to be performing for the people of Rome?"

"Is Rufio with us?" Felix said from somewhere behind a mountain of crates.

"I'm here!" Rufio called out, as he sat himself at the long table to eat some of the leftover bread and cheese.

"Good morning!" Felix appeared from the left of the stage to come around to Rufio. "How did you sleep?"

"Fine," Rufio said. "Though the noise of the city does keep one awake."

"You'll get used to it!" Felix said, looking at both Rufio and Clara and smiling most sincerely. "Together again!"

"So?" Rufio asked. "What play are you putting on?"

"We, Rufio!" Felix corrected. "*We!*" he put his finger to his lips and motioned for Clara to sit as well as he leapt onto the stage and turned around to address the company at their various workstations. "Etrurian Players!" he called out. "It is time! Gather at the stage!"

Slowly, the company emerged from their dimly lit corners throughout the warehouse to gather before the stage. Some sat upon chairs at the table with Rufio and Clara, others stood to the side, all of them looking up at Felix who waited for Electra to join them last at the far end of the table, her arms crossed as she stared at him.

Felix nodded to Electra and cleared his throat before looking at each of the faces before him, Rufio and Clara last. He smiled at his two old friends and proceeded.

"We are going to make history with this production, my friends."

"Just tell us already!" Silas blurted, more cantankerously than was usual, even for him.

"Silence!" Felix roared, his powerful voice crushing any more efforts to speak over him.

Silas pursed his lips and leaned back in a chair which he had dragged to the side of the stage.

"As I said," Felix continued. "We are going to make history with this performance. All others which we have done will pale in comparison, and the name of The Etrurian Players will be on the lips of everyone who has ever sat or will sit to witness greatness upon the stage.

Rufio raised his eyebrows and looked around at the rest of the company. Apart from Silas, he could tell that the rest of them truly believed Felix, believed in what he did and said. He was as Hector before the brave soldiers of

Troy, making them believe they could win with but a few words.

"When we were in Ephesus," Felix began, the Gods sent me a dream." He began to walk slowly about the stage, pausing at times as he spoke. "In that dream, the voice of a goddess spoke to me - I know not which - but she specified the particular play we were to put on, and who should be in it." Here, he presented his two friends who sat toward the middle of the table. "Rufio and Clara, my old friends," he said, smiling at them. "You were meant to be here. The Gods have demanded it."

The company turned to look at Rufio and Clara, some of them smiling, others looking clearly confused, but they all turned back to Felix a moment later.

"The Gods have told me that if this production is success-ful, then we will indeed be the greatest company in the Empire, sought and admired by all."

Clara noted that Felix did not mention the part about it being a matter of life and death. She knew why, however, for if he had, it would put added pressure upon his company that might hamper their performances. He was a man of focus and vision, and he required it of his company players as well.

Rufio took a bite of cheese and bread at once, he was so hungry, eyeing the dog looking up at him from the floor at his feet.

"And now for the play!" Felix's voice echoed about them. "The play the Gods commanded me to perform is a comedy."

There were pleased murmurs about the table from the company, for they had been performing a lot of tragedy of late and had found it most depressing at times.

"Which one, Dominus?" Castor asked aloud, unable to control himself.

Felix smiled again and stared at Rufio and Clara before speaking. "The Gods have demanded Plautus' *Menaechmi*."

In that moment, Rufio choked on the bread he had shoved in his mouth.

All heads turned from Felix to Rufio, whose face was now matching his red hair as he gagged upon the crust of bread.

"Damon!" Felix commanded the mute stage hand who promptly walked over to Rufio and slapped him hard upon the back.

The bread shot out of Rufio's mouth onto the ground at his feet only to be gobbled up by the dog who had been waiting patiently for just such a crumb.

Rufio gasped and spluttered and accepted the cup of water which Clara had thrust into his hand from the other side of the table.

Felix waited a moment, arms crossed, as he stared down the long table at Rufio. "Are you all right, Rufio?" he asked, his voice serious.

Rufio coughed a few more times, before fixing his eyes on Felix. "You can't be serious?"

"I've never been more serious," Felix said evenly.

"*Menaechmi?* Really?" Rufio looked at Clara and found that she was nearly as shocked as he was. "Why are you doing this?" he asked Felix.

"I am not *doing* this, my friend. The Gods demand it. You know why!"

"What's wrong with the *Menaechmi?*" Julius asked Rufio from down the table. "It is one of Plautus' greatest works!" The veteran actor turned back to Felix. "We'll have them rolling in the aisles!"

"That's the spirit!" Felix said, pointing at Julius.

But Rufio was shaking his head.

"What's wrong?" the youngest actor, Fausto, asked Clara.

She looked from Rufio to Fausto. "*Menaechmi* was the last play Rufio almost performed the last time he was in Rome."

"That's right!' Felix bellowed. "And now's your chance to see it through!"

Rufio felt the sweat beading on his brow then, the damp beneath his arms.

"Dominus," Beatrice stood, wiping her hands on her apron. "I don't know this play so much. What is it about?"

"How can you not know it?" Silas laughed at her. "Every actor knows it!"

Before Felix could berate Silas, Clara stood up. "I don't remember it at all, Felix. Can you summarize the story?" She winked at Beatrice when the younger woman looked over at her, sparing her the look shot by Silas.

"I was going to do exactly that next!" Felix declared, clearing his throat and stepping to the edge of the stage as everyone settled upon stools, benches or crates to listen. "*Menaechmi* is a fabula togata, and perhaps Plautus' greatest play. The story goes like this…"

Felix took a breath, his eyes closed for a moment as his mind reviewed the play in its entirety, for he had read it several times since that fateful dream in Ephesus. He began…

"*Menaechmi* is a story of twin brothers, Menaechmus and Sosicles who are separated one day when their father, Moschus, takes the former on a business trip to Epidamnus, in Dyrrachium. While there, young Menaechmus is abducted by a businessman who lives there, and Moschus is so distraught, he dies, and the two never return to their home in Syracusae."

Felix moved about the rough stage slowly, checking to see that they were paying attention.

They were.

"The grandfather of Sosicles raises the remaining boy in Syracusae, but he renames him Menaechmus in honour of the twin who never returned home."

"How sad!" Beatrice blurted out, unable to help herself.

"It is, dear," Felix smiled. "But wait for it! When he is of age, Menaechmus Sosicles goes on a journey to travel the Middle Sea to find his missing brother and father, and his path eventually leads him, and his loyal servant Messenio, to Epidamnus! In Epidamnus, a city of tricksters and reprobates, we see that Menaechmus of Epidamnus, the original Menaechmus that is," Felix clarified, "is wealthy and married to a shrew of a woman who is the most jealous wife one could ever imagine! But! He finds comfort in the arms of Erotium, the prostitute across the street who is kind and gentle. Menaechmus is so smitten with her that he constantly pilfers his wife's things to give as gifts to Erotium! This is all known by Menaechmus of Epidamnus' cheating, conniving slave, Peniculus, who is the worst sort of parasite!"

The company laughed at that, for they could already picture it!

"And so… Menaechmus of Syracusae, or Menaechmus Sosicles as we shall call him, arrives in Epidamnus with Messenio, who has warned his master of the depravity of the people in that city and urges him to give up the search for his long lost brother. Menaechmus Sosicles ignores the warnings of his servant, gives him a bag of coin for safekeeping, and heads out into the city to search for his brother. It just so happens that on that very morning, Menaechmus of Epidamnus has arranged for a breakfast full of pleasures with his mistress, Erotium. At the same time, Menaechmus presents her with a cloak that belongs to his wife. Erotium loves it and bids him return shortly after her servant, Cylindrus, and her maid have prepared the domus and meal for his arrival."

As Rufio listened, he remembered, with no little amount of nervousness, every twist and turn of the story. They had rehearsed it so much, so long ago. *Menaechmi* was going to be their breakout performance in Rome. He shook his head, and thought of running again, but for Clara's hand which reached across the table to grip his arm.

"Remember?" she asked, her whisper excited as it used to be, so very long ago.

He nodded and looked back at Felix.

"Menaechmus of Epidamnus leaves Erotium to take care of some business, but while he is away, Menaechmus Sosicles and Messenio arrive on the very street where Erotium lives across from her lover. Erotium mistakes the one brother for the other - they are twins, remember! She tells Menaechmus Sosicles that the breakfast is ready and that he should come inside. Menaechmus Sosicles is most confused, and loyal Messenio warns him that it is a trick to rob him. Menaechmus, however, is curious and accepts her invitation. He goes in, and sends Messenio to watch over the baggage and his money. Some time later..." Here Felix winked knowingly. "Menaechmus Sosicles emerges from Erotium's domus wearing a garland and carrying the expensive cloak the other Menaechmus gave to her. Erotium has asked him to get it fixed for her, and he so agrees, thinking that he has actually gained a new cloak as well."

Felix paused, took a couple of breaths, and laughed.

"When Menaechmus emerges from Erotium's home, he is met by Peniculus, Menaechmus of Epidamnus' hateful servant who accosts his perceived master for dining without him at Erotium's. While they are speaking, Erotium's maid rushes out to give Menaechmus Sosicles, whom she thinks is Menaechmus of Epidamnus, an expensive golden bracelet which Erotium asks him to have repaired for her. The bracelet is another gift taken from the other Menaechmus' wife! And so, Menaechmus Sosicles says he will do so and takes the bracelet, with the plan to keep it as well as the mantle. He berates the strange servant who has accosted him - Peniculus, that is, - and goes to tell Messenio of his good fortune. Meanwhile, Peniculus decides to turn on his master, Menaechmus of Epidamnus, and goes to tell the latter's wife of his infidelities and thefts."

"What happens next?" Fausto asked aloud, his face alight

with curiosity, for he had not known the play either, though he had been too shy to say as much.

"Well," Felix carried on. "When Peniculus tells the wife what her husband has done, she is furious and rushes out into the street to confront Menaechmus of Epidamnus, her husband, as he is returning from an overly long business dealing in the forum. She accuses him of everything, urged on by Peniculus, and they argue in the street. Menaechmus of Epidamnus goes to Erotium's to retrieve the items, but she too accuses him of lying because she already gave him those very items. Menaechmus of Epidamnus is confounded then, for the doors of both his own domus, and that of his mistress', are slammed in his face. He leaves to find his friends for advice."

Felix now sat on the edge of the stage, to be closer to his rapt audience. But he could not look in Rufio's direction then, for he did not want to scare him off, like a hunter spotting a deer in a wood. His voice was low now.

"Menaechmus Sosicles is returning to find his servant with the fixed cloak over his arm when the jealous wife of his brother sees him and demands that he confess his great shame. Of course, he knows her not, and so denies all, including the fact that she is is wife! The jealous wife of Menaechmus of Epidamnus is so distraught at this that she calls for her father who comes to confront Menaechmus Sosicles and tells him he must be mad to go on in that fashion with his own wife. Menaechmus Sosicles sees the merit of acting mad and plays along with it as a way to break free of the strangers. The father of the jealous wife then sends for a medicus whilst Menaechmus Sosicles gets away to look again for Messenio."

Felix clapped his hands.

"It is then that Menaechmus of Epidamnus returns at the same time as the father and the medicus and some men. They accuse Menaechmus of Epidamnus of being mad and try to apprehend him, and a great fight breaks out!"

"Excellent! A fight!" Pollux said, immediately quieting again with a look from Felix.

"Yes!" Felix agreed. "A fight! It is then that Messenio appears and thinks that the medicus and his men are fighting his true master, Menaechmus Sosicles. Brave Messenio rushes in to help him, and he does. Menaechmus of Epidamnus is so grateful for the help from Messenio, whom he does not know, that he says he is free! Messenio, thinking it is his real master, is very happy indeed and goes to get his possessions for him, that is, the money. Menaechmus of Epidamnus goes to Erotium's to ask about the cloak again, and while he is doing so, Menaechmus Sosicles returns to find Messenio with the purse and berates him for having been gone so long. Messenio protests, saying that he only just saved him from ruffians in the street!"

Felix paused as the great moment of revelation in the story approached.

"It is then that Menaechmus Sosicles sees Menaechmus of Epidamnus emerge from the house of Erotium and the two of them, upon seeing the other, are completely bewildered. Explanations bring about recognition and the two brothers embrace at last. Messenio is rewarded with his freedom by Menaechmus Sosicles for all he has done, and then he is asked by Menaechmus of Epidamnus, who is also grateful to him, to auction all of his possessions in the morning, including his wife, if there is a buyer!"

The company waited a moment to make sure that Felix was finished his great summary, and when they were certain, they exploded into applause and conversation about how fun it would be to put on such a play.

"You see?" Julius said aloud. "It really is one of the best!"

"I can see it all now," Beatrice mused.

"The crowd will love it!" Fausto added.

Meanwhile, Castor and Pollux were already enacting the fight scene with Damon.

Felix looked up then at Rufio and Clara and the two of them met his gaze with a mixture of terror and disappointment for the former, and reticence and excitement for the latter.

"Oh, Captain!" Julius addressed Felix with a flourish. "It is a wondrous choice! What sort of production do you envision? I know you have just had us begin on costumes and sets, but now can you tell us the grand scheme of what the Gods have shown you?"

"Yes, Julius!" Felix said, jumping down from the stage to stand among them. "This is going to be unlike any other production you have seen of this play. For this production, we will *not* be wearing masks."

"That's preposterous!" Silas accused. "Everyone wears masks!"

"Not this time. The Gods demand a production with a difference," Felix bit back.

Electra came to his side then. She had known this revelation would cause confusion, and had warned him as such. She stared down Silas for the moment, and he quieted himself.

Felix looked at her briefly and turned back to the company. "Neither will we be singing our lines."

"What?" It was Julius' turn to express shock. "Oh, Felix Modestus," he said without aggression, "it is one thing to forgo the use of masks - makeup can play the part there - but to forgo singing and music…" He shook his head and his thin hair twirled about his crown. "The crowd will dine upon our bones if we survive to the end."

"I know it is a risk," Felix said, nodding and placing his hand upon the older man's shoulder. "But I must follow the Gods' demands to the letter. Trust me, all of you. We must speak our words, as is done in the tragedies, so that the audience feels along with us. But, there will be music nonetheless! Do not worry. Between scenes, there will be music from Damon's flute, and the expert percussion of Castor, Pollux, and Beatrice. Of course there will be music and song!"

The company looked somewhat relieved, though terror was also etched upon their faces.

"We trust you, Felix," Julius said, standing up again.

"Thank you, Julius," Felix said. "I have not led you astray before, and I do not plan on doing so now. This will be our greatest performance!"

"And what plan do you have for the parts for this titanic production?" Silas asked aloud, standing before Felix, his arms crossed.

Felix waited for everyone to quiet down. "It just so happens that the Gods have shown me who plays what part as well."

"Of course they have!" Silas said, his voice slick with sarcasm. "Well, go on then!"

"Curb your tongue, Silas!" Julius said. "We should all count ourselves lucky to be here!"

"Maybe you should, old man!" Silas added bitterly.

"Enough!" Felix barked, and Peli echoed the sentiment from where he sat at Rufio's feet. Felix looked at Clara and Rufio then, and knew that they suspected what he was going to say. *If Rufio does not flee now, we may be safe,* he thought. "All right," he began, "I will play the part of Menaechmus of Epidamnus-"

There was applause from the company at that, for they knew he was as a god upon the stage.

Felix waved his hands to quieten them, nodding at the same time that he agreed with them. "Electra will play the jealous wife." He looked sideways at Electra who held a basket filled with scrolls, wearing a dark expression that said she was still not excited about the play, the role, all of it.

The others applauded, but she gave only the faintest of nods to acknowledge it.

"They seem afraid of her," Clara whispered to Rufio, but he was not listening for his head was straining forward to hear what Felix would say next.

"Rufio!" Felix then called out, staring directly at him. "You will play Menaechmus Sosicles, my long lost brother!"

The faces of the company turned to look at Rufio where he sat, wide-eyed and terrified at the prospect of, well, everything.

Felix could see it immediately and almost held his breath, waiting for his old friend to break for it, finding himself grateful for Rufio's temporary paralysis. "You'll be a wonder!" he declared, before turning to Clara. "Clara, my dear, you will play Erotium."

Clara nodded, searching her memories for the lines she had once known so well. She could see Julius, Fausto and Beatrice smiling at her, encouraging her.

"Now," Felix continued, "those are the primary roles. Now for the rest, which I know you will all perform to the best of your abilities. Remember! There are no small parts, only small efforts! We are professionals, after all!"

There were some scattered cheers at that.

"Fausto?"

"Yes, Dominus!" Fausto jumped up like a soldier at attention, grinning broadly.

"You will play Messenio, the loyal servant of Menaechmus Sosicles from Syracusae."

Fausto yipped at that and jumped up on a stool to bow to his comrades.

"Silas," Felix said immediately when he spotted the other contemplating kicking the stool from under the younger player.

Silas looked at him, his arms still crossed.

"You will play the role of the parasite, Peniculus, the slave of Menaechmus of Epidamnus and his jealous wife."

"Are you sure about that? Perhaps you do not recall your dream very well?" There was desperation in Silas' voice, and not a little anger. "I would do much better as Sosicles, no? You forget that I played the part a long time ago."

"Not with this company, you haven't!" Felix said curtly, before turning to the rest of them. "I am not joking when I tell you that the Gods have relayed everything to me perfectly. We cannot counter them…" For a moment, Felix's words stopped in his throat, for the thought of the threatened outcome, should all fail, still had its fearful claws in his gut. He shook it off quickly, before anyone could notice, and then continued. "Silas, you always play an excellent parasite. This will require all your skills to perform and make the discerning audiences of Rome believe!"

"I'm not worried about myself," Silas bit back. "I'm worried about the two new additions to our company. We are all depending on them for the success of this production, and we haven't even seen them act."

"By the Gods!" Felix roared. "*I* have seen them act, and I tell you they are excellent! That should be enough for you! Now put your tongue back in your mouth and clamp it shut!"

"Yeah, let the dominus finish, Silas!" Castor said from across the table.

Silas glared at him but said no more as he sat upon the crate behind him.

"Good," Felix said. "Now…Julius." He smiled at the older actor who always made the most of every production. "Julius, you shall play two roles - that of Moschus, the father of the twins who dies in the beginning, and then the role of the medicus whom the father-in-law of Menaechmus of Epidamnus calls to take his son-in-law away."

"I shall endeavour to make you proud, Felix Modestus." Julius bowed his head graciously.

"You always do, Julius. Thank you." Felix smiled. "Castor next."

Castor stepped forward, clearly overcome with excitement, for Felix only occasionally gave him roles as he was still new to performing, the same as his brother.

"Castor, you will play the father of Menaechmus of Epidamnus' jealous wife, the one who calls on the medicus to take him away."

"Woo!" Castor howled aloud and hugged his brother.

Felix laughed. "I'm glad you agree! And Pollux…you will play Cylindrus, Erotium's cook."

"Yes, Dominus!" Pollux said, saluting Felix as though he were Caesar himself.

"They are joyous for the scraps from his table," Silas grumbled to himself.

Rufio was the only one to hear the complaint, but he turned to look at the angry player whose discomfiting eyes turned in his direction almost at once without one iota of friendliness. At his feet, Peli began to growl, and Silas looked away.

"There is one more role to present!" Felix said then, and turned to Beatrice. "Beatrice, you shall play the role of Erotium's maid who rushed out into the street to speak with Menaechmus Sosicles and present him with the bracelet for repair."

From where she sat, Clara could see Beatrice's face light up.

"Thank you, Dominus!" Beatrice said, her hands clasped in her aproned lap.

"Thank the Gods, Beatrice," Felix replied before pausing. "But you are welcome." He turned to the mute Damon then. "Damon, as usual, you will provide some musical accompaniment with your flute along with Beatrice on the sistrum. I'm also giving some thought to using you as one of the brutes who tries to restrain Menaechmus of Epidamnus at the request of the father-in-law. But we'll see about that."

Damon clapped his hands and made a strange sort of howling sound that seemed to mean he was quite happy.

"Right!" Felix called out for their attention once again. "Now that you all know the play and your parts, the work you have been doing on the sets and costumes should make much more sense."

Most of them nodded, relieved to finally know what their direction was going to be, and where the work was leading.

"I have one last announcement before you all get back to work," Felix said. He waited for them to be silent before he spoke. "Electra and I met with the aedile the other day, the man sponsoring us, and he told me that he has secured a venue for us."

"Oh, please tell us it is in the forum!" Julius said, obviously excited. "The forum crowds are always so excellent!"

Felix shook his head. "It is far better than the forum, Julius!" Felix looked at everyone there, his gaze lingering on Rufio and Clara at the back. "We are to perform *Menaechmi*... in the theatre of Pompey!"

There was a stunned silence, and then an eruption of Vesuvian proportions that rebounded off of the warehouse walls with a mixture of excitement, terror, and incredulity.

"You can't be serious?" Fausto said, more scared than anything.

"I don't believe it!" Even Silas could not hide his eagerness.

Julius bent his head in awe. "Never in my life as an actor, have I had such an opportunity," he said, looking up at Felix with tears in his eyes. "Thank you, Felix."

"Don't thank me, my friend. Thank the aedile." To the larger group, he spoke then. "But we cannot move into the theatre until a week before the performance! In the meantime, we will rehearse in this space. I want the area on and about the stage cleared of debris so that we can get as close as possible to the scaena of the great theatre." Felix clapped aloud and turned to Electra who stepped forward with the basket she held. "I have had copies of the script made for all of you - I know you can read - so that you can all learn your lines to perfection. Electra has them in the basket. Get your copy, and then get back to work, Etrurian Players! I know we can do this!"

There was a great cheer as everyone went to Electra to get their own papyrus scroll and then return to the work they had been doing earlier that morning. When they had all gone, Felix went to the table to pour himself a cup of watered wine and sat down with Rufio and Clara.

Electra approached with the basket and handed both Rufio and Clara their own scripts, which they accepted.

Rufio looked as if the item might cause him some great harm as he looked up at the dark Hellene.

Electra scowled and turned to leave.

"Sit with us," Felix said to her.

"I am tired," Electra said. "I will-" She stopped just as Silas approached.

The four of them looked at him as he siddled up to Felix.

"I wish to speak with you," Silas said, his voice even, grave.

"What is it, Silas?" Felix asked as he took a sip of his wine.

"Now is not the time, Silas," Electra said.

"Shut up, woman!" Silas turned on her.

Electra's hand shot out quick as an asp's strike across his face.

"Enough!" Felix bellowed, on his feet and grasping Silas' arm tightly as he dragged him away from his friends at the table. When they were far enough away from Clara and Rufio, he spoke. "What is wrong with you?"

Silas shrugged free of Felix's grasp, but then returned with a hand upon Felix's chest, which the latter removed immediately. "Fine. I'll tell you. By putting those two amateurs in those roles, you are jeopardizing all we have worked for. If this fails, before the Roman audience, in that wondrous venue, it will be the end of The Etrurian Players."

"Silas…" Felix took a breath before continuing. "I know you would have liked the part of Sosicles. I understand. But it is as the Gods demand. I'm not joking about that."

"I'm not talking about the damn part!" Silas bit back, taking Felix by surprise. "I'm speaking to you as the account manager. All of this…" he waved his hands to indicate the entire contents they had brought to the warehouse, "…the expensive props and set pieces…the scrolls…the food…the drink…everything you have done to welcome your old friends… It has cost us a fortune. If this production is not the success you proclaim it will be - and I seriously doubt it will be - then Leno is going to kill you!"

"Shut up," Felix growled as he took Silas by the hem of his tunica and picked him up roughly. "I will pay Leno back every denarius he has loaned me for this production."

"And if you don't?" Silas said, having trouble breathing through the bunched-up collar of his clothing.

Felix set him down and pushed him. "If you don't believe in this endeavour, I can always sell you, you piece of shit!"

Now, everyone could hear and a strange silence fell over the work being done around the warehouse.

"You wouldn't!" Silas hissed, getting to his feet and brushing the dust from his tunica. "I know your secret about where all this money has come from. I could tell everyone."

Felix towered over him. "You think that because for one night you acted the cinaedus for me you can speak to me or to Electra in that way. Do that again, and I'll have your tongue ripped out so that that is the only role you will ever play for anyone. Got it?"

There was fear, anger, and betrayal in Silas' eyes, but Felix was not to be moved by it.

"I only care about the play and this company…and you, Felix."

Felix shook his head. "No, Silas. As ever, you only care about yourself." He waved his hand. "Go away. Back to work now, or I really will sell you."

Silas disappeared into the warehouse behind the piles of opened crates and work tables.

Felix stood there, alone for a moment before turning to go back to Clara, Rufio and Electra. "I straightened him out. It won't be a problem."

"Who is Leno?" Electra asked.

"Mind your own business!" Felix barked, stopping himself from saying more. "I'm sorry. Silas has angered me no end."

"He's going to be a problem this time, more than usual," Electra said, watching Silas' head disappear in the distance.

"No. He won't," Felix said, matter-of-factly. "He's a worm. That is all. The role of the parasite slave should be second-nature to him." Felix approached Electra and kissed her cheek. "Sit with us."

Electra looked down at Rufio and Clara who had remained sitting in stunned silence, and shook her head. "I am tired. I will rest and then read the script for myself." She inclined her head very slightly to Felix's friends, and went away.

Felix sighed and sat down heavily with Clara and Rufio, rubbing Peli's head playfully before taking a sip of wine. "It was much simpler when it was just the three of us."

Rufio looked doubtful.

"What was all that about?" Clara asked.

"Hmm," Felix grunted. "Silas has always thought he was better than the others, even though he is a slave among them. He is smart, good with numbers, but he has always had an attitude problem. I bought him out of necessity in Antioch years ago. He seemed keen to act and knew how to do accounts. It worked for a while, but his ideas got too big for his station. He is a good actor, it's true, but only for certain roles - parasites and villains, not for heroes or characters the audience must sympathize with. With a face like that, it's hard to find any sympathy!" Felix laughed, but Clara and Rufio were silent. "He thinks he could do a better job in the role of Sosicles than anyone."

"Well, maybe he's right, Felix?" Rufio said.

"I don't want to hear it!" Felix retorted.

"Why? It's probably true," Rufio continued. "I haven't acted since, well, since the last time we were together, and even then, I didn't see it through. I know that!"

"Yes, and both Clara and I know you were good at it, especially in this role!" Felix rubbed his beard. "Clara you agree with me, don't you?"

"He's right, you know," she said, turning to Rufio. "You can do this."

"My heart isn't in it," Rufio said.

"Well put your heart into it!" Felix said. "It's the will of the Gods that you're both here, and that we three do this together. We didn't get the chance before because you left us, Rufio!"

Rufio's face reddened. He stood, grabbed his papyrus scroll from off the table and pointed it in Felix's face. "Futuere!"

"You'll be amazing!" Felix called to Rufio's back as he strode toward the warehouse door and the sunlight outside. "You'll see!" He sighed and turned to Clara. "It'll be fine. Just like old times." He smiled, but his smile faded when she did not follow suit.

"But it's not like *old times*, is it?" Clara said, leaning toward him. "We're all different now. We've changed. You have to allow for that, Felix."

"Please don't tell me that you don't believe in this either, Clara. Of all people-"

She reached out and laid her hand on his arm. "Of course I do. And I want to try this, once and for all. But you need to give Rufio time. He has not led the life of comfort either of us have had. He has struggled."

"We've all struggled in our own ways."

"True," she said, "but we need to be patient with him. He'll come around. There is still a couple of months to the games, right? There is time."

"If he ever sits for more than a few minutes to talk with us, maybe," Felix looked to where he could see Rufio. He was sitting outside in the sunshine upon a crate that had been unloaded from one of the barges on the Tiber.

"I'll go talk to him," Clara said.

"Thank you," he said, kissing her hand, silent for a moment. "I'm so glad you're here."

She cleared her throat. "I… I am too." *Now is not the time,* she thought. Clara stood, picked up her scroll, and went after Rufio.

Felix sat there alone for a time, listening to the noise of hammering and sawing going on in the background, of muffled and excited conversations among his players about the roles they were to play. But his thoughts did turn dark for a moment as he thought of the man to whom he was indebted for an absolute fortune to put on the production. "Damn you, Silas, for reminding me!" Felix growled to himself before downing his wine and going to oversee the construction of the set by Damon, Castor, and Pollux.

Outside in the Spring sunshine, Rufio sat on the edge of a large crate, watching the dock workers move back and forth up and down the gangplanks of various barges. They carried innumerable wooden boxes and amphorae over and over, never pausing in their labours as they grunted and sweat. In the warehouse next door, the sound of chiselling could be heard quite loudly above the cries of the gulls overhead, and Rufio turned to stare at the tufts of marble dust that clouded from out of the large doors there.

"Apparently, there is some great artist working in there on commissions for the emperor."

Rufio turned to see Clara approaching from behind. He did not answer her right away, but took in the way the wind played about her hair, and the shift of her tunica as she walked over.

Some of the dock workers stopped for a moment too, to observe the woman walking their way.

Rufio turned and scowled at them. "Back to work!" he shouted, only to be treated to some obscene gestures before the sounds of unloading resumed.

Clara pet Peli on the head when she reached Rufio's box, and then hoisted herself up to join him on his perch. She tapped her scroll to his as if they were clinking cups, and tried to catch his eye. "Why are you so angry?"

"I didn't like the way they were staring at you. The docks are full of cutthroats."

"Possibly," she said casually, brushing blonde strands of her hair away from her face where the breeze played with them. "But I wasn't talking about the dock workers. What is bothering you, really?"

"I'm angry at Felix."

"Why?"

Rufio turned in his seat to look straight at her, shocked for a moment at how close she was. He shuffled his bottom back a little, almost to the edge of the crate. "He's tricked us. It's been years, and the first contact we've had from him is lies in order to get us to do his bidding. He's always thought his wants and needs were more important."

Clara's wide, clear grey eyes observed Rufio closely as she

turned the papyrus scroll over in her long fingers. "Are you sure you're not simply angry at being back here, in Rome? I mean…I find it uncomfortable. I'm guessing you do too?"

"Of course it's uncomfortable!" Rufio snapped, stopping himself immediately from going off. "I'm sorry. It's just that, nothing has gone right since I arrived here."

"Was anything right at home either?" she asked.

He was quiet for a moment. "No. Not really."

"Look, Rufio," she began. "I know you didn't leave Rome before to hurt us. You had your reasons, I suppose."

Rufio shut his eyes tight. *She just doesn't get it!* How he had, at times over the years, wanted to tell her why he had gone. That it wasn't anything to do with her or Felix. *They've already made their assumptions.*

"Clara-"

"Wait," she said. "Let me finish. The past is in the past, Rufio. We need to leave it there." She sighed. "We're all struggling with that."

He looked at her, for her voice took on a strange timbre then.

She met his gaze. "We've all led very strange lives since we were last together, very different lives. But we're not strangers, Rufio. We're still friends, aren't we?"

"Of course!" he said.

"And now, we're together again, in Rome, with a chance to pick up where we left off. How often do the Gods present people with such a second chance?"

"Pft! The Gods?" Rufio said doubtfully. "You mean, Felix."

"You know as well as I that Felix has always been touched by the Gods in some way. I know he can be a bit too much sometimes, especially before his company, but he means well. I think he really does care a lot for us and wants to help. Doesn't it mean something that he has not ever performed this play? It's one of the greatest comedies ever written! It held something special for him, something the three of us shared. I don't know about you, but I've often wondered what it would have been like if we had put on our show on those temple steps all those years ago." She looked away then. "Things would have been quite different."

"And I ruined it all."

"I didn't say that!" She turned back to Rufio.

"You don't have to." He held up his hand to stop her saying more. "Please, I know. I too have…thought…of what might have happened if I didn't have to leave Rome, if I hadn't left."

"So now, we're back to the present, and the second chance the Gods have given us."

"You mean Felix."

She shook her head, her frustration growing at his obstinance. "Does it matter?"

"Yes!" He waved the scroll of *Menaechmi* in front of her face. "I feel sick even holding this thing! I am *not* an actor!"

"You used to be," Clara retorted. "And a good one. And this," she held up her copy of the play, "this used to be your favourite play!"

Rufio looked down at the scroll in his hand. He knew that there was a part of him that longed to open it, to speak the words he had once been so familiar with.

Clara saw the shadow of great sadness in his eyes, and reached out to touch his hand. "Do you remember practising this play on the wooden stage in the wood near our homes?"

He smiled, if not a little sadly as he stared at her hand upon his. "Of course I do."

"Do you remember the freedom and joy we felt then?" She squeezed his hand.

Rufio nodded. "That was a long time ago, Clara."

"Yes. It was," she agreed.

He looked her in the eyes then. "You know what I'm most upset about?"

"Wh…what?" she hesitated.

"Lost time. Wasted time." He shook his head. "I remember those days as if they were only yesterday. And now, here I am in the late summer of my life with nothing to show for it. What's the point?" *I should have been the one to marry you!* he cried out inside, knowing he would never have the courage to say such a thing to her. His eyes burned, but he refused to let it show.

"Time has passed," Clara said. "You are right in that. But it is not fully gone, Rufio. We have been brought together again for a reason, be it of the Gods' choosing or Felix's design. It doesn't matter how. What matters is that Felix may be in trouble, and if we can help him, we absolutely should!"

Rufio looked up at the sky. Above it was the same blue expanse and sunshine that he saw in Etruria. Only when he looked down did he see a different world, a world he was terrified of. "I know you're right, Clara. I know. I'm just worried."

"Yes. You're a worrier. You always have been." She set down the scroll and held his round face in her hands so he would look at her. "I'm scared too, Rufio. I feel as though I've been asleep these past years. But I want to try this one more time, and I want you to do it with me, for yourself…and for Felix."

He smiled most sincerely that time, for like a Siren from an ancient tale, she had swayed him with her voice, and he wanted it to be so. "All right. I'll stay."

"You will?"

"Yes. I'll do it."

"No more talking about leaving? You will commit to this and give it everything?"

"Yes, Clara," he said. "I will. For Felix…and for you."

Peli barked then and pulled at his foot from below. "Not for you!" he said to the dog from his high perch.

"Thank you, Rufio!" Clara leaned in and kissed his cheek

quickly. "Now, let's get inside and see how we can help. Felix wants to start rehearsals tomorrow."

"Of course he does," Rufio muttered, as he held up the scroll. "I suppose I should get reading and reacquaint myself with Menaechmus Sosicles now that our long lost brother has tracked us down!"

Together, they and the dog went back inside the dark mouth of the warehouse to get to work.

THE REST OF THE DAY WAS SPENT LENDING A HAND WHEREVER they could, building the set pieces and giving input, if asked, about the colours to be used, the fabrics for the costumes, and the props that could dot the stage at various points throughout the play.

Most of all, Rufio, Clara and the rest of the company spent time reading and learning the lines from a play they had never put on. It was new territory for everyone in the company and most of them, apart from Silas, attacked their roles with genuine enthusiasm.

Felix had ordered that they would intersperse work on the set and costumes and props with work on the actual lines they were to rehearse. "I want this to develop organically, like a green-shooted garden in spring!" he declared. "By the time of the Ludi Apollinares, we shall have a garden in full bloom!"

The next day, with their bellies full from a hearty breakfast, Felix, Electra, Rufio, Clara and all of the company sat together the length of the long trestle tables with their scripts in hand, ready to read through the entirety of the play.

"Today, we will read through the entire work," Felix declared, standing at the head of the table, looking down its length at his theatrical troops. "I know we haven't performed this before, but I know that you are all capable actors. There is no doubt in my mind." Felix smiled at them, looked each of them in the eye and made them feel like the sun shone upon their faces for a fleeting moment. "I also trust in the Gods. I know Apollo and his Muses, and the goddess who directed me to this undertaking, are with us. They are watching…and waiting. They are eager to see what a heroic company you are."

Clara and Rufio watched Felix from the opposite end of the table where he stood before the stage and the three wooden doorways that had been erected there to represent the street setting of the play. Both of the newcomers felt strange indeed being there, finding their old familiarity with the words they had once been so intimate with. When Felix recited the prologus, they were thrown back, headlong into the past, and it sent a tingle up and down their respective spines.

They clapped with the others when Felix finished.

Then, Silas stood, and he took on an air then that demonstrated his potential as a performer of some skill. When standing, his face softened, his back straightened, and when he opened his mouth, the slave Peniculus began to speak. His words were cold and selfish, such that those listening knew immediately that this slave was not to be trusted in the least…

"He whom you wish to keep securely that he may not run away, with meat and with drink, ought he to be chained; do you bind down the mouth of a man to a full table. So long as you give him what to eat and what to drink at his own pleasure in abundance every day, in faith he'll never run away, even if he has committed an offence that's capital…"

Silas had obviously already memorized his lines, for his bulging eyes strayed from the papyrus scroll to rake over the variously contorted faces of his fellow cast members as he spoke.

For Rufio, it was most discomfiting, for Silas' eyes lingered on him directly, as if in challenge to his own skills which, the possessor knew to be greatly lacking, like the hinges of an unused door that are rusted tightly shut.

"But," Silas continued, "I have now had interval these many days, while I've been lording it at home all along together with my dear ones; for nothing do I eat or purchase but what it is most dear. But inasmuch as dear ones, when they are provided, are in the habit of forsaking us, I am now paying him a visit. But his door is opening; and see, I perceive Menaechmus himself." Silas turned to look upon Felix then. "He is coming out of doors."

Felix stood again from his chair, nodding to Silas, and then turning to Electra at his right. "Unless you were worthless, unless you were foolish, unless you were stark wild and an idiot, that which you see is disagreeable to your husband, you would deem to be so to yourself as well." In that moment, Felix shoved his chair backward, his breathing changed, his eyes filled with confused rage.

Rufio felt great discomfort then, for though he knew in his mind that it was an act, the performance of it was so convincing that he thought Felix and Electra would have at each other's throats in that moment.

"Moreover, if after this day you do any such thing to me, I'll force you, a divorced woman, turned out of my doors to go visit your father. For as often as I wish to go out of the house, you are detaining me, calling me back, asking me questions; wither am I going, what matter I am about, what business I am transacting, what I am wanting, what I am bringing, what I have been doing out of doors?"

The company, apart from those who were locked into the scene, laughed heartily at the supremely frustrated and confused man that Felix, or rather Menaechmus of Epidamnus, had become, like a strong-winged butterfly returned to the state of an awkward caterpillar, there for the kicking.

"I've surely brought home a custom-house officer as my wife; so much I am obliged to disclose all my business, whatever I have done and am doing," he went on until he lowered his voice to speak to the audience behind a tilted hand. "And therefore, that you mayn't be watching me in vain, for your pains I shall find me a mistress today, and invite her to dinner somewhere out of doors."

Silas stood again to give voice to Peniculus, and between him and Felix's Menaechmus, they entranced the others at the table with the scripted banter back and forth between them, both with such skill and device of facial features, that the newcomers to the company felt ill-equipped to meet the task they had accepted.

Where Clara began to feel a warm familiarity and excitement at the prospect of speaking her own words aloud, Rufio sat there contemplating the dog at his feet, and the warehouse door at his back, his heart pounding, his palms and pits sweating. Then he heard Clara's voice, and it was as if his soul fell back into his long-dead body once more, for the lilt and song of her voice aroused a hundred thousand long-dormant memories.

"My life, Menaechmus, save you," Clara said, bringing Erotium into the scene.

And with that, Rufio was back upon the stage in that Etrurian wood…

X

CHEESE AND DISCONTENT

"Call Cylindrus, the cook," Clara declared from the doorway of Erotium's domus upon the rehearsal stage. "Out of doors this moment from within."

Rufio watched Clara again from his seat, the same as he had done for many days during their rehearsals. In fact, all the company watched Clara slowly come into her own again - as Felix had said she would!

For days they had rehearsed the opening episodes between Erotium, Menaechmus of Epidamnus and Peniculus, and for days Felix had taken the time to help Clara bring to fruition his vision of Erotium, or rather to rediscover the Erotium that Clara had breathed life into so many years before.

During that time, Rufio had felt swept away in memory, as if the past had faded into some early morning mist hovering over the loamy earth of his farm.

There was sudden applause then as Pollux came rushing out of the doorway of Erotium's domus, an apron tied hastily about him to indicate his role in the household.

Clara turned to him, trying not to smile too much at the broad grin beneath his bearded scruff, so happy he was with the opportunity.

"Take a hand-basket and some money," Erotium said to her servant. "See, you have three didrachmas here."

"I have so," Cylindrus said, most eloquently, looking at the palm of his hand before his mistress.

"Go and bring some provisions," Erotium said, walking a few steps in thought, planning the perfect dinner for her visiting Menaechmus. "See that there's enough for three; let it be neither deficient nor overmuch." She looked up at Cylindrus to ensure he understood her instructions to the letter.

"What sort of persons are these to be?" he said, following his mistress a little into the street.

"Myself, Menaechmus, and his Parasite."

"Then these make ten, for the Parasite easily performs the duty of eight persons."

Everyone watching laughed at that, and Castor pointed a finger across the table at Silas, whose parasitic character was the butt of many jokes.

"I've now told you the guests; do you take care of the rest."

"Very well," Cylindrus caught up, trying not to smile at what was occurring in the audience. "It's cooked already; bid them go and take their places."

"Make haste back," Erotium commanded.

"I'll be here directly!" Cylindrus made his way down the street and Erotium turned and went back into her doorway.

"And that's the end of act one!" Felix declared.

Everyone began applauding as Clara came back out of the doorway upon the stage.

"Excellent, Clara!" Felix declared as Rufio stood beside him, still applauding and looking up at her.

Pollux returned to the stage as well and his brother hooted and hollered for him. He bowed playfully, making Clara laugh beside him, her cheeks rosy with the thrill of recent days.

"Well done, Pollux," Felix said, mounting the stage. "But I don't want you to be distracted by the audience. There will always be hecklers, and much laughter with this play. You must stay focussed, stay on task. Keep the story going, and do not break character."

"Yes, Dominus!" Pollux said, nodding very seriously now, as he wanted to do the very best he could.

"Good man!" Felix slapped him on the back and showed him the chairs about the table where he could sit and rest now. He then moved to Clara and spoke only for her. "You see? You're still magnificent."

She smiled. "I'd forgotten, truly," she said, her face beaming.

"You shine as ever," Felix said, leaning in to kiss her cheek. "I'm glad you're here."

Clara then descended from the stage to take a seat and a cup of water.

"You were wonderful," Rufio said to her.

"You think so?" she asked, her smile so brilliant that he did not want to take his eyes off of her.

Rufio nodded. "Yes, Clara…I-"

"Time for act two now!" Felix said loudly, staring down at Rufio. "This is Menaechmus Sosicles and Messenio's first scene! Rufio, Fausto! You're up!"

Young Fausto clapped his hands and jumped up onto the stage with the deftness his youth allowed him.

Rufio was stuck to the spot, however, for he had been dreading this moment for days. He had been learning his lines late into the night, every night, and yet he felt as though when he spoke them, they were as salty pebbles bouncing about on his tongue, more likely to choke him than emerge from his gullet with any semblance of the sonorous speech they were meant to be.

Clara reached up and held his face in her hands. "You'll be great," she said softly.

He nodded as she stepped aside, aware of everyone's eyes upon him expectantly.

"Opening music, Damon!" Felix directed, and the muscled mute twirled a playful tune from his flute that might have been the sound of gulls at the seaside.

Rufio mounted the stage, and went to stand beside Fausto who nodded kindly to him, encouraging him to the task. The two of them, Menaechmus Sosicles and Messenio, began to walk slowly to and fro across the stage, looking around as though they were newly-arrived upon the shores of that foreign land. Rufio could already feel the sweat beneath his arms and tickling his back beneath his tunica. He cleared his throat a couple of times.

"Begin!" Felix said, and the sound of the flute fell away…

There was only silence for a moment as Rufio contemplated the opening words, and then, Menaechmus Sosicles spoke.

"There…there's no greater pleasure to voyagers, in my notion, Messenio, than at the moment when from the sea they espy the land from afar."

"Not so stiffly, Rufio!" Felix commanded. "The word is 'pleasure' not 'torment'. Continue!"

Messenio, beside his master, began. "There is a greater, I'll say it without subterfuge, - if on your arrival you see the land that is your own. But, prithee, why are we now come to Epidamnus? Why, like the sea, are we going round all the islands?"

"Excellent, Fausto! Just so!" Felix encouraged. "Continue!"

"Erm," Rufio cleared his throat. "To seek for my own twin-brother born?" Menaechmus Sosicles answered his servant.

In that moment, some discussion broke out at the table of onlookers and Felix looked from them to the stage and back to them. "Yes! That's it! Keep talking amongst yourselves here. It is as though the very crowds of the streets of Epidamnus are all round Menaechmus Sosicles and Messenio. Carry on, Messenio!"

"Why, what end is there to be of searching for him? This is the sixth year that we've devoted our attention to this business." Messenio turned to look around the vast space of the warehouse that was Epidamnus. "We have already carried round the Istrians, the Hispanians, the Massilians, the Illyrians all the upper Adriatic Sea, and foreign Greece, and all the shores of Italy, wherever the sea reaches them."

"Continue walking!" Felix said as he paced at the bottom of the stage to see them from different angles as the other players continued their converse.

"If you had been searching for a needle," Messenio continued, "I do believe you would, long ere this, have found the needle, if it were visible. Among the living are we seeking a person that's dead; for long ago would we have found him if he had been alive."

Rufio looked down at Felix for a brief moment before Menaechmus Sosicles took over.

"For that reason I am looking for a person to give me that information for certain, who can say…" Rufio shut his eyes as he tried to remember the line. "…who can say that he knows that he really is dead; after that I shall never take any trouble in seeking further. But otherwise I shall never, while I'm alive, desist; I know how dear he is to my heart."

A relaxed feeling came over Rufio then as he found his comfort with the words and the eyes upon him, and as he waited for Fausto to carry on, he nestled into his role more happily than he had thought possible only minutes before.

"You are seeking a knot in a bulrush," Messenio continued. "Why don't we return homeward hence unless we are to write a history?"

Menaechmus Sosicles whirled on the spot to wag a finger at his servant. "Have done with your witty sayings, and be on your guard against a mischief. Don't you be troublesome; this matter shan't be done at your bidding."

Rufio caught Clara's gaze then and the smile upon her face gave him strength and impetus enough for the continuance of his performance as Menaechmus Sosicles and Messenio strolled the streets of Epidamnus, the sound of the gulls above and of the crowd around them.

Even Felix watched in pleasantly surprised silence.

"… For such is this race of people; among the men of Epidamnus there are debauchees and very great drinkers; swindlers besides, and many wheedlers are living in this city; then the women in the harlot line are said nowhere in the world to be more captivating."

Menaechmus Sosicles paused with his back to the side of the stage as though they were at the end of a street, and his eye caught sight of she whom he had always thought captivating.

"The name of Epidamnus," Messenio said, "was given to this city for the very reason, because hardly any person sojourns here without some damnable mishaps."

Menaechmus Sosicles held out his hand impatiently to his servant. "I'll guard against that. Just give me the purse this way!"

Messenio slapped the purse into his master's hand and Menaechmus Sosicles turned to walk away impatiently.

"Rufio!" Felix called out, but it was too late.

Menaechmus Sosicles disappeared from the unfinished scene with a loud crash as Rufio fell headlong down the stairs on that side of the stage to skip and trip and career into the side of a large crate. A dust cloud rose up into the air and a mixture of screams and cries went up as though the citizens of Epidamnus were overcome by an invasion of northern barbarians.

"Rufio!" Clara called, rushing to his side behind the dog who was the first on the scene.

"Futuo! My ribs!" Rufio said from dusty ground. "Get off me!" he said to Peli who was licking his face. He pushed the dog away, only to have it turn on its feet and lift a leg. "Ahh!" Rufio screamed as a stream of sun-yellow urine splashed into his nostrils. He swatted at the canine only to have it jump back and rush off to the outdoors beyond the warehouse.

Clara stopped short of Rufio, trying not to look too disgusted, and Felix emerged slowly at her shoulder, followed by all the other players.

"Very professional!" Silas mocked, ensuring that everyone could hear him. "We'll have them rolling in the aisles with that one!"

Felix pushed Silas with one arm, sending him backward upon his behind as he bent to give Rufio his hand. "Are you hurt?"

Rufio swayed on his feet, given a wide berth by all the others but for Clara and Felix. "I hate that dog," he growled.

"Did you break anything?" Clara asked, marvelling at the distance of his fall from the stage to the crate.

"I don't think so - Ahh!" Rufio shrieked as he gripped his side. "I'm sorry, Felix," he said.

"Don't worry about it," Felix said, putting his arm under Rufio's shoulder.

Electra stood back in disgust at the thought of the urine upon Felix's arms, but the latter did not seem to care, for he supported his friend without fail.

"That's enough for today!" Felix declared. "Get back to your other tasks of building, painting, and sewing. Learn your lines! We'll pick up the scene tomorrow."

Everyone began to disperse, not a little disappointed, for they had been enjoying the performance.

"You were exceptional!" Julius could be heard saying to Fausto. "The best Messenio I've seen in a long time!"

"I hope he's all right!" Beatrice said to Damon as they walked, the mute playing a tune, the sound of which was like to a pebble falling out of the sky. "It *was* a long fall," Beatrice agreed.

"Come," Felix said to Rufio and Clara. "I think we should visit the baths."

Rufio nodded.

"Electra, you come as well," Felix said.

Electra looked disdainfully at Rufio - her permanent opinion of him etched upon her godly features - and went to get her things.

Felix and Clara watched Rufio limp away.

"Did you see?" Clara said to Felix. "He had it!"

"I did see," Felix nodded, his eyes on Rufio's back. "He's still got the skill. He just has to believe it."

AN HOUR LATER, FELIX, ELECTRA, CLARA, AND RUFIO WERE making their slow way through the labyrinthine expanse of the baths of Trajan which were, at that hour of the afternoon, quite busy. At least, Felix, Electra and Clara made a slow progress together after exiting from the respective apodyteria for men and women. They had lingered in the tepidarium for some time, talking of the play in one of the private alcoves as they sweat and allowed the heat to envelop them.

Clara sat discreetly apart from Felix and Electra, but close enough to talk.

It was obvious that Electra would not leave Felix's side during their time there, for she was obviously distrustful of Clara.

She has no idea. Clara thought of the conversation she and Felix needed to have to clear up past transgressions, but it could not happen easily whilst Electra hovered like a tall, sleek Olympian ready to strike without remorse at any mortal who should approach her hero. "Where has Rufio gone to?" Clara asked Felix at one point, for Rufio had been sitting near her when they first sat.

Felix chuckled. "I think our friend is too embarrassed to sit in the open with us. Some things never change."

"He is not overweight. Why does he run?" Electra said.

"He's always been a shy one," Felix added. "But you're right. Rufio may not be built like Ajax, but he certainly is lean. Farming agrees with him."

Clara thought sadly of Rufio then, worried for his injury which he had been hiding since he emerged from the apodyterium without his clothing. "I'm going to go find him," she said.

"I'll join you soon," Felix answered as he ran a strigil along his oiled arms. He watched as Clara's naked form walked away toward the steaming entrance of the caldarium.

"You want her!" Electra growled at Felix.

"Stop it, won't you!" Felix bit back. "This jealous harpy role doesn't suit you at all, woman."

Electra turned her back, her long dark hair swaying down about her shoulders and back as she walked away, a backward glance at Felix.

"Gods, help me," Felix said to himself as he stood and followed.

"Ahh," Rufio cringed as he dabbed a sponge on his bruised ribs where he sat up to his chest in the least crowded pool he could find in the caldarium of the baths. "You idiot!" he chided himself.

Two women who had been talking in whispers about their neighbour's brother's former wife, who had taken her own house slave to lover, kept glancing over at him.

Rufio would have preferred not to have been in the same bath as the two of them, but it had been the least crowded when he arrived, and he had not seen them for all the steam when he had lowered himself into the water.

"There you are, Rufio," Clara said as she approached the bath.

Rufio looked for a second and then away quickly as her naked form emerged from the steamy air to settle into the water beside him.

"Are you all right? I've been worried about you," she said, leaning close to get a better look at his ribs. There, on his side, was a bruise the size of a man's hand. "Are any of the ribs broken?" she asked, reaching out to touch his side.

Rufio pulled back quickly. "Ouch! It hurts!"

"Sorry!" she replied quickly. "Maybe you should see a medicus?"

"No. He'll just tell me to put a poultice on and to make an offering to Aesculapius."

"Probably a good idea," she added as she settled beside him.

Rufio felt distinctly uncomfortable now. Of course, when they had all been young, the three of them had swum in the stream naked and thought nothing of it. Indeed a trip to the baths was not foreign to him either, but in that moment, he was distinctly aware of Clara's presence beside him, her hair that had turned dark in the water, and the swell of her chest just beneath the steaming surface. He sighed, desperately angry with himself, though he could not say why.

"It's good to see you again, Rufio," Clara said suddenly, turning to look at him.

He smiled. "It's…it's great to see you. I did miss you…and Felix," he added quickly.

She nodded. "So many years and yet…"

"What?" he asked.

"These past few days rehearsing the play…it feels like the past seven or so years never happened. I know it's silly, but-"

"It's not silly at all," he said quickly.

"What's not silly?" Felix asked from behind them as he approached and lowered his bulk unabashedly into the water before the two women across from them.

The women stared in awe at him, their silence in stark contrast to the gossipy giggles they had gone through when Rufio had jumped in.

"I was just telling Rufio that I feel like our years apart never really happened. Like we're back where we left off." Clara realized she did not truly believe that, especially with the two of them sitting to either side of her. "In some ways, anyway," she added a little sadly.

"I know what you mean," Felix added. "It's good to be together again, rehearsing, doing what we loved to do before… well." Felix dunked his head beneath the water and emerged again, his beard dripping.

"Where is Electra?" Clara asked.

"Oh, she's off pouting while a slave massages her. She wasn't happy about a eunuch touching her," he laughed. "She's never been one for public baths. Must be the Greek in her."

"You know she's scary, right?" Rufio suddenly said.

Clara stifled a laugh.

"She can be, that's for certain," Felix said. "I finally met my match in her, but she does cause me no end of headaches sometimes."

Clara stared at the surface of the oily water. "Why do you put up with it?"

Felix looked at her strangely then, surprised that she should say such a thing. "Why not? She's magnificent, and was a bargain to boot."

"You own her?" Rufio asked. "She doesn't behave like a slave."

Felix shrugged. "Why would I want her to do that? She's a fantastic concubine, make no mistake, but more importantly, she can act. When I saw her play her namesake in a production of Euripides' play in Alexandria, I knew I had to have her. She bewitches the audience no end!"

"Why did the previous owner sell her?" Rufio asked.

"He couldn't handle her!" Felix laughed heartily, the sound echoing off the walls and water. "He practically begged me to take her! Said she had his company in an uproar since the moment he had bought her."

"That I can imagine," Clara added, feeling a slight pang of jealousy she could not explain.

"Electra is my charm," Felix added, a bemused look on his face. "My life has been blessed since she came into it like a storm. Every production has been a success, and The Etrurian Players are the talk of every polis with a theatre."

"I'm not sure that is going to be the case with this one, Felix," Rufio said, setting the sponge aside to float across the pool. "I hate to break it to you."

Felix waved off Rufio's concern. "So, you had a rough start. It'll all come back to you. You'll see!"

"Will I? You heard how stiffly I recited my lines!"

"You're thinking too much about it. Feel the words like you used to. You've always been a gifted storyteller, Rufio. Use that!"

"He's right, you know," Clara added.

Rufio looked at the two of them, tried to remember a time when he felt confident in doing what they were now setting out to do. However, he found that he could not rekindle that feeling, for the memories were long gone and painful. He hated the feeling of guilt and self-hatred that had clung to him in all those years which, he admitted only to himself, had not flown by, but felt like an eternity. If Felix and Clara had been living in Elysium the last several years, he had been in Tartarus.

"Speaking of the production," Clara said, breaking into Rufio's dark thoughts. "How are you affording all of this, Felix?

I know the company is successful, but everything you've purchased for props, costumes - the decorations for the warehouse itself - it's all of the highest quality. I doubt Emperor Severus' apartments are so luxurious!"

"Don't worry yourselves about that," Felix dismissed. "With the success I've had, investors have been lining up. The aedile who is putting on the games wanted the very best, and we're going to give it to him. You should have seen the reception we received in Ephesus! I'm just reinvesting the gifts that have been showered on us into this production."

Clara observed him closely, how his eyes did not meet hers, but stared across at the two women who had been listening the whole time. She knew he had been bragging for their benefit, but that he was also hiding something. She shook her head, not wishing to pursue it. He had been successful for a reason, and lack of business acumen was probably not part of it.

Rufio looked at the two of them and felt suddenly very sad. "I'm going to the cold plunge now," he said. "I feel faint." He extricated himself quickly and disappeared into the mist.

"Why does he keep doing that?" Felix asked.

"I don't know." Clara went after Rufio and Felix followed, but not before looking back and smiling at the two women they had left behind in the pool.

RUFIO CUT HIS WAY QUICKLY THROUGH THE CROWD OF bathers, trying to find his way to the large pool of the frigidarium, and when he arrived at last on the tiled shore of those icy waters, he leapt. The cold shot through him like a knife, but he endured it, for he knew the swelling in his side might be aided by the chill, as much as it hurt to be there.

He tried to swim to the other side of the pool, feeling the painful stretch in his side, but was relieved to find that he could do the motion without shouting, which meant that nothing was broken. He had been afraid of that, after all, though he would not have admitted it to Clara and Felix. If anything, he was angry with himself for cutting his rehearsal time short with his mishap. Though he would not admit it to anyone, he had been thrilled with the fleeting exhilaration of the stage once more.

He emerged from the water to see Felix and Clara approaching together.

"Would you stop running off?" Felix said as he jumped into the water beside Rufio, followed by Clara.

"I'm just finished here," Rufio said.

"They have some of the best massage slaves here," Felix said. "Don't leave without getting a rub-down. You could use it!"

"Are you kidding?" Rufio said, lifting his left arm to show off his bruise. "If they touch me I'll clear this place out with my screaming."

"It's not that bad," Felix said. "I got worse in a riot in Caesarea when a woman's husband came for me with a cudgel to the ribs."

"Why did he do that?" Clara asked.

Felix shrugged. "He found us engaged in the peristylium of their domus."

"What?" Rufio could not help but laugh, no matter how much it hurt.

"She had seen me perform Ajax the previous night and invited me back to her domus for a night of fun. Told me she was a widow. Seems she lied, for the husband seemed very much alive when he was wielding his cudgel, newly back from a business excursion to Antioch."

"And he beat you?" Rufio asked.

"Of course not. He got in a lucky swing, before I hung him squirming from the bough of his own lemon tree. I kissed his wife goodbye and left them to question each other in the middle of their garden."

Clara shook her head. "Honestly, Felix! With the trail of satisfied wives and angry husbands you leave in your wake, it's amazing there isn't a bounty on your head!"

"There was!" Felix said. "You should have seen what happened in Sabratha-"

"I'm going!" Rufio suddenly burst out, jumping from the pool. "I'm going to get dressed and then get something to eat."

"We'll join you shortly!" Felix called after him.

"Something is not right with Rufio," Clara said, her voice sad as she watched him walk away, his fists clenched.

"You need not be Cicero to decipher that!" Felix added.

Rufio had to admit that it felt good to wash, to be freed of the malodorous combination of nervous sweat and dog urine. But how he hated public baths! The water was never truly clean, the mosaic floors were grimy, and people never kept to themselves. Never mind the frescoes and high, gilded ceilings of some baths. They were all the same to him - turds wrapped in eastern silks!

"Give me the stream back in Etruria any day," he muttered as he sat at a small table in the gardens of the baths of Trajan, sipping at a cup of wine and nibbling on roasted pine nuts and olives.

He closed his eyes and took a deep breath, listening to the shuddering leaves of the olive tree under which he sat, far from the other patrons. "Idiota!" he said, directing the vitriolic feelings at himself and reaching out to touch the trunk of the tree as if to ground himself in something familiar.

His mind whirled in a way it had not for some years, and the dejected feelings that harangued him were most unpleasant, though he did encourage them. For so long, he had missed his friends, and had thought of Clara. He had nurtured his own guilt, especially over Clara, and yet when he was finally with them again, he had fled the scene like an embarrassed guest at a dinner party.

Sitting there alone, it was safe to think again of the dreams he had had for himself and Clara all those years ago, of the two of them on a farm in Etruria, of children… "So stupid!" He shook his head violently, so much so that the other bathers at distant tables wondered if he was not having some sort of episode. "Sorry!" he said to them, adding a wave to his apology so that they returned to their drinks and food.

He heard familiar voices then, as if the Gods had latched onto his feelings of guilt and put him in his place once more, and looked up to see Felix and Clara walking across the gardens toward the missing piece of their triad. Rufio sat straighter and adjusted his tunica.

"There you are!" Felix said aloud so that all the other diners turned to look at him and marvel at his glimmering form.

Rufio sighed, and felt badly that he had done so at such a volume that the light somewhat faded from Clara's eyes when she heard.

She and Felix took their seats at the table with Rufio.

"Why do you keep running away from us?" Felix demanded. "Aren't you happy to be with us again?"

"You know I hate thermae," Rufio said.

"I don't know why," Felix continued as he waved one of the attendants over. "Two more cups and a pitcher of Falernian. More of the food as well," he said, pointing to Rufio's plate. He turned back to Rufio, shaking his head. "You're lean and muscular, Rufio. Most of the men in the baths are fat patricians who have bigger breasts than some of the women." Felix laughed.

Rufio shook his head. "I don't care. I've never liked such places. I prefer my bronze tub, or the stream back home. Do you remember?" He dared to look at Clara then, and there was a hint of a smile at the shared memory.

"Those were good days," she said before taking up the cup the server had just placed in front of her.

"They were," Rufio agreed.

"You two," Felix shook his head. "Every situation presents greatness if we have the courage to seize it!"

"Humph," Rufio snorted. "Maybe for you! You have adoring fans lining up to give you funds. It's not like a farmer has a series of patrons to fund his activities."

"Don't even go there, Rufio!" Felix bit back. "You could have had the same thing!" He slammed his hands on the table. "Right! I think the time has come!"

"Felix, no," Clara said.

But Felix shook his head. "No, Clara! It's time." He turned to face Rufio. "It's time you explained to us why exactly you left us in Rome all those years ago, on the day of our first performance no less!"

Rufio felt the blood pulsing in the side of his head, and the beating of his heart increase to a most uncomfortable pace. He wanted to flee again. However, when he locked eyes with Clara, he could see the hurt there, the longing to know exactly why he had chosen to change the course of all of their lives in such a cruel way.

"Please, Rufio," Felix said, his voice much softer then.

Rufio could see he had very much hurt the two people he had only ever truly cared about, and though they had both gone on to bigger and better things, they still carried the wound of his action. "Fine!" he said suddenly, making sure to calm himself before uttering another world. "I'll tell you." *It's time,* he told himself. *Just tell them the truth.*

Rufio sat up straighter then, and forced himself to look each of them in the eyes. He cleared his throat. "I… On the day of our performance on the steps of the temple of Antoninus and Faustina…do you remember I received a letter from a messenger?"

Felix shook his head. "No. I didn't see any messenger. Did you?" he turned to Clara, who simply shook her head.

"Well, I did," Rufio continued.

"Who was the message from?" Clara asked, leaning in slowly.

"My father," Rufio said, gathering the strength then as he relived the memory, the feeling of absolute deflation where he had been sat upon the temple steps, anticipating the biggest performance of his life, and then seeing it all dashed away.

"What did the message say?" Felix pressed.

"That my mother had died of a broken heart a few days after I left for Rome. He said I had broken her heart and that I needed to return immediately to the farm to bury her and help him run things. He said it was the least I could do after killing her."

"That bastard!" Felix growled.

"Oh, Rufio." Clara reached out to touch his hand. "Why didn't you say anything to us?"

"I don't know. I…I panicked. I had to get back to Etruria right away."

"You know, your father would have said anything to get you to abandon your dream of performing in Rome," Felix said, his fists hardened into hammy balls.

Rufio shook his head.

"Felix is right, Rufio," Clara added. "He always mocked you, and it was terrible of him to use your mother's death in that way. It wasn't your fault, you know that, right?"

Rufio shrugged. "It was done. I can't change any of it."

"I still don't understand why you had to leave without telling us," Felix said. "We're your best friends!" Felix's composure began to crumble such that it became obvious how much Rufio's abandonment had bothered and hurt him over the years. "We had dreamed all of it up together, Rufio. Together!"

"Things would have been very different if you had told us," Clara added, recalling the sharp feeling of devastation she had felt that night after Rufio had gone, how Felix had seemed like all she had left in the world.

Rufio looked down. "I know," he said, before looking back up. "I'm sorry. I truly am."

"Sorry doesn't cut it!" Felix said, unleashing many of the feelings he had forced himself to dismiss so long ago. He shook his head. "You betrayed us!"

"That's a bit harsh!" Rufio bit back.

"Is it?" Felix retorted. "We had made a commitment to each other. We three."

"Yes, well… It was always more your dream than mine," Rufio said. "I never really enjoyed performing the way you do."

"Landica! You know as well as I that is not true. I think you were afraid and you used your mother's death as an excuse to leave us."

"How dare you!" Rufio stood.

Clara was on her feet then, and moved around the table to his side. "He didn't mean it." She turned to Felix.

Felix stood too, his eyes closing slowly, his shoulders uncharacteristically slumped. "I'm sorry," he said. "Of course I didn't mean it. I just…I was so deeply saddened that you left. Clara and I were left there, alone, with an angry audience throwing food at us when we told them the performance was cancelled. It was humiliating."

"I can only say I'm sorry," Rufio added. "But…you may be right too, Felix."

Felix and Clara both looked back at Rufio.

"I was scared too. Sometimes I think I did leave because I was terrified. Before the messenger had found me, I was throwing up in the alleyway behind the temple. I told myself that I needed to help my father with the crops, the cheesemaking, and the animals. My mother had done much of the work… But you are right, my father never cared for me. I let him use my mother's death against me."

"But why didn't you come back to Rome after burying her?" Clara asked, desperate for a reasonable answer. "Or write to us to tell us what had happened?"

Rufio looked into her grey eyes, just a little glassy in the afternoon sunlight. "I was too embarrassed. I thought you both hated me after what I had done."

Felix frowned. "Hate you?"

"Rufio," Clara said, her voice as soft as the summer breeze in Etruria. "We could never hate you."

"I'm so sorry," Rufio said, this time reaching out to take her hand, and then Felix's.

The three of them were silent for a moment then, and it was as if the weight on each of their shoulders was a little less. After a few heartbeats, they released their grip on each other's hands.

"Well, now we know," Felix said, downing the rest of his wine. "This time, at least, you are here, and we will see the performance through, right?" He stared at Rufio who smiled sheepishly and nodded. "Good!" Felix clapped his hands. "Now, I have some errands to run. You two go back to the warehouse and rest. We have a big night ahead of us!"

"What do you mean?" Rufio asked.

"We're going to celebrate with the rest of the company at the Taberna Macedonica tonight. A reunion feast to really set things off!"

"Do you want us to come with you on your errands?" Clara asked.

Felix shook his head. "No. You two go and rest. I'll see you shortly."

"What about Electra?" Clara asked. "Should we find her?"

"She's probably back at the warehouse burning my clothes by now," Felix laughed. "I'll see you soon." Felix then dropped a few coins onto the table and left, leaving Rufio and Clara looking at each other.

"Well, that was sudden," Rufio said.

Clara shrugged. "Let's walk."

IT WAS AS STRANGE AS ANY DREAM RUFIO HAD HAD SINCE HE was last in Rome. He and Clara walked from the baths toward the Colosseum and then turned down the brightly-lit avenue of the via Sacra that led into the Forum Romanum. There was golden light everywhere, and birdsong washed down onto them from the gardened heights of the Palatine Hill above to their left.

The sound of hymns emerged from the tholos of the temple of Vesta on their left and to their right, a constant reminder of past hopes and errors, the steps of the temple of Antoninus and Faustina glittered in the dusk, the columns rising up to the pediment like trees on the slopes of a mountain.

"Where did he come from?" Rufio said suddenly, looking down to see Peli's head emerge from between them as they stood there. "I swear, he's like my own personal Lar following me about Rome!"

Clara smiled sadly and reached down to pet the dog. "Do you want to sit for a little?" she asked Rufio as they both looked from the hound to the temple.

Rufio shook his head. "No. Let's get back to the warehouse."

"Very well," she said, her voice not so melodic as it had been.

Rufio thought it was strange how life could wear down

one's personal instrument. It had done so for all of them. "It's funny," he said suddenly, "how my one act of cowardice led us all on vastly different paths from what we had hoped for ourselves when we were young."

Clara did not answer right away, but walked forward a bit more quickly as they turned onto the ramp that led up onto the Palatine Hill. She ignored the looks from on-duty Praetorians as they took the one public street through the tangle of imperial residences.

Rufio followed quickly, Peli silently at his heels. "Slow down, Clara!" he said, rushing to keep up.

She stopped suddenly and turned on him in the middle of the street. "Is that what you think? That all of it is *your* fault?"

Rufio squinted, as if tightening his eyes would help him achieve some form of understanding, but it was no use. "Why are you angry? I am admitting that it was all my fault. I'm so sorry, Clara!" His voice was pleading and he clasped onto her hands, a supplicant before the only woman he had ever truly cared for.

"Oh, Rufio. How can you ever be happy if you blame yourself for all the ills that befall the people around you?" She released his hands and began to walk more slowly up to the crest of the hill and on down the road with vine-covered walls on either side.

"I'm the one who left you both without a word."

"Yes. You did. But you had your reasons," she said.

"I should have told you what happened," he admitted yet again. "But I should also have seen the performance through."

"Rufio… Your mother had just died. How could you have possibly seen the performance through?"

"I don't know."

"You couldn't have. Yes, we could have helped you through it, but the Gods had a plan for each of us."

"You think so?" he said, a little irreverently.

She looked askance at him and shook her head. "Do you think your act convinced my father to sell me to an older merchant in Syracusae?"

"No. Of course not."

"No. Do you also think that your leaving, or your refusal to see the performance through, made Felix decide to go overseas to form his theatre troupe?"

"Of course not," Rufio admitted.

"Correct. Felix's plan had always been to form a group of players and tour the Middle Sea. And he did that. It was just with a different group of actors besides you and me."

"What is your point, Clara?" Rufio was getting annoyed now.

"Don't you pout at me!" she said, punching him in the arm. "My point is that, yes, Felix and I were saddened by your disappearance, but the only person you *truly* hurt by leaving that day was yourself-"

Clara's voice shuddered to a stop, and she quickly wiped at her cheeks which were hidden from Rufio's view by her hair which had fallen forward.

"Clara?" he said softly.

"I'm fine. It's just…the thought of you alone in Etruria with that horrible man. Your mother was always so kind, especially to me."

"She did love you."

Clara shook her head. "Gods, had I known, I would have come to help you."

"Really?" he asked, unable to hide the surprise in his voice as he took her hand again.

She looked up, her grey eyes now green from the tears which she had been wiping away.

"My father was no worse than yours," Rufio added. "I should have been there for *you!*"

"My father would have set the dogs on you, but yes, we

could have been there for each other. But we weren't, Rufio. We've each lived, and that is now a part of who we are. Yes, I was basically exchanged in a business transaction, but the man who took me in, though legally my husband, became the kind father that I never had. I was fine. I was cared for, while you… you were treated poorly in your own household."

Rufio shrugged. He did not really relish hearing about Clara's husband, except he did take some satisfaction in the fact that she called him more of a father than a husband. "Well," he said. "You needn't worry anymore. Pagano Pater is now Pluto's problem, and if I know my father, he's berating the God of the Underworld as we speak."

"Rufio!" Clara exclaimed. "Such sacrilege?" She could not help but laugh.

Without another word, Rufio turned about and clapped loudly to the sky so that his father could hear, wherever he was.

The Praetorians on guard began to take more of an interest in the two of them then, and so they hurried down the street toward the temple of Apollo and the stairs that led down the other side of the Palatine toward the Forum Boarium.

It felt like a veil had been lifted for both of them as they walked and talked, taking their time, not worrying about what lay around the next corner, even as the sun began to fall away.

Clara felt relieved to hear the old Rufio returning, slowly but surely. He joked, and smiled, and moved less and less like an old man weighed down by responsibility and regret. She knew, however, that she still held back, that she still clung to a part of the veil she herself had been wearing for fear of getting too attached, of being hurt, but also of hurting Rufio again, as she saw it in her mind. It was as if the old welcome and warm feelings she had once had were now warming the threshold of her domus, but she was not quite ready to let them in, despite the fact that she knew they would brighten her world. *Not yet,* she told herself. *I must clear things with Felix first.* She spoke as they settled on the base of the temple of Hercules in the Forum Boarium to watch some acrobats in the square. "I don't think Electra likes us very much."

"You think so?" Rufio laughed. "She certainly makes no effort to conceal her disdain."

"So, it's not just me imagining things?" Clara asked.

"No. But she does seem to have a particular dislike of you," Rufio added. "It's as if she's jealous of you and Felix!"

Clara did not speak at that, but focussed on the tumblers whirling across the square to the cheers of the audience.

"In truth, I don't think many of the players like us," Rufio added when she did not speak.

"Certainly that Silas is not happy we're there," Clara said, standing to leave. "But the others seem content enough with us."

"We just have to perform well so we don't embarrass them."

"True enough," Clara said, turning to face him. "And both Felix and I *know* you can do it, Rufio. You've got it in you!"

Rufio smiled. "Well…I'll certainly try. It beats being kicked by my horse back home!" He looked down at Peli. "Come-on."

THE WHOLE OF THE AFTERNOON, WHILE FELIX, ELECTRA, Rufio, and Clara had been at the baths, the warehouse had been alive with the sounds of rehearsing and building, despite the absence of the company's captain.

Julius had taken to coaching Fausto, and Castor and Pollux were dedicating themselves to their scant lines. Beatrice had continued her work on the costumes, and Damon had focussed his attentions on his flute and finding some new melodies to thrill the audience between scenes.

Meanwhile, apart from the others, Silas had been rehearsing his lines for the parasite, Peniculus. He was determined to show the company that he remained the best among them, even on a level with Felix Modestus. However, every time he began to delve more deeply, Fausto's young, happy voice broke into his thoughts and stoppered the words in Silas' throat.

"I should be playing Messenio, if not the role of Menaechmus Sosicles himself! Not that Etrurian bumpkin!" he growled from his dark corner of the warehouse to the left of the main doorway.

Silas had been nursing his lines and resentment when he spotted Electra returning alone from the baths, her face an image of silent fury that made him smile. He enjoyed her discomfort whenever it emerged, and this was one of those times.

Electra went directly to her veiled chambers without greeting anyone, and a moment later, the sound of smashing pottery could be heard.

Silas set down his scroll and edged his way closer to the chamber until his face was nestled against the hangings, his ears straining to hear anything.

The crashing waves of crockery had ceased, and now he could hear the deep, rapid breathing of a woman scorned, which increased his amusement tenfold, for if he hated anyone in the company, it was Electra. In Silas' mind, the woman had robbed Felix of his manhood, and himself of the latter's attention.

There was a whistling at the warehouse door to Silas' left and he turned to see Felix enter with a couple of packages in his arms.

"What are you doing, Silas?" Felix asked, his bulk blocking out the sunlight from the doorway behind him.

Silas bowed his head. "I was worried, Dominus. I saw Electra return in a most distraught state. There was a lot of breaking of things, and then silence. I worried that she had perhaps injured herself or worse. Did you have a fight?"

"Never you mind, Silas. Go on!" Felix growled. "There is time to fit in more work before we feast this night. I'll take care of this."

"As you wish," Silas said, skulking off into the dark corner where his scroll awaited him, only to return when Felix had disappeared inside the harpy's cave, as he saw it. He took up his position of eavesdropping again and settled down to listen.

WHEN FELIX ENTERED THE CUBICULUM, THE CRUNCH OF pottery under his sandalled feet stopped him in his tracks. Red Samian ware lay scattered about the chamber, and silk hangings wavered in tatters. Electra turned on him when he entered, a small dagger in her hand, the weapon with which she had slain her silky victims.

"What's going on with you?" Felix said as calmly as he could.

"What are those?" Electra said, her eyes dry now as she pointed at the packages. "Gifts for your pets?"

"For my friends, yes."

"And what of me?"

"You seem to have broken or torn the things I have given you," Felix said, casting another eye about the room. He sighed when he saw the broken, five-spouted lamp in the shape of an acanthus flower on the floor. "That was a costly one."

"Everything about this production is costly…too costly!" she accused.

Felix looked at the smaller of the two packages he carried, and set it down gently beside another bundle he had brought. "You know why I have put so much into this."

"Enough about your dream!"

"You are the one who told me to take it seriously!" he bit back.

"That was before *she* showed up!" Electra pointed the dagger at him.

"Who? Clara? She is my oldest friend, as is Rufio!"

"I saw how you looked at her at the baths! Her slim, white body, and her long blonde hair! So fair, so delicate!"

"I look at all women, including you!" Felix's voice had begun to rise and he forced himself to quiet so that the entire warehouse would not hear. "I don't know why you're so jealous. I give you everything."

"As a master throws scraps to a slave!" she said.

Felix waved his hands around the destroyed ornamentation of the room in which she slept with him. "This doesn't look like scraps to me."

"You love Clara, admit it!" Electra stepped forward and Felix slapped the dagger from her hand so that it fell with a clang beneath the hangings, skittering across the floor beyond the confines of their small arena.

"Yes, I love her, as I love Rufio. They. Are. My. Friends." he said, pronouncing every word most carefully.

"You still love her," Electra continued. "Admit it. You have known her since childhood. You shared the same dreams and aspirations. You were both hurt by Rufio when he left you. Admit it! You have lain with her!"

"I have lain with many other women!" Felix bit back. "Sometimes with you there! You never complained before! Why are you complaining now?"

"Because you love her!" Electra's hand swept out and caught Felix on the cheek.

In an instant he was carrying her to the bed and pinning her to the mattress, his eyes full of fury and shock. "Calm yourself!" he said, lowering his voice again. "You are right, in part," he said.

Electra's struggling eased almost immediately, though the distrust in her eyes still blazed.

"Yes, I love Clara, as a sister. Just as I love Rufio as a brother. Yes, we shared a dream, but not a bed. There was one night when we were in Rome last…the day Rufio left us and broke our dream. Clara and I were mutually saddened by his disappearance when he left us and we drank away our sorrows that night. She most of all. She was destroyed by his cruel departure. We may have kissed to comfort each other-"

"I knew it!" Electra stiffened again and spat in his face.

"But that is all!" Felix added, shaking his head to avoid the spittle flying at it. "Would you stop acting like a diseased cat and listen?" He released Electra and sat on the edge of the bed, his voice a bare whisper. "We comforted each other, and it may be that we would have lain together but for the fact that she was so inebriated in her grief, so deep into Bacchus' nectar, that she fell asleep. That was it."

"And you did not take advantage of her? Am I supposed to believe that?"

Felix shot her a dark look and shook his head. "Yes, Electra. I'm not a monster! I merely stood guard over her the whole of that night, praying that Rufio would return. He never did. Clara and I only gave each other emotional comfort before the final splitting of our trio. In the morning, she was obviously ashamed by her drunkenness. She bid me farewell, and returned to her father's home in Etruria. She didn't want me to accompany her or anything. She simply vanished, and I stayed in Rome to carry on with our dream on my own."

"That is all?" Electra finally seemed to believe him, to understand, though there was still an inkling of doubt behind the scrim of her impassioned features.

"I never heard from either of them again."

"You still looked at her differently at the baths today," Electra added as she lay back on the bed.

"What am I going to do with you, woman?" Felix said as he moved on top of her, their words at an end.

OUTSIDE THE CUBICULUM, SILAS BENT DOWN TO PICK UP THE dagger that had skittered to his feet beneath the hanging silks, and tucked it beneath his sleeve for safekeeping.

He could not help but smile to himself at what he had heard.

So, Clara Probita and Felix were lovers? he thought. *No wonder Electra is in such a state, the bitch!*

Silas was more than a little frustrated that he had not been able to hear the end of the conversation as they had lowered their voices too much to hear above the noise from the others in the warehouse. He knew, however, that Felix had no doubt denied any indiscretion with Clara. *Of course he would!* But Silas knew better. *Felix is far too selfish a brute not to have taken advantage of her. He does so of everyone!*

Just then Silas heard the voices of Rufio Pagano and Clara Probita arriving at the door outside, and he made a hasty retreat back into the darkness of the warehouse.

IT WAS NEARLY DARK WHEN CLARA AND RUFIO RETURNED TO the warehouse to join the others. When they arrived, they found the company sitting at the long tables, bent over some of the newly-created costumes which Beatrice had sewn that very day.

"What are you all looking at?" Clara asked, her voice friendly and upbeat once again as she, Rufio, and Peli approached the gathering.

"Beatrice has finished the medicus' costume for Julius!" Fausto said.

"And it looks brilliant!" Julius added, smiling at Beatrice who blushed beneath the praise.

"It does!" Clara agreed as she looked at the long tunica with matching cloak and skull cap. "The colours are brighter and more exaggerated than what a real medicus would wear," Clara noticed.

"That's true," Julius added. "But Felix has asked that all of the costumes be exaggerated so as to be highly visible in the great theatre."

"That makes sense," Rufio added.

"Oh, you agree, do you?" Silas said as he joined the gathering.

Rufio turned to look at the player, and in that moment he thought how perfectly Silas fit the role of the parasite to which he had been assigned. He shook his head and turned back to the others. Before he could say more, Felix's voice echoed over all of them.

"What are you all standing around for?" he bellowed.

"We were just admiring Beatrice's work," Julius said, stepping aside so that Felix could look.

Felix looked at the outfit, reached out, and ran his fingers along the hems and felt the expensive material. He nodded and looked up at the seamstress. "Excellent work, Beatrice! That's exactly what I asked for!"

"Thank you, Dominus!' Beatrice beamed.

"Now," Felix continued, "I want you all to put on your best tunicae and stolae."

"Why?" Castor asked.

"Because we're going to celebrate the start of this wondrous production at the Taberna Macedonica. They have a large table waiting for all of us and the food is cooking as we speak!"

There were scattered, excited exclamations as the company dispersed to dress and prepare for their night out.

As they did so, Felix approached Rufio and Clara with the packages he had brought back.

"Where did you run off to earlier?" Rufio asked Felix.

"The irony of that question is not lost on me, Rufio!" Felix laughed. "I told you I had errands to run. And here they are!" He handed Rufio the larger of the bundles, and Clara the smaller package.

"What are these?" she asked, seeing Electra peering at them from the distant entrance to the cubiculum.

"Open them!"

Rufio undid the strings that bound his package and when he opened it he found a pure white toga, neatly folded. "What's this for?"

"It's the one piece of clothing every citizen should have, but which I did not include in your wardrobe when you first arrived. Do you like it?"

"Well…yes…" Rufio's face twisted up in confusion as he held the extremely long garment up against him. "But I've never worn one. I don't even know how to put this on!"

"Ha, ha!" Felix laughed.

"I can help you, Rufio," Clara said. "I used to help Aeson with his all the time."

"All right," Rufio responded, though he did feel a sting of jealousy at the thought, as though he were a secondary citizen.

Clara then opened her package, and when she was done unwrapping it, she gasped.

From beneath the folds there emerged the brilliant glint of gold from an ornate, jewel-encrusted bracelet. She looked up at Felix with shock in her eyes. "This is too much, Felix!"

"It is for the production. The bracelet plays a role in the play, and for it to be convincing, we want something that will shine out to the audience. I want you to wear it for safekeeping." He took the thick bracelet and fastened it around Clara's wrist. "There! It looks beautiful on you!"

Clara held up her wrist and smiled. "I'll wear it tonight," she said, smiling. Though she loved it, she was relieved that she was only keeping it safe until the production was over. She did not want Felix to assume anything else untoward could happen between them, especially as she had not yet had the opportunity to tell him all she wanted to tell him.

"Now, both of you go and get ready!" Felix clapped his hands and spun on his heels to go back to his cubiculum. "We have much to celebrate!"

As The Etrurian Players made their way through the streets to the Taberna Macedonica, they were all resplendent in their finest clothes. Most sang as they walked, drawing the cheers of passers by, and Damon even played his flute for the procession. It was as if they were on the route of their own personal triumph.

Rufio walked awkwardly, grasping at the hem of his folded toga, worried that it would unravel and fall into the filthy puddles of the streets, but he managed to make it there without allowing that to happen, not without some help from Clara who walked beside him, coaching him on the proper way to move in such a garment.

"This is ridiculous!" Rufio said. "I can barely move in this thing!"

"You're just not used to it," Clara said, trying not to laugh at his discomfort.

Rufio looked down at the dog following them and wagged a finger at it. "Don't even think of pissing on me now!"

Peli eyed Rufio with his mismatched eyes, as if engaged in canine debate as to whether or not he should listen to the mortal man's command, or simply do as he wished. The dog refrained from blessing the new garment, though a sleeping drunk against the column of a small shrine was not so fortunate.

Finally, they arrived at the taberna and Felix entered first with a grand flourish.

"The Etrurian Players have arrived!" he bellowed, and there were cheers from the tavern owner, Philemon, and the patrons who filled the other tables.

"Your tables are ready, Felix Modestus!" Philemon called back from behind the bar and indicated the long row along the right wall. "Wine?"

"Need you ask?" Felix replied as he moved through the crowded taberna, a huge smile on his face. "Kraters of it! And a round for all of your patrons tonight, on me!"

There was another cheer that rose up to nearly crack the ceiling beams, and Felix laughed as he sat down at the head, Electra, Rufio and Clara to either side of him as the others filled the length of the table. Silas sat at the opposite end.

"Why do you pay for wine for everyone?" Electra said in a low, angry voice to Felix. "You are not so rich as that!"

"Hush, woman!" Felix replied. "There is always an audience to please. The emperor has his bread and circuses, and I have my words and wine."

"She's right though, Felix," Rufio said.

Felix turned to Rufio, and chuckled. "What? Now you wear a toga, you're a financial master?"

"Felix!" Clara said, her voice surprised. "We have seen how expensive the production is-"

"Please!" Felix put up his hands. "All of you. Don't fret. Just enjoy. Everything is well in hand. This is supposed to be a celebration of our burgeoning production. Of Plautus' divine shade and his partnership with The Etrurian Players." Felix was suddenly on his feet with his full wine cup held high in the air. "What did he do? Well, what?"

Rufio looked around as the taberna fell silent, all eyes upon Felix.

"I think he's performing," Clara whispered.

"Of course he is," Rufio turned to watch Felix.

"He gave bail. And never did I at any time see any person more clearly detected; three very adverse witnesses against all his misdeeds were there." Felix looked down at Electra, Clara and Rufio and winked. "May all the Gods confound him, he has so spoilt this day for me; and myself as well, who ever this day beheld the Forum with my eyes. I ordered a *dinner*," here he waved to Philemon, who bowed, "to be prepared; my mistress is expecting me, I'm sure; as soon as ever I had the opportunity, I made immediately to leave the Forum. Now, I suppose, she's angry with me…"

The taberna laughed at that, for an angry mistress could provide no end of comedy. Before Felix could continue, patrons were on their feet clapping uproariously as he held his cup to them and drank.

"Philemon, the dinner!"

As if by some instant alchemical process, servants emerged at that very moment from the kitchens carrying platters of roasted meats and fresh breads, boiled vegetables and salads alongside small pitchers of African garum. There were bowls of olives and figs, plates of dormice, milk-fed snails that had been cooked with cloves of garlic that matched the snails in size. There were roasted game birds too, and fish for those who craved it.

"Is it Saturnalia, Dominus?" Pollux asked from midway down the table.

"Only the best for the best players in the world!" Felix said aloud.

"To our captain!" Fausto proclaimed from farther down where he sat between Julius and Silas.

Everyone echoed the sentiment and drank before diving

into the food as the gentle hum of conversation settled over the entire taberna.

From the far end of the table, Silas watched the company eat and drink, and he wondered at Felix's stupidity at so much expense. He, after all, did the company's accounts, and knew from whence much of the money had come. And it was not the aedile who had funded it. He looked jealously at Rufio and Clara who sat where he once sat, to Felix's right hand. He noted the golden bracelet that now adorned the woman's wrist, and the new, white toga which the Etrurian oaf now wore like an imposter, trying desperately not to splatter it with food.

"What is wrong, Silas?" Julius asked. "You don't seem to be enjoying the food."

"I've not much of an appetite," Silas replied, not bothering to look at the older man, but instead staring at Rufio whose gaze constantly went to Clara as she ate from a plate of vegetables. Silas turned to look for one of the servants. "Girl!" he called and waved to Philemon's daughter.

The girl approached slowly, eyeing with distrust the jaundiced patron who sat at the end of the table. "Yes?"

"I want you to bring a platter of cheese to that senator at the end of the table. The one sitting beside Felix Modestus. He is a very important fellow and loves cheese."

The girl looked confused. "I thought Felix Modestus had specified no cheese at the table? That the actors should not have it."

"Oh, it's fine. He's not an actor," Silas laughed. "Have your father give it to the senator with his compliments. It will be good for his business."

"I'll do so right away, sir," the girl said before rushing off.

"What are you playing at, Silas?" Fausto asked, a frown marring his young face.

"Just shut up and eat, Fausto."

A few minutes later, Silas was pleased to see Philemon

come out of the back with a platter of various cheese, some hard, some young and creamy, and present it to Rufio with his compliments.

"For you, Senator," Philemon said, bowing slightly and turning to leave.

Even Electra could not help but laugh at the address he had received.

"You see?" Felix said. "A toga can change your life!"

Clara nudged Rufio into speech, for he seemed dumbfounded at being so addressed.

"Well I won't say no to cheese," Rufio finally spoke as he took a hunk of steaming bread to accompany the mucosal symphony before him.

"I wouldn't eat too much of that if I were you," Felix warned. "I would have returned it but for the look upon Philemon's old face. He seemed very proud to present it to you."

"Ah, don't worry, my friend. I love cheese! I eat it, and I make it!" Rufio said as he stuffed some into his mouth and took a sip of wine thereafter.

"I still can't imagine Rufio, the cheese maker!" Clara said.

"Back home, only the peasants make cheese," Electra said, put off by the sight of Rufio's degustation. She popped a grape into her mouth and looked down at Clara's bracelet. "That is a lovely bracelet, Felix has given you."

Clara turned her wrist over to look at it against the dark green of her stola. "Yes, it is. It will be visible to all in the audience when we perform."

"Yes, it will," Electra sighed. "Everything is for the audience. Just as this feast is."

"Will you stop, woman! You're like a dark cloud sent from Olympus to dampen our spirits," Felix groaned as he tore into a piece of wild boar, more like a hungry huntsman than a well-known player.

Electra smiled, most genuinely at Rufio and Clara who

looked from her to Felix and back. "I'm sorry. I do not like Rome, and it upsets me no end to be here."

"I agree with you there!" Rufio said spreading more cheese on his bread. "It's crowded and it stinks."

"Quite," Electra agreed reaching out to touch Rufio's hand as if she were happy of an ally.

Clara noted the touch, but continued to sip her wine.

"But I must be careful," Electra continued, "for if I complain too much, Felix has told me he will take me to the slave market to be rid of me."

"Felix?" Clara turned. "You wouldn't?"

Felix flushed at that and turned to Electra. "It was only talk."

"Really? You seemed quite serious when you said it. I am, after all, only a slave to you."

"Stop it. You are much more than that, and you know it." Felix set his piece of meat down and turned to her in earnest.

"Am I?" Electra asked.

Clara and Rufio turned to each other, eyebrows raised, their discomfort increasing with each silent second between the two beside them.

"I need the latrina," Rufio said suddenly, swaying to his feet.

"It's out back," Felix said, his eyes still on Electra while Clara was engaged in conversation about the costumes with Beatrice on her other side.

Rufio wove his way to the back of the taberna where Philemon indicated a small corridor lined with aged theatre masks presented to him by previous players. At the end, Rufio went out a back door that led to a curtained area. He entered the dimly-lit latrina and proceeded with his business as best he could, hoisting the lengths of the garment in which he was ensnared.

When he was finished his ordeal, he emerged from behind

the curtain only to be met face-to-face with Silas. "Oh, um, sorry...Silas... It's all yours."

Silas smiled, his face disturbingly demonic in the half-light of the brazier that burned near the doorway back into the taberna. "I just wanted to say how wonderful I think it is - all of us think so - that you and Clara Probita are reunited with Felix. It is a play in and of itself, how it all came to pass."

"Yes, I suppose," Rufio said, a little discomfited by Silas' proximity. But the toga did, he found, lend a certain power to his bearing and he stood straighter before the goggly-eyed Cacus.

"Over the years, he has spoken of you both often, and especially of Clara Probita and his time in Rome with her... after you left, that is."

"Hmm," Rufio said, only half-listening as he tried to find a way around Silas. "Well, yes...I did leave Rome in a hurry last time. A death in the family..."

"How sad," Silas said, clicking his tongue. "Yes, they had quite the time of it after you left."

Rufio's face screwed up at that, but he shook his head. "I'd like to pass, Silas."

"Of course! My apologies." He shifted so that Rufio could get around, but then held his arm. "Are you enjoying the meal? Felix has, as always, spared no expense. He's put this on just for Clara Probita...and for you."

"It's wonderful, yes," Rufio said, looking at the yellow hand gripping his arm. "The cheese is especially good."

Silas released his grip and smiled affably. "I will tell you a secret... Cheese is good for the voice. It makes it smooth and helps actors to project their voices in a most excellent way. Especially as one gets older, this is true. The more cheese the better."

"I'll keep that in mind," Rufio said. "There's still a lot left."

"Trust me. It will be worth it. Tomorrow, I believe we are rehearsing your big scene with Erotium."

"Oh, you're right!" Rufio had forgotten that, and was suddenly nervous. He felt the twinge in his ribs as a reminder in that moment.

"We're all looking forward to watching you," Silas said. He smiled and then went into the latrina while Rufio went back into the taberna. Midway down the hall he stopped, frowning to himself, and stared back toward the back door. *Quite the time of it?* He wondered what Silas had meant by that, but then hurried on back to the taberna interior.

When he arrived, the place was silent and Julius was standing up, all eyes upon him as he recited the part of the chorus from Euripides' *Bacchae* in honour of Philemon.

"Coming from the land of Asia, having left the sacred Tmolus, I dance in honour of Bromius, a sweet labour and a toil easily borne, celebrating the god Bacchus. Who is in the way? Who is in the way? Who is in the halls?"

The onlookers gazed about the room, as if entranced by Julius' bearing, the sincerity of his words, for they too wondered and looked around.

"Let him depart. And let everyone be pure as to his mouth speaking propitious things; for now I will with hymns celebrate Bacchus according to custom... Blessed is he, whoever being favoured, knowing the mysteries of the gods, keeps his life pure, and has his soul initiated into the Bacchic revels, dancing o'er the mountains with holy purifications, and reverencing the mysteries of the mighty mother Cybele, and brandishing the thyrsus, and being crowned with ivy, serves Bacchus! Go, ye Bacchae; go, ye Bacchae..."

Julius held up his wine cup and the place erupted all around him as everyone drained their cups and cheered for the spellbinding words which he had uttered with such skill and grace.

It was then that Castor stood up and placed a wreath of ivy about Julius' head, and The Etrurian Players cheered more loudly than all others for the veteran in their midst. "To Bacchus!" they all yelled.

Rufio smiled and laughed along with them, but that smile faded as Silas passed him to sit down again, his gaze reaching over to where Felix and Clara sat side-by-side, laughing and smiling with the rest of them.

"Quite the time of it?" Rufio said to himself, ignorant of the smile on Silas' face where he sat nearby.

XI

FALSETTOS AND FURY

"And music!" Felix commanded from the side of the stage.

Damon's flute trilled loudly, full of vigour and verve, the notes dancing about the rafters of the warehouse, demanding attention whether one wished to give it or not.

The flute's notes were then accompanied by Beatrice's tambourine, a sound to rattle one's teeth in the head.

"Silas!" Felix called out, and the player's voice rose high and wavering above the music to join in before the final flair. "Fausto, now!"

Just then, Fausto's lithe form burst from stage left in a tumble that bewitched the eyes as he spun in mid-air before landing. The four of them bowed to the audience.

Thunderous applause rose up from the rest of the company, apart from Felix who was thinking how to further mend the disconnection between the instruments and Silas' voice. When everyone calmed down, he stepped forward.

"That was good, but we need to work on the music more. Silas, your goal is not to crush the music, but to raise it up, like a tide lifting the boats in a harbour at once."

"It's hard to do so when Beatrice rattles that tambourine so loudly," Silas said.

Felix nodded. "Just a little lighter on the tambourine, Beatrice, all right?"

"Yes, Dominus," the girl answered, eyeing Silas when he was not looking.

"Fausto," Felix then added. "An excellent tumble. When we are in the theatre of Pompey, however, you will have much more room to work with, so you may need to add a couple more rotations."

Fausto nodded, wiping the sweat from his brow.

"Now," Felix called out. "Now, the fifth act… Let's work on the scene between the wife of Menaechmus and her father."

As Electra and Castor began to take their positions, Rufio breathed a sigh of relief once again. He used to think that Felix's rehearsal was haphazard, that it should have perhaps been in order, the way the play was performed, but that day he was not feeling so well.

The celebrations at the taberna the previous night had gone late, and they had all, including Rufio, drunk far too much of Philemon's wine. But that did not seem to affect the rest of the players who were, no doubt, used to such indulgences before a performance or rehearsal.

Rufio, however, was worse for wear, and Clara had noticed it and mentioned the situation to Felix.

"He'll have to get back up there soon!" Felix said. "His character nearly dominates the play!"

"Just let him practice some more and go later" Clara said.

Felix agreed, but he had waited long enough. He turned to Rufio. "After this scene, you and Clara are on for act two." He looked knowingly at Rufio, turned to the stage, and raised his vinerod, the sort carried by a centurion in the army. "Begin!"

All grew silent as Castor, dressed like an old man and walking with a stick, came onto the stage.

"Good, Castor," Felix said. "A few more paces…not so stiffly as that, and…now."

"According as my age permits, and as there is occasion to do so, I'll push on my steps and make haste to get along. But how far from easy 'tis for me, I'm not mistaken as to that. For my agility forsakes me, and I am beset with age; I carry my body weighed down; my strength has deserted me. How grievous a pack upon one's back is age. For... For...." Castor's face twisted up as he struggled to remember the line.

"For when it comes…" Julius prompted him from the table.

Castor nodded and dropped back into his character. "For when it comes, it brings very many and very grievous particulars, were I now to recount all of which, my speech would be too long."

Felix nodded to himself, pleasantly surprised as he watched Castor move about the stage, utterly transformed, the click clicking of his cane upon the wood an added effect to the illusion.

The rest of the company listened as the aged father spoke about his daughter's summons and whether she had quarrelled with her husband.

Felix stepped forward. "Use the cane, Castor, the way a referee uses his stick in the arena, as if you are preparing to separate the quarrelling husband and wife."

Castor flourished the cane, nearly falling over for the loss of his support as he described the situation for the audience, and everyone laughed at that.

"Excellent!" Felix said.

Castor continued his monologue as he approached the doorway that played the part of his daughter's domus. "And see, I perceive her before the house, and her husband in a pensive mood. 'Tis the same as I suspected. I'll accost her."

Electra emerged from the doorway of her domus, a dishevelled, seething and distrustful wife, completely distraught. "I'll go and meet him. May every happiness attend you, my father."

"Happiness attend you. Do I find you in good spirits? Do

you bid me be fetched in happy mood?" Castor shuddered with apprehension and not a little fear before the woman that was his daughter, and that made Felix smile. "Why are you sorrowful? And why does he," he said, pointing at Felix where he stood before the stage, "in anger stand apart from you? Something I know not what, are you two wrangling about between you."

The daughter made to speak, to unleash a diatribe, but the father held up his hand quickly, nearly falling over again.

"Say, in *few* words, which of the two is in fault: no long speeches, though."

The angry wife walked to the front of the stage to stand beside her father, all eyes upon her, all ears wary of the long speech that would no doubt burst forth from her full, pouting lips. "For my part, I've done nothing wrong; as to that point do I at once make you easy father. But I cannot live or remain here on any account; you must take me away hence imme-diately."

"Why, what's the matter?" the father asked, his voice surprised that she should be so concise.

"I am made a laughing-stock of, father."

"By whom?"

"By him to whom you gave me: my husband." Here, Elec-tra's eyes blazed as she looked directly at Felix.

The father shook his head, thoroughly exasperated. "Look at that - a quarrel now. How often, I wonder, have I told you to be cautious, that neither should be coming to me with your complaints?"

The daughter turned on her father then. "How, my father, can I possibly guard against that?"

"Do you ask me? …unless you don't wish. How often have I told you to be compliant to your husband? Don't be watching what he does, where he goes, or what matter he's about."

"Why, but he's in love with a courtesan here close by."

Upon this last line, Electra stared directly at Felix.

Felix tilted his head and anticipated Castor's next line with a self-satisfied grin.

"He is exceedingly wise," the father said, whispering to the audience. "And for this painstaking of yours, I would even have him love her the more!"

The company burst out laughing, and Felix stood to stop the scene. "I think that's good for now, my dear," he said to Electra as he leaned in close to her. "But you broke character."

"Life and fiction echo each other at times," Electra growled at him. "Go on, let your pets have a go now." She walked away, ignoring the applause the others gave her.

Felix shrugged and turned to Castor. "Excellently done, Castor!"

Pollux cheered his brother on along with the rest as Castor straightened up again and tossed the cane to Fausto who stood at the front.

"That was wonderful!" Clara said across the table to Rufio. "Don't you think?"

Rufio nodded, but said nothing for the hand to his mouth barred any sound. He groaned and coughed and cleared his throat.

"Are you all right, Rufio?" Clara asked, handing him a cup of water.

He cleared his throat more loudly. "Yes…I'm fine… Just clearing my throat."

"Well, I heard you practicing in your cubiculum this morning, so let's see if we still have it in us!"

"Right!" Felix bellowed. "Rufio…Clara! Act two. From when Erotium enters."

"What about mine and Fausto's parts at the beginning of the second act? Shall we not start?" Pollux asked, a disappointed look upon his face.

"You both have it down pat," Felix answered, making the

other two smile. "For now, I want Rufio and Clara to rehearse this part. It's an important scene."

"Come, Rufio. Let's show them how we used to do it!" Clara said, standing and moving down the table toward the stage.

Rufio stood slowly, and wondered how in fact he would be able to get through the scene, or indeed anything that day. He had not revealed so much, but he knew the truth that he had in fact, not been rehearsing in his cubiculum that morning, but rather groaning and shitting in a pot for all the disagreement the previous night's dinner had caused in his stomach like a rude friend one has brought home to dinner with family.

"Make haste, Rufio!" Julius encouraged the younger man. "Your lady awaits!"

Rufio focussed on Clara standing upon the stage at Erotium's door. She looked beautiful, as ever, and he would not have disappointed her in that moment. He cleared his throat again and walked up the stairs onto the stage.

"You all right, Rufio?" Felix asked as he passed him to go and sit at the table below.

"I'm fine," Rufio answered in passing.

Felix sat down beside Silas and across from Fausto and Julius. "Begin when you are ready…with Erotium addressing the servants within."

"That's us!" Pollux said to Beatrice, making her smile as she continued with her sewing.

"Begin!" Felix said.

Clara stepped out of Erotium's domus and turned back to speak to those within. "Leave the door ajar thus; begone. I don't want it shut: prepare, attend, and provide within; what is requisite, let it be done. Lay down couches, burn the perfumes; neatness, that is the charm for the minds of lovers." Erotium then spoke to herself. "But where is he whom the cook said was in front of the house?"

Rufio could hear Clara's lines bringing him closer and closer to the moment he would have to speak, but the sweat upon his brow distracted him no end, but less so than the strangulation of his gut which was battering him full-force now. He cleared his throat again, too loudly, which made Felix frown.

"I'll address him of my own accord," Erotium said, turning to walk toward Menaechmus Sosicles. "My dear life, it seems wonderful to me that you are standing here out of doors, for whom the door is wide open, more so than your own house," she gestured to the other door down the stage. "Everything's ready as you requested and as you desired…" Erotium batted her eyelids at the audience, making Fausto blush and Castor and Pollux hoot. "…you may go and take your place."

There was an awkward moment of silence as Rufio cleared his throat yet again, this time following it up with a choked cough. "To…to whom is this woman addressing herself?" he barely got the words out when a gob of phlegm lodged itself in his gullet like a chunk of underdone fowl's gristle.

"Why, I'm talking to yourself," Erotium retorted with a smile, suspicious that her lover was teasing her.

"Whatever busi…business have I…" Menaechmus Sosicles put his fist to his mouth and coughed hard so that the slimy projectile lay in his hand which he balled around it. "…ever had with you, or have I now?"

"You're not a cripple, Sosicles!" Felix said, standing briefly. "Nor are you sick. You're a young, vibrant man. Act like it. Speak like it!" He sat back down as Rufio nodded his understanding and began to clear his throat again as Erotium spoke.

"Inasmuch as Venus has willed that you singly above all I should exalt; and that not without your deserving it. For, by my faith, you alone make me, by your kindnesses, to be thriving."

More coughing echoed around the stage.

Silas looked up calmly from his perch beside Felix, and he

was unable to hide the satisfied smile that spanned his face. *This is the most enjoyable rehearsal to date!*

Fausto then took his position on the stage behind Rufio, so subtly attending the scene that the latter did not notice him there as he attempted to speak his next lines.

"For sure, this woman is…either…mad…" Menaechmus Sosicles coughed violently then, and this time he felt his gorge rise without mercy. "…or drunk, Messenio, that addresses-"

Menaechmus Sosicles spun on his heel, away from Erotium and vomited directly onto the chest of his servant Messenio.

A high-pitched, horror-struck falsetto burst from Fausto's throat as he received Rufio's offering.

Clara turned away then, unable to look for the feeling that now churned in her gut.

"What in Hades is happening?" Felix shouted. "Rufio?"

"I'm sorry!" Rufio said, bent over now. He looked up at Fausto, his eyes pleading. "I'm so sorry."

The young player's eyes were wide with disgust and disappointment, and it was in that moment that he returned the favour and presented his breakfast back at Rufio so that they both performed in concert.

Silas burst forth with a great laugh, while the other shocked players about the table let out a concerted "E-ooo!" Silas turned in his chair to speak to Felix whose face was going from red to purple. "Did he eat all that cheese that Philemon gave him last night?"

"Yes," Felix answered.

"I told you, Felix. He's an amateur!" Silas added.

Felix grasped Silas by his tunica and lifted him out of his chair. "Shut up, Silas!" Still grasping the slave, Felix turned to the stage. "Fausto, Rufio, get cleaned up right away. Clara? Are you going to be ill?" he asked.

Clara simply put up her hand and shook her head before disappearing inside Erotium's doorway.

Even as Silas hung limply from Felix's grasp, he laughed at the scene he had just witnessed, and the retreating forms of both Fausto and Rufio.

"You think it funny, do you?" Felix snarled. "Then you can clean up the stage!" He pushed Silas up the stairs. "NOW!" Felix turned to the others. "Everyone take a walk while we clean up. Gods!" Felix raged before going from the warehouse like a swift storm over the hills.

Rufio spent the rest of the day within his cubiculum resting and wrestling with his ailing guts and guilt. He knew Felix had tried to warn him about eating too much cheese at the taberna, but he had been so hungry, enjoying his food so much, that he had barrelled on without a thought for the consequences. *That Silas doesn't know what he's talking about!* Rufio thought, remembering the player telling him it was good for the voice.

He felt for poor Fausto, who had received the brunt of his display, but more than anything else, from that morning, he regretted the discomfort he had caused Clara. *She performed so well, and I ruined it!*

There was a knock on the door then.

"What is it?" Rufio called out.

The door opened and Felix stuck his head in. "How are you feeling?"

"Better than poor Fausto, I suspect."

Felix chuckled. "Not so. There was this time in Caesarea when-"

"Please, Felix. My stomach is still not my own!" Rufio put up a hand to spare him the details.

"Of course. Just promise me you won't eat any more cheese until after the performance, all right?"

Rufio nodded, and sighed. "Is Clara…is she very upset?"

Felix smiled. "Not in the least. She's worried for you, but I didn't think you would want her to see you like this right now."

"Please no. I just need to rest."

"Yes, do. But tomorrow, we're back at it, Rufio. You and Clara again. Just be ready."

"I'll be fine by tomorrow."

"Good." Just then, a flash of white and black burst into the cubiculum from beside Felix. "This one's been waiting around, pining for you."

Rufio turned upon his bed and was startled then to see Peli's face upon the edge, staring at him.

The dog barked once and planted his muzzle on the bedside.

"Want me to get rid of him?" Felix asked.

"No. It's fine. You can leave him. He can't piss on me from down there."

Felix laughed. "I wouldn't worry. He just pissed on Silas' satchel. He won't have to go for some time now."

Rufio laughed but then gripped his stomach.

"Anyway, rest," Felix said. "Tomorrow, we'll witness your greatness. Sosicles and Erotium, together again!" Felix backed away and closed the door behind him.

Rufio looked at Peli. "What a day!" he said, reaching out to pet the dog only to have it bite his hand. "Ow!"

THE WHOLE OF THE NIGHT, RUFIO FRETTED OVER HIS constricting gut until the pain abated, only to be replaced by a worry over his next scene with Clara. He never actually stopped thinking about Clara, how lovely she looked, how her voice made him feel again after such a long numbness of emotion in his life. *And I'm messing everything up!* he chided himself.

When morning came, he rose early, washed himself thoroughly in the basin of fresh water in his cubiculum, and dressed in a fresh, floor-length tunica of soft, grey silk which Felix had provided him with as part of the extensive and expensive wardrobe.

Might as well make use of all of this and feel the part of the successful businessman! Rufio thought.

When he went out, the dog at his heels, he found that Clara was the only one sitting at the long table eating only a little fruit and bread.

"How are you feeling?" she asked. "I wanted to check on you last night, but Felix said you just wanted to rest."

"I'm much better now. A little embarrassed, but better."

Clara tried not to laugh, and Rufio could see that she was not at all disgusted anymore.

He simply shook his head.

"Poor Fausto," Clara said before the laughter burst from her lips like spring rain.

Rufio sighed. "I'll do better today, I promise."

"I know," Clara said, reaching across the table to hold his hand. "Just eat sparingly for now."

Later that morning, once everyone had worked at various props and costumes, the company gathered at the table again for rehearsal.

"Right!" Felix declared. "We still have a long way to go on this production, but as we all know, this is a process. We have ups, and we have downs." Felix looked at Rufio. "And some of us have both at once!"

Everyone laughed, even Fausto, despite the small hiccup of disgust that he stoppered in his mouth.

Rufio sighed and stood. "My apologies, everyone! I know

now that cheese is *not* good for once's voice, or gut." Here he looked at Silas, but the player ignored him and went back to writing in his account book. "I'll do better today!" Rufio declared.

"We know you will, Rufio!" Felix added. "Now, we'll pick up with Menaechmus Sosicles, Messenio, and Erotium in act two. Rufio, Fausto, and Clara…you're up!"

The three of them moved onto the newly-scrubbed planks of the stage and took their positions together before the house of Erotium.

Rufio began.

"For sure this woman is either mad or drunk, Messenio, that addresses me, a person whom she knows not in so familiar a way."

The words emerged clearly, and with sufficient projection that Felix relaxed on the spot and sat to watch. *He's back!*

Fausto relaxed visibly too, having worried over another incident, but as soon as he saw that Sosicles was well and present, Messenio stepped forward.

"Didn't I say that these things are in the habit of occurring here?" Messenio warned. "The leaves are falling now; in comparison with this, if we shall be here for three days, the trees will be tumbling upon you!"

The scene played out perfectly well then, with Messenio giving voice to his warnings to his master, and Erotium trying to decipher the problem, convincing the confused Menaechmus Sosicles that he was indeed the one who was invited to a pleasurable time with her.

Felix watched Rufio and Clara perform, their banter together perfectly-timed, their expressions at once hilarious and yet sincere as they performed the parts they had once known back to front as intimately as any pair of lovers. They spoke of the mantle which Menaechmus of Epidamnus had given to Erotium, stolen from his wife, and Rufio expressed

Menaechmus Sosicles' confusion with accuracy and innocence, having decided to enter into Erotium's domus.

"Don't you do it," Messenio warned. "You are undone, if you enter inside her threshold."

Rufio felt the once-familiar thrill of his performance, and he began to revel in it. He did not see the audience of players, nor think on the specifics of the direction which Felix gave here and there, though he aligned with them instinctively. He saw only Erotium before him, heard only the warnings of Messenio beside him.

"…there's some spoil for us here," Menaechmus Sosicles said to his servant as he stepped toward Erotium who stood in her doorway.

"Excellent!" Felix piped up. "Now, here, I want you to insert a kiss!"

Rufio broke character. "What?" He turned to face Felix.

"We want to titillate the crowd a little before the door closes on both of you," Felix said.

"Go on!" Castor shouted. "Kiss her!"

"I'm serious, Rufio. You should kiss now."

"Should I grab her backside too? Or she mine?" Rufio could feel his temper rising.

"No, Rufio," Felix stated flatly. "Just a kiss. A good one."

Rufio swallowed and turned to face Clara who was, to his astonishment, blushing as much as he.

"It's all right, Menaechmus," she said. "Kiss me."

Rufio rubbed his beard, and took a deep breath. He had dreamed of doing just that for so long, but this had not been how he envisioned it. *Carpe diem, Rufio!*

And with that thought of self-encouragement, Rufio stepped forward with verve and pressed his lips to Clara's.

It was a strange and inexplicably exhilarating moment for both of them, one in which they lingered, ignorant of the clapping and hooting from the onlookers.

Rufio felt dizzy, as if he had only just stepped into a dream. He could not believe the profound feeling of joy he felt as his mouth pressed against Clara's soft, warm lips. And what's more, she kissed him back!

It was the most tenderness he had received in ages.

"That's good!" Felix called out, but Rufio did not stop.

Only when Clara began to pull away did his mind come back to the warehouse and the people watching them. He wanted to declare himself to Clara, to tell her all that he felt, and had felt, for so very long. He very nearly got the words out but that she spoke first.

"Uhm…Rufio?"

Rufio opened his eyes to gaze into hers, but when she looked back, it was not with love, nor desire, but rather the shy, head-tilting look of one who is embarrassed.

Clara glanced down, a very slight smile upon her lips, and when Rufio followed her gaze, he became all too aware of the display he was putting on for her and everyone else watching.

"Rufio!" Felix's commanding voice chuckled over the jollity of the rest of the company. "You do know there is no Priapus in the play, right?"

Peels of laughter rang out when Rufio turned, the silk of his long tunica protruding like the pole of a legionary's tent. He looked at Clara, and when he saw the amusement there, he could no longer stand it and rushed from the stage and out of the warehouse with Peli at his heels. The momentary joy he had felt was snuffed out like a lamp in a gale.

Everyone was buckled over with laughter except for Clara who, though briefly amused, felt a sting in her heart for Rufio as he had fled, the players pointing at him as he passed. Even Electra had emerged to chuckle at his humiliation.

"Tell us what you *really* want, Rufio!" Pollux howled after him, even as Damon beside him fell to the floor from off the chair on which he was perched.

"All right, everyone," Felix said after a few moments, rubbing his eyes from his own laughter. "Settle down! We'll let Rufio collect himself, and move on to the beginning of act four and the scene with the wife of Menaechmus and Peniculus. Electra, Silas…you're on!"

OUTSIDE THE WAREHOUSE, CLARA SEARCHED THE STACKS OF crates and masses of amphorae which lay there in the bright, afternoon sun. It was quiet, for the dock workers were at their midday rest, leaving there a silent canyon of commerce with peaks and valleys leading all the way to the edge of the Tiber.

A loud bark drew her eyes and there she saw Rufio silhouetted against the blue sky where he sat hunched upon a tall mound of crates gazing at the flowing river below. The image saddened Clara greatly, for she thought then that the lonely scene before her, of her dearest friend in the world sitting completely alone, was how he had spent his life for the last eight years. She also felt that, though she had lived with someone kind, she too had had an inkling of such loneliness, and it hurt. She knew it.

When she arrived at the base of his mound of wood and iron nails, Clara found Peli with his paws on the first crate, barking up at Rufio.

"Just bugger off!" Rufio shouted without looking.

Clara placed her hand on the dog's head and it calmed immediately. Then, she looked up at Rufio. "May I join you?" she asked.

Rufio turned briefly to look down, and then his eyes went back to the flowing river. The sunlight glinted off the water, sending flecks of light over his face as though he stood over a golden mosaic. "Please," he said, his voice low and deeply sad, "leave me alone."

For a moment, Clara thought of acquiescing to his wish,

but then she remembered how many times she had felt alone in the past, and how good it would have made her feel to know that someone cared enough to sit in silence beside her. She began to climb.

"Clara," Rufio began, "I just want to be alone."

"Yes," she said as she pulled herself up onto the final crate on which he sat. "I understand, and I'll be alone with you, if that's all right?"

"I'm not sure you understand the concept of 'alone'," he answered scowling grumpily.

Clara said nothing more, but settled beside him to gaze out over the river as it wove its way through the city of Rome like a giant serpent of silver and gold. When she dared to grasp Rufio's hand, she was relieved to feel him squeeze back.

After several minutes, he spoke.

"Who am I kidding, Clara? I'm not cut out for this. I'm no actor. I'm a laughing stock. A clown."

Clara brushed back her hair the better to see Rufio as she turned. "Rufio… You can't go back to singing that same song each time you think you slip up. I thought you were going to stop that and just get on with the work?"

"Let's see… I ate a mountain of cheese, and vomited all over poor Fausto. He hates me now, by the way-"

"He doesn't hate you. Don't be silly."

"No. Silly is what happened just now. I…I…" Rufio threw his hands in the air and turned away. "I can't even look at you. I'm so sorry for embarrassing you like that."

"Rufio, please… We…we're old friends, right? Can't we just laugh about it?"

"Oh, there was quite enough laughing without us adding to it, don't you think?"

"Rufio," Clara pleaded. "Don't be so hard on yourself."

"Everything is hard, it seems!" he barked, and Peli did the same from below.

There was a brief moment of stifled laughter as Clara bit down on her lip at this remark.

Rufio turned quickly to look at her, and he could not help but join her so that, together, they burst out laughing from their high perch. The tension dissipated immediately, and Rufio marvelled that she could make him relax so easily when before, he would have clung to such embarrassment for weeks, berating himself no end.

"Well…" Rufio said when he caught his breath. "I think I'll just avoid the silk from now on in favour of heavier garments."

"Yes," Clara laughed. "You do that!"

Rufio held her hand to his mouth and kissed it.

Clara saw his eyes close as he did so, and as the joyous laughter abated, they sat together to look out over the river and Rome once again.

Inside the warehouse, Felix sat at the table watching the rest of the company on the stage, practicing the songs they would sing between acts, of masters and slaves, men and mistresses.

He could not understand it, but it seemed that Rome had robbed them of their usual ease of concert. Castor and Pollux's baritone voices were like crumbling rock, and Beatrice's normally dulcet tones were more feline than avian. Fausto found it hard to keep his time, and Julius seemed to have gotten older overnight. And Silas, well, he had barely made an effort since arriving in Rome.

Damon, with his flute, had been trying to keep them in time and tune, but it seemed of no use.

"Save your breath, Damon!" Felix said to the mute, shaking his head. "Today is not a day for music."

The sound of the flute floated away to nothing, and the rest of the company skittered to a halt.

"I don't know what it is, but you are all singing terribly today!" Felix said, his face in his hands. "Just…just go back to working on the props and costumes. I've had quite enough of rehearsing!"

One by one, the players dispersed to go back to their manual labours, except for Silas who descended from the stage to walk toward Felix.

"I need to speak with you," Silas said as he took a chair beside Felix without waiting for permission.

"I'm really not in the mood for your complaints, Silas," Felix said.

"Well, you'll hear them nonetheless!" Silas bit back. "Felix, this production is going to be an epic failure. It will ruin you and this company for good! You see that, don't you?" Silas poured himself a cup of wine, took a sip, and carried on. "The woman is passable good, but the peasant…" he shook his head, "…he's the worst actor I've ever seen. This is not the time for amateurs! We're professionals, Felix!"

Felix looked up slowly, his eyes hard and angry. "Those are my friends you're speaking of, Silas. And you are my slave. Remember yourself, or I'll make you remember."

"You've changed," Silas accused. "Ever since that dream you say you had, you've shunned me. You listen to nothing I say. You used to let me advise you."

Felix wanted to slap the hurt look off of Silas' face then, for he knew how he actually treated the others in the company. He hated how Silas thought of himself as better than all the others, somehow superior. A part of him wanted to tell Silas that in the dream the Gods had sent him, Silas had not been there. He had been watching from the sidelines, contorted and angry.

"This is the last time I will say this, Silas," Felix stood and looked down on the other man. "You are not better than anyone here. You have your uses, yes, but make no mistake…

If you persist in trying to tear down the others, or comment on people above your station, on my friends, I will have no qualms about dragging you to the slave market tomorrow and being rid of you once and for all. Do you understand?"

"How can you say that, after everything I've done for this company?" Silas stood now, but backed away from the wall of Felix's bulk before him.

"Do you understand?" Felix repeated.

"Yes."

"Yes, what?"

"Yes…Dominus."

"Good. Now I don't want to hear anything more about replacing Rufio or Clara in the play. It will be as the Gods deemed it, and we shall not stray from that script."

Silas said nothing. It was then that, beyond Felix's shoulder, he saw three men walk into the warehouse from outside.

"Do you understand?" Felix asked.

Silas nodded, but it was not in agreement, but rather to indicate the men approaching Felix from behind. "Leno is here," Silas whispered.

"Futuo!" Felix mumbled, taking a breath before turning to meet the intruders. "Leno!" he said, a forced smile spanning his face. "What a pleasant surprise! What are you doing here?"

The man named Leno stepped forward to meet Felix. He did not smile, and his icy blue eyes betrayed no sign of friendship or joy. He was a man of business, and that was all. A deep scar where a dagger had cut him during a street fight ran from the right side of his mouth to his ear, giving him the air of one prone to violence without a thought. He wore a tunica of black and gold, and his fingers were covered in jewelled rings. Behind him, two plainly-dressed thugs in brown tunicae and short cloaks stood, each with a pugio tucked into their cingula.

"I've come to check on my investment, Felix Modestus," Leno said.

Felix looked around. "As you can see, things are well under-way. It's all going very well!"

Leno eyed Silas for a moment, as if searching for some indication of a lie, but the slave only stared at the ground behind his master.

"Let's talk outside, shall we? We don't want to disturb the others while they rehearse, or work on the expensive materials for the production." Felix led the way, and for a moment he thought Leno would not follow.

But he did, and soon they were standing out in the sunshine.

Felix looked down the road to the next warehouse where he saw his neighbour, the sculptor Emrys, leaning against the wall looking up at the sky. Felix waved to him and turned his atten-tion back to Leno and his two men who hovered uncomfort-ably close.

"You need not worry, Leno. This is going to be the greatest production I've ever put on. We've even secured the theatre of Pompey for the performance."

"Yes, I heard," Leno said, the Suburan aggression in his voice unmistakable. "That's a lot of pressure. A lot of expecta-tion. That is why I thought I should check to make sure every-thing is on track."

"Well, as you can see, it is. All is good. The Gods smile on us!" Felix tried to smile, but there was something in Leno's face that caused him worry.

"The Gods do not always smile on you, Felix Modestus," Leno added darkly, running a hand over his oiled black hair. "I've run into some troubles in my other business dealings and need to make up shortcomings in other areas."

"Meaning?" Felix felt nervous, but tried not to show it.

"Meaning, the interest on the loans I gave you is going up. You'll need to pay forty percent rather than twenty-five."

"What?" Felix said, stepping forward. "That's outrageous!"

At that moment, the two men behind Leno put their hands to their daggers.

Felix stopped and spread his arms wide. "You can't do that. We had an agreement!"

"Yes, we did," Leno said. "And yes, I can! I can do anything I wish, Felix Modestus. Remember, you came to me. You made promises, and you have to keep them. I, on the other hand, am altering the deal." Leno smiled. "I have to adapt with the times and the cost of doing business."

"But…but-"

"What? Felix Modestus at a loss for words? That doesn't sound like you," Leno mocked. "You claim to be the best company around the Middle Sea. This is your chance to shine and prove it to the world. If this is as successful as you promised it would be, then we will both be extremely wealthy after this, and you will be the greatest theatre company in the Empire. Not too bad, eh?" Leno reached up and laid his hand on Felix's shoulder, squeezing hard. "And if it doesn't work out you know what will happen, right? I'll take everything, including that pretty Greek concubine you have." Leno sneered. "She'll look good scrubbing me down in my bath at home."

Felix shoved Leno hard so that he fell back into his men, but before he could do anything else, the blades of both men were at Felix's throat, pressing into his flesh just to the point of breaking the skin.

Leno straightened his tunica and the golden chain about his neck and stepped up to face Felix. "Careful, Felix Modestus. If you're dead, I get everything anyway."

Felix looked aside to see the sculptor approaching with a heavy mallet, and waved him off, not wanting him to get involved.

The sculptor paused and watched from a distance as the daggers were slowly pulled back from Felix's throat.

"Don't forget who you're dealing with," Leno hissed into Felix's face before patting him on the chest and turning away. "I'll be watching you!" he said over his back as he and his sneering men walked away, past the sculptor and on toward the Forum Boarium.

"I'm fine, Emrys," Felix called out to the sculptor. "Thank you."

The neighbour waved and went slowly back into his workshop.

For a few minutes, Felix stood there, fists clenched, jaw working. He had been avoiding thinking of Leno, but the reminder of what he stood to lose now terrified him. He took a few deep breaths to calm his racing heart, and when he had composed himself, he turned to go back into the warehouse.

"Felix!" Clara called just then as she and Rufio came walking out of a laneway of crates and amphorae. "Who was that? We heard some raised voices."

"Yeah, is everything all right?" Rufio asked.

Felix smiled. "Oh, everything is grand. Just some admirers come to visit me, that's all. We were reminiscing about old times."

"You sure?" Clara asked, clearly suspicious.

"I'm sure," Felix lied. "Are you both recovered then?" Felix asked, though he seemed fidgety.

"Yes. Look, Felix," Rufio began, "I'm sorry about before...I-"

"Don't worry about it, Rufio. It's fine. We'll pick it up again tomorrow." Without another word, Felix went back into the warehouse, leaving Clara and Rufio staring after him.

"Something's off," Rufio said.

"I think you're right," Clara said. "Let's keep an eye on him."

The two of them followed Felix inside, and did not notice

Silas crouched behind one of the large crates that had been deposited just outside the warehouse door.

When they had passed, Silas peered to either side, and then ran in the direction of the Forum Boarium where he had seen Leno and his men go.

XII

THE INCIDENTS WITH THE DOG

As inevitably happens, whether people like it or not, time passed. More and more days elapsed between Rufio's embarrassment, and Felix's encounter with the Suburan thugs. However, try as they might to forget, the incidents lingered in their respective memories.

The weeks skittered by like dry leaves upon a frozen pond and, against great odds, the production began to shine with each passing day as every player achieved greater and greater comfort with his or her part.

Rufio especially enjoyed the scenes in which he and Clara performed together, in addition to those moments when they sat back to watch the others. When Clara was upon the stage, Rufio marvelled in silence, as though he had found a window to Olympus to which only he was privy.

Likewise, Clara and Felix enjoyed those moments in which they could spy Rufio as they remembered him: calm and filled with an enjoyment of life, displaying a vitality upon the stage which he had lacked in the day to day of life.

It was after a particularly long stretch of gruelling rehearsals that the three friends and their attendant hound found themselves walking through the Forum Romanum. It was a sunny afternoon, and they had enjoyed a visit to the baths of Titus and the markets of Trajan. There was an indescribable freedom in the air that made Rome shine. The marble was whiter, the colours more brilliant, the people more joyous.

As the Ludi Apollinares approached, more and more theatre companies, large and small, began to arrive. It was also whispered that an army of poets, philosophers and other artists had been invited to Rome to take part in intellectual symposia held by Empress Julia Domna who, it was said, could hold her own with the most brilliant among them.

"I just hope I don't get an invitation to one of her gatherings," Felix was saying as the three of them stood leaning against the newly unveiled arch of Septimius Severus. "At least not until after the performance. I don't need the distraction."

"I'm sure you'd be fine in the company of the empress," Rufio commented.

"No doubt," Felix said, "But I prefer to focus now."

"At least we have this!" Clara presented the blue skies and warm, brilliant surroundings in which they found themselves.

"True!" Felix added. "I think even Rufio is enjoying it!" He pushed his friend playfully.

Rufio pushed him back, but lost the last bit of honeyed pastry he had been eating only to see Peli gobble it up at once. For a moment, he was silent, and then burst out laughing. He bent down to rub the dog's neck energetically. "Oh, even you have grown on me! You're a good boy!" He stood again and pointed to where a small mime group was setting up on the steps of the temple of Concord opposite them. "You're right, Felix, I am finding Rome much more delightful. The city seems so different!" he said as he looked around noting the greenery spilling over the edge of the Palatine Hill above the forum, as if the temples and basilicae were crowned with ivy.

"I think you're the one that's changed, Rufio," Clara said softly, touching his arm.

Felix smiled to himself.

Rufio pat her hand and relished her proximity as the sun shone warmly on his face. For the last weeks, he had enjoyed every moment he was able to spend with Clara, and with Felix. It was as if they were back in Etruria again, completely at ease.

The ease of course, was something of an illusion, however, for Felix had been displaying an occasional discomfort whenever someone not of the company arrived at the warehouse. Rufio and Clara had put it down to the visit by the so-called fan some weeks before which had upset Felix for some strange reason. Sadly, every time they tried to broach the subject, he dismissed it out of hand with a chuckle and moved the conversation on. They decided to let it be.

Rufio too struggled with his own worm of doubt which he fought in the wings of his mind. The passing comment made by Silas at the taberna many nights gone by, about Felix and Clara, had lingered in his thoughts. He knew he could not trust Silas, for he had never been friendly, and had grown more sullen and silent as the rehearsals went on. Still, the thought of them having *quite the time of it* hampered his full enjoyment. There were times when he thought of asking Clara, but every time he considered bringing it up, his courage evaporated like drops of water on the cobbles in summer.

For her part, Clara too had held back on the conversation she had long wanted to have with Felix about their time in Rome, and the delay of that conversation had held her back when it came to Rufio who was the last person she wished to hurt. Her guilt kept her awake many a night as she worried that if she were to bring it up, the rekindled friendship between the three of them would be doused for good. And she did not want that. She felt alive again since their reunion, since the re-emergence of their shared childhood dream.

"Let's watch!" Rufio said as a lone man and woman in theatrical masks began to move about the steps of the temple in front of them. They strolled casually, baskets in hand as they perused the produce in a market. From the end of the steps, a child of about eights years shook a sistrum each time the husband presented his wife with a fruit or vegetable.

The small crowd that had gathered to watch laughed each time the wife raged at her poor, downtrodden spouse for his poor choice of produce. As he persisted in his efforts to choose the perfect piece of food to add to their basket, inevitably a fig was too ripe, a bunch of greens too limp, or a basket of plums too expensive. And each time the wife refused his offerings, the husband then turned to the audience and lobbed the piece of food at them to be caught most gladly, some devoured on the spot.

"Look at their faces!" Felix said to Rufio and Clara. "See how happy they are? People don't always want tales of gods and goddesses. Sometimes, the performances that bring the most joy are the ones to which people can relate."

"You're right," Clara agreed.

Felix continued, now watching the faces of the audience members rather than the players. "For some of them, this might be the high-point of their day, perhaps their week?" He leaned back against the marble of the soaring arch and crossed his arms. "It's wonderful!"

Rufio and Clara smiled at that, for there they spotted the true Felix, the one who had always sought to bring joy to others. They both turned back to watch the performance, waiting for the moment when the husband, who grew more and more hunched and downtrodden as he went on, would choose a piece of food to his wife's liking.

Peli barked then, and Rufio looked down at him.

"Quiet, Peli. You'll get something to eat when we get back to the warehouse. Let the people enjoy!"

Clara smiled at the unlikely pair beside her and then looked back to the players.

At last, the husband found a perfectly red pomegranate

which he held up to the sky as if to thank the Gods for it. He presented it proudly to his wife who, at long last, nodded her approval and accepted it. And as she held it in her hand, her arm lowered as she leaned in to present her suffering man with a kiss.

It was this moment of theatrical climax which Peli chose to break from Rufio's side and charge the temple steps to snatch the pomegranate from the wife's grasp. With the ruby orb in his mouth, Peli returned to Rufio's side, plopped himself down, and crushed the fruit in his mouth.

Rufio looked up to see the faces of the audience turned to look at them, but even more disconcerting, the masked faces of joy and sadness of the wife and husband upon the temple steps whose kiss Peli had so rudely interrupted.

"Sorry!" Rufio said, his neck growing shorter as he tried to disappear into the hem of his tunica.

The audience turned to look back to the temple steps where the husband attempted to return to the kiss he had been so enjoying, and they howled when the wife turned her cheek and slapped him across the face for having allowed such a thing to happen. She then stormed off, and the husband followed, downtrodden as ever, pointing at Peli as he quit the stage and returned home.

The audience cheered and clapped then, some even throwing coin onto the temple steps which the actors' child quickly scooped up on her parents' behalf.

"Brilliant!" Felix called out. "It's the only way it could have ended!" He turned to pet Peli whose mouth was stained red with pomegranate juice. "There may be a life in theatre for you too. Good boy!"

"Beatrice, you've made my stola too loose!" Electra was saying as she tried on the latest costume for Menaechmus of

Epidamnus' wife. "I want my breasts to be pushed up, not flattened!"

"But Dominus said that the wife's costume should be less revealing than Erotium's!" Beatrice was obviously flustered under Electra's dark gaze, however used she might have been to the taller woman's strong opinions when it came to her wardrobe. "I only did what was asked of me."

"Well, I'm telling you I would like it tightened up," Electra said, her voice angrier than ever, though she knew it was not meant for the young seamstress. She sighed. "Please, just do it. I'll speak with Felix about it."

"All right, but if he gets angry-"

"He won't," Electra said as she removed the yellow stola and tossed it to Beatrice before sliding her own over her head and going out of the cubiculum. "Felix!"

"Shh, woman!" Felix hissed from the stage where he and Clara were rehearsing a scene from act four between Menaechmus of Epidamnus and Erotium.

Electra stopped suddenly and went to sit down between Rufio and Julius who were watching with the rest of the company.

Beatrice joined her, the costume in hand, and began to rip at the stitching as the rehearsal went on.

"Who's enquiring for me here?" Erotium said as she looked out of her door.

"One that's more of an enemy to his own self than to yourself," Menaechmus of Epidamnus said, a look of perfect exasperation upon his bearded face.

"My dear Menaechmus?" Erotium held her hands out, her smile at once brilliant and understanding. "Why are you standing before the house? Do follow me in-doors."

"Stop. Do you know why it is that I'm come to you?"

Erotium smiled and winked, reached out to touch his shoulder. "I know well; that you may amuse yourself with me."

Rufio watched Felix and Clara work together and thought that their performance was indeed flawless. It was as if no time had passed at all, that they were even better than they had been all those years ago. It made him feel inadequate, though he tried to suppress the feeling, for it did him no good. However, he could not ignore or dampen the feelings of jealousy that he was experiencing in that moment, seeing Erotium's hand upon Menaechmus' shoulder, the tilt of her head atop her long, soft neck, and the soothing timbre of her voice.

The decision not to sing the play had been a bold one, risky, but Rufio knew that it would draw the audience in more to be able to focus upon the humour of the actual words spoken, of the mantle given to the Menaechmus that was not Menaechmus, the very mantle which lay upon the table in front of Rufio.

The back and forth between Erotium and Menaechmus drew the other players to the long table, away from their various labours, in order that they should better hear, better witness the contempt in which Erotium increasingly held her lover when he asked for the return of the mantle which he had gifted her.

Everyone clapped as the door was slammed in the exasperated face of Menaechmus, laughing as he stood in the middle of the street without a friendly refuge, locked out by both his wife and his lover.

Rufio stood and clapped when Clara returned to the stage, and the look upon her face - a look of purest joy - made his heart flutter. He clapped for her loudly and her eyes sparkled like two sunlit jewels in the light of the brazier before the stage.

"That was excellent!" Julius said, also upon his feet.

The players crowded around Clara as she descended from the stage to sit at the table and have a drink.

"Very good, Clara!" Felix said. "Are you sure you haven't been practicing all these years? It's like you never stopped!"

Elextra shot Felix a dark look, her jawline shifting back and forth. But she remained silent as Felix came to speak to her and Rufio.

"Tomorrow, we will begin with the fifth act and the scene between Menaechmus Sosicles and the jealous wife, yes? I can't wait to see how you work your way to the climax of the play. Remember, Electra, you will be ready for a fight with your false husband who is not your husband."

"Oh, do not fear, I *will* be," Electra said steadily, and the look in her eyes was not a little terrifying to Rufio.

"And you, Rufio," Felix said, sitting down beside him with Clara across. "You have been so good. Almost as good as you were before. You just need to let go, let the words emerge more naturally from your mouth. You know this play back to front."

"I used to," Rufio said, distracted by Clara's lips upon her cup. "I don't know, Felix... I...I feel like it's all a little forced for me."

Felix was quiet for a moment, the smile definitely evicted from his face. He shook his head. "What do you want, Rufio? Do you want to quit again?"

"No!" Rufio looked at Clara in that instant. "No, of course not!"

"Because if you do," Felix continued, "I would rather know now than on the day of the performance."

"That's not fair, Felix," Clara said.

He looked at her, but did not speak.

"I think you forget that I haven't done this for ages!" Rufio bit back at Felix. "While you've been travelling the Middle Sea, lauded in every city, I've been shovelling shit and trying to scrounge a living."

"Yes, and now you have a chance to leave all that behind, if you would just commit fully, Rufio! The Gods have given you this chance. Take it!"

"I don't want to leave my life in Etruria! As sad as it sounds, I like it!"

"You're a terrible liar," Felix said, more mockingly than anything, but Rufio's face was changing colour quickly.

Rufio was about to unleash on Felix, to tell him that he was the one who asked for Rufio and Clara's help, not the other way around, when a loud slurping sound echoed about them.

"What is that sound?" Electra said, her nose turned up. "Where is Damon? Is he tasting the paints again?"

"It's not Damon," Fausto said. "I saw him go outside just as the scene ended."

"Perhaps it's the shade of some worker who died in here?" Beatrice suggested, putting down her needle and thread very slowly.

"Nonsense," Silas answered. "Shades don't haunt the living during the day."

"Shut up for a moment!" Felix said. "That's no shade."

Everyone about the table looked around as the sound got more and more urgent, the pace quickening.

At that moment, Pollux burst out laughing. "It's Rufio's dog!"

"What?" Rufio said.

And as the slurping reached a crescendo, everyone peered beneath the table to see Peli gulping at the engorged version of himself most excitedly before he let loose.

The release struck Rufio's bare legs square on and the latter had no time to dodge the slimy bolt, pushing back from the table clumsily before landing upon his back. "Ahh!" he cried out in disgust.

Everyone stood back quickly from the table to look down with twisted features upon Rufio and then Peli who wagged both his tails about most joyously while attempting to lick his adopted master's face.

Rufio tried in vain to fight off the overzealous cur.

Felix approached carefully and looked down on Rufio as he lay upon his back. "At least *he* knows what he wants!" he said, pointing at Peli before walking away.

Everyone roared with laughter, except for Clara and Electra who had retreated a safe distance from the curious pair upon the floor.

"That dog is always trying to upstage the actors," Julius observed, and the comment aroused further jollity among the group, even Felix who could not remain angry any longer.

"I take it back!" Rufio said as he pushed the dog away. "You're very bad!"

Peli's ears went back, his toothy smile now a frown to match Rufio's. As if to display his disappointment, the dog turned again, urinated upon the prostrate man, and ran for the outdoors before Rufio could lay hold of him.

"Hahaha…" Felix laughed, now feeling sorry for his friend. "Rufio, get yourself to the baths, for tonight, The Etrurian Players are throwing a bacchanal!"

Everyone but Rufio cheered at that.

"You were very good today," Rufio said to Clara as they walked past the western end of the Circus Maximus toward the Forum Boarium. "I couldn't take my eyes off of you."

Clara smiled as she walked, looking down at their partnered foot falls upon the cobblestones. "It feels good to be back on the stage, even one tucked inside a warehouse."

Rufio looked sideways at her, unable to voice how he felt in that instant. He was glad she had accompanied him to the baths that afternoon, for he had expected to go alone and angry, a brooding version of himself, abused by his dog and mocked by his fellow players. But Clara's presence, and the clean waters of the baths of Titus, had washed all of that away.

As the sun dipped red behind the high arches of the circus, Rufio sighed.

"What is it?" Clara asked.

"I don't know… A part of me misses Etruria, the country-side. I miss fresh air and trees. I miss my animals."

Clara chuckled at that.

"Laugh if you must, but most of them are loyal. They don't piss on me at every chance they get. Not like this one." Rufio nodded his head behind them to where Peli had fallen into step as their rearguard. Rufio craned his neck to look at the confused canine. "You're worse than my horse, you are!"

Clara laughed again, but that subsided as she laced her arm through Rufio's. "What's it like back home? Have things changed much? It's been so long since I was there."

"It hasn't changed much at all. The senator on the other side of the hill has quite a large operation now, but I have no dealings with him. None that are pleasant anyway. The family stopped coming some time ago, and he shows up once-in-a-while by himself. Occasionally, the forman of the latifundium and his wife visit me with a gift of their olives or oil, or some vegetables, when their dominus is not there. They're a nice couple, but I don't know how they can stand working for their master."

"I remember my father speaking highly of the previous owner, the senator's father," Clara said, wishing her own father had not popped into her head.

"Yes, he was. He protected his neighbours. Some people called him 'the Dragon', but his son fell very far from the tree. Anyway, I mostly just mind my own business and try to grow enough food to eat. It's not easy, I won't lie."

"And yet, you love it?" Clara asked.

"Well...yes," Rufio answered. "I may not be a good farmer, but I am a part of that place. When I'm away from it, I feel something missing."

"Do you regret coming here?" Clara stopped and turned to him.

The dying light only just caught her green eyes for a second, but in that moment, Rufio knew he would not have wanted to be anywhere else. "How can I? We're together again," he said, his voice low. "We three..."

"Yes," she said. "We three." They continued to walk toward the warehouses which lay ahead of them. Even before they reached the first stack of dockside crates, the faint notes of music reached their ears, and then laughter which became louder and louder the closer they got. "I don't know what Felix has planned, but it sounds like there are more people than our company there."

"Oh, Gods..." Rufio muttered. "I don't know if I'm ready for this."

Together they walked toward the brilliant glow of the open warehouse doors, the music and laughter louder with every step. They stopped abruptly as a flash of glistening skin rushed past them, followed by another, both of them laughing and crowned with ivy.

"Was that..." Rufio's voice died away.

"Yes," Clara confirmed. "A nymph and a satyr."

"Looks like Felix wasn't kidding," Rufio sighed.

Peli barked then and ran off in pursuit of the naked duo that had just rushed into the warehouse.

"Of course he would be up to this," Rufio said, pointing after the dog.

"Come on," Clara said. "Let's get some wine, and see what's going on?" She took Rufio's hand and pulled him inside the gaping maw of the warehouse.

. . .

THE WAREHOUSE WAS UTTERLY TRANSFORMED. NO LONGER WAS it the working storage and stage of a company hard at its labour to put on a production - all props, raw materials, paints, and tools had been hidden away to be replaced with vine-clad carts groaning with amphorae of wine, and gatherings of couches and low tables where faces unknown to Rufio and Clara laughed and drank and caroused as if it were Saturnalia.

The long trestle table that had been their work and eating space before was now laden with platters of meat and fowl, fruit, fish and salads. Pitchers of garum rose up from the surface like beacons among the dishes, people coming and going to help themselves.

To the side of the stage, a group of musicians honoured Apollo and the Muses with tambourines, sistra, reed pipes, drums, a curved cornu and even a lyre. Among them was sat Damon, his face red and sweaty as he played his flute along with the others. He waved with one hand when he saw Rufio and Clara approach.

Clara poured a cup of wine for herself and one for Rufio, which she handed to him. "Where is Felix?" she asked.

Rufio's eyes scanned the warehouse, down the length of the cornucopic table to the stage. "There he is!"

As a group of players from some other company descended the stage, it revealed both him and Electra together upon a couch, he like Marcus Antonius, and she like Cleopatra, draped over him, observing the goings on as if they were returned to Alexandria once more. Beside them, upon another couch, reclined a bright-eyed, red-haired man with whom Felix spoke most intently.

"Rufio!" Fausto called from nearby where he was engaged with a young woman.

Rufio waved, embarrassed, and turned back to Clara. "I

don't think I can do this tonight," he said.

"Oh, yes you can!" she replied. "You're not leaving me alone in all of this." She smiled. "Come. Let's drink and have some fun. It might be the last time before the performance!"

"There they are!" Felix bellowed from atop the stage, sitting up and adjusting his ivy crown. "Rufio! Clara! Come here! I want you to meet someone!"

Clara pulled Rufio in the direction of the stage and up the stairs.

"My friends, this is Longus."

The man smiled, his red curls dancing about his smiling face. "I am happy to meet you both. Felix has told me about you."

"He has?" Rufio said.

"Longus is a gifted novelist. His latest book, *Daphnis and Chloe*, has caught the attention of the empress and her entourage. Everybody's talking about it!" Felix said.

"I know!" Clara added suddenly. "I've read it!"

"You have?" Longus sat up, smiling even more.

"Yes," Clara said, sitting on the couch beside the poet. "When it was night, they all lead the bride and bridegroom to their chamber, some playing upon whistles and hautboys, some upon oblique pipes, some holding torches. And when they came near to the door, they fell to sing, and sang, with the grating harsh voices of rustics, nothing like Hymenaeus, but as if they had been singing at their labour with mattock and hoe. But Daphnis and Chloe lying together began to clip and kiss, sleeping no more than the birds of the night. And Daphnis now profited by Lycaenium's lesson; and Chloe then first knew that those things that were done in the wood were only the sweet sports of children."

Longus jumped to his feet and clapped at that. "You *have* read it!"

Clara beamed. "Such an ending!"

The poet took Clara's hand and kissed it. "I thank you, lady." He turned to Felix. "You weren't joking, my friend. She does have a voice!" Longus turned back to Clara. "Felix has told me of your talents. I can't wait to see you play Erotium!"

Rufio noted that Longus still held Clara's hand, and cleared his throat.

Longus released Clara and turned to Rufio. "And you must be the third member of the original Etrurian triad?"

"Yes, I am," Rufio answered with unusual confidence. "Where do you and Felix know each other from?" Rufio could see Electra observing him and Clara closely.

"Longus and I met at a banquet when we were performing in Mytilene. He had just started his work then, and now it is finished and has found titanic success!" He raised his cup to the poet.

"Not titanic," Longus said, "but enough to make a name for myself. I have to admit, though it is an honour to attend the empress' intellectual circle, I get far more enjoyment out of smaller gatherings." He sat himself down again upon the couch beside Clara. "Why just this past Veneralia, I was invited to the home of my good friend Alene Metella, where they asked me to recite the story to them. Good food, good wine, and excellent company. It was an evening I shall never forget. Your neighbour," he turned to Felix, "the sculptor, he was there as well." He sighed. "Perhaps the best part of that night, however, was seeing the budding love between the young man and woman who were also there. The Gods could not have picked a finer couple!"

"A subject you know well!" Felix added.

"Quite. I do have a knack for spotting deep love, even before it blooms." Longus looked at Clara, and then quickly at Rufio. He smiled. "But come, this is a joyous night of revelry. You don't need to attend on me alone!"

"Nonsense!" Felix said.

"Where is Julius?" Longus added. "I wanted to commend him on the last time I saw him perform. His Priam was heart-wrenching!"

"I'm sure he would love to hear from you," Felix added, looking around.

"Julius is engaged with a young lupa on the other side of the wine cart," Electra said, smiling to herself.

"In that case, I shall wait," Longus said. "He is older and may require a bit more time to properly entertain the she-wolf."

Electra laughed, her hand to her mouth.

Rufio noticed how very beautiful she was when she smiled. He turned to look around the warehouse from the high vantage offered by the stage. He spotted Castor and Pollux with a group of four women, unable to discern where one person started and another began for all the flashing skin he spotted in the firelight. *At least they're not near the food,* he thought. At the long table, a young man plied Beatrice with questions that made her blush. Beyond her, to the right of the table, Silas seemed to be engaged in heated discussion with a group of men who also appeared to be players. "Who is Silas speaking with?" Rufio asked Felix.

Felix looked over. "Ah. Yes. He is speaking with Titus Gallicus, the master of one of our rival groups, The Messenian Masters." Felix indicated the tall, lanky, dark-haired man with whom Silas was speaking or, rather, arguing.

Even from a distance, the man's cold eyes made Rufio shiver, for he looked more like a back-street poisoner than a player.

"I wouldn't pay to see that man act in any part," Longus said. "He's far too ugly."

Clara and Electra laughed at that.

Rufio rolled his eyes.

"I saw The Messenian Masters perform in Syracusae

once," Clara said. "They weren't very good, I have to say."

Felix chuckled. "No! They're not! But they think they are. He'll be so mad when he finds out we're performing in the theatre of Pompey."

"You are?" Longus asked, his eyes wide.

"Yes."

"Well, I will definitely be there, my friend," Longus added.

Felix watched as the discussion between Gallicus and Silas appeared to become more heated. "I'd better go and diffuse things," he said, rising with a grunt from his place of comfort beside Electra. "Rufio, you sit with Electra. Mind no one comes to accost her."

Rufio looked at Electra and shivered. She really did not seem to be in need of protection. "I think I'll get some food first," he said to her.

Electra stared evenly at him. "Yes. You do that," she said as Rufio descended the stage. "Don't eat any cheese!"

Rufio looked back. "Yes, *mother*." He shook his head, unwilling to admit he was grateful for the reminder.

Electra turned to Longus. "He ate a whole platter of it the day before a rehearsal."

"He didn't!" Longus' golden eyes popped wide.

"It was messy," she added.

"Is he new to acting?" Longus asked. "Even poets know one does not eat cheese before a performance."

"Quite the amateur," Electra added.

"Come now, Electra!" Clara said. "He made one mistake. And he is no amateur!"

"We'll see, Clara Probita." Electra's voice was dark and at odds with the frivolity circulating all about them.

Longus felt the awkwardness of the situation acutely in that moment.

"Tell me of Mytilene," Clara said. "I've never been before. Is it quite beautiful?"

"It is exactly as I describe it in the book," he said.

FROM THE TABLE, RUFIO COULD SEE LONGUS AND CLARA engaged in discussion, a sight which, he had to admit, upset him, but no more than Electra's heated gaze as his hand hovered over the platter of cheese. "Look, cheese!" he called out to Electra, and a second later, he had a chunk in his fingers which he held aloft and pressed into his mouth for her benefit.

Electra shook her head and seemed quite agitated, for the next day he would have to rehearse a scene with her.

When Rufio saw that she was sufficiently annoyed, he turned his back to her and spat it out onto the floor.

Peli, who had been dogging his heals since he came off of the stage, quickly snatched up the evidence.

Rufio sat alone upon one of the stools nearby, like a boy at a new school, to eat the meat and bread he had served himself. He looked over to where Felix was nearly nose to nose with Titus Gallicus. From the waving of their arms, the conversation seemed to be getting more heated with every second, at least on Gallicus' part. Felix seemed to be comfortably confident, even as Silas shouted insults from behind his shoulder at the other player and his troupe who were gathering around him.

"Ooo, I like your dog!" a voice said from very close, followed by a loud hiccup. "May I pet it?"

Rufio looked to see a short, extremely buxom woman in a too tight stola standing before him. She smiled, her dilated eyes looking hungrily from the dog to him.

"Are you a player?" she asked Rufio, swaying upon her feet.

"No," he answered. "Not really. Are you a lupa?"

She howled like a wolf and burst out laughing. "Yes, darling!" she reached out to touch his cheek with a clammy hand. "And I'm in need of a mate!" She winked. "I saw you here, all alone, and I wondered why so handsome a lad is not yet engaged."

Rufio looked to the stage where Clara was coming down in order to get some food for herself. He looked pleadingly at her, but found his chin grasped in the lupa's hand.

"Don't worry, boy," the lupa said. "I may be small, but I can handle big things."

"Nice," he said with not a little sarcasm, noting that she was anything but small. *Boy?* She seemed blind as well as deaf, and how she had managed to squeeze into her clothes was beyond him, for her rebellious breasts kept escaping the confines of her insufficient stola.

She looked down at her heaving, wine-spattered chest. "They are, aren't they?"

Rufio saw that as Clara was about to approach, the player, Titus Gallicus, who was no longer engaged in conversation with Felix, was now speaking to her at the long table.

"I hear you are playing Erotium in Felix's production," Gallicus said to her.

Clara tore her eyes from Rufio to speak to the man. "Yes, I am," she said.

"Are you sure you're up to it?" Gallicus laughed. "I mean, the theatre of Pompey? During the Ludi Apollinares? I think Felix has finally overstepped his skills to hire such as you."

In that moment, Rufio jumped up, tore himself from the lupa's grasp, and went to Clara's side. "What's all this about then?"

"Ah," Gallicus said, looking down. "And here is the other one. I hear you are a complete amateur." He looked around to see where the rest of his own players were. "Silas told me that-"

"What?" Rufio said. "What did Silas tell you?"

"Leave it, Rufio," Clara said.

"Yes, leave Rufio…" Gallicus said, looking back at Clara.

"Leave so that Clara and I may engage in some rehearsals of our own."

The music in the warehouse was getting louder as Damon and his musical companions began to parade around the place as they played. A convoy of laughing nymphs and satyrs trailed after them in various stages of undress, wine splashing, voices raised.

Gallicus reached out to touch Clara's hair, and Rufio pushed him hard.

Rufio heard Peli growl, and looked to see the lupa bent over him, trying to ply kisses upon the dog. Peli did not seem happy. "I wouldn't do that if I were you," he warned the drunken lupa.

"Oh, he just wants to play, doesn't he?" she said.

Suddenly, Gallicus came back and pushed Rufio into Clara so that the two of them fell against the table.

It was at that moment that the lupa screamed as Peli latched onto her errant breasts.

"I told you!" Rufio cried out. "Peli, no!"

"You set your dog on a helpless lupa?" Gallicus accused, his men now gathering behind him.

Rufio shook his head. "No. It's her fault. But I will set him on you, you shit!" Rufio turned to Peli. "Attack!"

The dog wove his way around the screaming lupa, lifted his leg and pissed on Rufio.

Rufio looked up at Gallicus, just as the latter's fist connected with his face.

Rufio spun and fell at Clara's feet, and then she, with such force, swung a water pitcher at the attacker's head, only to have him duck. The jug connected with the lupa who was, at that moment, running in to kick Rufio.

It was then that chaos broke ranks and the world of the warehouse exploded with violence and confusion accompanied by frenetic music.

Amongst flailing feet, Rufio scrambled onto his own, ducking, swinging every which way as he searched for Clara in the fray. He could hear Felix's battle cry above everything as he rallied The Etrurian Players for the fight, and then he caught glimpses of the naked forms of Castor and Pollux, like Olympic competitors, wading into the melee.

Fausto emerged with his own naked companion, howling like a young wolf as he and his lupa, grabbed whatever they could find to come to the others' aid.

Rufio then spotted Julius standing quite confused on the sideline, shouting something to Felix, a sort of director in the wings crying out for the company to rally in the chaotic scene. Rufio kicked at one of Gallicus' men, sending him backward into a naked trio so that all of them tumbled into the wine cart, sending an amphora to the ground in a tidal wave of wine that washed under the table.

Rufio then turned to join the battle line which he could see Felix had formed, on the other side of the seething crowd of confused Bacchae running to and fro.

"Get them!" Gallicus roared behind Rufio.

Rufio made to join his fellows when the lupa jumped in front of him, her face raging, her teeth bared as she tore open her stola to reveal her bitten breasts. "Look what your dog did to me!" she shouted.

"I'm sorry!" Rufio said. "He's a bad dog!"

Without another word, the lupa kneed Rufio in the figs so that he crumpled to his knees, and she followed it up with a hammy fist grasping a wine jug from the table.

Rufio swayed there, his vision failing. The last thing he spotted was Felix rushing in like Hercules wielding a club, and Clara and Electra to either side, waving wooden prop swords, like Hippolyta and Penthesilea, to finish the battle.

Then, darkness, and the taste of wine as he splashed down, unconscious beneath the table.

ACT IV

LOVE AND THE GAMES

XIII

A BURIED LOVE

"How is he?" Clara asked. "Will he survive?" Her voice was laced with concern, so tremulous that Felix put his arm around her.

"Tell us, Medicus," Felix said in a voice so low one could still hear the flickering of the flames in the brazier near the bed.

The medicus, an older man with black, curly hair that matched his wizened beard, hoisted his long tunica and put his ear to the patient's mouth. He listened intently, his hand also on the wrist. After a few moments, the medicus stood and looked at Felix and Clara. "He has received quite a trauma to the head. The cuts were not deep, but head wounds do tend to bleed more easily, so you will need to change the bandages I've applied, regularly. Can you do that?"

"I can, yes," Clara said.

"Good. When you do, try to be as gentle as possible. The muscles in his neck are very stiff and will need massaging once he is awake." He looked down at the patient. "Check on him frequently to ensure he is breathing and that there is no fever. Right now, sleep is the best thing. Let him dream, for Aesculapius helps to heal therein." The medicus turned and reached down to the floor to pick up a small box. "I have brought with me one of our sacred serpents from the Aesculapium on Tiber Island."

Clara inhaled audibly.

"Oh, do not worry. These are not venomous. Let it live here in the room with him while he heals. It will help with his dreaming." He pulled out a young snake with markings like to a leopard's, its scales a glistening mosaic of pale browns and black.

"It looks like an adder," Felix said, shaking his head. "We can't have that here."

"A common confusion," the medicus corrected. "This is an ochendra. It will help to heal, not harm. If you see it on your friend, do not remove it. Let it roam freely over him, even lick him. It means the god is at his work."

Clara stiffened.

"If you like, I can also bring one of the sacred dogs from the island too. When they lick the patients, it also aids the process of healing."

"Erm…" Felix shook his head. "We've got the dog part covered. The snake will suffice."

"Very well." The medicus put the box the snake was in beneath the bed with the lid open. "Notify me if he vomits or if he begins to bleed in excess. Also, I must know when he is awake so that I may check his biles. Would you say this man is phlegmatic or choleric?"

"Definitely the latter," Felix said.

"He is prone to anger?"

"Oh, yes," Felix said. "Lately for certain."

"And is he melancholic or sanguine?"

"He is prone to melancholy," Clara added.

"Then, I will monitor his black and yellow bile when he is awake, for both are indicators of imbalance."

"Is there anything else we can do?" Clara asked.

"Speak to him," he said, glancing up at the scrolls in the

wall. "Perhaps read something if that is what he enjoys. Someone familiar to him. You can also make offerings of votive heads at the temples of Aesculapius and Apollo on his behalf since that is where the main trauma was inflicted. You say he also received an injury to his testes?"

Felix raised his eyebrows. "You could say that."

"Then some votive bollocks would be required, especially if he has trouble urinating." The medicus began to pack up his things. "I'm leaving some clean bandages for you. When he is awake, and I've had a chance to speak with him, I will also bring the appropriate elixirs to help balance his humours."

"Thank you," Felix said. "Come, I will show you out." Felix opened the door and led the medicus out. "Tell me, do you like the theatre?"

"Of course," Clara heard the medicus say as their voices trailed off behind the closed door. "In fact, at Epidauros…"

She sighed, and found her hand shaking. She looked down at it and the scratches there from the brawl the night before. She then looked at Rufio and shook her head. "Always an adventure of some sort," she muttered, remembering her anger when the lupa had struck him. Clara had not been able to control herself upon seeing that, and had waded in with her wooden gladius to chop at the woman's hefty rump.

She wondered how much Rufio would remember, for she herself remembered only small glimpses of the sad battle. It had all happened so quickly, but even in such a short amount of time, the detritus had covered almost every inch of the warehouse. She also wondered that Felix had perhaps expected such a spectacle, for he had ensured that most props and materials had been safely stowed away prior to the bacchanal. She reached out and touched Rufio's cheek. "At least we won," she said, trying to smile, but finding that she could not, for the bruise upon the right side of his face marred what was to her, beautiful.

She felt something glide past her foot and looked down to see the serpent slither beneath the bed. She stood and leaned over to kiss Rufio's cheek. "Rest now, Rufio. Dream and heal. I'll be back shortly to read to you."

With that, she went out into the warehouse where the sound of sweeping and the clink of broken pottery echoed above the recited lines of their shared Plautian epic.

"I've paid the medicus," Felix said as Clara sat down with him and Electra at the partially-cleaned table. "I gave him something extra so he will not neglect us. He's also going to come to the performance."

"If there is a performance," Clara said.

"What do you mean *if?*" Felix sat up. "Of course there's going to be a performance!"

Clara's eyes blazed as she turned on him. "Is that all you can think of? Rufio could have been killed, and you're still thinking on the play?"

"It was a small brawl," Felix said. "It happens every day. He'll recover. That medicus is one of the best. I spared no expense."

"So you keep saying!" Clara bit back. "But are you sparing our friend? For his one mistake in the past, we have guilted and cajoled him into doing this when maybe, just maybe, he really doesn't want to do it!"

"Of course he does!" Felix said. "Besides, it's the will of the Gods."

Clara stood quickly and began to walk away.

"Where are you going?" Felix called after her.

"To buy the votive offerings for Rufio."

"Wait! Let me give you some coin!"

"I've got my own, Felix! You just focus on the rehearsals for your precious play, and I'll take care of Rufio!"

When Clara was gone, Electra turned to Felix most casually. "She's stronger than I took her for. She's also right."

"What do you know of it, woman?" Felix said, leaning heavily on the table, his arms flexing and un-flexing.

"You're being selfish. What if your friend does not get well?"

"Of course he will," Felix said, his voice lower, more fretful.

"I've been watching the three of you and, though you have told me little of your time together as friends, I have noticed that there is much more going on with Rufio than mere stage terror. He is deeply unhappy in some part of his life."

"You barely know the man, and you think you can divine his life?" Felix shook his head.

"No. But my sight is not clouded by past events the way yours is." Electra stood, straightened the lengths of her stola down her hips and legs, and turned to leave. "I don't know what it is, but you three need to work things out. You're all as tightly wound as a Numidian's lock of hair."

Felix watched her walk away and he felt his anger seething, so much that he wanted to throw a water jug, but he realized there were none left to throw, for they had all been broken. "Futuo!"

"Erm, Dominus," Beatrice said from beside him.

Felix turned to see her, Julius, Fausto, Damon, Castor and Pollux looking at him. "What is it? What's wrong?" He looked at Silas who was alone upon the stage, practicing his lines and movements. "Why are you all standing around? We still have a lot of work to do today after all this is cleaned up."

"We know, Dominus," Fausto said.

Pollux stepped forward. "We just wanted to ask you if Rufio is all right."

"What?" Felix asked.

"Yes," Beatrice added. "We're worried about him."

"Will he pull through, Felix?" Julius asked.

Felix was silent for a moment, taking in the worried and haggard faces of his company. *They really are worried for him,* he thought. "In truth, I don't know. The medicus is a good one, but only time will tell."

"What can we do?" Fausto asked.

Felix shrugged, but then he stood to face them all. "Pray to the Gods that he is well again."

"We will," Beatrice said, and the others nodded, going back to their work silently.

"Why don't you hold your peace?" Silas' Peniculus was saying from on the stage, oblivious to the air about the warehouse. "I'll let you now catch him in the fact; do you only follow me this way. In a state of drunkenness, with a chaplet on, he was carrying the mantle to the embroiderer's, which he purloined from you at home today..."

Felix watched Silas move about, his arms dramatic in their arching description as he spoke. He never felt like slapping him more than at that moment.

THE HOT AIR WAS RUSHING AROUND RUFIO, AND THE SOUND OF cicadas clamoured in the depths of his ears, muffled at first, and then as clear as could be. Light dazzled his eyes as he opened them to find himself standing in the middle of the orchestra of a great odeon.

He had never seen anything like its enormity, the auditorium fanning out and away like smooth mountain slopes to a tree line at the top. Behind him was a short stage, not the usual scaena frons that one might see in a theatre in Rome.

This is not Rome, he thought, noting the feeling of great and foreign antiquity about him.

He turned around and noticed the orchestra was completely round, with an altar at the centre, the thymele.

"Where am I?" he said, and his voice echoed up the aisles

to the top.

There was no answer of course. He was alone in the middle of that hot, bright space. He looked up at the strangely fast-moving orb of the sun, like a fiery jewel in the blue setting of the sky. Sweat beaded on his forehead, and he wiped at it, wincing as he touched his brow. He turned again and saw that beyond the orchestra, set in distant trees, there appeared to be a temple of sorts, as well as other low structures. He began to walk in that direction, but when he reached the edge of the circular orchestra, he was immediately back at the altar in the middle. He tried again, this time walking with more determination.

Again, he found himself in the middle of the orchestra.

He tried a third time but running, and the same thing occurred.

"What is happening?" he called out, but the only reply was the echo of his own voice about the theatre, and the incessant chorus of cicadas chattering from the distant trees.

For some time, Rufio walked about the circle of the theatre's orchestra, occasionally making a surprise sally to puncture its confines, only to find himself back in the middle.

The light in the sky began to shift from bright blue, to pink, to red, and then to a deep indigo and purple that nearly blended with the peaks of the distant mountains. With nightfall, Rufio grew weary and, after a final attempt to clear the confines of the theatre, he sat upon the ground and leaned against the altar. His lids grew heavier and heavier. He struggled to stay awake. For a moment, he thought he spied a strange movement in the dirt at the edge of the orchestra. He scratched his head, and it felt strange to him, tingly and a little painful. The action made him dizzy and so he shifted to lie upon the ground and gaze up at the star-whirling sky.

As Rufio's eyes closed, he heard the soft notes of a beautiful, vaguely familiar voice, blanketing him like soft rain out of

that cloudless night sky. His heart rate slowed, and he focussed
upon the words he thought he could hear…

*I throw myself down; and watering the couch with profuse tears, Here,
(I cry,) we pressed thee together: bring us together again. Hither we both
came; why not both also depart? Perfidious bed, what is become of my
dearer half? What shall I do? Whither, thus desolate and forsaken, shall I
fly? The island lies uncultivated, and affords no prints either of men or
cattle. The sea encompasses me. No mariner appears, no ship to bear me
through the ambiguous tract. And suppose a ship, companions, and winds
were in my power, what could I do? My native country denies access. Even
if in a prosperous ship I should traverse the quiet seas, Aeolus restraining
the murmuring winds, still I should remain an exile…*

*…For you have I betrayed them, when, anxious lest the victor should
be bewildered in the labyrinth, I gave you a clue to guide your uncertain
steps: when you deceived me by false protestations, and swore by the
dangers from which you had escaped, that, while life remained, we should
be inseparably one. We live; and yet, Theseus, I am no longer thine; if
indeed an unhappy woman, oppressed by the treachery of a perjured man,
can be said to live… Now I not only figure to myself those ills which I
shall suffer, but every mishap that can befall one in my forlorn condition. A
thousand shapes of death wander before my eyes. Death itself appears less
terrible, than the lingering life that threatens me…*

*…I, who boast of Minos for my father, who was born of the
daughter of Phoebus; and, (what is still more to me) who was solemnly
engaged to you. If I turn my eyes toward the sea, the earth, or the winding
shore, both earth and waves threaten me with a thousand dangers. Heaven
only remains, and yet even here I fear the forms of the Gods. I am left a
prey, and food for savage beasts. If men inhabit or cultivate these fields, I
am apt to mistrust even them. Already a sufferer, I have learned to be slow
in giving credit to strangers…*

Rufio's eyes widened, struggled to stay awake for the words
that wove about him, those words that fell from the sky to
pierce his heart, words of leaving and of grief, of loneliness
and fear. He felt shame choking him, as ever it had, and tried

with all of his might as he lay there to pry those clawing hands from about his neck. His lids, however, so heavy, began to close, only just spying the slithering form approaching his paralyzed shape in the dark.

He was then in the middle of a broad island field where wheat swayed, and summer poppies bobbed their gently-compliant heads. It was day again, and he felt his lungs fill with sweet air. He turned where he was, looking for the altar, but found none. He began to walk, and almost at once, he saw the form of a lone woman standing among the wheat.

Rufio waved to her, but she made no reciprocal movement. She simply stood there, tears running down her dark cheeks, her black hair swirling about her shoulders in the hot wind. He walked toward her and when he stood but a few paces from her, he spoke.

"Are you lost, lady? How can I help you?"

She raised her head, her pale grey eyes strangely familiar. Streams of tears trickled slowly down her cheeks as she looked upon him. "He left me here…alone…"

"Who did?" Rufio asked.

"You did!" Her voice was hurt and accusing, so filled with pain and torment. She clawed at her face with shaking hands, wiping her tears with such sad violence until those hands were still, a curtain before her grief.

"Are you all right?" Rufio asked, taking a step toward her, reaching out to her.

She lowered her hands to reveal a different face, her countenance no longer the dark visage he had first seen, but one of pale and sad beauty which he recognized all too well.

"Clara?" he said.

"How could you?" she asked.

He began to shake his head, his own tears breaking the barriers of his lids. "I'm sorry!"

"You did this!" she accused. She then turned to leave.

"CLARA!" Rufio yelled after her. He felt rooted to the earth of that blood-red poppy field, but he pulled at his legs with all his reserves of strength and broke free to go after her. He got closer, his hands out to catch hold of her, his voice pleading silently to the wind and air, and then, he fell hard upon the earth.

When he opened his eyes, he was back at the centre of the orchestra with the sun shining hot upon him, baking his streaming tears upon his bearded face. "I'm sorry, Clara!" he wept out loud. "I'm so sorry!"

He felt something about his neck then, and reached to find it moving and writhing.

"Ahh!" he screamed, and pulled at it, throwing the serpent from off of him into the dirt at the far edge of the orchestra. "Leave me alone!" he shouted at it, but it turned toward him again where he knelt in the dirt with the altar at his back.

The scene shifted before his eyes and he caught a glimpse of the woman in the field once more.

"Clara, I'm sorry I left you!" he pleaded with open arms. "I love you!" He crumpled to the ground as the theatre re-appeared to envelope him.

It was night again, and the stars' fires burned brightly overhead.

Rufio wept in the dirt as the serpent approached, making for his face. He closed his eyes and felt his tears falling. "I always have…" he muttered, just as the serpent came to a stop before his sad and sodden face.

"OH IF YOU COULD HAVE VIEWED ME FROM THE STERN OF YOUR ship, the mournful figure had surely moved compassion. As you cannot now observe me with your eyes, only imagine me to yourself, hanging over a frightful rock, undermined by the waves that dash against it below. Consider me with my hair disheveled, and carelessly spread over my disconsolate face; behold my clothes heavy with tears, as from a shower. My body trembles like corn shaken by the north winds; and the letters proceed unequal from my faltering hand. I do not urge you now by my merit, since my favours were so ill bestowed, nor expect any retribution, as due to my kind offices: but then, what pretence have you for ill usage? Had I not contributed in the smallest degree to your safety, even this is no reason why you should be the cause of my death. To thee wretched Ariadne stretches over the wide sea her hands, faint with often beating her sorrowful breast. Disconsolate as I am, I remind you of the few mangled tresses that yet remain. I conjure you, by the tears shed for your cruel departure, turn your ship, dear Theseus, and bear back your inverted sails. If I die ere you arrive, you may yet collect my scattered bones…"

"Are you sure Ovid is the best thing to read to him while he is in this state?" Felix's voice came in at the doorway, surprising Clara and making her jump. "Sorry, dear. I didn't mean to startle you. I did knock."

Clara wiped the tears from her eyes and set the scroll down. "I was deep in the words."

"It's been three days, Clara," Felix said. "You need to rest."

"I can't while he's like this."

"The medicus said…" Felix choked back his emotions. "He said that if Rufio hasn't awakened by now, he may never awaken."

"He said my name, Felix!" Clara said. "While I was reading to him. He said my name. I'm not going to stop! He's going to be fine. He *has* to be!"

Felix nodded, unwilling and unable to gainsay her, for he knew when Clara had her mind set upon something, that she was not to be swayed. "I'll fetch you some food and drink. If you want, I can take over reading to him."

When Felix was gone, the door closed once more behind

him, Clara turned back to Rufio's still form upon the bed. She noted the wetness about his eyes and felt her heart wrenching at the sight. She leaned forward to stroke his hair, and as she did so, a silent whining came from beside her feet.

"It's all right, Peli," she said to the dog who had refused to leave Rufio's side. "He'll be fine," she said. "Gods, please help him to pull through."

THE SOUND OF THE CHORUS ABATED, AND RUFIO OPENED HIS eyes slowly, blinded by the hot white light of the sun above him. He pushed himself to his feet and looked around.

"Still here? Why am I stuck in this theatre?"

He was about to walk around the orchestra again when he remembered her, the woman in the field, sad, alone, disconsolate…

"Clara!" his voice rose and fell about the odeon like the cry of a gull by the seashore.

He fell to his knees before the altar, his eyes shut tight, his hands clasping the smooth marble edges as he bowed his head.

"Gods… I know that I've made mistakes and betrayed my friends… I also know that I've betrayed myself. I love Clara. I've always loved her…since we were young. If there is any way she could feel the same about me, if ever she did, I promise to be better than I was…better than I am." He shook his head with his eyes still closed. "My mind is racing and filled with hopes and dreams… Let them not consume me, but rather let them come to pass. I will tell her. I will."

Rufio opened his eyes again, and it was night, the theatre lit by the brilliance of a full moon in the overhanging firmament. The cicadas were silent now, and only the sound of crickets pierced the night. Rufio scanned the orchestra, turning on the spot to take in the skene behind him, outside the orchestra, newly adorned with the doorways of a street setting, silk clothes wavering in the breeze. He recognized it, the setting, and knew then what had to be done. He turned back to the altar bowed his head again.

"I will see the play through, for my friends…and for me. I will not abandon them the way I did before, I swear!"

His eyes stung and he felt the tears come once more. He nodded to himself, giving action and motive to the determination he felt, and when he opened his eyes, he saw her.

Half-way up the smoothly-curving seats of the auditorium, a goddess sat looking down on him, watching, smiling. Her hair was long and golden and she wore a stola of purest white that cast its own light in the space about her. Even from so far away, Rufio could see her wide, kind eyes as she leaned upon her knees to stare at him.

"I accept your prayers," she said, and her voice was a beautiful song that filled the theatre, the words rushing down to Rufio at the thymele.

Rufio felt a great weight lifted within his heart, and as he did so, the serpent slid out from beneath his sleeve onto the altar. He did not baulk at that, but looked down with great curiosity at the serpent where it curled up and closed its tiny black eyes. He stood and looked back up at the goddess. "Thank you."

She smiled and looked beyond Rufio.

Rufio smiled back, bowed and turned to leave. He walked hesitantly toward the edge of the orchestra, and to his great relief, he stepped beyond its confines. "Thank you," he whispered, and continued to walk.

His eyes sought the pathway that led behind the skene, but then he stopped himself and turned to look upon the stage, set as it was for a great performance. He turned and went slowly up the stairs, stepping past the hangings until he stood in the middle of a street before three doors.

To Rufio's surprise, the goddess yet sat there, watching him.

He bowed to her, spread his arms wide, and spoke…

IT WAS COMING ON MORNING, AND CLARA HAD REMAINED AT Rufio's side the whole of yet another night, dozing on and off in the chair at his bedside. For days she had worried more than ever she had, about Rufio's life, about the serpent that had slithered beneath the sheets, about the dog at her feet and whether he would eat the serpent.

Fortunately, Peli had behaved himself, rising only occasionally to lick Rufio's hand, or venture abroad from the room to relieve himself and then return.

As voices from somewhere in the warehouse reached her ears, Clara wiped her eyes and bent closer to Rufio. Not until he was near death in the summer of their lives did she fully allow herself to remember the love she had felt for him since the spring of her youth.

But even as the warm memories enveloped her, the poison of her guilt seeped into her veins to flood her brain, and she bent with the weight of it until her forehead touched his hand.

"I love you, Rufio, but I have wronged you. I'm haunted by my past actions. I was angry, sad, and desperate. Felix and I both were, when you abandoned us. We drank too much, and found comfort with each other. We forgot ourselves, Rufio, but I have never forgotten you since. I…I just don't know how to make things right. I don't deserve you, my friend, my love…"

Rufio's hand shifted and squeezed hers.

Clara sat up and looked down in shock at his face only to see the serpent glide down from off the bed to its basket beneath.

Shockingly, Peli observed its passage without movement, his strange eyes following it warily until it was gone.

Clara watched as Rufio's mouth worked a little of its own accord.

"And you, whom with many and anxious labours I have ever been seeking up to this time, and whom I rejoice at being found…"

"Rufio?" Clara leaned down most suddenly when she heard his voice, her hand yet clasping his. She turned toward the door which was slightly ajar. "Felix!" She turned back to Rufio. "Can you hear me? It's Clara, Rufio. I'm here!" Her voice shuddered and her eyes welled, and through her tears she could see his eyes opening slowly to search his surroundings like a man lost at sea to find himself on some strange and foreign beach.

"Rufio?" Clara repeated.

"What's happening?" Felix burst into the room and froze when he saw Rufio's eyes opening and closing slowly and Clara leaning over him. "Is he-"

"He spoke!" Clara said. "Something about anxious labours he has ever been seeking up to this time, and someone he rejoices at being found…" She shook her head. "That sounds familiar, but-"

"Ha, ha!" Felix clapped his hands and beamed. "He's reciting some of the Menaechmus Sosicles' final lines of the play!" Felix went around to the other side of the bed and knelt at Rufio's side. "Rufio, can you hear us?"

Rufio nodded very slowly and then his eyes opened again to look from side to side at both of them. "What…what happened?"

"You were injured in the fight," Felix said. "But you're all right now. The medicus did his work well, as did Clara." He looked up at her and smiled and nodded, before turning back to Rufio. "How do you feel?"

"Thirsty," Rufio croaked.

"Here is some water." Clara released Rufio's hand and turned to get the clay cup that sat upon the small table beside the bed. "Here."

Felix helped Rufio sit up a little and Clara pressed the cup gently to his lips.

Rufio coughed at first, choking on the water, but then drank more smoothly. He sighed and lay back down heavily.

"You gave us quite a scare, my friend," Felix said, clearly moved as he brushed back Rufio's hair from his sweaty brow. He cleared his throat and stood. "I'll send for the medicus. He wanted to know if you woke…or, as soon as you awoke."

"If?" Rufio asked. "Why? Did he think I was going to…" The words stopped in his throat.

It was then that Clara bent over him, and he could feel her tears wet upon his neck.

Felix looked down at his friends and sighed. "You're back. That is all that matters to us, Rufio. I'll be back soon."

Rufio watched Felix leave and then raised both his arms to hold Clara's shuddering shoulders. "I'm here, Clara. I'm all right now. You brought me back. I heard your voice."

Clara sat up and wiped her eyes. "I was so worried, Rufio. But when you spoke in your sleep, I knew you would come back. I just knew it."

He smiled at her. "I spoke? What did I say?"

"You…you spoke lines from the play just now. You said other things too, but I wasn't able to understand all of it. You said my name."

"I remember saying your name, and-" Rufio paused, searching the vague memories that trickled into his consciousness. He then remembered the lone woman…the goddess… and… He looked up at Clara's shining eyes. "You were reading to me?"

Clara nodded and smiled. "Yes. From Ovid."

"I think I remember." He grasped her hand more tightly now. "Thank you, Clara, I-"

There was a sudden bark as Peli rose up from the floor and set his front paws upon the bed.

"You!" Rufio said. "Don't you dare!"

Clara laughed. "It's all right, Rufio. Peli has been standing guard over you the entire time. He did piss on Damon once in the night, but that is all."

Rufio eyed the dog suspiciously and then smiled.

Peli licked his hand with feverish relief, and Rufio then wiped his spittle-covered hand on the dog's head.

They sat in silence for a time before Rufio turned to Clara. "Clara…there is something I want to say to you."

"Yes, Rufio?" She stared straight into his eyes.

He looked upon her with such gratitude in his heart, so beautiful, so wondrous. "Clara, I-"

"I've brought the medicus!" Felix said suddenly as he rushed in with the man in tow. "Here he is! Awake and talking!"

Rufio released Clara's hand and turned a little annoyed toward the doctor.

"How are you feeling?" the medicus asked, taking Rufio's wrist and looking into his eyes in a most discomfiting way.

"I'm fine!" Rufio snapped. "I'm hungry, and thirsty, and I need to piss!"

The medicus nodded, satisfied, and turned to Felix. "You were right, most choleric." He turned back to Rufio. "I must inspect your bile."

Rufio recoiled. "No one's inspecting anything else!"

"Did the serpent bite you?" the medicus persisted.

"Serpent? Bite me?" Rufio had a vague memory of a serpent. "I…I don't know."

The medicus reached under the bed and pulled out the serpent. "This one."

"AHH!!!" Rufio screamed, and when he did so, Peli sprang up to grasp the serpent from the medicus' hands and bolted out of the bedroom door into the warehouse.

The medicus screamed in return, and went after the

mischievous hound. "That is sacred, you cur!" he yelled as he ran after Peli.

"Back to normal!" Felix said as he went after them.

When they were alone again, Rufio and Clara looked at each other. She waited expectantly for him to say something, to pick up where he had left off, but he was silent in his exhaustion.

"I'll go and get you something to eat," she said.

"Thank you." Rufio smiled at her as she went out. "My love," he whispered to himself before pounding the bed with his fist.

Rufio SPENT THE NEXT THREE DAYS IN HIS BED, STILL FEELING too weak at first to be up and about, his mind reeling in residual tumult from his period of unconsciousness. He slept fitfully, and ate and drank, regaining his strength. He tried to distract himself from the chilling things he had heard and seen in the theatre of his mind, those visions the Gods or, rather, that goddess, had given him. For as long as it did not hurt his aching head, he rehearsed his lines from his bed, sometimes alone, other times with Clara.

Finally, on the fourth morning, he felt well enough to get up out of his bed, wash his face in the bronze basin, and get dressed. He swayed on his feet at first as he stood before the rack of variously-coloured tunicae until he chose a long, indigo tunica which he belted with a brown cingulum to match his sandals.

When he was finished, he turned to the door of his cubiculum and looked down to see Peli, standing and waiting for him, his tail wagging back and forth and his tongue lolling happily out the side of his jaws.

"You going to be good for once?" Rufio asked the dog, bending down to rub his face.

Peli sighed and whined.

"Thank you for staying by me," Rufio said, a little reluctantly. "You can be quite good at times."

Peli barked.

"When you're not pissing on me." Rufio stood. "I guess I should get out there." He opened the door and went out to find the warehouse exploding with colour and sound.

Things on the production had progressed quite a bit since he had last been out in the world. An array of colourful costumes hung on display where they were newly-stitched and ready for final flourishes, and long painted curtains that were part of the staging wavered in the hot breeze that blew through the warehouse, representing the walls of domi in the play, painted in red and white with faded images of acanthus leaves and hovering images of the god, Eros.

The elaborately embroidered mantle that belonged to both the jealous wife, and Erotium hung in pride of place where Beatrice and Felix observed how it sparkled in the half-light, above the travelling trunks of Menaechmus Sosicles and Messenio.

Damon trilled on his flute, practicing his melodies which would accentuate the performance while the rest of the company sang the songs which would delight the audience between acts.

Rufio took a deep breath and made for the long, repaired, trestle tables where most of the company sat.

Silas saw him first and scowled as if he were disappointed Rufio yet lived, but when the others spied Rufio, there was a cheer.

"Rufio!" Fausto shouted. "You're up?"

"Salve, Rufio!" Julius added. "Returned from the land of the Gods!" The older man walked up to Rufio and pat him on the shoulder. "How are you feeling? You had us worried."

"I'm well again, Julius. Thank you," Rufio said, smiling at Clara who sat at the table with Felix and Electra.

Castor and Pollux came up to Rufio then and nudged his shoulder. "You can walk! That is good. After a kick like that to the figs, you should be hobbling around!"

"Yes, well…" Rufio did not know what else to say to that. He was sore, but had suffered enough embarrassment for a lifetime and just wanted to move on from it. "How are rehearsals going?" he asked everyone.

"All is well, Rufio!" Felix said, standing and coming over to him. "Come. Sit and eat and regain your strength."

"I'm fine, Felix. Thank you." Rufio looked down at the ground and back up at his friend. "Thank you for hiring the medicus. He did help."

"I would not have done otherwise, my friend. I'm just glad you're all right."

"Beatrice, your costumes look wonderful!" Rufio said as he passed her display on the way to the table.

"Thank you!" she said, beaming with pride. "It is much easier when I have such fine materials to work with!"

"Nothing but the best!" Felix said. "Come. Sit, Rufio."

Rufio made his way around the table and sat beside Clara, who smiled and kissed him on the cheek. "Have you rested?" he asked her, remembering how she had sat by him the entire time.

"I have, yes," Clara said.

"Good."

"I am happy you are well again, Rufio," Electra said from across the table, handing him a plate of bread, olives, figs, and hazelnuts.

Rufio looked at her, stunned. "Tha…thank you… Electra."

She smiled at him for a brief moment, further deepening the sense of surreality which seemed to accompany everything he saw. The world seemed different, brighter and more colourful to him. The people about him - apart from Silas - seemed happier, ready to face whatever the day may bring them.

Rufio felt as though a Herculean weight had indeed been lifted from off of his own shoulders too. He knew the Gods had indeed helped him pull through, and that he must, that very day, go to the temple of Apollo to offer his thanks for his healing.

Rufio ate and drank in silence, content to sit beside Clara as they watched Castor, Julius, Felix and Messenio rehearse the large, confrontational scene at the beginning of the fifth act. He and Clara laughed along with the other observers, marvelling at Felix's skill and the anger which the others took for madness in his character. When they were finished, there was loud applause.

Clara turned to Rufio, a wondrous smile upon her face. "It's going to be a magnificent production, Rufio. I just know it!"

Rufio nodded, but did not say anything.

"What's wrong?" Clara asked. "Are you feeling ill?"

He shook his head. "Not at all. I... I just feel very fortunate. Glad to be here with you."

Clara leaned into him and touched her golden head gently to his brow. "I prayed every moment that you would be safe."

"I know," Rufio said, his voice barely a whisper. "This morning, I'm going to go to the temple of Apollo to offer my thanks."

"Good idea," she said. "I can come with you, if you like."

Rufio thought about it for a moment. *I should go alone, for I want to thank the Gods not only for getting better...* "You stay. I feel I need to go alone to do this."

"Are you sure you're able to walk so far?" Clara touched his arm and squeezed, her pale brow knitted as she looked upon him.

"I'll be fine. I'll just go to the Palatine and back."

Rufio finished eating and prepared to leave.

"Here," Felix said. "Take this. You need to buy a suitable offering." He handed Rufio a small pouch of coins.

Rufio would have refused, except that he had very little to his name anymore. "Thank you," he said to Felix.

"Go. Pray…give thanks to Far-Shooting Apollo and his son for helping you."

"And to the goddess who helped me…" Rufio said to himself.

"Who's that?" Felix asked.

Rufio shrugged and smiled. "I don't know!"

Felix watched him go out into the sunlight beyond the confines of the warehouse.

"I hope he's all right," Clara said.

"He'll be fine," Felix answered. "He's his old self again. I can see it!" Felix clapped loudly then and turned to the company. "Right! Electra! Silas! From the beginning of the fourth act, between the wife and Peniculus!"

Electra was already on the stage waiting, looking around for her partner in the scene, but when she did not see him, she spread her arms wide to Felix.

"Where is Silas?" Felix bellowed.

"He said he needed to run out and purchase some new sheets of papyrus," Julius piped up.

"Now?" Felix said, rubbing his beard roughly. "Fine. Castor?"

"Yes, Dominus!"

"You, Electra and I will go through the scene between the wife, the father and Menaechmus Sosicles. I'll play Rufio's part for now. He knows it well anyway."

. . .

It felt strange to be outside in the bright, sunlit streets of Rome. It was warm and colourful, and Rufio began to feel more and more revived with every step he took. It felt good to go beyond the confines of the warehouse and his small cubiculum, so much so that he did not mind the crowds pressing around him as he passed through the Forum Boarium, past the end of the Circus Maximus, and on toward the stairs leading up to the temple of Apollo on the Palatine Hill.

Once he reached the top of the stairs, Rufio had to sit for a moment to rest, and from there he looked about the square before the temple. He wrinkled his nose at some foul odour that attacked his senses then, and wondered what it could be.

It was with no small amount of embarrassment that he realized the odour rose up from his own person.

"Gods!" he said to himself. "I can't go before Apollo in such a state!" He stood then and made his way across the hill, down into the Forum Romanum and on toward the baths of Titus.

"Ahh," Rufio sighed as he lowered himself into the hot water of the caldarium. "That's better."

It had felt good to rub the oil over himself and then scrape it away with the strigil before getting in the hot water, so much so that he felt like a new person. In a way, he felt like that man the Christians sometimes referred to, the one who died and returned to the world of the living. "What was his name?" he mused to himself as he sat in the water. "Lazy? Lazaroo?" He shook his head. *Whomever it was, he must have gone straight to the baths.*

Rufio was grateful for the quiet in the baths at that time of day. For once, he seemed to have much of the space to himself. He stretched his leg so that it rose up out of the water, straining the muscles behind his knee. "What?" He peered closer at the inside of his thigh at what appeared to be bite marks in the form of two rows of tiny dots. He shivered as he recalled his dreams, and immediately, his mood darkened.

"There was the theatre," he reminded himself. "I couldn't get out until…" He smiled then and his heart felt light. "Clara."

For so long, Rufio had been silent about his love for Clara, his deep and abiding affection for her, that he had become accustomed to the veil in which he had wrapped his feelings. Now, it seemed unnatural to him. He knew he had never told her because he had wanted to spare her the disappointment he no doubt would have been to her, and later that he had been.

His father's cruel words over the years had cut deeper than any blade, bruised him more darkly than any switch from the cherry trees on their land.

But Clara had sat by him throughout his long sleep. "She cares for me," he said, his mouth just above the surface of the water. "I'll tell her. I've waited too long. Just after the performance. I'll prove myself first, and make her proud."

Rufio leaned back against the wall and looked up at the high, arched and echoing ceiling. He was still not feeling his best, especially where the whore had kicked him, and he reached down to ascertain the damage done to his manhood.

"Ah!" a creaky old voice said from behind him.

Rufio turned to see the naked form of an aged senator scowling down at him, his jowls most disapproving.

"You young people are so disgusting! Cease that behaviour at once!"

Rufio shook his head and stood. "No, no! You misunderstand, sir. I have an injury, that is all."

"Well it's no wonder you do, pulling at yourself in such a violent way!"

"What?"

"You cinaedi are spoiling everything!" The old codger pointed.

"I beg your pardon?" Rufio was shocked. "I'm an actor!" he declared, sticking his chest out most rebelliously.

"Ha! Even worse! Now get out of there so that I can have my bath!"

"Futuere!" Rufio waved his arm angrily. "I was leaving anyway!"

The old man pushed past Rufio and lowered himself into the water just in time to push out a whistling bit of air from his behind which sputtered on the surface of the water.

"You're the disgusting one!" Rufio called back as he stormed off to the frigidarium.

RUFIO TRIED TO SHAKE OFF HIS SOUR MOOD AFTER THE interaction at the baths. He walked with a purpose back through the Forum Romanum and up onto the Palatine Hill to seek the temple of Apollo. His mood was further disturbed by the feeling that he was being followed, and he wondered if the old man was not grasping at his shadow to further accost him, or worse, proposition him. He turned around several times, but saw nothing but the marketing crowd.

"Why is it that this city always ruins things?" He began to miss Etruria most acutely then, the quiet, the air, his animals… *Well, some of them anyway.*

He thought of his dilapidated farm, his strange old servant, and his moody animals, and wondered if any of it would be enough for Clara.

"Stop it!" he said to himself, angry at his wild propensity for building scenarios before anything had come to pass, especially when it came to Clara. "You have to make things right first!"

"Who are you talking to, Citizen?" someone asked.

Rufio looked up to see an offering seller standing behind a table to the left of the temple stairs. "Ah, salve!" *What was his name?* Rufio wondered.

"I remember you from Veneralia. On the steps of the temple of Venus."

"Ah, yes…um…"

"Numonius," the man said, hoping to save Rufio the embarrassment.

"Right. Apologies. Numonius." Rufio stood before the table.

"Rufio, right?"

"You have a good memory. I'm afraid mine is not so good. Especially now. I received a blow to the head."

"You seek Apollo's aid, then?" Numonius asked.

"To offer my thanks. I almost didn't make it."

"Was the blow coupled with a slap to the face?" Numonius observed Rufio's reddened face. "I must apologize for my fellow Romans' behaviour."

"Coupled with a kick to my manhood, actually."

Numonius' face crinkled. "Ouch! No wonder you're talking to yourself!"

"Oh, I wasn't… I was…rehearsing my lines."

"For what?"

"For a performance during the Games of Apollo," Rufio answered proudly.

"Really? How wonderful! You didn't say anything about being an actor when we met!"

Rufio shrugged and smiled sheepishly. "It's a new development."

"I do love the theatre!" Numonius said, nodding to some other customers who were browsing along the table. "What play?"

"The *Menaechmi*, by Plautus," Rufio answered.

"I love Plautus!" Numonius clapped. "Will you be

performing in the forum?"

"Well…no."

"Where then? I'd like to come and see it!"

Rufio was touched that Numonius seemed genuinely pleased for him and excited by the prospect of seeing him perform. It did make him nervous, but he knew that the enthusiasm was truthful. "In the theatre of Pompey."

"What?" Numonius' eyes bulged. "Ladies and gentlemen!" he announced to the few people about the square. "We are in the presence of greatness!"

"Shhhh!" Rufio hissed. "What are you doing, man?"

Numonius laughed and slapped Rufio on the shoulder. "I'm just excited for you. I can't wait to see it! I'll be there!"

"You might regret it," Rufio grumbled.

"Nonsense! I can see you have it in you! You survived grievous injury unscathed. The Gods must have a plan for you."

"Sometimes I wonder."

"But I am keeping you. You came for offerings to Apollo. In addition to your thank-offering - for which I would suggest some oil and bundled herbs - you may wish to offer something for the success of your artistic endeavour. How about this?" Numonius held up a small clay votive statue of a cythara.

"Those will do just fine." Rufio fished in the pouch that hung from his cingulum. "How much?"

"One sestertius."

"Really?" Rufio looked up. He expected it to be more.

"Remember me in your prayers after your success." Numonius smiled.

"Thank you." Rufio felt his previous anger fall away. "See you at the performance."

"Absolutely!" Numonius said as Rufio made his way up the temple steps. "How can I help you, lady?" he said to the next customer.

Rufio stopped on the steps to look up at the high pediment and the statue of a great palm tree there which, he presumed, was the Delian tree beneath which the god had been born. After a few people filed out of the temple in a cloud of incense and smoke, Rufio waded in, cradling his offerings gently in his hands.

It was as though he had stepped into another world, dark, and fire-lit, but smelling as sweetly as Olympus, he imagined, rather than Hades. For that, he was grateful indeed.

Rufio made his way toward the cella of the temple and the large statue group of Apollo and the Muses. The high altar was covered in offerings of various sorts - fruit and other foods, herbs bundled with decorative ribbons, votive statues, and even a pugio.

"Do you wish to make an offering to Apollo?" a white-robed priest asked as he emerged from the shadows behind the statues.

"Oh, um, yes. I do," Rufio said. "I wish to make a thank offering to Apollo for my healing, and for artistic greatness in the time to come."

"Greatness?" the priest repeated, a slight smile behind his white beard.

"Well...I'll settle for passable goodness in that area," Rufio added.

The priest nodded and smiled. "Your health and healing are the greater of the two. You may make your offerings to Apollo and his son, Aesculapius, at the altar over there. You will not be disturbed." The priest pointed to a small alcove along the far wall of the temple, to the left of the great altar.

"Thank you," Rufio said, bowing his head awkwardly and making his way over to the altar where statues of both Apollo and Aesculapius stood, their faces illuminated by the flames of five flickering oil lamps at their feet.

The altar, Rufio noticed, was covered in votive offerings of every sort - feet, ears, livers, legs, and eyes made of clay, bronze, or even of glass. Rufio spotted a large clay head and what appeared to be...

"Bollocks," he said.

"Shhh," the priest hissed from the high altar.

"Sorry," Rufio returned, and then looked back at the altar to see the large head and bollocks which sat together.

Felix had told him Clara had gone to purchase votive offerings, and he wondered if those were indeed the ones she had given.

He felt a little embarrassed at the thought of her purchasing such large votives, but was grateful to her for having done so. He then set down his own offering of the bundled sage and rosemarinus over which he poured the oil from the tiny glass phial.

Bending his head, he prayed before the Gods. "Oh Apollo and Aesculapius... I offer these sacred herbs and oil in thanks to you for helping me to heal. I was afraid...in that other place...that I would not return, that I would not see her again. But through your help and healing, I am back, and I am grateful to you. Thank you, Gods. Thank you."

Rufio looked up at the faces of the father and son gods and wondered what they might have been thinking seeing him, Rufio Pagano, there praying before them. Had they not cared, they would have let him die. And so he thought they must have had some purpose in mind for him. He then picked up the miniature cythara and raised it to Apollo before setting it upon the altar beside Clara's offerings.

"Lord Apollo...master of the Muses... I don't know exactly what skill lies within me to be able to do justice to this performance. I only ask that it is sufficient to erase my past wrongs in the eyes of my friends." He pressed his head to the edge of the altar. "I betrayed them long ago, and I would make it up to them. Guide me in the performance to come. Inspire me to be better." He looked up and, in that moment, he remembered the ancient odeon…the dirt beneath him…the serpent circling him. "And if you know the goddess who watched over me, please let her know of my gratitude, whoever she is. Thank you."

THE SUN WAS ALREADY REDDENING IN THE LATE SPRING SKY when Rufio exited the temple. He saw that Numonius had packed up his wares and moved on. The square was empty but for a few stragglers enjoying some lazy conversation in the late light, or just standing looking out from the crest of the Palatine Hill.

Rufio knew he should get back to the warehouse, but he was so happy to be out of doors that he decided to go for a walk. He made his way down the stairs and around, along the base of the Capitoline Hill, and then along through the thinly-crowded streets in the direction of the Saepta Julia and the law courts.

Of course, he did not know where he was going. He did not care that day, for everything about him took on a new lustre. At one point, he looked down to see Peli strolling along beside him.

"There you are!" he said to the hound. "Where have you been?" He rubbed the dogs head roughly and the two of them carried on. "No. Don't tell me! I don't want to know."

"I see you two have become fast friends!"

Peli barked and ran toward the voice, and Rufio looked up to see the lupa, Meretrix, leaning against the doorway of her domus.

"Hello, Meretrix!" Rufio said, hailing her with a friendly wave as he approached.

"My, my! Rufio Pagano! You are a changed man!" Meretrix said, her jewellery jingling in agreement as she leaned in to kiss him, making him blush. "I've been wondering what happened to you!" She paused in her enthusiastic reception to stare beyond his shoulder at someone skulking in the shadows down the street. "Anyone bothering you on your way here?" she asked, her voice lower.

Rufio shook his head. "No. Not that I'm aware of. I'm just happy to be out. So much has happened!"

Meretrix stood back, her friendly face a joy for Rufio to behold. She looked down the street again. "Why don't you come inside for a drink with me. Don't worry! I won't try to tempt you." She leaned in to whisper. "I know your heart belongs elsewhere."

"It does." Rufio beamed.

"Well, come inside and tell me all about it!" Meretrix threaded her arm through Rufio's and led him inside. "Peli, you stand guard, all right?"

Peli barked again, pissed against the wall, and turned to sit before the door.

"Good boy!" Meretrix said. "Now Rufio, tell me everything that has happened to you since you left me…"

"Damn dog!" Silas cursed as he stood peering from around the corner at the doorway where Peli sat, shooting him an occasional canine glare and growl whenever his head poked around the corner. "So, Rufio has a lupa," he said to himself. "Interesting."

Of course, Silas knew many men did visit brothels, but he thought the information might come in useful. Truthfully, he did not know why he followed Rufio that day. The urge to go after him, however, had been overwhelming. He had been fed up with Felix and the company anyway, and needed to get away. He knew it could cost him a beating from Felix, but at least the dominus would pay him some attention then. *He's all but ignored me since that peasant and arrogant bitch joined the company!*

The wait at the baths had been annoying, but he had simply eaten a honeyed pastry in the shade of a tree while he waited for Rufio to emerge. There had been several times when Silas worried that Rufio had seen him tailing him through the streets, but Rufio was so befuddled by the city, he knew he did not have to worry. *What a bumpkin!* Silas laughed to himself at how easy it was, at least until the cur showed up!

He looked at the window of the upper storey of the lupa's tenement where a warm light bled out into the darkening street, and heard laughter emerging.

"I'd better get back to the warehouse. He'll be a while, the shit."

With a final glance and dark grin, Silas retreated from the corner and walked quickly back through the streets to the warehouse and his inevitable beratement.

"WHERE IN HADES HAVE YOU BEEN, SILAS?"

Felix's voice shook the walls of the warehouse the moment Silas entered, and all eyes of the company, who were eating at the long table, turned toward him. There was not a friendly face among them, for Silas had missed many a scene in which his Peniculus should have been present.

"The games are nearly upon us, and we need to rehearse more than ever now. But YOU, you go out for a day-long walk!" Felix's face was red as he stood there staring at him.

Silas approached slowly, his eyes on the ground leading up to Felix's colossal stance. "I know I abandoned my post today, but I needed to get out."

"You *needed* to be here, Silas. Not in some alleyway buggering little boys!"

"I wasn't!" Silas looked up now. "You can punish me if you

like…beat me, even! But I wasn't doing that. I was out for a walk. I went to the temple of Apollo to pray for our success," he lied. He looked at the table then and saw Clara and the others looking up at him, a familiar look of disgust and distaste upon their faces.

None of them cares for me. None of them ever has, he thought. *Except for Felix, once-upon-a-time.* "I won't do it again, I swear, Dominus!" Silas said, his pleading almost believable.

Felix shook his head. "You do anything like that again, and I *will* sell you!"

"Yes, Dominus," Silas bowed before Felix.

"You can eat now," Felix said. "There are some scraps left for you. Clara has already set aside a platter for Rufio when he returns."

Silas looked at Clara and back to Felix. "Oh, I don't think he'll be coming back tonight."

"Why do you say that?" Clara asked.

"Oh, he's fine. Nothing to worry about. I just saw him on my walk, from a distance, that is. He's visiting with a lupa near the Saepta Julia."

"How do you know, she's a lupa?" Julius asked.

"Oh, she's a lupa all right. Pretty one too. They seemed quite friendly." Silas looked around, confused, and shrugged. "Anyway, he'll probably be a while. He was thrilled to see her, it seemed."

"It's probably the one who helped Rufio out on his first night in Rome," Felix said to Clara.

She did not answer.

"She seemed eager to help him now," Silas added with a raised eyebrow.

"Just shut up and eat, Silas," Felix growled as he sat back down and looked across the table at Clara.

She would not meet his eyes.

XIV

A STAGE FOR THE GODS

The Kalends of Iulius finally arrived, and there was a new energy in Rome, a vitality beyond the calm of soothing Spring. The days were hot, and the nights clear and raucous in almost every quarter. The markets were brimming with new wares from every corner of the empire with traders arriving daily by river or by road from the great port at Ostia.

The people's enthusiasm always built at the beginning of the month of Iulius for they anticipated the Ludi Apollinares and all that it entailed, including bursting markets and fairs, the thrill of races in the Circus Maximus, blood on the sand of the Colosseum and, most importantly and pleasing to the Gods, the theatrical performances that would grace the stages and steps of temples throughout the city.

Of the myriad theatrical companies that descended on Rome, The Etrurian Players were most frequently the subject of excited discussions in the tabernae and fora. This was in part due to the carefully-placed hints of Felix Modestus and his crew in every interaction with the people of Rome, as well as the occasional bundle of flyers they let drop in the crowded Forum Romanum to blow about the sandalled feet of pedestrians.

The aedile, Sextus Annius Sabinus, also played his part by advocating for the magnificence of the production in the halls of power of the Roman elite, so much so that the masters of wealthy domi discussed with excitement the forthcoming production of Plautus' *Menaechmi* with every guest who dined with them. The slaves of those very masters then whispered amongst each other and their compatriots in other great houses of what they had overheard.

And so it was that by the Kalends of that summer month, every person with even a passing interest in the theatre, knew of the forthcoming production of Plautus' masterpiece of hectic hilarity and confusion.

"The entire city's talking about us!" Felix said loudly as he entered the warehouse. "I've never heard such buzz! Gods love the Romans and their propensity for gossip!" He clapped his hands loudly. "Quickly, everyone! Today's the day we move to the great theatre. Pack up everything but your beds and get them into the wagons!"

Rufio and Clara watched as the rest of the company loaded the convoy of wagons Felix had hired with every crate, set piece, and prop with the efficiency of a legion on the march.

"Rufio, Clara!" Felix went to them where they stood in the middle of the maelstrom of activity. "Make sure you put on your costumes for the procession to the theatre of Pompey. We want the people to see Menaechmus Sosicles and Erotium in all their splendour!"

"We're getting into costume to go to the theatre?" Rufio asked, clearly unprepared for this.

Felix nodded his head and turned around. "Etrurian Players!" he shouted. "Gather round!"

From every corner of the warehouse, and down from off of the various wagons, the players gathered around their captain, sweaty and grunting, eyes excited at what the day before them held.

"Listen, everyone!" Felix said. "This will be Rome's first proper glimpse of us, and so we must make an impression on the people, one they will never forget. We want them excited! Full of anticipation! Once the wagons are loaded, I want them properly decorated. They are to be rolling stages with us upon them. I want each of you to wear your costumes. Put on your makeup, and arrange your hair. We need to surprise and delight the people as we pass through the streets from here to the theatre of Pompey. We will take a bit of a circuitous route there to draw things out."

"But wagons aren't allowed in the streets during the day," Rufio said.

"Ah!" Felix smiled. "We *will* be allowed! The aedile has arranged for a special dispensation for The Etrurian Players to be able to do so. We cannot stop and block the streets, but we may roll on at a slow pace so long as we entertain the crowds along the way. Damon!" Felix turned to the mute. "I want you playing your flute the whole way. Beatrice, Castor, and Pollux, you accompany him on the tambourine, sistrum and drum. The rest of you will raise your voices in our practiced songs while I proclaim us from the head of the procession."

"What do we do besides sing?" Clara asked.

"You need to be Erotium, Clara. Dress the part of the beautiful lupa, tantalize the crowd, smile, wink, let them see a glint of the bracelet, let them admire the cloak.

"What about me?" Rufio asked. "Do I just stand there?"

"You and Fausto - that is, Menaechmus Sosicles and Messenio - shall smile and wave, jingle your money pouch, and toss out the occasional coin."

"What?" Silas barked. "We're throwing money at the crowd now?"

"Yes!" Felix bellowed.

"What money pouch?" Rufio asked.

"This one!" Felix reached beneath his own cloak and tossed a leather pouch at Rufio. "It's full of bronze asses, but the sound of coins on the cobbles will drive the crowd mad!"

"What order do you want the wagons in, Dominus?" Fausto asked.

Felix smiled and pointed to the outside where the wagons were waiting. "Menaechmus of Epidamnus and his jealous wife will be in the first, then Erotium for all to admire, with her two servants Cylindrus and the maid. After them will come Menaechmus Sosicles and Messenio. The fourth wagon will be carrying Julius as the medicus accompanied by the jealous wife's father." Felix turned to Silas. "Peniculus will go last, Silas, and I want you looking angry and dejected as you look suspiciously upon the crowd. I want your face to haunt and taunt them!"

"Shouldn't be too hard," Castor whispered to Pollux, making his brother laugh.

"The wagons with the larger set pieces will follow, but I want every wagon decorated with flowers, and ribbons!" Felix turned to look outside. "I want the horns of the ox on the first wagon to be painted with gold, and the hooves of the horses in bright colours."

"We're painting the animals now?" Silas asked. "We've never done that before!"

"We've never performed in Rome before, Silas!" Felix said. "Besides, we're paying the cart owner extra for that. Make sure you only pay half now before we leave, and the other half when we're at the theatre."

"And where did all of this coin come from?" Silas asked.

Felix leaned in so that only Silas could hear him. "Just shut up and do it! You know where the money is coming from."

"Why can't I sit in the first wagon with you and Electra? Peniculus is your servant, after all!"

"Because, Peniculus is an outcast, something to behold all on his own!" Felix slapped Silas on the back and went to the others. "Any questions?"

Nobody said anything.

Felix clapped loudly. "Then let's get to it!"

The company spread out to finish loading the wagons and then dress for their first true appearance before the people of Rome.

Electra went directly to her curtained cubiculum to dress herself, not to degrade herself with loading the wagons, and Felix was about to follow her when Rufio held him fast.

"Felix, are you sure it's safe for Clara to display herself like that? It is Rome, after all!"

Felix glanced at Clara who was standing behind Rufio. "Clara, does this make you uncomfortable?" he asked.

Clara stepped forward and shook her head. "Of course not. It's all part of the show!" She turned to Rufio. "You don't mind lupae, do you Rufio?"

Rufio shook his head, clearly confused by her tone. "What? No! I...I just worry that someone will try to grope you on the way."

"Don't worry, Rufio," Felix said, almost laughing. "Clara will have the high ground from atop the wagon, and Pollux will be there with her in case anyone tries to climb aboard to accost her."

Rufio looked uncertain, but he was distracted by Clara who had, of late, been quite cool with him. At first he had thought it was nerves as the performance approached, but that was doubtful.

In the last weeks, as the company had rehearsed the play in its entirety, from start to finish, several times over, it had become apparent that Clara knew every one of her lines and was completely at ease in her role. Everyone, in fact, knew their part perfectly well, but for Rufio who yet stumbled here and there over Plautus' lines for Menaechmus Sosicles.

"Don't worry, Rufio," Felix said. "You just keep on top of your lines. You can slip up in rehearsal, but on the day, with all of Rome watching and listening, it must be perfect!"

"No pressure, then," Rufio grunted.

"Loads of pressure!" Felix said, reaching out to place his hands on both Rufio and Clara's shoulders. "But we can do this. We've always dreamed of doing this, and now it's happening." He smiled at them, most sincerely, and in that moment they glimpsed the Felix of their youth from whom they had always borrowed courage. "Now go, both of you. Climb into your characters so that you can dazzle these Romans as you pass." Felix turned and went to find Electra, leaving Clara and Rufio alone in awkward silence.

"What is wrong?" Rufio asked her, unable to stand the silence she had inflicted on him for a while now.

"Nothing," Clara said, forcing a smile. "I'm just getting a little overwhelmed."

"Let's step into the sunlight," Rufio suggested. He knew that was not what Clara meant, but she followed as he went outside the warehouse where the train of wagons was groaning under the weight of the crates and set pieces, the animals lowing where they stood, flies buzzing annoyingly about their faces and the piles of excrement that had begun to build up beneath them.

"Rufio, Clara!"

The two of them turned to see the neighbouring sculptor, Emrys, waving. They walked over to him and the short-haired, blonde girl who was his apprentice. "Good morning, Emrys!" Clara said, her voice much more friendly than it had been moments before.

Rufio felt a pang of jealously then which, of course, he knew to be ridiculous, but which he could not help. *Things were better between us when I was injured,* he thought to himself as Clara traded pleasantries with the sculptor.

"I see you are getting ready to move to the theatre itself," Emrys said. "Most exciting!"

Rufio shrugged, and Clara smiled.

"Are you nervous, Rufio?" Emrys asked.

"Of course I am!" Rufio admitted. "Who wouldn't be? Besides Felix, that is."

Emrys smiled, his grey and black beard stretching wide. "Felix Modestus is indeed a true artist. He seems to revel in performance."

"He does," Clara said. "Have you finished the two statues you were working on, the ones of the young man and the young woman?" She turned to Rufio. "I've never seen anything like them. It's almost as if they are alive." Clara smiled at the sculptor. "I just don't know how you do it."

Emrys inclined his head graciously. "We all have our talents. Mine almost pale in comparison to Carissa's." He smiled at his apprentice but she was slightly distracted. He turned back to Rufio and Clara. "I don't think you need to be nervous. Felix Modestus knows acting and if he believes in you both, that is for a reason."

"Yeah, a bad dream!"

Clara smacked Rufio playfully.

"I don't know much about the theatre," Emrys added, "but I do know about creating art. Whatever skills the Gods have graced us with, we are duty-bound to pursue them, to enrich the lives of others with our work. The most divine, long-lasting thing one can do is to create something beautiful and enjoyable for the world. I believe this applies to your theatrical performance too. Think of the thousands of people who will fill the theatre of Pompey on the day of your performance."

"I'd rather not think about that," Rufio muttered.

Emrys pressed on. "In a short span of time, you will have the ability...the opportunity...to make them laugh as one, united community. To share a unique experience that will never repeat itself in that exact way. Your performance will be a marker in time for all of them, for they will go away with the goodwill and feelings which you gave to them." Emrys shook his head. "It is amazing to me. My statues will look the same always to the people who behold them daily, for they will not change, but then your performance will be different every time. Unless you are only performing the once."

"By Apollo, let's hope so!" Rufio said, smiling to himself as he watched Emrys' apprentice kneel down to pet Peli.

Clara smiled sadly at Emrys. "Rufio has always been doubtful of his skills, though I know he is a wondrously-natural performer."

"A clown, perhaps," Rufio said, crossing his arms.

"You should not belittle yourself, Rufio. I've watched you both rehearse from the warehouse door, and though you may not be professional actors in the sense that Felix's company is, I see real feeling in what you are doing on that stage. That is your job, is it not? To make the audience feel?"

Rufio shrugged. "I suppose."

"Clara! Rufio!" Felix bellowed from inside the warehouse. "Time to get dressed for the procession!"

"We're coming!" Clara called back, and turned to Emrys and his apprentice. "Will you come to the performance?"

"We will certainly try," Emrys said. "May Apollo guide you in the days to come."

"Thank you," Clara said, reaching out to squeeze Emrys' hands before turning to Rufio. "Let's get ready." She went inside the warehouse leaving Rufio behind, silent for a moment.

"What is it, Rufio?" Emrys said, walking up to stand beside him as they watched Clara go.

"Oh, nothing. Just…" Rufio's words faded away as though he were standing in a gale.

Emrys smiled. "You know, Rufio. Life is so much more worth living if we open our hearts and tell the people we care for what they truly mean to us."

Rufio pursed his lips. "Sometimes things are better left in dreams, I think."

Emrys pat him on the back. "Go now. Your army is departing soon."

Without another word, Rufio walked away, and Emrys and his apprentice turned to go back to their own work and the final touches they were putting upon the statues.

CLARA STOOD IN HER CUBICULUM WITH BEATRICE AND ELECTRA who were both helping her into her costume as it was the first time she was putting it on since Beatrice had finished the alterations. Even in her late husband's home, she had never worn so rich a garment as that, nor so revealing. At first, she had shuddered at the sheer, pink tunica which she had slid over her head and body, for it did not leave much to the imagination. But then Electra and Beatrice wrapped the many-layered stola about her. It was violet with embroidered hearts of gold and of the very finest eastern materials that could be bought in Rome.

"The dominus certainly has spent a lot on the materials," Beatrice said as she finished adjusting the folds.

"Yes, he has!" Electra said as she took up a long crimson ribbon and handed it to Beatrice.

Clara dared a smile at Electra and was surprised when the other woman smiled back, for the Hellene's moods toward her had been as changeable as the seasons. But that smile told Clara that Electra was in full summer, and for that she was grateful. *She must love performing as much as Felix!*

It was true, in fact, for the entire company, for they all seemed to be excited and abuzz at the prospect of donning their costumes and appearing before the Roman populace.

Whilst Beatrice wrapped the crimson ribbon about her, from just beneath her breasts to just above her knees to highlight her slight figure, Clara turned around to face Electra. "You look beautiful in your stola."

"Yes. I do. I was not sure about the burnt orange colour with embroidered flowers, with the black tunica beneath, but Beatrice is a wonder, as ever, with her needles."

Beatrice looked up at Electra from where she was fastening the ribbon. "Thank you, Electra!"

Clara smiled at that, for the surprise upon Beatrice's face told that she had long wished for a kind word from the older, more glamorous woman.

"At first, I was angry to be so covered up," Electra continued, but I know that I am playing the jealous wife. All eyes will be upon the desirous lupa," she said, stepping back with Beatrice to look Clara over from head to foot. "The golden sandals go well."

"Yes," Beatrice agreed. "Now for the mantle." She turned to the bed and took up the crimson mantle laced with golden thread that caught the light at every angle, and which would be one of the main props for the performance. She placed it over Clara's shoulders.

"It covers you too much, I think. Felix will want the crowd to see you," Electra said.

"What if I drape it on the chair behind me on the wagon?" Clara suggested. "That way, they will see it."

"Yes," Electra agreed. "That will work."

"And Pollux can bash anyone who might try to take it from off the wagon!" Beatrice added.

"They wouldn't!" Clara gasped.

"These Romans are uncouth," Electra said. "Of course they will try. They will also try to touch your legs."

"What?" Clara was getting nervous now.

"If they do," Beatrice said, "just give them a kick in the face and smile at the crowd."

"And be sure when you wave to the people that you do so with the bangle visible. Gold catches everyone's attention."

"Rufio is going to hate this," she said to herself.

"Shall I help him get his costume on?" Beatrice said, an uncharacteristically cheeky smile on her face.

"No need, girl!" Electra laughed. "Felix is helping him, that is, unless *you* wish to, Clara Probita?"

Clara did not look at Electra when she said it, but merely shook her head. "No need," she said, and sadly at that.

"WHAT DO YOU THINK?" FELIX SAID TO RUFIO. "NICE, ISN'T it?" He stepped back to look at Rufio in his deep blue tunica bordered with a meander pattern in golden thread, and belted with a black cingulum. "Beatrice has done well."

"I've never worn a wool so soft," Rufio commented. He looked from himself to Felix and noticed that, though the tunicae were the same colour and pattern, Felix's was shorter than his own, that it stopped at the knees while his went all the way to his calves. "Why are they different lengths?"

"We are twins, but the audience needs to differentiate between us a little. That is why your cingulum and coin pouch are black, and mine are brown, the same as our sandals. The lengths are different because they suit us. I have nicer legs and should have a shorter tunica, while you look taller with a longer tunica."

Rufio looked himself over. He felt like an imposter in such finery, and was quiet then.

"What's wrong?" Felix asked.

Rufio shook his head. "I don't know if I can do this, Felix."

Felix lowered the bronze mirror he was holding up to check the makeup Beatrice had applied to accentuate his eyes for the parade. He sighed and sat on the bed beside Rufio. "Listen my friend… No…my *brother*. For that is what you are to me, Rufio. You have always been so. And now, we are going to play brothers upon the stage, as we almost did before. There are no hard feelings now, all right? You are here, now, with me and with Clara. And we're going to do this. The Gods themselves have asked it of us!"

"That doesn't help my nerves."

Felix smiled. "I know. I like to tease you. But I'm being serious. You can do this. You know this play back to front. And I've seen you rehearse out there!" He pointed to the cubiculum door. "You are as good as you have ever been. You know your lines, and you make everyone laugh. The company respects you, Rufio. Sure, you've had some embarrassing moments, but we all have. That's part of the thrill of this profession. The ups and downs, the triumphs and the failures." Felix stood up and straightened his tunica. He then reached out for Rufio's hand and pulled him to his feet. "Let's go, and show the people of Rome what magnificence awaits them."

Rufio could not help but smile. "All right. For you, my brother."

"For us!" Felix corrected. He then threw open the cubiculum door and strode out with Rufio. "The Menaechmi are ready!"

WHEN THEY STEPPED OUTSIDE INTO THE BRIGHT, MIDDAY sunlight, Rufio's breath caught when he saw Clara as Erotium, already standing atop her wagon. It was as if he were staring at Helen herself, before she was paraded before the people of Troy.

Clara smiled down at him. "Are you ready?"

Rufio nodded. "You look beautiful," he said as he approached the second wagon where she stood, the scent of the fresh flowers decorating the wagon filling his nostrils.

"Remember!" Felix said as he strode along the length of

the wagons to address the company and make sure they were all in their assigned places. "You are not yourselves now! You are your characters! Play to the crowds! Smile or skulk, depending on who you are!" He turned to Rufio. "You search the crowds for your long lost brother."

"But you'll be two carts in front of me."

"Yes, but you don't know that, Rufio," Felix said, exasperated.

Rufio laughed, and Felix relaxed.

"Go on, then!" Felix said. "It's time. Messenio's already waiting for his master."

Rufio turned to look at the third wagon where Fausto was standing, waiting for him amid the props of travel trunks and two miniature ship's masts that stuck out of the wagon for both of them to cling to as they went. He smiled once more at Clara, wishing for a smile back, but she was already in character with Beatrice and Pollux, her maid and her cook. He climbed up into the wagon with Fausto who wore a slave's collar over his clean, pale blue tunica with a matching head band.

"Are you ready, Dominus?" the younger man asked.

"You don't need to call me that, Fausto," Rufio said.

"Who is this *Fausto*? My name is Messenio!"

"Fine then. Have it your way." Rufio looked down and saw Peli watching him intently, tail wagging, tongue lolling. "Are you coming?" He waved to the dog and immediately Peli charged to the wagon and leapt onto the bench, startling the hired driver, and then clambered over the wall into the bed behind to sit by Rufio. "Good boy."

Peli barked.

"I don't like dogs!" the driver said. "Keep him away from me, you hear?"

"Don't worry, good man! He's very well-behaved!"

"But-" Messenio began to protest.

"Shhh!" Menaechmus Sosicles put up a hand.

Messenio smiled and nodded, winking at his master.

Rufio looked down at Peli and put the flat of his hand out, indicating that his name was written upon his palm, just for him if he did misbehave.

Peli barked once and laid his paw upon Rufio's leg.

At the front of the wagons, Felix gave some final instructions to the main cattle driver as to the route they would be taking, then he climbed up into the cart beside Electra. He turned to address everyone.

"Etrurian Players! Forward with grace, music, and song! Begin!"

The crack of a loud whip ruptured the air and the great ox at the front bellowed and heaved at the first wagon, its painted horns glinting in the sunlight, swaying side to side.

The draft horses of the wagons pulled then, and the procession moved forward in concert.

It was silent for a moment, but then, Damon's flute exploded all around them in a playful reel as he danced and bobbed about the wagons. Beatrice's tambourine shivered and shook, and the sistra and drums of the others roused the ear as their voices rose up like the chatter of a crowd at first, but then settled into a melodic song that might have been sung upon the deck of a fast-moving ship in summer.

The procession turned slowly to roll along the length of the Circus Maximus and there, for the first time, the crowds of Rome looked in their direction, at carts that rolled through the city streets when none were allowed, at people on splendid display and richly adorned, waving to them, singing and smiling.

"The Etrurian Players have come to town!" Felix roared from the lead wagon where he and Electra stood like Jupiter and Juno looking down on gobsmacked mortals. "Come and witness the pageantry and hilarity of the greatest production to ever grace the theatre of Pompey!" Menaechmus of Epidamnus shouted, his arms wide.

A great crowd gathered around to walk with the moving wagons, many a man and boy casting admiring looks up at Erotium in the second wagon, who waved and smiled, and teased, her golden bangle glinting in the sun, her rich mantle drawing the eyes behind her.

One rough-looking citizen tried reaching up to grab the mantle, but Cylindrus was prepared and beat him down with great efficiency so that the man fell to the cobbles, gripping his face while his fellows howled at his failure.

Another young scamp reached out to touch Erotium's leg, but she was quicker than he, and her leg snapped out to plant a foot flat upon his nose, sending him back into the crowd, thoroughly beaten back by the beautiful lupa.

In the third wagon, Menaechmus Sosicles held his hand to his brow, searching the crowds for his lost brother as he clung to the ship's mast, and all the while, his loyal servant, Messenio, kept an eye upon his dangling money purse which the pickpockets of Rome eyed greedily.

In the fourth wagon, the medicus held aloft the serpents that were a part of the tools of his trade. With one extended from each hand, the medicus seemed to reach out to heal the crowd, his wise old face kind and caring, clearly the opposite of the grumpy father who sat beside him, shaking hands resting upon his solid cane.

Behind the medicus and the father, the slave Peniculus, that hated parasite of the great Plautus' play, scurried back and forth upon his wagon, worrying, plotting, shouting obscenities, and making rude gestures. In return, the crowd tossed rotten fruit and vegetables back at him, some of which he caught and threw back in retaliation. They booed and hissed at him, and all the while, Peniculus knew that he was not with his master and mistress for the very reason that his cart now filled with rubbish and filth.

The final wagons, adorned with flowers and tripods of burning incense followed, carrying the larger set pieces and crates where Damon climbed up to pipe his gleeful tunes before leaping back onto the street and dancing about as the procession carried on, turning onto the via Appia and moving past the Colosseum and then turning again and going past the fora of Vespasian, Augustus, and of Trajan where enormous crowds gathered and pressed in upon the street to see the vision that passed.

Children clapped and laughed upon the shoulders of their parents, flyers for the performance were tossed onto the hot wind. Women gazed upon the handsome Menaechmus in the lead wagon, obviously willing to set his dark and beautiful wife aside for a bit of pleasure. Men sighed as Erotium waved her slender arms and opened her hands to release soft flower petals which blew onto their faces like kisses. The crowds jostled as well for the occasional coin of largesse tossed high into the air by the second Menaechmus in the third wagon.

The parade of players moved on through the streets at a steady pace, their appearance the talk of the city from the heights of the Palatine and Esquiline hills to the tenement slums of the Suburra. It was as if the emperor's triumph had paled in comparison and faded from memory. Such a magnificent sight had not moved through Rome, nor been as pleasing to the people, since the time of Cleopatra's grand entrance into the city so long ago.

By the time, they reached the eastern end of the Circus Flaminius, exhaustion began to set in, especially for Rufio and Clara who were not so used to the prolonged exertions of character which the rest of the players were accustomed to.

Crowds of onlookers still harried them, and cheered for them, attempted to touch and rob them only to be beaten back. And so, it was with great relief that the procession turned into an enormous arched gate set in an impossibly long, arcaded wall, and came to a stop before a row of ancient temples.

They were free of the crowds at last. They were exhausted, as though after a night of pleasure, and had left the people titillated and wanting more.

"Well done, everyone!" Felix cried out as he jumped from off the first wagon, helping Electra down after him. "That went much better than I expected!" He clapped loudly and the group cheered.

"Where are we?" Rufio asked as he climbed down after Peli, his legs stiff and shaky. He looked at the row of four temples and rubbed his eyes, smearing the makeup which he had applied, the same as the others. It felt strange not to have the roar of the crowd in his ears, eerie even.

"We're at the back of the quadriporticus of the great theatre," Felix said as he looked around. "This is the easiest way to get all of the wagons into the complex to unload, another gift from our patrician patron."

"These temples are old," Electra commented, making a sign of respect as she looked upon them while Felix spoke with the cattle driver.

"Everybody gather here, off the wagons so that the drivers can take them in. We will walk from here."

The company moved to stand before the temples while the wagon train turned slowly and sharply down a smaller path between the temples to disappear beneath the arcades behind them and into the theatre complex.

"They will be waiting for us." Felix looked up at the temples and closed his eyes. "Gather round," he said again.

It was quiet before the four temples, each of them different, each of them dedicated to a different deity. The first was dedicated to Juturna, a water goddess, and the second, a round tholos, to the Aedes Fortuna Huiusce Diei, the luck of the day. Just beyond the open doors of the temple, they could spy the colossal marble statue of the goddess, her dress all glinting bronze in the fire-lit interior.

Felix strolled silent before them with Electra and the others following. Rufio and Clara brought up the rear. "Ask the Gods for their help in our endeavour, for we can use all the divine aid we can get," Felix said.

The third temple, more ancient than the others, had a short staircase leading to a black and white mosaic floor below an inscription above the lintel that spelled the goddess' name.

"Who is 'Feronia'?" Fausto asked.

Rufio looked up. "She is a goddess of fertility. Some of the folk in Etruria still worship her in the woods." He thought of home then, the calm of the forests, fields and streams, and would have fallen into a melancholic state again if Clara had not stood beside him.

"I remember seeing her shrine in the woods," she said.

Rufio nodded.

"The last temple," Felix said, pointing to the largest of the four, "is dedicated to the Lares." He turned to everyone. "We will need all of their help here, so I want no disrespect to any of them. We are here because the Gods told us to be, and because we are professionals. Does everyone understand?"

Clara and Rufio looked at each other, both surprised by Felix's sudden, serious bent of mind.

"Now," he said, more excitedly. "Follow me!" Felix walked more quickly then, down the path the wagons had taken between the temples and beneath the arcade.

"Cacare!" Silas shouted, his voice echoing beneath the covered walkway.

"Quiet, Silas!" Felix bellowed.

Rufio chuckled when he saw Silas extricating his foot from a large pile of excrement left behind by one of the oxen or horses.

"How about I make you eat this?" Silas growled at Rufio.

Rufio ignored him and walked with Clara after the others, leaving Silas rubbing his foot upon the pebbled pathway.

"My Gods!" Clara said the moment they cleared the arcade and came into the open.

The interior of the quadriporticus spread out before the company, an elaborate, sprawling field of gardens and tinkling fountains where birds sang and flitted among the boughs of shivering trees. Peacocks squawked where they roamed at will, their tails fanned out to display their greatness to the newcomers.

"Incredible, isn't it?" Felix said. "It's quiet now, but during a performance, patrons roam back here to eat and drink and escape the sun or rain. They also talk about the plays they see!"

"I never thought to return here, Felix," Julius said. "Thank you for making this happen."

Felix put his hand on the older man's shoulder and smiled. "We all made this happen. And now, we shall perform before the spirits of those who have gone before us." Felix pointed to the statues which stood about the vast gardens.

"Who are they?" Castor asked.

"They look quite splendid, don't they?" Beatrice added.

"They are our great predecessors," Felix said, "poets and playwrights all, and the greatest actors to grace the world's stage. They are all here in the Porticus Pompei, among the statues and paintings…"

"There's Accius," Clara pointed at one particularly noble-looking statue.

"And here is Andronicus!" Rufio added, indicating the statue nearest to himself.

"And Naevius!" Electra said.

"Yes! They are all here." Felix looked up at the statue of Clodius Aesopus, the great tragedian. "They say he was brought out of retirement for the first performance here."

"What did they perform?" Clara asked. "Do you know?"

Felix put his arm around her and squeezed. "I believe it was *Clytemnestra*, and *Equos Troianus*. Two magnificent plays."

"And both tragedies," Electra added. "Is that a sign, Felix?"

"No," he answered her curtly and removed his arm from Clara. "They are both excellent plays."

"I would have been much better off playing Clytemnestra than the jealous wife!"

"But you are such a good one!" Felix bit back, shaking his head.

Rufio walked a bit farther and stopped where two statues flanked the pathway, one across from the other, as though they were in conversation. He looked from one to the other and smiled sadly.

"Rufio," Clara said, her voice softer now.

He turned to her. "Are you all right after the parade? You got a lot of attention."

She smirked. "Didn't I? Yes, I'm fine. I gave a few good wallops to some."

"I saw!" he laughed, but then turned back to the statues, trying to ignore Fausto who was screeching on the other side of the garden where a peacock was chasing him about. "Plautus and Terence…they always made me laugh."

"They still do, don't they?"

"Perhaps, when this is over. For now, I'm too nervous to laugh."

"Except when Silas steps in shit," Clara added.

Rufio raised his red eyebrows. "Except for that!" He looked to see Silas trying to clean his sandals in one of the shrubs nearby.

Felix stepped up to join them and turned to the looming

statue of Plautus with his finely trimmed beard with a hint of a cheeky, knowing smile beneath. "There he is," Felix said to Rufio and Clara. "Our shared father."

"He would be proud of what you have put together, I'm sure." Clara grasped Felix's hand and squeezed.

Rufio looked askance at them, and back up at Plautus before kicking at the pebbles.

It was then that Peli roamed up from behind the statue and urinated upon the pedestal.

"Peli, no!" Beatrice cried out.

"Ha, ha!" Felix laughed. "It's all right, Beatrice. If anything, our theatrical father would find that amusing! Everyone!" he called to the group. "Pay homage and make offerings - other than urine - to the master whenever you pass him. Ask his daemon for guidance and inspiration that we may bring his play to life like never before!"

Silas hobbled up, his face red, his eyes bulging with frustration after having dragged his dirty foot the length of the gardens.

Peli growled at him, and Rufio stifled another laugh.

"Can we please go into the theatre now?" Silas shouted.

Everyone turned to him, and he looked up.

"The wagons are waiting for us!"

"You're right, Silas," Felix admitted. "Let's go and unload. We don't want the drivers breaking any of our creations.

The company moved on through the gardens toward the spot where the wagons were stopped in the shadow of the soaring stage house at the other end. All heads turned upward to look with wonder upon the edifice before them.

Rufio and Clara slowed. "It's enormous," Clara said, her voice almost a whisper.

Rufio gulped and looked with her while the rest of the company followed Felix and began to unload the wagons, small as ants carrying leaves into their mound and back. "I've always known about it, but…when we were here, we never saw it up close.

"No, we didn't," Clara confirmed, still standing there looking up while the hot breeze played with the hem of her stola.

The back of the stage house of the theatre built by Gnaeus Pompeius Magnus rose up before them like the face of a mountain, a solid wall at the end of the gardens decorated with columns and arches to which the roofed colonnades of the quadriporticus connected on either side.

Rufio and Clara walked slowly forward, intent on helping the others, but their attention was drawn upward to the tiled rooftop.

"I can't wait to see inside," Clara said as they walked into the shadow cast by the structure.

"Careful of your costumes!" Felix shouted to everyone. "If you have to, take them off for unloading."

Rufio looked down and saw that Beatrice and Julius had already done so, with the others following suit before getting back to work. He picked up a crate with rope handles, hoisted it off one of the wagons, and followed the others beyond the columns and into the stage house.

It was dark within, apart from a few torches, and the other players' voices echoed strangely in the dark. There was a wide open area in the centre of the interior where many of the crates and props had already been placed, and to either side, stairs rose up into the dim dark to reach the second and third levels.

Rufio looked down to see Peli at his side for a moment before darting off into a corner to chase an unfortunate rat which squealed and made a hasty retreat.

The floors all about him were of worn marble, and he wondered how many of the great actors and playwrights he admired had been in that place. Then, directly ahead, he caught a glimpse of light through one of three impossibly tall doorways, and knew that the stage and auditorium lay beyond it.

Rufio shook his head. *Not yet,* he told himself before turning and going to get another load.

The company worked quickly and carefully, all the while accompanied by Felix's voice which resonated off of the high-ceilinged hall of the stage house. Things were organized by stations with all of the costumes being set aside to the left, and set pieces and props to the right. The makeup tables, which they had also brought with them, were set down near the costumes.

After some time, the wagons were finally emptied and the scene behind-the-scenes was set like a more spacious and luxurious version of that in which they had been working for weeks.

Felix hopped up on the large flat area of the stage floor that was behind the scaena, where more stairs went up to the other levels, and turned to look down at everyone. "It's been a very successful day," he said, clapping loudly when they did not hear him at first.

"Quiet!" Silas shouted, and the sound of excited talk burned out. He looked up at Felix, pleased, but only received a frown.

"As I was saying," Felix continued, ignoring the screaming of the cattle driver outside as he and his fellows whipped their beasts into action to get them out of the gardens. "You did very well today, all of you! Rome now knows that there is something special coming. The people are excited!"

"Yes!" Pollux shouted.

"I'm glad you agree, Pollux," Felix said, one eyebrow raised. "Now, we will be spending our days here, but we will sleep back at the warehouse."

"Why don't we just stay here the whole time?" Fausto asked, brushing his hair out of his face.

"Because this place is a shrine to our artistic endeavour, Fausto," Felix said. "It is sacred, and we don't want to sully it with whatever activities you get up to in the dark of night."

Fausto blushed.

Felix continued. "We will finish setting everything up today, and then the rest of the week we will be rehearsing in full, right up until the performance itself. The Ludi Apollinares start in the next couple of days, so we have little time now."

"What do you want us to do then, Dominus?" Silas asked. "What's next?"

"Well, before we set our stage, we should probably see the theatre, no?" Felix smiled. "Come, everyone. It's time."

Clara looked around at the players and realized that they had all been silently waiting for the same moment - the chance to walk the space in which they would pour out their hearts and souls for that singular performance before the people of Rome, the performance that would make or break their company.

Felix helped Electra up the stairs and then released her hand to hold it out to Clara and Rufio. "Come, my friends. Let's see what the goddess has in store for us."

Everyone filed up the two staircases that led onto the stage and stood before the three enormous doorways that led out of the scaena frons and onto the main stage.

"These doorways are for giants!" Fausto exclaimed, straining his neck to look up.

"Fausto," Felix began, "while we are performing here, we shall be giants."

"Except for you, piglet," Silas hissed in Fausto's ear as he pushed past him and went through the left doorway.

The rest of the company followed Felix through the central door and, together, they stepped onto the planks of the stage floor.

Their gasps carried to the uppermost seats of the marble auditorium, each person turning on the spot to look about.

If the back of the stage house was solid and imposing, the scaena frons, which faced the auditorium, was an inspiration. Above the smooth, polished wood of the stage's floorboards there rose a facade as beautiful as any temple to honour the Gods. About the three titanic doorways rose two levels of finely polished columns of gold and crimson marble from Aegyptus and Africa Proconsularis. Between the columns, statues of the Gods, the Muses, and the great generals of Rome's past stood sentry over the stage, staring down on the players and the seating for the would-be audience.

It was obvious that whomever sat in that auditorium, they would not be alone. There were silent witnesses to everything that happened in that place.

Rufio felt his spine tingle.

"It's more like a temple than a theatre," Clara said as she walked up to Felix and Electra.

Felix tore his gaze from the statue of Apollo, to whom he had been silently praying, and smiled. "It *is* a temple!" he said, before turning and pointing to the central structure at the back of the auditorium seats, hovering like a gilded Olympus above everything.

"What is that, Dominus?" Beatrice asked.

"That, my girl, is the temple of Venus. Pompey the Great, who built this magnificent theatre, dedicated all of this to her."

Floating above the theatre, the temple was faced with six columns of golden, veined marble, which supported a pediment that displayed a golden statue of Venus Victrix. It was so beautiful and imposing that it was as if the entire place were a temple and not a theatre.

"So the goddess will be watching us the whole time?" Beatrice said softly.

"All of the Gods will!" Felix said, pointing up at the statues above the stage. "Have a good look around everyone, and then we'll get to work putting the sets in place."

The company spread out as each of them strolled about the massive stage, imagining his or her role in the greater scheme of the production they would be bringing to the people of Rome. It was strangely quiet for a few moments as each of them contemplated the time to come. Of course, they had tread the boards of many a stage across the empire, but somehow, this felt different.

"I feel a little insignificant in this space," Rufio finally said. He looked to Felix who stood with Clara and Electra. "It's too big!"

"Too big?" Felix laughed. "Well, it certainly is larger than the steps of the temple of Antoninus and Faustina." Felix turned a full circle to take it all in. "It's perfect!" He strode over to Rufio and grasped him by the shoulders. "You must claim your space upon the stage, Rufio, just as you must do in life!"

"You a philosopher now?" Rufio joked, unable to keep from smiling.

Felix shook his head. "No. Just a player making his way through the world and trying to learn what I can along the way." Felix slapped him playfully across the cheek, stepped to the edge of the stage, and turned to look at the scaena to envision where things would go.

Rufio knew Felix was right, for he had always filled the space around him with his presence. He had no idea how Felix did it, but it was evident that he was successful at it. Whenever he entered a room, all eyes turned toward him. Whenever there was a conversation, Felix was at the centre of it. Rufio shook his head and silently chided himself. He felt like he was more one to shrink in on himself than claim any space beyond a couple of inches.

"You all right, Rufio?" Clara asked.

Rufio turned to her, unable to hide the quizzical look upon

his face. It felt good to hear her voice warm toward him again. When he had been sick abed, he knew that something had happened between them, he had felt it, heard her words reach him through the fog of his illness. But, ever since the day he had awoken and gone out alone, she had been more distant. He could not decipher why, and the unknowing of it had, he only just realized, trampled his enthusiasm.

"Rufio?" Clara said again.

He smiled sadly. "I'm sorry. It's just all a bit much."

"It is, isn't it?" she agreed, looking around at the company moving about the stage, arranging and re-arranging set pieces. They positioned crates for the harbour, a fountain for the street of Epidamnus, and arranged the enormous hangings that would cover the three doors of the main houses.

"How about you two go sit in the auditorium and rest a little," Felix said. "Clara, you can let me know how things are looking from there. You've always had a good eye for set-up."

"All right," Clara answered.

She and Rufio made their way to the right side of the stage and went down the stairs that led onto the semi-circle of the orchestra which was made up of a polished marble floor of differing geometric shapes and colours. They then made their way to the central section of the cavia, the seating for the auditorium, and settled themselves upon the cool marble seating to look upon the scaena frons in its entirety.

"It's magnificent," Rufio could not help saying.

"It certainly is," Clara agreed as she motioned for Felix and the others to shift the fountain a little to the right. "That's good!"

Felix turned to them. "It's a wonder, no?" he called out, his voice perfectly clear.

"Yes!" Clara answered.

Felix turned to the others. "We'll secure the fountain pieces later," he said as they wiped sweat from their brows.

"I can hear him breathing!" Rufio added, shaking his head. "We're a long way from our play stage in the forest in Etruria."

Clara turned to him. "For me, that was the greatest stage."

"Castor and Pollux are going to test the aulaeum to make sure it hides the fountain sufficiently. Let me know!" Felix said.

Castor and Pollux disappeared into each of the wings and descended beneath the pulpitum of the stage where they each grasped a large crank.

"Now, lads!" Felix called out.

After a moment, a rich red curtain began to rise up out of a pit in the floor just in front of the stage. It rose higher and higher until it reached its extent and locked in place.

"So?" Felix asked. "Is everything hidden?"

"Yes!" Clara answered. "Even the massive doors from where we're sitting."

"At the top, the spectators will see a bit of the fountain's top, and the doorways, but not very much!" Rufio called back.

"You don't need to shout, Rufio!" Felix said. "I can hear everything!" Felix turned to tell Castor and Pollux to retract the aulaeum again.

"Bugger yourself," Rufio joked.

"I heard that!" Felix said.

At that moment, Peli's tail was visible as he trotted around the auditorium seats toward Rufio and Clara. He arrived and plopped himself down beside them.

"Where've you been then?" Rufio asked the dog. "Chasing rats?"

Peli barked, and Felix covered his ears.

Soon the aulaeum was back in its pit in the floor and ladders were leaned against the scaena frons in order to hook up the thick hangings that indicated the house of Erotium, the house of Menaechmus of Epidamnus and his jealous wife, and the tavern near the port where Menaechmus Sosicles and

Messenio would be staying. The setting was now transformed, and made their own.

Felix disappeared back into the stage house to give some more direction to the others, leaving Rufio and Clara sitting alone in the cavia with Peli dozing at their feet.

"Have you been angry with me lately?" Rufio asked Clara without any preamble.

"What? No!" Clara said, a little embarrassed. "Wh...why would you think that?"

"I don't know. You've been a little distant since...since I got better."

Clara thought about it for a moment and knew that she had been colder with him. She had wanted to ask him about the lupa he had visited, but knew it was none of her business. She had only been greatly disappointed that he had gone, especially after the words they had exchanged upon his sick bed.

"I'm not angry with you, Rufio. I...I'm just preoccupied with all that is going on." *I can't say anything about it. Not now!* she told herself. "I'm of two minds with this. On the one hand, I'm so excited to finally get to do this with you and Felix, to perform before the people of Rome. On the other hand, the audience we will be performing for is much bigger than ever I would have dreamed or wanted. The Ludi Apollinares? Unbelievable!"

"Not long now," Rufio said, feeling his heart bounce around like an overturned cart of sanguine oranges.

They looked around and both imagined the seats of the cavia full, the front rows filled with senators and maybe even members of the imperial family.

Clara shook her head. "And look at me? Dressed like a... like a lupa? It's a bit ridiculous, don't you think?"

"I think you look beautiful, Clara," Rufio said, unable to stop himself from staring at her. "The audience won't be able to take their eyes off of you."

She smiled, grasped his hand, and sighed. "I haven't been this happy in a long time."

"Me neither." He turned to look up at the temple of Venus above them where Electra was just coming out of it, smoke from the incense she had just offered to the goddess wafting out behind her as she descended the steep stairs of the cavia toward the orchestra.

"Everything all right, Electra?" Clara asked.

"I thought you were helping set up backstage," Rufio said.

"Don't be ridiculous, farmer boy!" she chuckled. "I don't do such things!" She worked her jaw and gazed toward the stage, her eyes searching for Felix. "That man!" she said, carrying on her way to go to him.

"What's with her?" Rufio asked. "So grouchy."

"Well, wouldn't you be?"

"What do you mean?"

"She's good at what she does. She's a better actress than I've ever been, and yet, Felix treats her like a concubine. He's quite harsh with her, I've noticed. Once you get to know her, she's not so bad."

"But she *is* his concubine!"

Electra heard Rufio and turned to scowl at him from the stage.

He blanched, and whispered. "Felix is quite open about that."

"Yes, he is," Clara whispered back. "But maybe she would like more than that. Maybe she deserves more?" Clara looked to the temple of Venus where Electra had just come from, the sweet scent of the offerings tickling her nose even there.

"There you are!" Electra shouted, and the sound crashed onto the seating. "Felix, I was waiting for you in the temple!"

"I'm busy, woman!" Felix shouted back from the other side of the stage where he and the other men were setting up what appeared to be the prow of a ship.

Rufio stifled a laugh. "I guess art imitates life!"

Clara did not laugh though.

They watched Felix and Electra go off backstage toward the gardens, while the others carried on with their work.

Rufio glanced at Clara and he realized that no matter how nervous he was for the performance, he was in fact the happiest he had been in years. He looked up at the temple again, as if he felt the goddess urging him to speak to Clara, to tell her that he now knew she was his world, or that he wanted her to be. *Go on, Rufio! Tell her!* "Clara, I-"

Before Rufio could speak, a shadow crossed Clara's face and he followed her gaze to the far right of the stage where, behind one row of seats, Silas was approaching Fausto, the latter pushing him away only to be slapped across the face.

"What in Hades is he doing?" Rufio said, as Silas leaned in against Fausto, his hands pressed upon the younger man's shoulders. Rufio stood up. "Silas? What are you doing?"

The two of them pulled apart and looked up awkwardly at Rufio and Clara.

"Fausto, you all right?" Clara asked, but Fausto only pushed back his hair and disappeared backstage, leaving Silas standing there alone, staring daggers up at them. "I don't like him," Clara said to Rufio. "He tried to tell me that you were visiting with a lupa the day you felt better. Trying to get a rise out of me, I'm sure."

What she said just clicked in Rufio's mind, like a harsh master's snap when calling his servant. "That...that's preposterous." It was all he could say.

"I knew it," Clara said. "He just likes to start trouble that one."

"He...he does that. Yes."

"Should we tell Felix what we just saw?"

"I don't know. They've all been a company together for a long time. It must be part of the dynamic. Felix isn't stupid.

I'm sure he knows what goes on. Let's not stir things up before the performance."

"I suppose," Clara said, the uncertainty in her voice unmistakable.

"Come." Rufio stood and held out his hand to her. "Let's go back onto the pulpitum and see what it feels like with all the set pieces there."

Peli only woke as they stepped onto the orchestra floor, and followed after them, his claws tickling the marble flooring as he went.

It was only a few days until the start of the Ludi Apollinares, and it seemed the company was being robbed of hours more quickly than was normal. The Etrurian Players battled against dwindling time, rehearsing for the bulk of each day, quitting the great theatre but to eat at the taberna and sleep at the warehouse, before returning in the drowsy hours of pink dawn.

The play was rehearsed from start to finish in an ongoing cycle of hilarity and misunderstanding on a daily basis, with Felix tweaking an action here, and a musical note there. The set pieces found their precise spots, and the hanging doorways of the houses of Erotium, of Menaechmus of Epidamnus and his jealous wife, and of the taberna and inn of the wandering Menaechmus Sosicles and his Messenio all fluttered upon their hinges which jutted from the rich marble of the scaena frons.

With but little time for Felix to perfect the staging and ensure that everyone knew their positions and movements with absolute precision, Rome was preparing to honour Apollo with fervour.

Clara sat with Felix and Electra in the auditorium of the theatre for the first scene with Menaechmus Sosicles and Messenio at the beginning of the second act. They had seen it many a time, but like every other scene, Felix wanted them to know every movement or expression, every word and syllable, by rote. The murmur of the other players behind the scaena replicated the busy hubbub of the port, complete with the sound of gulls overhead which Damon expertly replicated upon a reed pipe.

From the right of the stage, the mock prow of a ship with a glaring eye pushed into view then, and upon it stood both Menaechmus Sosicles and his servant, Messenio.

Clara smiled as she watched Rufio standing there, searching the port of Epidamnus with Fausto beside him. She knew he had been terrified when they first arrived at the theatre of Pompey, as she had been, but as the rehearsals went on, and they all made the space their own, it became less a thing of terror and more something to be relished. She looked aside at Felix for some indication that he saw the same transformation in Rufio, but he was too taken up with perfecting every nuance to acknowledge her, and so she settled back to listen with the summer sun upon her face.

"There's no greater pleasure to voyagers, in my notion, Messenio, than at the moment when from sea they espy the land afar," Menaechmus Sosicles said as he gazed out from the prow of the ship upon their next port of call.

Messenio stepped up beside his master, shaking his head in dismay. "There is a greater, I'll say it without subterfuge, - if on your arrival you see the land that is your own. But, prithee, why are we now come to Epidamnus? Why, like the sea, are we going round all the islands?"

"To seek for my own twin-brother born?"

"Why, what end is there to be of searching for him? This is the sixth year that we've devoted our attention to this business. We have been already carried round the Istrians, the Hispanians, the Massilians, the Illyrians, all the Upper Adriatic Sea, and foreign Greece, and all the shores of Italy, wherever the sea reaches them. If you had been searching for a needle, I do believe you would, long ere this, have found the needle, if it were visible. Among the living are we seeking a person that's dead; for long ago, should we have found him if he had been alive."

Menaechmus Sosicles turned to his servant. "For that reason I am looking for a person to give me the information for certain, who can say that he knows that he really is dead; after that I shall never take any trouble in seeking further. But otherwise I shall never, while I'm alive, desist; I know how dear he is to my heart."

"Now…louder," Felix whispered to himself as he watched, and on perfect time, the sounds of the crowds in the port grew louder as the ship approached its berth. "Excellent!"

While Messenio worried over their expenses and warned his master of the perils of dealing with the people of Epidamnus, the ship came to a stop and Menaechmus Sosicles turned to him with his hand out and a reassuring smile.

"I'll guard against that. Just give me the purse this way."

"What do you want with it?" Messenio asked.

"I'm apprehensive then about yourself, from your expressions."

"Why are you apprehensive?"

"Lest you should cause me some damnable mishap in Epidamnus. You are a great admirer of the women, Messenio, and I'm a passionate man, of unmanageable disposition…"

Clara smiled to herself as she always did at that part of the scene, for she saw not Menaechmus Sosicles speaking, but rather Rufio who was truly finding his rhythm at that point. She realized that Erotium would soon be joining, and made her escape from the auditorium to go backstage.

Messenio gave him the purse most reluctantly. "Take and keep it; with all my heart you may do so."

Then, as the two set foot on land, adding a little comedic

weaving as their sea legs settled, Cylindrus the cook wandered on with a basket of provisions for the aforementioned breakfast Erotium had ordered.

"I've created well, and to my mind. I'll set a good breakfast before the breakfasters. But see, I perceive Menaechmus...."

The scene wore on, building apprehension upon misunderstanding until Erotium emerged from her doorway on the far side of the stage, she speaking to her servants within.

"Leave the door ajar thus; begone. I don't want it shut: prepare, attend, and provide within; what is requisite, let it be done. Lay down the couches, burn the perfumes; neatness, that is the charm for the minds of lovers..."

Erotium looked about for her cook, and spied him near the port where he was speaking with someone she recognized to be her Menaechmus, unaware he was the wrong Menaechmus.

It was Rufio's favourite scene of the entire play. His world shrank in that moment, for he and Clara exchanged words as if the dialogue itself were an old, familiar friend, though their characters were less acquainted.

While Menaechmus Sosicles admired Erotium's beauty where she stood, so alluring, so lovely, Messenio made his comic attempt to warn him off.

"Didn't I say that these things are in the habit of occurring here? The leaves are falling now; in comparison with this, if we shall be here for three days, the trees will be tumbling upon you. For to such a degree are all these courtesans wheedlers out of one's money..."

The scene wore on tantalizingly toward the end with Erotium and Menaechmus Sosicles playing with words and innuendo back and forth, and Messenio attempting, to no avail, to extricate his master until, put in his place, he watched Menaechmus Sosicles disappear into the courtesan's domus. He turned to the audience, his hair disheveled, his frustration written clean upon his face.

"I'm undone. Are you going away then? He is certainly ruined; the piratical craft is now leading the board straight to destruction. But I'm an unreasonable fellow to wish to rule my master; he bought me to obey his orders, not to be his commander. Follow me, that, as I'm ordered, I may come in good time to meet my master."

Messenio walked off in the direction of the tavern and disappeared inside.

When the music and singing of the chorus came to an end, marking the act's finish, Felix and Electra stood and clapped loudly.

"Well done!" Felix yelled, and his praise wound about the theatre. "Very well done!"

Rufio and Clara emerged from Erotium's domus, all smiles and clasped hands, but they looked to the far left where Fausto emerged from the confines of the tavern, his face red as his fellow players emerged, clapping and calling his name.

"Bravo, Fausto!" Felix shouted, his praise further reinforced by the others.

"Rome will witness the rise of a new star!" Felix said, and Fausto, unable to contain himself, did a back flip on the spot.

It was then that Silas walked onto the stage from where he had been standing behind the ship's prow, to speak to Fausto as he passed.

"He is only using you like he uses the rest of us," he hissed at Fausto. "Your performance was average at best. Don't expect the adulation to last."

Fausto's smile faded, but as Clara and Rufio moved in to congratulate him, it returned, and the sun chased the errant cloud away into the wings.

XV

LET THE GAMES BEGIN

The Etrurian Players were in their element in those days leading up to the start of the games, working hard at every aspect of the performance and production, each doing his or her part with utmost professionalism and a will to help their leader succeed in his grand endeavour. The Gods had, after all, demanded that Felix Modestus do this thing, that he dazzle Rome itself.

If they succeeded - something of which they became more and more certain with each passing rehearsal - they would be the most sought-after company in the whole of the empire. They lifted each other up by their performances, and by their mutual encouragement, brothers and sisters in costume and in song, with Plautus as their emperor, and Felix as their general.

As the hours and days wore on, it also became apparent to the rest of the seasoned company that it was no mistake to have brought on Clara Probita and Rufio Pagano. They had shown their metal and knowledge of the play such that they even contributed ideas which Felix had not thought of.

As the veteran among them, Julius told the others that this was no doubt due to the fact that their dominus and friends emerged from the same forest grove where they used to play-act as children, and that this gave birth to the love of theatre which they shared, though expressed in different ways.

As such, the company's perception of the triad of friends became something more religious than parochial. The Gods had intended things to align exactly so. The company believed that, and they revelled in the feeling.

Except for Silas.

For so long, Silas had been Felix Modestus' right hand, and though he had enjoyed the literal and figurative nature of that relationship for several years, he could now feel it all slipping painfully away. All those years of bowing to his dominus, of grovelling, of being used, and of caring, had turned to ash in the palm of his hand, and it had all started with the arrival of the two strangers which Felix had invited into their company.

Silas was the shadow in their great comedy, and while the others blossomed and bloomed in preparation for Apollo's games, he shrivelled with anger and resentment.

I've given my life to this company, Silas told himself as he sat alone in the auditorium during the rehearsal for the fifth act. *I've kept his secrets and cooked his accounts expertly like a palace cook. And what thanks do I get? Shoved aside for amateurs…given the role of the hateful Peniculus!* "I guess that shows how much he thinks of me now," he muttered beneath his breath.

He watched Rufio and Electra upon the stage, and felt hate for both of them as they were joined by Castor who had always been an oaf to him, but now robbed him of Felix's adulation. The sight of them working together - and well! - enraged Silas. The production was indeed excellent, he knew. It was the best they had ever put on, the most richly-appointed. *If not for my dealings with that scum, Leno, on Felix's behalf, he never would have been able to fund this!*

The imminent success, which Silas could see coming, ground at his heart and mind. He could feel his loyalty dissipate with everything he saw in that theatre.

In the midst of it all, he had turned to Fausto for some sport. The lad was an easy target after all. But now, even that was proving difficult, for Felix's meddlesome friends were always calling for the boy when Silas tried to engage him.

I should have been Messenio! he kept telling himself, harping on about it to whatever dark gods might lend him an ear. He spat on the marble floor, and slinked away to roam the gardens behind the stage house.

FROM WITHIN THE MIND OF MENAECHMUS OF EPIDAMNUS, Felix Modestus watched the final scene's rehearsal unfold before and around him with awe - the appearance of his long-lost brother and his servant, the realization that they are brothers, and the great re-union of brother and brother that fully displayed the genius of Father Plautus. He spoke to Messenio - now freed by his brother - of auctioning off all of his belongings, including his slaves, and his wife.

And when Messenio finished the play off with his request for applause from the would-be audience filling the great theatre, there was a momentary pause, a silence in which Felix thought, *This is the best production we've ever put on!*

The company cheered themselves and applauded on and off the stage, patting Fausto on the back, singing and dancing.

Even Electra beamed a great smile that made Felix kiss her.

"There is absolutely no doubt that we're ready!" Felix announced, smiling when he looked upon them all, his gaze resting upon Rufio and Clara who stood in the midst of his players, smiling in a way he could not remember seeing since they were in the spring of their lives together.

The beaming pride that emanated from Julius and Fausto, Castor and Pollux, Beatrice, and even Damon, made Felix realize that he had been right to trust in the dream the goddess had sent him. He spied Silas leaning against the prow of the ship at the end of the stage and waved him over.

"Silas! Come join the celebrations!" Felix said.

"Peniculus!!!" Pollux roared, clapping Silas on the back.

"Well done, Silas!" Julius said as the younger man passed him by, only grunting at the veteran actor's praise.

Kissing Electra's hand, Felix released her and jumped up onto the edge of the completed prop fountain to address the company.

Everyone shushed as they gathered to look up at their leader.

Felix took in the sight of them, in costumes of embroidered and shivering silk, and glittering gold and silver thread. He smiled at the rosy hue upon each of their faces which, he now felt certain, would delight the audience more than any mask.

"We are doing something that has never been done before, my friends. When we perform this play for the more than twenty-thousand Romans who will be seated in the auditorium before us, we will be setting a new standard. Unmasked we may not please every one of them, and our musical interludes may not meet expectations, but… But! We will surprise and delight the majority of them, and their laughter and joy at the sight of what we are doing here will drown out any naysayers among them. We will thrill them, of that I have no doubt!"

Everyone cheered at that, Castor jostling Silas who stood with his arms crossed.

"I feel very proud of what we have accomplished," Felix added, bracing himself for a moment, willing himself not to get too emotional when he looked upon Rufio and Clara. "I'm extremely proud," he repeated, looking directly at his friends. He sniffed and clapped his hands. "Beatrice, I want you to have a final look at each player in costume to make sure there are no rips, missing jewels, or frayed borders. I want it all perfect for the performance."

"Yes, Dominus!" Beatrice replied with confidence. "It will be!"

"That's a girl!" Felix said. "Now, I have an errand to run in the city, but I want you all to see Beatrice one by one, and then remove your costumes and stow them carefully. No wrinkles!"

"What about your wrinkly ass?" Rufio called out to the laughter of the rest.

Felix scowled and turned his buttocks to everyone. "Does this look wrinkled, Sosicles?"

"Only when you scowl!" Rufio retorted.

"Then I shall go about with a smile upon my face!" Felix jumped off the fountain, and found himself in front of Silas. "Cheer up, Silas! All is well!"

"You'd better hope so. You owe a lot-"

Felix got in his face immediately. "That's enough!" he growled. "It's all in hand. This is going to be such a huge success that no one will be able to stop us after this. Believe, Silas! Everyone else does."

Silas stared back, his eyes steady and bulging, his jaw working as he nodded up at his master.

"Good. Now, I'll see Beatrice first, and then go. See that everything is put away properly, all right?"

Silas nodded and went away without another word.

"What's with him?" Rufio asked as he and Clara joined Felix.

"He's grumpy. It's normal," Felix said, before taking Clara and Rufio, one in each arm. "Thank you for being here, my friends."

"We wouldn't miss it!" Clara said, reaching up to scratch Felix's beard.

"Ahh!" Felix roared. "Let the games begin!"

THE LUDI APOLLINARES FINALLY ARRIVED IN ROME, AND THERE was pure merriment in the air. It was one of the most exciting festivals of the Roman calendar, and the people wasted no time jumping into the celebrations for which they had been holding their collective breath. Every square echoed with the sound of music, and the steps of every temple were a stage for groups of players who offered their wares of tragedy and comedy to the people of that ancient city of glory.

The atria and peristyle gardens of many a rich home bore witness to the words of poets who cast a spell over their audience with as much skill as a northern barbarian bard about a warm forest fire. Guests wept and cheered at what they heard, at the feelings the words and music aroused, and the poets bowed graciously as pouches heavy with coin were deposited into their skilled hands.

Apollo and his Muses were present in Rome for the games of that god of wonder and creativity, and the city was so much the better for it.

Whilst the people of Rome honoured Apollo with art and offerings, and celebrated his gifts to the world, The Etrurian Players continued to prepare for their theatrical battle, rehearsing in the days leading up to their great performance. They only quit the great theatre to eat and to sleep, before returning in the drowsy hours of pink dawn.

"Excellent!" Felix applauded after one of their final run-throughs. "We've ironed out the kinks so much that I think it would make the shade of Father Plautus blush!"

"Are we going through it again this afternoon, Felix?" Julius asked, wiping his brow and sitting upon one of the crates.

The sun beat down on them intensely, as the days had come into their full summer heat. Even with the velaria fully extended over the auditorium for shade, the theatre yet baked.

Felix looked around and could see the company's energy flagging.

"I think they could use a rest, Felix," Clara said. "You don't want them exhausted before the performance.

Felix nodded. "True enough. We've got it down." He clapped and walked up to them. "You've all done very well, and you are ready. Tomorrow, we will have our very final dress rehearsal. Today, I give you all permission to go and enjoy the games!"

There was a collective cheer from the members of the company, and the joy upon their made-up faces made Rufio smile, for he too had worked hard, and the labour made him feel alive.

"We will feast at the Taberna Macedonica tonight!" Felix added, arousing an even greater cheer. "But in the meantime, while you are enjoying the delights of the city, you are forbidden to fight, and you must spend the night at the warehouse. I don't want to go from brothel to brothel looking for you again…Damon!"

The mute blushed and spun a playful note upon his reed pipe.

"AND…" Felix put his hands up for quiet. "You are only to enjoy a modicum of inebriation."

There was silence and an exchange of confused looks.

"Don't get too drunk!" Felix clarified.

They all laughed.

"Now, secure the set pieces for the night, and put your costumes away carefully in the stage house. Hop to it!"

As the players set excitedly about their tasks, eager to head out into the city streets, Rufio and Clara got stuck into the work as well, for after so many weeks, they too had become a part of the company, Julius going so far as to call them 'founding members' of The Etrurian Players.

Rufio watched Clara emerge from the scaena frons where she had gone inside to change out of her costume into her blue gap-sleeved tunica, so as not to damage the fine materials Beatrice had worked so artfully upon. Clara and Fausto were setting the smaller props carefully into a crate, laughing at some joke Pollux just made. The sight of her so happy, so free, brought him a greater joy than he had felt in years.

In that moment, Rufio realized with certainty that he had been happy himself simply because he had been with her, around her, and hearing her on a daily basis.

He dreaded all of that coming to an end after the performance. And with that dread, worry and panic began to worm their way into his new-found joy, like a weevil that has happened upon a freshly-baked loaf of bread.

Rufio Pagano had forgotten in the ensuing years of loneliness how very much he had loved his childhood friend. Up until his recent injury, he had told himself that his betrayal of her, and of Felix, would have overshadowed any feelings she might ever have had for him. For years, he had believed that he did not deserve her.

But Rufio knew with absolute certainty that he loved Clara, and it made him feel brave, for once in his life.

He looked down at Peli who had come to sit at his heels and was looking up at him with his mischievous, mismatched eyes. The dog turned around to face the sloping seats of the vast auditorium, and Rufio followed his canine gaze until his eyes locked on the goddess' temple at the top.

"Who are you?" he asked the fidgety beast.

Peli barked and quit Rufio's side to weave in and out of the busy members of the company.

Rufio looked at them, and then back at the temple, and decided to make his way across the orchestra floor and up the steep steps of the auditorium's central aisle toward the temple.

He reached the shade cast by the velaria, and moved upward to the temple entrance until he stood before the six golden columns, his eyes seeking the sanctum of the cella like a tramp before a bakery, uncertain if he should dare enter.

As he began to mount the steps, Electra emerged from the interior in a waft of smoke. She startled Rufio who froze before her, not because it was her - she had, in fact grown much warmer toward him over the weeks - but because he noticed that her eyes were wet, making the kohl about them run as if she were a freshly-painted statue left out in the rain.

"Electra? Are you all right?" Rufio asked, surprising her in return.

She looked up suddenly from her clasped hands and pushed back the veil she had over her head for her prayers. She breathed deeply to compose herself before speaking. "I...I was just making offerings to the goddess."

"Why are you weeping?"

"Why don't you mind your own business!" she snapped, her blue eyes boring into him like an oncoming storm over the sea.

There she is. "I don't mean to pry," Rufio said, his hands up. "Only to help if I can."

She sighed, but not with exasperation. "There is nothing you can do. Only Venus can help me in this." She looked at him then and her eyes strayed to the stage far below. She smiled. "I suspect you are also asking the goddess for aid?"

"I am unused to praying for such things," he admitted, "but in this case, I could use her help."

Electra smiled knowingly at first, but then sadly, for though Felix had told her the truth of what had happened, she could see that as the weeks had worn on, he and Clara had grown closer and closer, so much so that she suspected he had lied to her from the beginning. She looked back to Rufio and smiled sadly. "You will need all the help you can get, Rufio. We both will."

He did not say anything, but stepped aside so that she could descend the temple steps.

Electra stopped beside him and placed one arm about his waist, the scent of the incense she had lit filling his nostrils. She leaned in close to his ear and whispered. "I am grateful you came to Rome for Felix, and I wish you well in whatever you are praying for."

Without another look at him, Electra moved on slowly, like a silent Medea floating across the stage.

Rufio watched her go for a moment, confused, and then turned to go inside the temple.

It was dark, but for a single brazier that burned in the middle of the floor before the altar and statue of Venus.

Rufio felt small immediately, but pressed on toward the high altar that sat at the goddess' sandalled feet.

Venus looked down on him, a serene and understanding look upon her lovely face, unlike the seemingly-heartbroken wraith he had just met on the steps outside.

He realized that he had not brought anything to offer the goddess, and thought of abandoning his prayers for the moment, but then he spied a small pedestal table to the right with a bronze bowl containing chunks of incense. He went to the bowl, chose a particularly hefty piece, and then went to the brazier to light it. He rushed back to the altar, bowed awkwardly up at the goddess, and set the burning offering upon a broad bronze plate which sat in the middle.

The smoke began to rise, encouraged by his hesitant breath, and once it began to encircle the Venus' face and hair, Rufio leaned upon the altar and bowed his head.

"Goddess Venus... I have not often prayed to you. I...I never felt that you would smile on me...until now." He looked up to seek the wisdom in her timeless eyes. "I don't know if it was you, oh Goddess, who gave Felix the dream that brought me here to be reunited with Clara, but if it was, I thank you with all of my heart."

He felt light-headed as he prayed, as if in the goddess' presence, he was unable to maintain his strength. But he persevered and fell to his knees with his palms up in supplication.

"I have loved Clara since we were children, but I never had the courage to tell her before it was too late. My past cowardice robbed me of the chance to be happy with her. And I *want* to make her happy, oh Goddess. Truly." Rufio felt his eyes burning, not for the smoke, but for lost time and the gift of a second chance, a chance at redemption. "Fill me with courage, Goddess Venus. Please grant me the right words to tell Clara how I truly feel for her, how I would spend the rest of my life with her if she will have me. I pray that she feels the same as I do." He shook his head. "But if she does not, may she truly be happy, for her joy is all the world to me. I know that now. I see it every time she smiles and laughs. I would help nurture her joy and amplify her laughter for all the world, be she with me or not."

Rufio stood then, pulling himself up by the cool marble edges of the great altar which he kissed before looking up at Venus.

"Guide me, oh Goddess, and I will obey."

He backed away, his gaze lingering on the smoke-shrouded image of Venus, before turning and going toward the brilliance of the sunlight outside. When he emerged, he found that his eyes were wet with tears, and he then understood a bit more of the woman who had emerged before him, and the sting of love she felt acutely.

THE COMPANY SPREAD OUT INTO ROME FROM THE THEATRE OF Pompey that afternoon to enjoy the festivities the Ludi Apollinares had to offer. It was a time of well-deserved rest before the imminent big day.

Castor, Pollux, and Damon were the first to rush from the theatre to try and gain entry to the Circus Maximus for the chariot races that were taking place. Castor and Pollux were keen fans of the Veneti, the blue team that tended to dominate the sands, but Damon insisted with waving hands that the Russati, the red team, were the ones to beat.

"Good thing you're mute, Damon," Pollux laughed. "Otherwise we would get in a fight!"

Damon signed a futuere fist at him as they joined the crowds filing into the circus.

Julius, Fausto and Beatrice headed straight for the Forum Romanum where many of the smaller theatrical performances were taking place, not because they wished to spy upon the competitors, but because they loved to watch, to feel, to get outside of their own heads for a while and experience stories through the skill of other performers.

Julius walked more quickly than his two younger escorts had ever seen before. "Quickly!" he said to them as he ploughed through the crowded streets. "I heard that Fabia Arete is going to be performing today."

"No!" Fausto jumped excitedly as he caught up with the veteran actor.

"Who's she?" Beatrice asked.

"She's one of the finest actresses to ever perform, the greatest archimima. Her dancing…her singing - such a voice!"

"Don't tell Electra that!" Beatrice worried.

"I think Julius is in love!" Fausto joked.

The older man blushed and nodded. "Truly," he agreed. "The first time I saw her, Eros struck me dumb with his sharpest barb! Electra is one of the greatest actresses I have seen, it's true. We're fortunate to have her! But Fabia Arete is a gift from the Gods themselves!"

"I can't wait to see her then!" Beatrice clapped her hands and skipped along with the other two. "Maybe I'll learn something?"

"You always learn something when you watch her," Julius said. "If she performs any bits from her most famous role, that of the plotting wife, Charition, then we're in for a special treat!"

The three of them rushed headlong into the forum crowds

which were already as thick as honey in a hive, the bees gathering to catch a glimpse of the queen herself.

Back at the theatre of Pompey, Felix, Electra, Clara, and Rufio had finished securing everything and set off across the gardens of the quadriporticus for the baths of Titus.

"You don't want to see any performances, Felix?" Rufio asked as they stopped in front of the statue of Plautus.

They never passed the progenitor of their play without paying their respects.

Felix shook his head. "No. Electra and I never watch others perform before we are due to perform."

"Julius mentioned they were going to see Fabia Arete in the forum," Clara said. "Is she really as good as they say?"

Electra shrugged. "She was good once. Now, she is old and ugly, and her voice sounds like a cat."

Felix looked at Electra and shook his head. "Fabia Arete is a wonder. She's still got talent. You know it. You're just jealous because of that time in Caesarea when-"

"I don't want to hear any more of your escapades!" Electra shouted before storming off down the path. "Let's just go to the baths and wash the dirt of this filthy city away!"

Felix sighed as he looked up at Plautus. "Oh, father... You must have had stories!"

Rufio laughed uncomfortably as he watched Electra go, unable to shake the sight of her wet eyes back at the temple. "Let's catch up with her," he said. "It's a lonely time before a performance, and the city's crowded." He gulped at the thought, snapped his fingers for Peli to follow, and went after Electra.

"Come on, Felix," Clara said, pulling him by the arm away, from Plautus' statue.

"Where's Silas?" Rufio asked as they rushed after Electra.

"Who cares," Felix said, his eyes on his concubine's lustful and angry form.

When they were gone, the gardens of the quadriporticus were silent but for the tinkle of the fountains, and a single pair of footfalls across the pebbled pathways.

"Who cares?" Silas said through his clenched teeth as he stepped out from behind one of the columns at the far edge of the gardens. "You'll care!"

He had been waiting for everyone to quit the theatre before leaving, and when he was sure they were gone, he went to sit on the steps of the tholos of Aedes Fortuna Huiusce Diei. His heart beat quickly, but he was determined. He had had enough of Felix's constant dismissals.

"He's given me no choice," Silas said to himself, jumping up when he heard the familiar, gravelly voice come in off of the street. He waited until he saw the one scar-faced man attended by two others, former gladiators by the look of them. Silas swallowed hard as they approached. "Salve, Leno!" he said, his attempt to sound strong and forceful crumbling like dried bits of bread from his mouth.

"Silas," the man said cooly.

"Come," Silas said, showing him the way. "Let me show you what your investment has got you…"

They walked back toward the theatre, one of the gladiators kicking a peacock along the way.

The afternoon had flown by in a flurry of excitement and awe, like a happy storm that swept through Rome leaving everyone flush-faced and ready for a drink.

The Taberna Macedonica was packed, but Philemon had made sure, when he received word from Felix Modestus, to reserve the usual, long table along the wall for him and his company. It was the busiest time of year, but there was always room for The Etrurian Players at the Taberna Macedonica!

When Felix, Rufio, Clara and Electra arrived, clean and

fine-looking after their thermal ablutions and massages, they found the other players, apart from Silas, already drinking and laughing, and awaiting the platters of food which Philemon's cook was preparing for them. The high hum of the taberna's conversations filled their ears immediately as they wended their way through the crowd to their saved seats, like late arrivals in the auditorium.

"You're late, Dominus!" Castor called out. "We've got a head start on the drinking!" He held up his cup to Felix.

"Worry not! I'll catch you up!" Felix bellowed as the others clapped.

Soon enough, Philemon was there with another pitcher of wine and four more cups which he promptly filled.

"Thank you, Philemon," Felix said, laying his hand on the proprietor's shoulder. "You're busy tonight!"

Philemon was sweating, working hard for his living that evening. He nodded and smiled. "It's good to be busy, Felix Modestus!"

"Yes. It is!" Felix agreed, and reached to his belt to take a pouch heavy with coin. "My company has been working hard." He put the pouch into Philemon's hand. "Keep the food and drink coming all evening!" He leaned down. "But water the wine well, my friend."

Philemon winked. "As you wish, Felix Modestus."

Felix stood at the end of the table and stared down its length at his company. He was about to address them when Silas came stumbling up and seated himself at the far end of the table, facing Felix.

"Silas!" Pollux said. "Why are you limping?"

"I'm not limping, you oaf!" Silas bit back, sitting gingerly on the stool that was left for him.

"Yes, you are!" Pollux countered. "You're walking funny."

"Maybe he went to the brothel?" Castor mused, winking at Silas.

"Catamitus in angiportum?" Pollux enquired, hinting at a quick encounter.

"Futuere, Pollux!" Silas shouted.

Pollux shrugged. "No. But seems you did."

"All right, that's enough!" Felix shouted across the table. "We're here to celebrate and relax! I want no squabbling. You've got through the day without fighting, so don't start now. Eat and drink, my friends! You deserve it!" Felix sat down impatiently and refilled his cup.

"That's your speech?" Rufio asked.

"Fine words will be lost on them right now. Their blood is up for some reason."

"Maybe if you had not told Philemon to keep the wine coming?" Electra said, taking a small sip from her cup.

"It will be fine," Felix added. "I don't need to play nurse-maid to them all the time. Besides, I'm still quite relaxed and I want to enjoy this evening." Quite unexpectedly, he took up Electra's hand and kissed it.

She let his lips linger there, but then slowly pulled it away.

Rufio spied the beginnings of a smile at the corners of her full lips, but it faded, as if Electra was reluctant to let her guard down.

"Do you feel better after the baths?" Clara asked Rufio, leaning in to speak so that he could hear her above the racket of the taberna.

He nodded. "Yes. But at the time I felt like the German massaging me was going to snap my bones."

She laughed. "You were quite red in the face the whole time!"

"You think that's funny, do you?" he said, elbowing her playfully.

Clara shrugged, her bare shoulder touching his arm. "I just like seeing you relaxed." She sipped her wine. "I'm surprised really."

"Really? Why is that?" Rufio asked.

"Well, the performance is in just a couple of days. I thought you would be much more nervous." She set her cup down. "I know I am."

"Of course I'm nervous," Rufio said. "But…I'm with you. And Felix!" he added quickly. "It feels right. Besides," he turned to Felix, "the Gods demand it, no?"

"That's right, my friend!" Felix said, reaching across the table to grip the back of Rufio's head playfully. "Nothing can stop us now!"

Just then, a party of three men, a magistrate of some sort, and two men who appeared to be warriors, one dark and the other clearly a Roman, entered the taberna. Then, the older man unexpectedly spread his arms wide to address the drunken assembly.

"Boy server of old Falernian,

Pour me out more pungent cups

As toastmistress Postumia rules,

Who's drunker than the drunken grape.

Pure water, find your level elsewhere.

You ruin wine. Shift to the sober.

Here is unmixed Thyonian!"

"Bravo!" Felix and the rest of the company cheered, followed by the other patrons as Philemon showed the newcomers to a table. "What an entrance!" Felix said.

"The man knows his Catullus," Rufio added.

"So did you, once-upon-a-time," Clara said, nudging him.

"That's right!" Felix said, turning to Electra. "Rufio does have a knack for Catullian verse."

Electra looked across the table at Rufio. "I would love to hear some. Go on!"

Her voice was such that Rufio found it hard to refuse, the same as any audience who watched her could not but listen to every syllable that emerged from her lips.

"Let me think..." Rufio rifled through his memory for one of his favourite verses, cleared his throat.

"Stand up, man!" Felix said before he could start.

Rufio stood, and looked at the faces along the table, resting finally upon Clara beside him. He smiled at her lovely face staring up at him, borrowing the courage to begin...

"In Diana's trust are we,
Girls and boys unblemished.
Of Diana, unblemished boys
And girls, let us sing.
O Latona's daughter, great
Progeny of greatest Jove,
Whom thy mother bore beside
The Delian olive,
To be mistress of mountains
And the greening forests
And unfrequented passes
And strident streams:
Thou art called Lucina Juno
By women in labour pains,
Called powerful Three-Ways and Moon
Of borrowed light.
Goddess, by Thy monthly course
Measuring the year's journey
Though fillest up with good fruits
The farmer's barns.
Hallowed be Thou by the name
Of Thy pleasure, and protect
As in days of old from ill
Romulus' race."

As Rufio recited the poet's words, words that he had often spoken to the moonlit night when he was alone in his Etrurian pasture, he remembered the last time he had recited it before others, and he felt his heart tighten at the memory, as though his once-dead heart were now being pumped, and the blood began to flow once more from his heart to his mind and limbs and face.

Rufio did not notice that the entire taberna had gone silent at his words, the patrons listening intently to the feeling he expressed in their utterance. It was only when the applause erupted, like a quake in the countryside, that he rounded back into himself, his hand still gripping Clara's, as he had been the entire time.

"Bravo, Rufio Pagano!" Felix roared, on his feet and clapping with the rest of the revelrous crowd.

Rufio felt his face burning, but managed a smile and a bow before sitting back down.

"That was beautiful," Electra said, smiling as she looked across the table. "Thank you, Rufio."

"Typical choice for a peasant farmer, no?" Silas blurted at the end of the table, only to have the back of his head smacked by Pollux's thick hand.

"Shut up, Silas!"

Felix was suddenly on his feet again, this time turning to address the crowd. "This man will be in one of the lead roles of The Etrurian Players' production of *Menaechmi*, at the Theatre of Pompey, in a couple days' time. Make sure you all come and see it! Spread the word!"

"Like a lupa spreads her legs!" Castor called out.

Felix frowned at him. "Castor, more water in your wine! Your metaphors are getting sloppy!"

There were scattered cheers and laughter, and the entire company roared and clapped as more wine and food were brought.

"I remember how you like cheese, Rufio Pagano," Philemon said as he brought up a platter he had put together just for Rufio. The man smiled kindly as he did so, happy for the joy that his recitation had brought to all of them. "I love that poem by Catullus."

"Thank you, Philemon. Truly. But," Rufio put up his hand, "I cannot eat cheese so close to the performance, as good as it looks and smells." Rufio could feel his mouth salivating at the sight of the lactic display.

"Good man!" Felix said to Rufio, before turning to the proprietor. "Worry not, Philemon," Felix said, smiling. "After the performance, Rufio will be back to eat all of your cheese, like a field mouse returned to the kitchen from the desert."

"My apologies," Philemon said, inclining his head and leaving the table. "I would not want to jeopardize your performance." He turned to Felix. "My daughter and I already have our tickets!"

"I'm glad to hear it, Philemon!" Felix said, patting the man's thick shoulder and smiling broadly.

"You did very well, Rufio," Clara said.

He turned to face her, and felt his heart lighten even more, if that were possible in that moment. *I've wasted too much time away from her. I can't lose her again!* he told himself, his rushing thoughts chiding his constant deliberation and delays.

Clara continued. "I remember the last time I heard you recite that poem."

"You do?"

She nodded and tucked her hair behind her ear. "It was the night before the three of us set out for Rome." She leaned forward and looked down the table. "Do you remember, Felix?"

"I certainly do! The forest grew silent!"

Rufio felt something against his leg then, and looked under the table, shocked to see Peli resting there. "Sneak in, did you?" He looked to make sure Philemon was not there. The sight of the dog beneath the table brought back memories he would rather forget, but he did not have the heart to send the dog away. "You going to behave yourself?"

Peli sighed, and lay down across both Rufio and Clara's feet at once.

"I guess that's a 'yes'," Clara said, laughing and reaching down to pat Peli.

For some reason, in that moment, Rufio wondered how things were back on the farm. He had been away for so long, a part of him worried that Stella, at least, would be fretting over his absence.

"So, Clara," Felix asked. "Tell me more about life on Sicilia. Was the villa very grand?"

Clara released Rufio's hand and leaned on the table to speak to Felix and Electra. "Yes. It was a beautiful place. Fields and olive groves stretching into the distance, away to the sea which lent us a cool breeze that wafted through the house. I had a beautiful, shaded terrace on which to read."

"You must have felt like a princess there?" Electra asked.

"Sometimes, but…"

Clara's voice faded in Rufio's ears as he tried not to listen. It upset him to hear about her former life, not because he begrudged her that life, but because they were years which he could have spent with her.

"I pissed it all away," he muttered.

"What was that, Rufio?" Clara asked.

He looked up, embarrassed. "Oh, nothing. I was just thinking out loud about…about Errol. He's probably drunk all the wine at home."

"I can't believe Errol's still alive!" Felix said. "Still kicking, is he?"

"Well, no, not kicking. That would be my horse. Errol is Errol. He does his grumpy best."

"So, tell me more," Felix said to Clara again.

Rufio listened to her describe the beauty of the home in

which she had lived, and he felt downcast at that, for he knew he could never provide her with such a place. He imagined his dilapidated farmhouse, the potted road leading up to it, and the fields that yielded only what they felt like as he was unable, it seemed, to coax better harvests out of them. Not like the great farm production that Clara's dead husband had.

Down at the other end of the table, Rufio could hear catches of drunken narration from Castor and Pollux, and a bit of added music from Damon's flute. Beatrice sang bits of a song, and Fausto hooted like a pretty owl, upon a fence post beside her.

"They've drunk too much," Felix said to Electra, but his smile never wavered. "But they'll pull through."

"They needed this," she acquiesced. "They'll be slow to start tomorrow, but they'll be fine."

Felix took her hand and kissed it, then accepted the plump grape she pressed to his lips.

It was then that Julius stood, swaying upon his feet a little, cleared his throat, and spoke with a voice of age and wisdom that grabbed hold of everyone's attention with an iron fist worthy of Mars...

"Arms and the man I sing..." he began, and people sighed with joy at the famed and familiar poet's words, "...who first from the coasts of Troy, exiled by fate, came to Italy and Lavine shores; much buffeted on sea and land by violence from above, through cruel Juno's unforgiving wrath, and much enduring in war also, till he should build a city and bring his gods to Latium; whence came the Latin race, the lords of Alba, and the lofty walls of Rome.

Tell me, O Muse, the cause; wherein thwarted in will or wherefore angered, did the Queen of heaven drive a man, of goodness so wondrous, to traverse so many perils, to face so many toils. Can heavenly spirits cherish resentment so dire?

There was an ancient city, the home of Tyrian settlers,

Carthage, over against Italy and the Tiber's mouths afar, rich in wealth and stern in war's pursuits. This, 'tis said, Juno loved above all other lands, holding Samos itself less dear. Here was her armour, here her chariot; that here should be the capital of the nations, should the fates perchance allow it, was even then the goddess's aim and cherished hope. Yet in truth she had heard that a race was springing from Trojan blood, to overthrow some day the Tyrian towers; that from it a people, kings of broad realms and proud in war, should come forth for Libya's downfall: so rolled the wheel of fate. The daughter of Saturn, fearful of this and mindful of the old war which erstwhile she had fought at Troy for her beloved Argos – not yet, too, had the cause of her wrath and her bitter sorrows faded from her mind: deep in her heart remain the judgment of Paris and the outrage to her slighted beauty, her hatred of the race and the honours paid to ravished Ganymede – inflamed hereby yet more, she tossed on the wide main the Trojan remnant, left by the Greeks and pitiless Achilles, and kept them far from Latium; and many a year they wandered, driven by the fates o'er all the seas. So vast was the effort to found the Roman race."

Julius' voice faded out, and every person who had felt the spell of his words, like those of a bard around a midnight fire, emerged from the trance with wetted eyes, and clapped as loudly for the old veteran as if he were a general in his triumph.

Julius bowed graciously and sat down.

Clara turned to him. "That was the most beautiful narration I've ever heard of Virgil's words."

"Thank you, my dear," Julius said, patting her hand.

Rufio spied this, and felt uncomfortable at the relinquishing of his own hand in favour of the older man's. *Don't be stupid!* he chided himself. He tapped Clara's shoulder then. "Clara," he said.

She turned, wiping a tear from her eye. "Yes?"

"Narrate something for us…for me?"

"Yes!" Beatrice said, her words echoed by Fausto and the others. "Go on, then!"

Clara smiled and protested, though weakly, before agreeing to the demands of the jubilant table. "All right, all right!" she said, laughing and standing. "Let's see… Julius has inspired me to this…"

Rufio frowned again, but his discomfort quickly evaporated as the words slipped like a cool breeze from Clara's lips…

"It was night, and over the earth weary creatures were tasting the peace of slumber; the woods and wild seas had sunk to rest – the hour when stars roll midway in their gliding course, when all the land is still, and beasts and coloured birds, both those that far and near haunt the limpid lakes, and those that dwell in the thorny thickets of the countryside, are couched in sleep beneath the silent night. They were soothing their cares, their hearts oblivious of sorrows…"

Clara looked around at the faces tilted upward to her sunny face, but then a cloud passed over, her smile fading at the words to come.

"But not so the soul-racked Phoenician queen; she never sinks into sleep, nor draws darkness into eyes or heart. Her pangs redouble, and her love, swelling up, surges afresh, as she heaves with a mighty tide of passion. Thus then she begins, and thus alone revolves her thoughts in her heart: "See, what am I to do? Shall I once more make trial of my old wooers, only to be mocked, and shall I humbly sue for marriage with Numidians, whom I have scorned so often as husbands? Shall I then follow the Ilian ships and the Trojans' uttermost commands? Is it because they are thankful for aid once given, and gratitude for past kindness stands firm in their mindful hearts? But who – suppose that I wished it – will suffer me, or take one so hated on those haughty ships? Ah! Lost one, do you not yet understand nor perceive the treason of Laomedon's race? What then? Shall I on my own accompany the exultant sailors in their flight? Or, surrounded by all my Tyrian band, shall I pursue, and shall I again drive seaward the men whom I could scarce tear from the Sidonian city, and bid them unfurl their sails to the winds? Nay, die as you deserve, and with the sword end your sorrow. Won over by my tears, you, my sister, you were the first to load my frenzied soul with these ills, and drive me on the foe. Ah, that I could not spend my life apart from wedlock, a blameless life, like some wild creature, and not know such cares! The faith vowed to the ashes of Sychaeus I have not kept." Such were the cries that kept bursting from her heart..."

On the last words, Clara's gaze lingered on Rufio, and he could not help but look away, for in those glossy orbs which he so loved to gaze into, he felt the sting of accusation, though he was certainly no Aeneas, and she was, to him, far greater than Dido.

The cheers of the taberna crowd lingered for a long time, accented with whistles of admiration for the moving performance given by such an actress.

Silently then, as if emerging onto a mist-shrouded stage by the sea at morning, Felix's bulk rose up, and his eyes locked onto Clara's...

"Not far from here, outspread on every side, are shown the Mourning Fields; such is the name they bear. Here those whom stern Love has consumed with cruel wasting are hidden in walks withdrawn, embowered in a myrtle grove; even in death the pangs leave them not. In this region he sees Phaedra and Procris, and sad Eriphyle, pointing to the wounds her cruel son had dealt, and Evadne and Pasiphaë. With them goes Laodamia, and Caeneus, once a youth, now a woman, and again turned back by Fate into her form of old. Among them, with wound still fresh, Phoenician Dido was wandering in the great forest, and soon as the Trojan hero stood near and knew her, a dim form amid the shadows – even as, in the early month, one sees or fancies he has seen the moon rise amid the clouds – he shed tears, and spoke to her in tender love: "Unhappy Dido! Was the tale true then that came to me, that you were dead and had sought your doom with the sword? Was I, alas, the cause of your death? By the stars I swear, by the world above, and what-ever is sacred in the grave below, unwillingly, queen, I parted from your shores. But the gods' decrees, which now constrain me to pass through these shades, through lands squalid and forsaken, and through abysmal night, drove me with their behests; nor could I deem my going thence would bring on you distress so deep. Stay your step and withdraw not from our view. Whom do you flee? This is the last word Fate suffers me to say to you." With these words amid springing tears Aeneas strove to soothe the wrath of the fiery, fierce-eyed queen. She, turning away, kept her looks fixed on the ground and no more changes her countenance as he essays to speak than if she were set in hard flint or Marpesian rock. At length she flung herself away and, still his foe, fled back to the shady grove, where Sychaeus, her lord of former days, responds to her sorrows and gives her love for love. Yet none the less, stricken by her unjust doom, Aeneas attends her with tears afar and pities her as she goes…"

As the applause exploded like a tidal wave upon the shore, deafening and all consuming, Rufio stared into his cup and drank fully of the red wine therein. The guilt he felt, hurt far too much and, unlike Aeneas, he could not look upon his love, though he did feel like weeping.

The night air was cool when they emerged from the Taberna Macedonica, the warm glow of wine heating them and flushing their faces. Most of the company, exhausted from the day's exertions and activities, returned to the warehouse for some well-earned sleep.

Felix, Electra, Clara, and Rufio, however, decided to walk through the Forum Romanum, for the night was beautiful and moonlit, and cool air was needed to clear their heads.

"The city is still active!" Felix said. "Let's go and see who is performing in the forum at this hour!"

And so they strolled easily along the open streets, past parties of other revellers, until they arrived within the scented confines of the heart of Rome where many were still gathered to watch the mimes and pantomimes by firelight.

Torches and braziers burned everywhere, casting the shadows of pedestrians as if they were wild Bacchae dancing through the semi-dark. People drank and ate and nuzzled and laughed in a great release that came with most festivals in the city.

As Felix led them through the Forum, claiming the space before them like Hercules stalking a midnight wood, they came to a stop where there was a small crowd before the temple of the Divine Julius. There, all heads were turned toward the steps of the temple of Castor and Pollux where a mime troupe performed.

Rufio and Clara paused to watch.

"Oh faith of Gods and men!" an angry Laches of Terence's creation was saying, arms waving, head shaking. "What a conspiracy is this! That all women should desire and reject every individual thing alike! And not a single one can you find to swerve in any respect from the disposition of the rest. For instance, quite as though with one accord, do all mothers-in-law hate their daughters-in-law. Just in the same way is it their system to oppose their husbands; their obstinacy *here* is the same. In the very same school they all seem to me to have been trained up to perverseness. Of that school, if there is any mistress, I am very sure that she," he pointed at the woman on the other side of the steps, "it is."

The audience laughed, and some husbands gave their wives knowing looks, only to receive the edge of an elbow or have them cross their arms.

"Wretched me!" Sostrata replied upon the steps. "When now I don't so much as know why I am accused!"

"Eh! You don't know?" Laches asked, his arms wide to the audience.

"So may the Gods kindly prosper me, Laches, and so may it be allowed us to pass our lives together in unity!"

Laches turned most conspiratorially to the audience. "May the Gods avert *such* a misfortune!"

There was more laughter, and Clara turned to Rufio. "I always loved Terence."

"Yes. Another great," Rufio agreed, "but I prefer Plautus."

"Naturally," Clara smiled and stepped close to him. "Where are Felix and Electra?"

Rufio turned, a little panicked, only just then realizing how much the crowd was pressed around him. "I don't know. Come, let's get out of here." He took Clara's hand and pulled her through the audience.

As they walked, Rufio looked aside at Clara, observing her most intently. His heartbeat quickened. He had so many questions, wanted so desperately to be sure of himself, and of her feelings.

"Did you like living in Syracusae?" he asked suddenly.

She looked surprised, but shrugged. "I suppose. The weather was nice. The people were not that friendly though. I was always an outsider."

"I'm sorry to hear that."

"It's fine. I *was* an outsider and, truth be told, I kept to myself."

"And your husband. Aeson?"

"What about him?" Clara asked, feeling slightly guilty that she had not thought of Aeson in some time.

"Did you love him?" Rufio asked.

"As I told you before, I did, but as a daughter loves a doting father. Nothing more. He was kind to me at a time when I most needed it. I was so alone after…"

It was as if the temple steps nearby emerged on purpose, a statement, a reminder of Rufio's past mistakes.

He abandoned his questions, and they found Felix and Electra sitting before the temple of Antoninus and Faustina, kissing in the silver moonlight where it cast its glow upon the marble steps.

"Erm!" Rufio interrupted them. "We wondered where you'd gone!"

Felix turned to him, and Electra looked annoyed. "I always come here to think."

"And play, it seems," Clara said winking.

"Come now, Clara. Jealousy does not become you!" Electra bit, before standing and walking slowly along the via Sacra.

Felix sighed.

"You didn't want to see any of the play?" Rufio asked, looking at Clara a little strangely for her comment. "It was Terence's *The Mother-in-Law*."

"You know I don't watch any other performances before I am finished with my own. My world is of a Plautian air for now," Felix said.

"Where is Electra going?" Clara asked, seeing her outline leaving. "We shouldn't let her go alone."

"You're right. Even she shouldn't be alone at night in Rome. Come." Felix left quickly to catch up with her.

Rufio and Clara followed.

"She's so touchy, that one," Clara said as they walked briskly after them toward the arch of Titus.

"Well…" Rufio muttered, "you did practically accuse them

of fornicating on the temple steps. It's almost as if you were jealous!" He had meant to say it in a funny manner, but that is not how it was received.

Clara pulled away from him, a scowl marring her lovely face. "I can't believe you would say that!"

"Say what?"

But Clara was already speeding off after Felix and Electra, leaving Rufio behind in a fog of confusion.

Rufio finally caught up to Felix, Electra, and Clara along the side of the temple of Venus and Rome. He arrived breathless after running up the stairs. "Why are we here?" Rufio asked.

"I'm going into the temple to make an offering," Electra stated. "Wait here for me."

Rufio looked at Felix who shrugged and went in with Electra.

"I never thought I'd see a woman have such a hold on him," Clara said, as she looked out over the dark plaza of the Colosseum to their left, and walked slowly in that direction.

"Oh, it's not so bad, is it?" Rufio asked.

"Not if she keeps him from being who he is. It is not like Felix to bow down before anyone."

Rufio frowned. "I don't think he is. You hear how he speaks to her sometimes, don't you? I mean, he does own her, right?"

Clara did not answer, but kept walking. Suddenly, she greeted someone. "How nice to see you, Astarte!"

"And you, fine lady!" the woman replied from her seat upon the temple steps.

"Oh, no," Rufio grumbled, as he joined them.

"And Rufio Pagano!" Astarte cried, her smile broad. She sat there with her bowl of coin, as usual, this time covered with a multi-hued shawl that warded off the evening chill. "I thought I might see you both together!"

"You did?" Clara asked, looking from the priestess to Rufio.

Astarte nodded and winked. "I did," she said proudly before turning to Rufio. "You are a naughty boy, aren't you?"

Clara looked quickly at Rufio who shrugged as if he did not know what the woman was talking about.

"I don't know what you mean?" he said to Astarte.

"Meretrix misses your company, you know?" Astarte said. "She had hoped for the occasional visit after she helped you out on your first night in Rome. You've quite ignored her." She wagged a plump finger at him.

"Well…I…uh…have been quite busy. We're putting on the play and-"

"Yes, I know! Everyone is talking about it!" Astarte's white teeth shone as she smiled.

Clara interrupted. "I'm sorry… Meretrix?"

"My friend," Astarte said. "She's a lupa here in Rome. One of the best actually. She's taken quite a liking to our Etrurian man here!" She laughed and pointed at Rufio.

Rufio shook his head.

"She has, has she?" Clara said, crossing her arms.

Rufio shrugged. "She helped me out."

"I'll bet," Clara said curtly. *So, Silas was not lying for once.*

Just then, Peli came bounding up the temple stairs and plopped himself down next to Astarte, proceeding to lick the rolls of her oily neck, making her giggle.

"All right, Peli!" she laughed. "That's enough!" She turned back to Rufio. "Anyway, both Meretrix and I have our tickets for the play. We can't wait!"

"That's great, Astarte," Rufio said, distractedly. "But I have to go now!" he said, going after Clara.

"You must try harder, Rufio Pagano!" she called after him, before turning to Peli. "Go on then." She pat him. "Keep a watch, Peli. There's something in the air tonight."

Peli shot off after Rufio.

. . .

As Rufio rushed after Clara toward the end of the temple facing the Colosseum, he wondered how things had gone so awry so quickly. The warm and loving glow of the night seemed to have been blown away by a sudden gust of spiteful wind, and now, he would be lucky to get in a word edgewise.

He had thought that night would be the night when he would tell Clara how he felt about her, emboldened by their imminent success upon the stage, but also by his prayers to Venus who, he felt certain, had heard his pleas.

Of course, he had been extremely nervous, still unsure of himself and of Clara's feelings toward him. More so now since her comment to Electra shortly before. *Friends can get jealous, can't they?* he asked himself. The truth was that he had been living alone for so long in isolation, he was not yet sure of what social interactions were acceptable. He only knew how he felt, and what he felt was a deep love for Clara Probita, a love that he had hidden away since their childhood.

"Clara, please stop and listen to-" Rufio stopped when he saw Clara, Felix and Electra speaking with the offering seller, Numonius, at the top of the temple stairs. "What's going on?"

Felix turned to Rufio. "Numonius says it is not safe here."

"There's been trouble brewing all day," Clara added.

They all looked to the crowds of men gathered beneath the fire-lit arches of the Colosseum. There was some shouting and pushing, an intensity in the air that said violence was about to erupt.

"Well, why are you standing about then?" Rufio asked Numonius. "Let the Vigiles take care of it."

Numonius was distracted, half listening to Rufio and the others, his main attention focussed on one particular party in the group of ruffians. He stepped toward the edge of the stairs and peered out to see a group of three men turn right to avoid the violent group and go around the other side of the Colosseum.

Just then, some of the ruffians broke off from the main gathering.

"I'm sorry, my friends!" Numonius said to Felix and the others. "I have to go!"

Numonius rushed off at a run, toward the darkness of the plaza and the far side of the amphitheatre.

"Well, that was strange," Clara said.

"Very," Felix added, putting his arm around Electra. "Come. Rome has lost its lustre for today. Let's get back to the warehouse.

Felix, Electra and Clara began to walk back the way they had come, but Rufio stared after Numonius who had run off so suddenly.

There were shouts then, from the distant darkness, cries of distress and what seemed like the snap of bowstrings.

"I hate this city!" he said, turning to run after the others with Peli at his heels.

ACT V

DEUS EX MACHINA

XVI

SNAKE!

It was a beautiful summer day in Rome. The sun dawned in lovely pink hues, and proceeded to make its leisurely way across a sky of purest blue absent of any clouds. In the tops of cypress trees in the gardens of Rome, larks sang to the early morning, pleasing to the Gods' ears, and mourning doves accompanied them from the pediments of temples, arches and arcades throughout the city.

Aedile Sextus Annius Sabinus awoke feeling a great deal of hope for the day to come. He could not help it, for as the sun arose and laid a blanket of brilliant rays upon him and his wife where they lay abed, the world seemed about to change. He felt that Fortuna had favoured him for all his hard work.

The Ludi Apollinares had been going well since their start only a few days before, and he was congratulated by everyone he met for putting together such magnificent entertainments. The gladiatorial combats in the Colosseum had proven highly entertaining for those who lusted after blood most, with bread being distributed to all attendees, and the chariot races in the Circus Maximus had exceeded all expectation with the Russati nearly robbing the Veneti of their victory. Apparently, it had been one of the most exciting races in recent memory, well worth the great expense it had cost him, with a talent of gold and a pair of Iberian stallions going to the winner.

As Sextus Annius Sabinus rose, bathed, and partook of his porridge for ientaculum in the garden, he thought on the theatrical performances he and his wife had enjoyed to that point in the games. They had been his favourite part, and it was widely whispered - to his secret satisfaction, it should be noted - that these games had seen the most theatre troupes in the city in an age. There were performances in every square and theatre, and upon the steps of every temple. Wherever one went, there were companies of mimes and pantomimes with large crowds before them, hanging off of every word and action and musical note that fell upon their crowns.

It was all very exciting, but not nearly as exciting as the main performance to come, the *Menaechmi* of Felix Modestus and his Etrurian Players.

It had been something of a gamble, having the great theatre of Pompey taken over by the one troupe for an entire week with no other performances, but Sextus Annius Sabinus knew it would be worth it. And he would get a peek of the performance that very day as Felix Modestus had invited him to view their final dress rehearsal.

"Are you sure you don't want to come, my love?" Sextus Annius Sabinus said to his wife when she joined him in the garden. "It will be a full performance." He smiled broadly, so much so that it made his wife smile to see his childlike enthusiasm come to the fore. He had been quite stressed in the time before the games, but he was now enjoying the fruits of his labours and the fortune he had expended on them.

"I'm quite sure," she said, reaching out to touch his hand. "I want to experience it with everyone else there, to feel the energy and laughter of the crowd."

"I understand. I just can't help myself!" he added. "When Felix Modestus extended the invitation to watch the final dress rehearsal, I just couldn't refuse."

"I know," his wife said, giggling at how he bounced upon

his chair. "Did you write back to him to tell him of the news you received yesterday?"

Sextus Annius Sabinus shook his head. "No. I want to tell him in person today."

"Might it not make his company too nervous?"

He shook his head. "No. They are professionals, through and through. They'll be thrilled. And if this works…if it goes off the way I've hoped, then my political career will be secured for good."

"It must work, Sextus, for if it does not, we'll be ruined." For the first time, the conversation turned serious, and her smile faded. "You've spent more on this production than on anything else."

Sextus Annius Sabinus reached over to take his wife's hand and squeezed it. "I know, and by Apollo and the Muses, it will be a great success. How can it not be? The Etrurian Players are the greatest in the empire. To be a part of their performance…well…" He was thoughtful. "If all goes according to plan, I shall invest in them on an ongoing basis."

"Let's not tempt Fortuna to throw you into the dirt," she whispered urgently. "One performance at a time, Sextus."

"Yes. You are right, my love. One performance. A beginning to please the Gods!"

They ate slowly and easily for a time, and as the sun rose higher into the sky, Sextus Annius Sabinus donned his toga, kissed his wife, made his daily offerings in the lararium of their home, and then climbed into the litter which would bear him away to the theatre of Pompey for his preview of the play. As he went through the streets of Rome with the curtains of his litter open, he accepted the congratulations of many a citizen on such magnificent games.

"Thank you!" he said to his commentators. "Just wait until the performance tomorrow. It will be the greatest Rome has ever seen!" His words left a buzz of speculation and excitement in his wake.

It gave Sextus Annius Sabinus great joy to see the people of Rome so happy, and it made him happier still to know that there had been no rioting as often happened during other festivals. The only violent incident he had been made aware of that morning was some sort of attack late the previous night beside the Colosseum. He had been assured the Vigiles were looking into it, but it was thought to be some sort of personal vendetta in an isolated incident.

Still, it upset him to think of the violence. *That's Rome, I suppose,* he told himself, his dark thoughts dissipating as the litter entered the quadriporticus and gardens of the theatre of Pompey. "So beautiful!" he exclaimed to himself as the tinkle of the fountains and birdsong entered into his hearing above the tramp of his litter-bearers upon the gravel pathway. "You can set me down here!" he said.

"Dominus?" said the lead litter-bearer. "Do you not want us to take you all the way to the stage house?"

"No. I want to walk," Sextus Annius Sabinus said. "I want to roam through the gardens. You can rest in the shade near the temples behind us. I will be some time."

"Yes, Dominus," the man said before giving the order to the others to set the litter down.

Sextus Annius Sabinus descended and stretched, straightened his toga, and strolled down the pathway toward the statues of his beloved Plautus and Terence ahead.

Two peacocks darted in front of him, and he jumped, laughing at himself. *Calm down, Sextus,* he commanded. *It will go well!* He took a breath and dipped his hand into the water of one of the fountains, the reflection of which showed a flock of birds soaring high overhead.

He shut his eyes quickly averting his gaze from the reflection in the water, or the grouping in the sky. He avoided all sight or talk of auguries with so much invested, for the stress of it all would surely have killed him. He focussed on making daily offerings and prayers that were pleasing to the Gods, and then focussing on the work of the day, hoping that any Olympians watching would look favourably on him.

When he was sure the birds had passed, he carried on toward the statue of Plautus, and paused there to look up at the poet.

From within the theatre, the sound of music floated to him, accompanied by the sound of Felix Modestus' strong baritone voice. That made Sextus Annius Sabinus smile. He looked into Plautus' timeless eyes then. "If you are watching from the other side of the dark river, please bless this production of your work. Let it be pleasing to all."

He froze then, for from behind the statue's plinth, a black serpent emerged, taking in the sight of his sandalled feet. Beads of sweat began to form upon his brow, but he did not move, did not speak, though he wanted desperately to shout *Vipere!* to his litter bearers so that they could come to his aid. But he dared not.

The serpent slithered closer until it was upon his foot, the vein of which was pulsing beneath the leather straps. The forked tongue could be felt ever-so-slightly, the smooth scales running over the skin as it wound itself about his ankle.

Oh, mighty Apollo, Sextus prayed. *If you keep me safe, I shall build a new shrine to you and your Muses in the gardens of my home. Let me live to see the glories upon the stage tomorrow.*

He felt the serpent tighten upon his ankle for a brief moment, but then to his great relief, it quit its perch upon his skin and carried on across the path behind him. He sighed and wiped the sweat from his brow with the hem of his sleeve. *Thank you, Apollo... Thank you!*

Just then, a loud bark from nearby startled him and this time, he squealed in surprise, turning to see a black and white dog with a naughty air about him standing in the middle of the path.

"What is it with this garden?" he asked himself. "Go! Shoo!" he said to the dog.

But the dog approached him at a run, swerving at the last moment to turn to the statue of Plautus and piss upon the plinth.

"What sacrilege, you cur!"

"Aedile! Welcome!"

Sextus Annius Sabinus turned with relief to see Felix Modestus striding up the path to meet him, resplendent in his belted tunica of deepest blue with a gold meander border. "Ah, Felix Modestus! S…salve!"

Felix was all smiles as he approached the aedile, putting the man at instant ease. "Are you unwell? You look white as asphodel!"

"I, ah…I just had a fright with a serpent here, and then this dog accosted me. He urinated upon Plautus!" He looked up at the statue.

Felix laughed. "Oh, don't mind our Peli. He has adopted our company and makes his daily offerings to the master of our comedy."

"I see," the aedile said doubtfully. "I feel like I've seen this dog before."

"Everybody in Rome has seen Peli at some point, it seems. He's like our own personal Lar of the city!"

"How fascinating." The aedile smiled. "I suppose even the Gods love a bit with a dog!"

"Ha! So they do!" He also kills the serpents he finds in the gardens. See!" Felix pointed to the other side of the garden where Peli was holding something black in his jaws.

"Ah," the aedile sighed. "Yes, that's the one." He turned back to Felix. "Thank you for inviting me to view the rehearsal today. I'm very excited to see what you've done!"

"You won't be disappointed, I can assure you," Felix said, putting his arm about the aedile in a most friendly fashion. "Come. We have refreshment for you in the auditorium while you watch. The company will be ready to start as soon as you are seated."

Together, they walked toward the stage house, the artist and his patron.

The Etrurian Players were, in fact, not ready that morning. Despite Felix's warnings about indulging too much in Bacchus' nectar, large quantities of wine had been drunk by many of them the previous night.

As a result, Felix had had to resort to kicking them awake in the morning, urging them to get clean and refreshed for the final dress rehearsal to which, he told them, their rich patron was coming.

"Get the puke out of your systems now!" he commanded them. "Get clean and clear your heads! Only water today!"

Rufio awoke to Felix's raging and wondered if they were under attack or something strange, but when he heard Damon's flute pipe up to rouse the others like a cornu in a legion's camp, he recalled the big day ahead.

They had returned to the warehouse late the previous night, rushing away from the violence they had witnessed, hoping that they could avoid being drawn into anything. All four of them had worried about Numonius, but he had shot off before any of them could stop him.

Upon returning to the warehouse, Felix had been dismayed to find that Castor, Pollux, and Damon had not returned yet, and suspected they had hit the tabernae or brothels to indulge themselves when they should have been getting rest.

"If this dress rehearsal isn't perfect, I'll have your hides!" Felix threatened.

Clara had been awake already when the raucous chorus of threats exploded in the warehouse, but it had been no less surprising than if she had been awoken by it. She had been sitting quietly in her cubiculum, looking at the painted walls displaying their childhood haunt, thinking of Felix and of Rufio, and of all that she had said and not said. She wondered briefly what Aeson would have thought of her plan to appear on stage before all of Rome, but then dismissed the worry. He had always been interested in her thoughts on theatre, and may even have enjoyed watching her. She hoped his shade would be pleased, and did so without an iota of guilt. However, she did feel guilty when it came to Rufio.

When he was sick, she had wanted to tell him how she felt, how she had missed him, how he had upset her by leaving the last time they were in Rome. She had also wanted to tell him the truth of what had happened between her and Felix, but as had been the case since she arrived in Rome, she had not been able to pluck up the courage to do so. Add to that, Rufio's seemingly jealous behaviour at times, and she worried that he would take it the wrong way.

"We must see the performance through before anything else," she told herself as she dressed.

The company eventually emerged from their dark corners in the warehouse, as the light only just dawned over the Tiber outside, and each sat groggily at the long table to eat sparingly of the bread and oil that had been laid out for all of them.

"We'll have more food at the theatre later," Felix said. "No use feeding you all only to have it puked up!"

Rufio and Clara sat beside each other at the table, both noting the stress Felix was under. It was only when Electra emerged from their curtained cubiculum and kissed his bearded cheek that Felix seemed to calm, but only a little.

"The production is solid, Felix," she told him. "The aedile will be most pleased. Do not worry."

"How can I not worry when they look like this!" Felix gestured down the table at the pale-faced players, hunched over their food and water cups, red-eyed and dishevelled. "Even Julius!"

"Worry not, Dominus!" Julius said, sitting straighter and looking to their company's leader. "We'll pull through for you."

Felix rubbed his face.

"Nothing a little makeup and Beatrice's magnificent costumes won't fix!" Electra said, trying hard to calm him, like Juno soothing her Jupiter.

"A LOT of makeup!" Felix countered.

Electra looked at them all and smirked. "Yes. Quite a lot."

EVENTUALLY, THE COMPANY REACHED THE THEATRE OF POMPEY and, refreshed and rejuvenated after their walk along the river, they immediately set to preparing the stage for the rehearsal. When that was finished, they each donned their costumes which Felix and Beatrice went over individually to make sure nothing was amiss. That done, cheeks were whitened and rouged, and eyes highlighted with kohl so as to be seen from the auditorium. It was a lot more work without masks, but this was a production Felix wanted everyone in Rome talking about, and for that to happen it needed to be different from anything they had seen before.

"I feel ridiculous!" Rufio said as he stood before Clara, the hum of the others' vocal exercises ringing in the background. "Look at my eyes! It's like I've been punched."

"Oh, nonsense!" Clara laughed. "You're just not used to the makeup."

"Farmers don't wear any," he grumbled.

"Yes, well, right now, you're not a farmer. You're an actor, and so am I! Just like we always dreamed, Rufio." Clara took him by the shoulders and held him fast. She stared into his eyes directly then, her beauty only enhanced by the pink and violet stola and the makeup Beatrice had so expertly applied. "How do I look?"

Rufio felt his heart tighten at the way she asked the question, for there was uncertainty there, a lack of confidence he had not expected. He smiled. "So beautiful," he said.

She blushed behind her makeup, and looked down the length of her costume to her sandalled feet. "Rufio...I want to tell you something-"

"Me too!" he said, unable to stop himself. "Sorry. You first."

"Since we've been together...here in Rome...I've realized that-"

"Quickly! Everyone get on the stage! Felix and the aedile are coming!" Electra said, taking charge in Felix's absence.

"Go on," Rufio urged Clara, but she shook her head.

"It can wait. Come. Felix needs us now."

They both began to make their way to the stage with the others, noting Silas hanging back.

Silas crossed his arms and frowned. He had always found the Helene insufferable and arrogant, but now she was taking the role of second-in-command when it had always been him who stepped in for Felix. He followed the others to the stage.

"Everybody line up!" Electra said, arranging them how she and Felix had discussed with her on the end, then Clara, then Rufio and Fausto, Silas, Julius Castor and Pollux, Beatrice and then Damon who adjusted his ivy crown and held his flute at the ready. "Damon, some light music to set the scene."

Damon mumbled something incoherent, but the music that flowed like a gentle rain from the tip of his flute was anything but incoherent. It was soft, and beautiful.

They all waited a moment, and then from the central door of the scaena frons, Felix and the togate aedile emerged.

"Right this way, Sextus Annius Sabinus," Felix said as he led the way onto the stage.

The aedile smiled like an excited child, his eyes wide as he took in the wondrous set pieces which displayed the greatest attention to detail and quality. "Magnificent..." he said to himself and he turned to look about in awe. "Absolutely stunning, Felix Modestus! I feel as though I am in the streets of Epidamnus." He looked to the ship's prow at the end of the stage, shocked by the sight of it. "I can almost hear the gulls."

Felix looked to Damon, and the latter altered his tune to sound like sea birds in the port.

The aedile turned to the musician. "Wonderful!"

"Thanks to your generous support, Aedile, we have built the set pieces and created costumes with the greatest quality materials so that they will dazzle the audience even from the upper tiers of the auditorium."

"That you have indeed, Felix Modestus! I could not have dreamed up a greater stage for Plautus' masterpiece." He walked over to the hanging that was Erotium's front door and reached out to touch the painted fabric that was so alike to brick and stone that he wondered if his eyes were playing tricks on him. "Simply beautiful." He turned to Felix. "Which artisans did you hire to do all this?"

"No one," Felix said proudly. "The members of my company have many skills. We have done all of this ourselves."

Sextus Annius Sabinus looked shocked. "Then you are very talented indeed!" he gasped. "When the performance is over, I should love to have your people paint me a fresco in my domus to commemorate our partnership."

"We can certainly arrange that!" Felix responded.

"Simply magnificent!" the aedile added as he looked at the fountain with its running water, trickling just softly enough so as not to drown out the voices of the actors upon the stage.

"May I introduce you to the company?" Felix said.

"Yes, absolutely!" Sextus Annius Sabinus pulled his attention away from the set pieces and looked over the line of actors.

He did not have the haughty air of others whom they had encountered on their travels across the empire. He was, rather, an enthusiast who enjoyed every aspect of production. It became quickly apparent that he was one who appreciated the skill it required to bring a theatrical performance to life. He might have wished he could have done so himself, but was gracious enough to acknowledge the fact that he did not possess the skill. He smiled most genuinely as Felix introduced everyone.

"Aedile, you remember Electra? She is playing the jealous wife."

"Of course!" he said, reaching out to take Electra's hand. "My dear, how wonderful you look. I cannot wait to see you perform!"

"It is lovely to see you again, Sextus Annius Sabinus," Electra said, her manner like that of a well-bred Roman lady. "I trust your lovely wife is well?"

"Yes. She is. Thank you. I did invite her, but she prefers to see the performance in all its glory with the rest of Rome."

Felix continued. "These are my dearest childhood friends from Etruria. Clara Probita and Rufio Pagano. They are playing Erotium and Menaechmus Sosicles."

"It is a pleasure to meet you both," the aedile said. "Lady, you will mesmerize the audience, of that I have no doubt."

"I will endeavour to do so," Clara said.

"And you, Rufio Pagano…with your costume the same as Felix Modestus', I can see how the audience will be confused and not." He turned to Felix. "An ingenious way of using the costume to indicate the twins without…" he gestured to Rufio's small frame in comparison to Felix.

Fausto chuckled beside Rufio.

"I should say, Aedile," Felix added quickly, "that without Rufio and Clara, I would not have been the actor I am today, and this production would not be going forward. The Gods have brought us together for this occasion."

The aedile grew serious. "Then I am most grateful to them." He smiled at Clara and Rufio and moved on with Felix.

"Fausto here will be playing Messenio. It is the largest role he has played to date. He is our rising star, to be sure."

Fausto looked up at Felix with awe and pride, unaware of the scowl directed at him by Silas beside.

Felix frowned. "Next we have Silas who, as you can see, is already in character for the parasite, Peniculus."

"Yes, I can see that!" the aedile laughed, though the sound of it faded quickly.

"I have often played the supporting roles for Felix Modestus in our productions," Silas stated out of nowhere.

The aedile looked confused. "Yes, well… I'm sure your dominus knows what he is doing. Peniculus is an important character, is he not?" He turned to Felix. "Every play needs a villain!" He moved on from Silas. "Ah, the great Julius!"

"Aedile," Julius inclined his head most graciously. "Thank you for your support of our humble production."

"I don't know if humble is the word for this production, but it certainly does you all justice. I remember seeing you in a production of Terence when I was a boy. *Adelphi*, I think it was."

"That was a long time ago," Julius said. "I am honoured that you remember it.

"Julius will be playing both the roles of Moschus, the twins' father, and that of the medicus."

"I look forward to seeing you perform again, Julius," the aedile said, grasping the older man's hands.

"We have our own set of brothers in the production," Felix continued. "Castor and Pollux have not only built all of the set pieces, but they are also performing in the roles of the father of the jealous wife, and Cylindrus, the cook."

"Aedile," the brothers said in almost comic unison, bowing just the same.

"And here we have our Beatrice," Felix said, presenting the young woman.

"Hello, my dear," the aedile said, smiling most kindly. "Who are you playing?"

"Oh, ah…I'm playing Erotium's maid," she answered, so shyly one might have thought she was addressing the emperor.

"Beatrice is the one responsible for all of our magnificent costumes," Felix said, and this made the aedile's eyes widen.

"Really? Well, I'm sure my wife would love to hire you to create some new stolae for her. You have a rare gift, my dear."

"Thank you, sir!" Beatrice said, trying to curtsy but making it look more like a bounce.

"And lastly," Felix continued, "we have Damon, our gifted musician and muscle when we need it."

"How are you, Damon? You have a lovely skill with the flute!" the aedile said.

"He is mute, Aedile," Felix added quickly, "but his musical skill is exceptional."

"Ah, I see. Well, if you can make birds flutter from the tip of your pipes, then I can imagine that the music you create will cast a spell over the audience!"

Damon smiled and bowed his head, the leaves of his ivy crown dancing as he did so.

"Well," Felix said, "now that you have met the company, I think it time that you witness the wonder that your support has created!" He gestured to the awning that had been set up in the orchestra, beneath which was a cushioned couch and a table with a platter of fruits, cheese and bread, along with a pitcher of watered wine.

"Before we go any further, Felix Modestus, I would like to make an announcement to you and your company."

Felix turned, surprised by the sudden statement, and a little nervous. "By all means, Aedile." He stepped back and gave the stage over to Sextus Annius Sabinus.

The aedile cleared his throat and looked over The Etrurian Players with a great smile spanning his shaved face. "It is an honour for me to be a part of this production. I rejoiced when Felix Modestus accepted my invitation to come to Rome for the games. I know it will be a great success. And so much the better for the news I bring you today." He looked over the faces before him, at Felix last. "I received word last night that Emperor Severus and Empress Julia Domna will be attending the performance tomorrow."

Everyone gasped at that, their painted eyes straining wide in shock and excitement, and not a little fear.

Futuo! Rufio screamed in his mind. *I don't believe this is happening!*

Sextus Annius Sabinus nodded, acknowledging the excitement of the announcement, the general murmur that could not be helped among the players. "I know it is a heady thing to perform before the emperor and empress. I have staked a fortune upon this production, but I trust you and your dominus implicitly."

Clara reached down to grip Rufio's hand and she felt it sweaty. "How exciting," she said, her words aimed at tempering the panic she could feel radiating from Rufio.

"It is very exciting!" Felix said aloud, echoing Clara's sentiment. "Sextus Annius Sabinus, we will not let you down."

"I know you won't," the aedile said. "Now, I will take my seat, and witness what you have put together."

"Please do," Felix said, showing him to the stairs that led down to the orchestra. "We'll just need a few moments to prepare."

"At your leisure, Felix Modestus," the aedile said as he made his way across the polished, sunlit surface of the orchestra. He settled himself upon the couch beneath the awning, served himself some wine and food, and watched as the players took their places.

The sound of soft music wafted around the theatre like the sweet smoke of a newly-lit offering, and the voices of the players stilled completely behind the scaena as Felix Modestus walked onto the centre of the pulpitum to address his lone audience member for the prologus.

Sextus Annius Sabinus looked up at the magnificent man standing there, and from that moment he could not rip his eyes from the stage.

A moment passed, then another as Felix composed himself. Then...

"In the first place now, Spectators, at the commencement, do I wish health and happiness to myself and to you. I bring you Plautus, with my tongue, not with my hand: I beg that you will receive him with favouring ears. Now learn the argument, and give your attention, for in as few words as possible will I be brief..."

THE FINAL DRESS REHEARSAL COULD NOT HAVE GONE BETTER. By the time the sun had tilted beneath the high rim of the theatre of Pompey, and Messenio had closed out the performance with his declaration of the auction of all of Menaechmus of Epidamnus' possessions, including his wife and servants, Sextus Annius Sabinus was on his feet, red-faced, and teary-eyed from laughter, clapping so loudly one would have thought that the theatre was at capacity.

"Bravi!" the aedile shouted, accompanied by barking from Peli who had settled himself at his feet for the duration. "Bravi, players! Well done!" he cheered as the company lined up on the pulpitum for a bow to their patron.

Smiles spanned everyone's faces as they looked upon him, for it was that moment of absolute joy and awe which they had given to him, that often made the blood, sweat and tears worth the while.

The aedile crossed the orchestra before Felix could come to him, and ascended the steps at the side of the stage until he stood before the players, taking hold of each of their hands and praising their efforts. "Most well done! Excellent! The emperor and empress will be most pleased! All of Rome will, indeed!" he added, taking Silas' hand. "A most hateful Peniculus. I am awed by your talent…"

"Silas."

"Silas. Yes. Very well done." The aedile turned to Fausto then. "And Messenio! You certainly surpassed your performance in Ephesus…Fausto, is it?"

"Yes, Aedile!" Fausto said, beaming.

"All of you!" He then turned to Rufio and Clara who stood at the end. "I don't know why you both were not members of this company before, but I tell you, the play was perfect for your being in it. So funny…so lovely and alluring!"

"Thank you, Aedile," Clara said, still feeling the rush of the performance in her veins.

He shook his head in disbelief. "This will truly be the pinnacle of the games. I know it!" He turned to Felix again. "If you can pull this off exactly so tomorrow, well…we will all reach such heights as we can only have dreamed of until now, Felix Modestus. Truly!"

"I'm very happy you are pleased with your investment," Felix said.

"Investment!" Sextus Annius Sabinus shook his head. "This is no mere investment. This is my religious duty to Rome and the world, to be able to help you bring this to life!"

Felix put his hands up in a show of modesty that made Electra smile to herself.

"I mean it most sincerely!" the aedile added. "Every person shall leave this theatre uplifted and feeling so much better about life." He stopped himself and glanced at the player who had brought Peniculus to life. "Well, maybe not the servants who accompany their masters here!" He howled with laughter. "But they shall be much better behaved for fear of being sold!"

Everyone laughed at that.

Rufio stood there, shoulder to shoulder with Clara, his mind a maelstrom of confusion, for he had well and truly enjoyed what they had just done. *It felt so right!* he thought, as unbelievable as the thought might have been. *I wasn't even nervous!* It was true. He had not been nervous once the performance had begun, and seeing Clara there with him, and Felix at the helm, and all of them in their assigned places speaking their words to perfection… It truly was magic, and one that he had forgotten about for a very long time.

Rufio turned to Clara. "You were amazing."

She looked at him and smiled. "So were you, Rufio. I couldn't stop watching you." The memory of their staged kiss still lingered then, and she grasped his hand. "I can't imagine doing this without you, you know?"

"I do," he said, reaching up to trace a finger along a strand of her golden hair that had fallen in front of her cheek. "I'm trying not to be nervous about the fact that the emperor and empress are coming."

"Well, let's try not to think about that. There are other things…" Clara smiled and kissed him on the cheek.

Rufio smiled and blushed through his makeup as he gripped her hand in his, no words needed in that moment. In the background, he could see Felix and Electra leading the aedile back through the stage house to the quadriporticus behind where his litter bearers were waiting.

Clara frowned then, and Rufio stepped back.

"What is it?" he said, his heart plummeting.

"Silas."

"What?" his brow furrowed deeper than the loamy earth of his Etrurian holdings.

"He's harassing Fausto, look."

While the rest of the players had gone into the stage house to remove their costumes and makeup, Silas had pulled at Fausto's tunica, and appeared to be pressing distasteful words upon the younger man in a most aggressive fashion.

"You think you were that good, do you?" Silas hissed, his hand gripping Fausto's arm tightly. "That should have been my role. I would have been much better than you. You're an upstart and an embarrassment! The aedile only praised you for your ass and nothing more. He's probably just looking for a new catamitus for his domus! Just the role for you!"

"Let me go!" Fausto growled, and pushed Silas, but the latter came at him again.

"You think you're so good, but you're not. You're just a pretty face and ass, boy! Nothing more. Why do you think Felix took you on?"

"Shut up!" Fausto said. He had begun to ball his fist when Clara and Rufio appeared behind Silas.

"What's going on here?" Clara demanded. "Silas?"

Silas wheeled around to find Clara and Rufio standing in front of him, scowling with disapproval.

"Why do you keep harassing Fausto?" Rufio asked, looking beyond Silas at Fausto whose face was as red as sun-ripened cherries.

"Ah!" Silas stepped forward into Rufio's face. "The lotium-breathed loser speaks!"

"What's the matter with you?" Rufio pressed. "You're always harassing Fausto!"

"He's right!" Clara said. "In fact, you're always bothering everyone in the company."

Some of the other players had emerged from the stage house again to see what the shouting was about, and Silas spied them all, staring at him, judging him.

"What do you know of it, landica?" Silas spat at her.

Rufio was on him in a second, and they tumbled against the fountain's edge and fell in, all splashes and sputtering.

Everyone shrieked and rushed to pull them apart, but not before Felix and Electra returned, the smiles that had spanned their faces quickly replaced by anger.

"What in Hades is going on here?" Felix roared, rushing without hesitation to the fountain to pull Silas out of the water by the hem of his tunica and hold him upright with one strong arm like a cat that had fallen into a pool. "There had better be a good explanation for this!" Felix shouted. "What is happening here? Rufio? Silas?" He shook the latter violently.

Damon howled and pointed a finger at Silas.

"It looked like Rufio attacked Silas," Beatrice said, most disappointed.

But Clara stepped forward to Rufio's side. "We saw Silas harassing Fausto again and asked him what was going on."

"Again?" Felix said, looking at Silas.

"He insulted Clara!" Rufio said. "So I gave him one!"

"Like a little girl!" Silas tried to kick at Rufio but Felix held him back like a wet cloak upon a peg.

More shouting ensued, and Felix dropped Silas. "Shut up, all of you!" He turned to look at everyone. "What is happening here? We just gave a magnificent performance and might have ensured patronage for our company for the duration. And you're all fighting?" He turned on Silas. "Why are you harassing Fausto?"

"So this is my fault?" Silas stood then, wiping his face violently. "You always have favourites! You're blind to the truth as usual!"

"The truth?" Fausto stepped forward. "Dominus," he addressed Felix. "He keeps telling me I have no skill. And I'm tired of him trying to use me as a *cinaedus* at every turn. I haven't been sleeping because he's always lurking!"

Everyone was silent as the shock of what Fausto was saying came to light. They knew he had not been sleeping well, and that there were circles beneath his eyes to attest to that. But everyone had put it down to nerves before the biggest performance of his young career.

Felix turned on Silas. "What do yo have to say for yourself, Silas? We're supposed to be a *familia*, no? To help each other? To lift each other up?"

"You mean to lift you up!" Silas hissed back. "It's all about you, Felix, isn't it? You and your amateurish friends and your stupid dream that you keep saying some goddess sent you!"

"Careful, Silas." Felix's voice was low and even, his demeanour dark.

"It's you who should be careful! All of Rome is coming to see us - the emperor and empress! - and you're putting your faith in this bunch!" He waved a soaking arm at the entire company. "You think you can trust the opinion of that fool aedile? He's an idiot and wouldn't know a good performance if it struck him across his fat face!"

"I am your company leader Silas…your dominus. You will apologize to everyone here right now, or you will find yourself in the slave market tomorrow!"

"Some leader you are!" Silas shouted, standing without fear now before Felix, as he had never done before. "Why don't you tell them where *all* of the money is coming from to fund this farce?" He looked at the rest of the company now to make sure they had heard him correctly. "Did you all know? He didn't just get money from the aedile! Most of it came from a Suburan thug named Leno!"

"What of it, Silas?" Pollux growled. "Wherever the money comes from, we'll make it back tenfold!"

"Oh you think so, you idiot?" Silas turned to him, and then back to Felix. "Why don't you tell them about the deal you struck with Leno? Hmm?"

"You go too far, Silas," Felix said.

"No, *you* go too far! Felix is in so much debt, he'll never be able to keep this company alive! If Leno doesn't get back all of his money, plus interest, he will take over the company and own all of us!"

"What did he say?" Julius asked. "Felix?"

"You're lying, Silas!" Castor said, pointing a finger at him.

"Oh, am I?" Silas almost screamed. "Why don't you ask our *dominus*?"

"We have investors, and we will pay them back easily!" Felix declared, and saw the shock in everyone's faces. "You heard the aedile. It is the greatest production he has ever seen!"

"A dress rehearsal!" Silas said. "It will be different tomorrow! Felix, your hubris is going to bring us all to ruin, and it all stems from your ridiculous dream about these two idiots!" He pointed at Rufio and Clara.

Without a moment's hesitation, Felix's arm struck out and landed a backhand across Silas' face, sending him into the side of the fountain.

Everyone gasped.

Silas was still for a few moments before he stood up, his nose bleeding, and spat at Felix's feet.

"I'm finished with all of you. Good luck tomorrow, because when you all fail in front of the emperor and empress, you'll enjoy a life of servitude to one of the foulest men in Rome. I QUIT!" Silas roared, turned, and rushed off the stage.

"Silas, you snake!" Felix shouted. "Get back here! SILAS!"

XVII

POISONED WORDS

That evening, panic began spread through the company like blood in the water when a ship wrecks itself upon the rocks, and the sharks begin to circle and feed. To have gone from such elation and excitement, to view the world that could have been theirs after performing before the emperor, empress, and all of Rome, but then to have that vision blown away… well… It is a sad thing when dreams perceived are so suddenly dashed.

However, what concerned the members of the company, first and foremost, was not the fact that they had to put on the play without the frowning visage of their Peniculus but, rather, what Silas had revealed about Felix's funding sources for the production. In a terrible way, it all began to make sense to them - the lavish set pieces and materials, the renting of the enormous warehouse for so many months, the seemingly endless budget. It was not all due to the generosity of the aedile who, they all realized, also had to fund the rest of the Ludi Apollinares around Rome. Felix had bet all of their lives on this venture, and Silas had just put the seal on their papers of servitude.

Felix raged for some time about the theatre while the rest of the company cleaned up the stage and secured everything for the night. "He's left us hanging at the most crucial moment in our career as a company!" Felix kept saying. "I'll kill him!"

"I can't believe you've done this to us!" Electra said as she stood in the middle of the orchestra floor facing Felix who sat beneath the dark shadow of the awning where the aedile had sat before. She shook her head when he looked up at her. "You've killed us all with your ambition, Felix."

Felix Modestus looked up to see Electra at the forefront of his company, like the rebellious woman in *Lysistrata* leading the masses against him.

"How could you do this to me?" she demanded. "To all of us?"

"Shut up, woman! I'm trying to think!" Felix barked.

But Electra did not back down. "You've had your time to think. And it did not go well for any of us!"

There was ire in Felix's eyes then. He stood and took a few steps toward her.

It was then that Rufio and Clara stepped in from where they had been sitting to the side, numb from all that had happened, trying to think clearly about a way out of things.

"Felix, don't," Clara said, her hand upon his chest as she stood between Felix and Electra.

Felix looked at her, a shocked expression upon his face that she should think he was about to strike Electra for, in actuality, he had been going to hug her tightly. *I can't lose her to Leno!* he screamed inside, though he was not going to say it aloud. "I'm fine!" he barked. "Don't worry, everyone. We'll figure this out."

"How are we going to figure this out, Dominus?" Castor said. "I've heard about this Leno. He's one of the worst thugs in Rome!"

"I don't want to make clothes for someone like that," Beatrice said, her face ashen since the earlier fight.

"I don't think making clothes is what he'll want you for, Beatrice," Pollux said, most unhelpfully.

Beatrice did not understand immediately, but as it dawned on her, her lip began to quiver with fear and she clung to Julius.

"There, there," Julius comforted her. "Felix will figure this out, girl. Don't worry." The veteran actor looked up at Felix, his disappointment plain, though he did not voice it.

"No one is going anywhere!" Felix stood tall and walked among them, like a general addressing his troops. "I'm sorry I got you into this mess. I know I've let you down. We could not get the funds we needed in order to put this production on unless I went elsewhere for the coin."

"Yes, but you gambled our lives!" Fausto burst out, his face red, terror written plain upon it as if it were a lead curse tablet etched in anger.

"I know, Fausto," Felix said, trying to be calm and fatherly toward the young man. "I also know now that you've been putting up with Silas' attacks. I'm sorry I did not see it, but you should have come to me."

"Well, he's gone now, and we're screwed!" Castor said.

"Fu-tuoooo!" Damon howled, his eyes darting like a cornered dog.

"All right, all right! Everyone shut up!" Felix bellowed. He looked at Electra and Clara who stood there arm-in-arm, and the sight of it wrenched his heart. "Rufio," Felix said. "What do you think?"

"I think you're an idiot!" Rufio said.

"Not helpful right now!" Felix growled.

"We need to get Silas back so that he can perform the play."

"And how are we going to do that?" Felix asked.

"Can you hire some slave catchers?" Rufio suggested.

Felix shook his head. "I thought of that. Even if they find him, it would mean Silas might be locked up or beaten, and then unable to perform anyway. No. I want to coax him back somehow so that he willingly performs. Then, after the play, I'll figure out what to do with him."

"And if he is not found, or if he doesn't come back?" Julius asked.

Felix was silent for a few uncomfortable heartbeats. "We'll need to try and find him first. Then, if we're not successful, we'll go back to the warehouse and re-assign some roles to make it work. It won't be that difficult. You all know the lines." *More or less,* he thought with unaccustomed terror. "Is everything packed up for the night?"

"Yes, Dominus!" Pollux said.

"Good. Now, let's go in pairs. Take roundabout ways to get back to the warehouse. Visit any places Silas has been to - tabernae, brothels, anywhere - and report to the warehouse directly."

"What do we say if we see him?" Beatrice asked, wiping her nose.

Felix thought for a moment. *What would bring him back?* "Tell him that I am very sorry for what happened and what I said, and that I will make it up to him. Maybe one of the lead roles in our next production."

Everyone stared at him.

"We want him to come back, right?" Felix asked his company. "That is what's required. Castor and Pollux, you take the Suburra. Beatrice and Julius, try the Aventine. Fausto and Damon, check the taverns. Go now. I'll see you back at the warehouse."

The three groups set out, eager to find their hateful colleague and somehow save their company from the ruin that hung over all of them.

When they had all gone, Felix turned to Rufio. "Take Peli with you and Clara. Try the Forum Romanum. Maybe the dog can sniff out Silas somewhere. He hates him."

"That he does," Rufio said. "But the streets are going to be crowded with revellers. It's not going to be easy to find him."

"I know," Felix agreed, "but we have to try."

"Felix why didn't you say anything about the money?" Clara asked. "I could have helped you."

"Please, Clara. I appreciate that, but the costs were beyond you, trust me."

Clara decided not to say anything. *It's too late anyway.*

"I think Leno knew something would go wrong, and that he would acquire much more. Who knows how men like that think?"

"You should have," Electra said. Her usually strong demeanour had nearly crumbled with the recent revelations, and she now appeared like one of the tragic characters she so often performed.

"I know." Felix took her hand which she gave reluctantly, and pulled her to him. "I should have." He hugged her. "I'll fix this."

"Well, we'd better start searching," Clara said, turning to Rufio.

"Yes. Felix, we'll see you back at the warehouse," Rufio said, not sure if Felix had heard him. He then joined Clara and Peli and the three of them wandered through the gardens behind the theatre and out into the torchlit streets of Rome.

THE SEARCH FOR SILAS HAD, UNFORTUNATELY, COME UP EMPTY. In pairs, they had visited the assigned places and more, but to no avail.

Rufio and Clara, with Peli in tow, had gone into the forum to search the crowds that had gathered there for performances. They had checked the alleyways between temples, the porticoes of the Basilica Julia, and even the quieter streets of the Palatine that hung over the forum. The whole time, Peli had seemed undisturbed, trotting along casually beside them, stopping only briefly to urinate on the leg of some poor, unsuspecting audience member whose attention was taken up with a pantomime upon one of the many stages that had been set up.

"He's nowhere to be seen," Clara said to Rufio as they turned to head toward the Forum Boarium and back to the warehouse. "I meant to thank you for stepping in earlier. With Silas, I mean."

Rufio shrugged. "He insulted you."

"Do you think we shouldn't have confronted him like that?" Clara asked him. "I mean, if we hadn't done that, maybe he wouldn't have left?"

"I think Silas was just looking for a reason to disappear."

"Maybe you're right, but I can't help but think that this is all going to fall apart. I worry about the others, but mostly about Felix."

"I do too," Rufio said. He reached out to take her hand in his as they walked, and to his delight she gripped his back.

"We have to try and help Felix somehow. Let's get back to the warehouse and talk about who can play Peniculus. This is too good a company to be broken up now!"

Rufio smiled at her, and kissed her hand.

"You forgot to change out of your costume," Clara added with a smirk back at him.

He looked down at the deep blue tunica and the golden border glinting in the passing light of a brazier. "Ha! So I did! I knew I felt different. I'll be careful not to soil it." He looked down at Peli. "You too!"

The dog gazed up at him with his mismatched eyes.

The mood back at the warehouse was grim. Rufio and Clara were the last of the search parties to return, and when they entered the heads of everyone sitting at the long table turned to look hopefully at them.

"Did you find him?" Felix rushed forward to greet them.

"I'm sorry, Felix," Clara shook her head, "no sign of him."

Felix nodded to himself as if he had made a decision, his mind racing to go over the best course of action so that they could salvage all that they had built together. He sat back down at the head of the table with his players, all of them looking to him for reassurance.

Rufio could see that Felix's body was far more tense than usual, his eyes darting, and he was speaking more quickly, not with his usual energy, but with a growing panic. He walked over to him and placed his hand upon Felix's slumped shoulders. "We can fix this."

Felix looked up from where he sat. "I'm open to ideas. Tell me."

Clara took her seat across from Electra and they all looked up at Rufio.

He felt the heat around his neck, but he also felt emboldened by Clara's warm hand in his as they had returned from their search. "Peniculus is a big role, to be sure, but he is not on stage all the time, not with all of the others. Julius?"

"Yes," the older man replied.

"It's not really said that Peniculus is a young man, is it?"

"No. I don't think so."

"And people often have older servants."

"I believe they do." Julius was sitting straighter now.

"I *know* they do!" Rufio laughed, picturing Errol and his dry antics back home. "Do you know Peniculus' lines?"

"I believe I do," Julius answered.

"I see what you are doing," Felix added, "but we have Peniculus lurking in the fifth act, and as part of the fight, even though he doesn't say anything."

Rufio shrugged. "Just don't have him lurking or fighting. Stick to Plautus' direction completely. Peniculus is not there in the fifth act." Rufio turned back to Julius. "Could you play Peniculus for the first four acts, and then revert to the Medicus for the fifth?"

Julius was silent for a moment. He turned over in his old mind the lines he had been hearing for months, lines which he had visited off and on over the course of his career. "It will be a challenge," he said, scratching the side of his head, "but I can do it. Certainly. For our dominus!"

Felix felt his heart fill with pride and gratitude for the older man, and immediately felt himself beginning to calm.

"There you have it," Rufio said, taking his seat beside Clara.

"Right!" Felix clapped his hands loudly. "Silas is gone, but we will press on without him! Now, I know you are all tired, but we should run through all of the lines just once to make sure."

There was a collective sigh from the group, but they knew it was better to be safe than utterly sorry if things went awry the following day.

"Come on, friends!" Julius said aloud. "We can do this!" He paused for a few seconds, and then, without looking at the script on the table before him, he began. "The young men have given me the name of Peniculus, for this reason, because when I eat, I wipe the tables clean..."

Felix gazed down the long table at Julius and smiled.

IT WAS WELL INTO THE NIGHT BY THE TIME THE READING WAS finished, and everyone made their ways to their sleeping cots or cubicula to get some rest for the following day. The performance was not until later in the day, so they had time to sleep in if they could.

Felix stood from the table and held his hand out to Electra. "Come. Let's rest."

Electra, who had been quite upset earlier in the day at

the revelations about Leno and the deal Felix had struck, had calmed now that she saw a way out of it. She knew Julius was an accomplished actor, and knew the production was safe again. His instincts on stage were good enough that he would be able to perform the actions as if he had been practicing them for months. With a loud sigh, she followed Felix, but not before she turned to Rufio. "Well done, Rufio Pagano."

"It was just an idea." Rufio smiled back at her. "Julius is the hero."

"Yes he is," Felix added. "Anyway, good night, you two. Rest. Tomorrow is the big day. Let us hope the goddess who started all this is pleased, whoever she is."

Rufio and Clara watched Felix and Electra disappear into their curtained sanctum.

"Well, I guess we should get some sleep," Clara said as she turned to Rufio.

"Can I speak with you first? Alone?" Rufio asked the question, but he had not planned on it. *Now is as good a time as any!* he thought. *I can't hold it in anymore!*

"Are you sure it can't wait?" Clara said.

"No. It can't." He smiled and took her hand again, wanting the familiar feel of it.

Clara smiled back, and nodded. "All right."

Rufio led her through the warehouse to his cubiculum, his heart racing as they went. He did not quite believe what was going on in his mind, but he felt a sudden urgency to tell her all that he felt, and all that he wanted and hoped for them. *No more wasted time!*

They entered the cubiculum and Rufio lit the small brazier that was there. As the fire took, the wall of scrolls illuminated alongside the flickering paintings upon the walls. He sat on the edge of the bed and looked up at her.

Clara's eyes sought his, and without a word, she sat on the

edge of the bed beside him, her hand once more in his. "What is it?" she asked, her voice so very soft in his ears.

"Clara, I…" he felt his breath shallower, and paused to catch it. "I have loved these past months together. I feel like… like we've been given a second chance. I mean, how many people are given such a gift by the Gods?"

"Not many," she answered. "For us to be given a second chance at performing in Rome, and the same play too? It's unheard of! We owe Felix a lot for this."

"Yes…yes we do. But that's…that's not what I'm talking about."

"What are you talking about, Rufio?" Clara's eyes were wide and glossy as she looked upon him. She knew, of course, what he was getting at. But she wanted him to say it. They had been dancing around the thought for too long. She had avoided it before Rome, for all the pain it had caused her. But since seeing Rufio again, all of her past feelings of love and warmth had resurfaced from the depths into which she had plunged them. She had forgiven him, and it was not until his injury that she had truly understood.

"I'm talking about us, Clara. I…I love you." *I said it!* "I always have. I always will. And I-"

"I love you too, Rufio." The words burst from her lips like the first notes of birdsong in spring. "Since we were young… I've loved you, with all my heart." *You have to tell him before this goes further!* she told herself, afraid of ruining the moment.

The smile that stretched across Rufio's face hurt it was so wide, but he did not care, for he felt life bursting within him as if he were ten years younger. It was as if a whole new world of possibilities suddenly became clear in his mind. "Clara you've made me the happiest man…" *Wait, you idiot! You're moving too fast. Slow down! Enjoy the moment!* "I…I think we should pour a libation to the goddess for bringing us together again."

"I think that's a fine idea," Clara said, laughing a little at how red he was in the face.

Rufio went to the broad table where he had a wine jug and two cups sitting there. He poured wine into the cups and was about to hand Clara one of them when he saw a small, rolled papyrus in the middle of the table. He set the jug down and reached for the scroll.

"What is it?" Clara asked.

"Someone has left a note here. It says 'Urgent' on it?" He turned and held it up for her to see. "It...it looks like Silas' hand. I remember it from when I watched him do the accounts."

"Really? What does it say?" Clara was on her feet right away.

Rufio looked at her, and wondered for a moment whether he should just leave it and continue on the course of love he had been determined to follow before. But then he thought of Felix and the production. If they could figure out where Silas was, then they could make everything well again.

"Read it!" Clara urged.

Rufio unrolled the papyrus and held it to the firelight.

Rufio Pagano,

I never liked you and I think you are a terrible actor and idiot.

However, if there is one thing I hate, it is lies, and daily I have watched your friends lie to you.

You should know that things have happened without your knowing, that all those years ago, when you left Rome like a coward, Felix and your beloved Clara then spent a night of passion together, drinking and comforting each other. As soon as you were gone, they took the opportunity to do so, and they have kept that secret for years. You've seen the way they are together, haven't you? If not, then you're a fool.

That they were lovers is plain for all to see, except, that is, for you. But, as I said, you're an idiot.

I'm not telling you this because I like you, but rather the opposite. I hope this news ruins you and any false chance for happiness you thought you might have had.

If I were you, I would get out now, before you humiliate yourself anymore.

Silas

"What does he say?" Clara said, but her heart sank when she saw the changed expression upon Rufio's face, the way he looked up at her, utterly disappointed.

He handed her the papyrus scroll.

Clara read the words that Silas had all but spat onto the page, and she felt herself grow dizzy. There was a ringing in her ears for a moment, and she sat on the edge of the bed.

"Why is he saying those things?" Rufio crossed his arms and looked down at her.

"Rufio…I…" *This can't be happening.* Clara felt her head spinning, and the walls about them wavering upon their joists. "I can explain-"

"You mean Silas isn't lying?" Rufio felt his chest heaving, and the muscles of his entire body shuddering. "Clara? Tell me this is not true!" He pointed at the papyrus grasped in her hands. "How could you do this to me? To us?"

"YOU LEFT US!" Clara shouted suddenly.

Rufio took a step back at her sudden vehemence.

"You abandoned me, and Felix, and all of the dreams we had built together!" Tears were rimming her eyes then, but she wiped them away violently and stared at him, her irises like broken shards of pale glass. "We were utterly destroyed, and so we drank to numb the pain you had left us with!"

"And threw in a night of lovemaking? Just for kicks?" Rufio shouted back.

"For *comfort*, Rufio! You broke my heart when you left!"

"My mother had died!" he bit back. "What was I supposed to do?"

"To tell us! Us, your best friends! But instead, you snuck off without a word, just before the performance, because you were too scared to go on!"

Rufio felt his anger getting the better of him. He did not want to indulge in it, but it had a hold of him like nothing else he had felt before. "You speak of a broken heart? That!" He pointed at the paper, shaking his head. "There is no coming back from that! You've broken mine…after I have loved you since childhood…for the whole of my cursed life, I've loved you."

Tears were forming on the lids of Rufio's eyes as he stood there, not knowing where to go or what to do now. Everything he cared about had just gone up in flames.

"And I have loved *you*, Rufio!"

"You have a strange way of showing it." He danced on the spot. "Oh, no! Rufio's gone! What shall we do? I know! Let's screw and everyone will be all right!"

"Stop it!" Clara shouted at him. "Rufio, it was just one night!"

"And this has been just a few weeks…just a lifetime… Mundus stercoris!"

"Rufio? Clara? What is going on?" Felix called from outside the cubiculum door. "What's all the shouting about? Everyone's awake again!"

Rufio turned back to Clara. "There's your lover! Shall we see what he has to say about this?"

"Rufio, no! Please, just leave it!" Clara pleaded.

But Rufio was already opening the door. "Oh, it's you! Hello!" Rufio said, and without a second thought, his fist swung up and cracked Felix on the jaw, hard enough to send him stumbling backward, out the door and onto his back. "Ahh!" Rufio grabbed his wrist and stormed out. "I hope you're happy together!" he shouted as he bolted past Felix and the others, and out of the warehouse into the night.

"What in Hades is going on?" Felix shouted.

. . .

FELIX WAS RESIGNED TO HIS DEATH. THE DREAM THE GODDESS had sent him had been clear, explicit, and now it had burned to cinders before his eyes.

He wiped the blood from his lip, checking that his nose was not broken or crooked, and then looked at his company.

They all looked to him, absolute fear in their eyes now. They had lost Silas, and that had been bearable, almost a relief in some ways. But now, with Rufio gone, it was almost too much to bear.

Felix took a deep breath and approached them. He noted Clara off to the side, but focussed on those who would be directly impacted by the play's failure. He was quiet, like a bear who knows the hunters are closing in. "We're not done yet, my friends," he said to them, trying with all the strength he had to insert a calm hope into his voice. *This performance is one of your most important, Felix!* he told himself. *Don't let them down!*

"Dominus, what are we going to do?" Beatrice was beside herself, Castor and Pollux flanking her as if to protect her already from the grasping hands of Leno and his thugs.

"I'll tell you what we're going to do," Felix said, his voice certain, deep and clear. "We're going to put on the best show that Rome has ever seen. Do you think a legion stops fighting after losing a few men?" He shook his head. "No. The troops fight on, and so shall we." He stepped closer to them, his mind recovered from the shock, a strategy emerging from out of the tangled wood in his mind. "Silas seems to be gone for good, and I don't know where Rufio has gone, or whether he'll come back." *I can't believe he's done this to us again!* "We have to assume neither of them is performing." Felix rubbed his chin. "Castor?"

"Yes, Dominus?"

"You are now going to play Menaechmus Sosicles instead of Rufio."

"Me?"

"Yes. I know you can do it. This is your chance to shine."

"I won't let you down."

"I know it. Pollux?"

"Yes, Dominus."

"You're playing the Medicus now."

Pollux nodded grimly.

"And Julius…" Felix stepped up to the veteran actor and laid his hand on his shoulder. "As discussed, you will play Peniculus instead of Silas, but can you also play the father of the jealous wife, now that Castor is playing Sosicles?"

"Of course!" Julius said with more gusto than they had ever seen in him. "We can do this, everyone!" he turned to his compatriots. "We are The Etrurian Players, is that not so?"

"Yes!" they answered with the dark certainty of a Euripidean chorus.

Felix could see Electra staring up at him, the only one, apart from Clara, who said nothing. She sat still, her arms crossed, looking up at the man who had been supposed to protect her, who owned her in more ways than she would ever have allowed any other mortal.

"And what happens if the play is *not* a success?" Electra asked. "What then? Do we just line up in chains for this Leno to take us away?"

Felix walked up to her, took her hand, and raised her from off the chair on which she sat. He shook his head. "No. I am going to make arrangements right now to get all of you safely out of Rome. We will know immediately if the play is a success or not. If not, you will be out of Rome before the theatre empties."

"But what about you, Dominus?" Fausto asked. "Won't you come with us?"

"No, Fausto. I'll need to delay Leno and his thugs." Felix held his head high. "It will be the grandest exit I've ever made, it if comes to that."

There were tears forming in Electra's eyes at that, though she said nothing.

Felix smiled at her. "Don't worry. I have faith yet, that the goddess is on our side."

She hugged him and then, without another word, went back to the cubiculum to try and rest.

"Everyone get some sleep if you can. The city will be awake all night, but you cannot be."

The rest of the players went to find their cots for the second time that night, like silent, thoughtful wraiths seeking corners in which to hover.

Felix sighed and turned to Clara, his smile gone, his expression dark and fearful. "What happened?"

Clara shook her head and rubbed her eyes, tears falling as she removed her hands. "We argued…about the last time we were in Rome," she said through the broken sound of her voice. "He was very angry."

"Yes, I got that." He rubbed his jaw. "But why would you bring that up the night before our performance? This was our second chance, Clara!" Felix's voice had begun to rise to a shout, but he stopped himself.

"Rufio received a letter-"

"You know what? I don't have time for this!" Felix turned to leave.

"Wait! Let me explain!" Clara pleaded as he began to leave. "Where are you going?"

"Later!" he said. "Right now, I have to make arrangements to get everyone safely out of Rome." He stormed off, leaving Clara with her face in the palms of her hands.

XVIII

PAGANUS INVICTUS

Rufio Pagano tore from the warehouse and through the streets of Rome as if he were a dog with its tail on fire. His vision blurred with tears of rage and betrayal, and yet his fists were balled as if he were in search of a fight at the close of the taverns.

"Where you going, you ginger knob?" a group yelled after him as he ran through them and into the Forum Romanum.

Peli raced at his side, nipping at Rufio's ankles as if he were trying to halt his progress away from the warehouse.

"Leave me alone!" Rufio shouted at Peli, but most of the people about him saw only the well-dressed, teary-eyed sprinter who cut his way past. Even the players upon one of the makeshift stages took notice.

"Look!" one of the pantomime actors said, his huge prosthetic phallus waving in the firelight. "There's a man who has forgot himself!"

The crowd laughed in Rufio's wake.

He looked back briefly to scowl at them, but in doing so he did not see the honeyed pastry stand into which he was headed, tucked in front of the Regia, before the temple of Antoninus and Faustina. He spotted the seller too late, and flung himself to the left to avoid crashing into the shelves of sticky food.

Off balance, and dancing aside like a drunken tumbler, Rufio skipped across the street toward the temple, tripping toward the ground, or what would have been the ground, except that it was the street priestess Astarte.

"There he is!" she squealed as he fell directly toward her to land on her naked chest.

"Ahh!" Rufio yelled as he flailed around on her sweaty bosom like a freshly caught fish gasping and sputtering on a broad deck.

"I knew you would come to me at some point!" Astarte sang, as she smiled and laughed and wrapped her leviathan arms around him.

All around them, people laughed and pointed.

"Look! Astarte's caught one!" someone shouted.

Farther off, another group shouted. "Look! Another play's about to start! A bawdy one!"

More people gathered around, but as Rufio extricated himself to land on his behind on the temple steps, he shouted at them. "Get out of here! There's no play! Cunni!"

"No need to be rude!" one matron said, her nose wrinkled as she looked down at the red-faced man and naked priestess. "Actors!" she said with disdain before moving on with her group.

Astarte reached out more slowly now, her hand seeking Rufio's arm.

"Don't touch me!" Rufio snapped.

Peli growled at him for that and was about to turn up his leg when Rufio's own flung out to kick the dog away.

"Something's happened," Astarte stated.

Rufio turned his sodden, sweat and tear-speckled face to look at her. It was only then he saw that Meretrix was seated with her. He laughed darkly.

"Things not going well, Rufio?" Meretrix asked with a

mixture of amusement and compassion. "You certainly know how to make an entrance."

"You could say that nothing at all is going *well*! Everything has happened!"

"Should you not be resting for tomorrow?" Astarte asked. "Meretrix and I have our tickets. We can't wait to see you and The Etrurian Players. Everyone's talking about it!"

Rufio shook his head. "Go ahead." He turned then to look up the steps of the temple and laughed. "Back at the beginning. History repeats itself, I suppose."

"What are you talking about? Relieve yourself of your burden to us, Rufio Pagano. We can help." Astarte reached out to touch his face.

He slapped her hand away. "I'm not interested. I told you before."

"Not *that*, silly man! Though it would do you some good!" It was her turn to shake her head, her lips pouty. "I meant, tell us what's happened. I'm a very good listener. And so is Meretrix, as you know."

Without any preamble, Rufio told them. "The last time I was in Rome, we were going to perform right here, on these steps. It was going to be the beginning of something great for me and my best friends."

"This Clara you told me of before?" Astarte asked.

"Yes. And Felix."

"Ah…" she sighed. "Yes. Felix Modestus. I've seen him."

"He *is* a sight," Meretrix smiled and winked at Astarte.

"Yes, well… Just before we were going to perform, I received word from Etruria that my mother had died. I panicked. I needed to go back."

"Did they understand?" Astarte's eyes were wide.

"I didn't tell them. I just left." Rufio could see it all, and worse still, he was now reconnecting with those feelings of guilt. *I'm doing it again!*

"I see," Astarte said. "What happened?"

"After I left, Clara and Felix were distraught and, apparently, they laid with each other that night after getting very drunk. Probably on some shit posca!"

"And you just found this out? Is that why you were running so wildly to me just now?"

"I wasn't running toward you, Astarte!"

She shrugged her plump shoulder, an action that made her breasts appear to grin across her chest. "The Gods have their ways, Rufio." She winked.

Meretrix giggled, not unkindly, and came around to sit on Rufio's other side. "So, you left your friends without explanation - though your reason was valid, of course. They were distraught at being left without explanation?"

"Yes. I suppose."

"They felt abandoned by you?" Astarte asked.

"Supposedly. Probably."

"Their dreams of performing in Rome were dashed."

"Yes."

"And they found comfort in each other, the only other person each of them knew. Best friends, really? At a time when their world seemed like it was ending?" One of Meretrix's painted eyebrows was raised, and there was a half smile on her lips.

"Y..yes," Rufio said.

"Can you blame them?" Astarte looked directly at him.

He was speechless, looking from one to the other of them. Until he had been together with Felix and Clara again, learned of the course of each of their lives during the years of absence from each other, he had not realized the effects of his actions.

"Had I only told them about my mother, they would have come with me, and we would have performed the play another day."

"Most likely," Astarte confirmed. "They are your friends, no?"

"Maybe I was too afraid to perform? Maybe that was the real reason I left so quickly?"

"And now the Gods have given you a second chance, you are thinking of doing the same thing, aren't you?" Meretrix put her arm about Rufio's shoulder, and he did not push her away. "Remember Felix's dream that you told me about?"

"So many wasted years…" Rufio thought, and a sadness came over him that was so sharp, so deep, that he felt he could see with new clarity for all the pain it caused him.

"Were they a waste though?" Astarte asked. "The Gods have a plan for us all, do they not? Some roads are just longer than others."

"Think about it, Rufio," Meretrix continued, her bangles jingling as she removed her arm from him. "All that has happened was meant to be. You were meant to come back here, to meet me, and Astarte, to reunite with your friends."

Astarte shifted to turn toward him, her face more serious than he had seen it. "The goddess arranged for all of it, Rufio. It's clear. Your future happiness and the lives of your friends depend on you putting aside your fear. And taking this second chance."

Rufio looked down the length of the forum to see crowds of citizens laughing in the moon and firelight, their joyous faces turned up at the performers upon the stages. They would remember that night, those games. *Some roads are just longer than others?* He repeated Astarte's words to himself. He then turned to look at Meretrix, confused by the sudden wisdom to come from the street priestess on his other side. "Do you think I should stay?"

"Why not?" she said, petting Peli who had curled up on the step beside her.

Unbidden, as if some god of mischief and discontent

sought to undermine him, to fuel his wavering anger, Rufio suddenly imagined Felix and Clara together, and the thought made his guts churn. He stood suddenly. "I can't. I just can't!" he said before walking away from the two women.

THE STREETS OF ROME GREW QUIETER AND DARKER AS THE night wore on, but Rufio did not care. He wandered by himself, letting the Gods lead him where they would, and if it was to his death at the hands of cut-throats in a dark alleyway, so be it!

He longed for the peace of Etruria, the sweet smell of the air, the scent of the earth around his home. He even missed the leaky-roofed, mouldy domus where he lived. It was not much - a supreme understatement - but it was his, and that was fine with him.

He wiped his forehead from sweat, for it was a hot summer's night, and the air was still and very close now that he had, unwittingly, entered the confines of the Suburra. Rickety tenement blocks seemed to have sprung up all around him like a forest of gnarled trees growing out of a stinking bog. To his right, a man urinated into the pot outside of a fullo's laundry, the sting of urine making him gag. A few feet up the road, an unsavoury lupa pleasured one of her customers outside the entrance of a noisy taberna with its windows thrown open.

"That slave, Silas…" someone was saying.

What? Rufio stopped suddenly in front of the taberna window. *Silas?* He dared a peek inside and spotted a table of three thugs.

They were huddled together over their cups of wine. Even from where he stood outside, the smell of garlic on their breaths wafted in his direction.

"Get out of here, you!" the man with the lupa hissed. "I don't want you watching!"

Rufio turned, annoyed. "Then get out of the street!"

"You'll have to pay if you want to watch," the lupa said, turning with a near toothless grin.

Rufio shook his head and made his way into the taberna to try and sit by the group he had heard talking.

It was noisy inside, and the stink of rancid wine stung his nostrils. The smell of cooked sweet meats hung in the air. The clientele was much rougher than any other place he had been to in Rome, but Rufio was too focussed on the three men and their mention of Silas to care what was going on around him.

"Wine?" asked a woman server whose bust was nearly exposed for the looseness of her tunica, pulled at by many a lecherous patron. "Well?"

"Ah, yes. Wine. Yes," Rufio mumbled. "And bread if you have it."

The woman went away and returned a few moments later to set the wine cup down with a slosh, and a small plate with a crust of hard bread.

Rufio looked at the bread questioningly.

The woman shrugged. "End of the day." She walked away. Rufio sniffed at the cup and took a sip that stung him all the way to his ears.

"So where do we have to go tomorrow?" one of the thugs asked.

"The theatre of Pompey," the one who appeared to be the leader replied, shaking his head. "I already told you."

"Ah! Who cares? Just tell us who we have to hit!" said the third, downing his wine and pouring some more from the chipped jug that sat in the middle of their table.

"Like I said," the leader continued, "Leno told this Silas he doesn't want the production to be a success anymore. He hates that Felix Modestus. Just wants to ruin him now."

"I hear a lot of people talking about the play. Should be good."

The leader and the one thug looked strangely at the one who had just spoken.

"That don't matter no more," the leader said, slapping the other across the face.

Rufio jumped in his seat, but forced himself to stare at his own table, his ears straining for more information. Outside, the idiot with the lupa was reaching his climax, which only made it harder to listen.

"He's getting some then, isn't he?" one of the thugs laughed.

Soon after that, the man from outside joined them at their table. He sat down and stared at Rufio. "You get off on that, did you?"

Rufio shook his head. "Just drinking my wine, friend."

"I'm not your friend," he growled.

The others stared at Rufio for an uncomfortable space of time before turning back to each other.

"So, what's the plan for tomorrow?" asked their newly-sated colleague.

The leader looked around, and then leaned in closer. "This Silas, the one staying at Leno's right now… He's going to go back and join the players for the performance."

"He is?" asked one of the others. "I thought he hated that lot? He went on about it enough when he showed up."

"Well, that's all part of his and Leno's plan, you see?" the leader continued. "This Silas is going to sabotage the play somehow, right in front of the emperor and empress."

"Sabotage? How?"

The leader shrugged. "He didn't say. All I know is that we're to show up back stage during the performance and hide ourselves from the others. When Silas gives us the signal, we're to rush in and help an *accident* befall this Felix Modestus Leno mentioned. It'll be chaos! And when the play fails we're to round up all the players for Leno, and then dump this Felix Modestus' body outside the walls along the via Aurelia."

"What kind of accident?" asked one of the others.

The leader shrugged. "I don't know. That Silas is working that out now with Leno."

"We'll need a cart," said one of them. "I've heard this Felix is a big man."

"Big men fall harder," the leader said with a grin.

Rufio felt his blood run cold. *Felix's dream!*

The leader continued. "Leno stands to make a lot from this company. He's promised to let this Silas run it in return for him making a mess of things."

"Tell him about the women!" one of the men elbowed the leader.

The leader smiled. "Apparently, there is some pretty sweet landica in the group. Very nice. Leno's promised us all a go, just to break them in."

The men all laughed at that, and clinked their cups.

Rufio felt sick. The rising panic inside his gut and chest was almost too much to bear. A part of him wanted to pick up a stool and strike each of them over their stupid skulls for what they had said, but he knew that would get him killed. He was staring hard at them, willing them to fall down dead.

"What are you looking at, fancy man?" the leader suddenly said, standing from their table and reaching across Rufio's to grab the hem of his indigo tunica. "Look at this one!" he said to his friends. "Pretty pricey tunica. Is that real gold thread?"

"Leave me alone!" Rufio snapped, pushing the man away.

The others were on their feet in an instant.

"I mean…" Rufio started to panic. He spotted the taberna server watching them, wary of yet another brawl. "I mean, how about I buy you lads a jug of the taberna's finest vintage?"

They eyed him suspiciously, but then relaxed, too tempted by his offer.

"Suit yourself, fancy man," the leader said. "Make it quick."

"I won't be a moment," Rufio said, looking at each of them.

"Do you have the money?" one of them asked. "I don't see a purse on you."

They all glared at him.

"Oh, well… I…ah." He winked at them. "I keep it hidden in my carriage, if you know what I mean."

The man from outside twisted up his face. "I thought you was walking funny."

Rufio shrugged.

"You need help getting it out?" one of the others asked him with a sly grin.

"Thanks. I've got it," Rufio said, and then went in the direction of the server.

"You shouldn't be messing with those men," the woman said.

"I know," Rufio said, leaning against the bar. "They said they would pay my bill, and asked for a jug of your finest wine."

"The Falernian?" Her face betrayed her utter astonishment.

"What else?" Rufio said. He turned to look at the group and the leader nodded and waved the woman over.

"All right," she said doubtfully. "They must have had a good night of gambling." She went to the back of the taberna and returned with a finer jug filled with a sweet vintage. "Here," she said. "Have a drink on them." She poured some into a cup for Rufio.

"You're too kind, lady," he said, taking up the cup with a shaking hand and downing the sweet nectar. He watched her go over to the table and pour for them.

The men drank immediately and greedily.

In that moment, Rufio bolted for the door and ran down the street, the shouts of the men and the taberna server echoing in the stinking dark behind him.

THE SUMMER NIGHT WAS HOT AND HUMID, AND THUNDER rumbled in the distant countryside outside of Rome as Father Jupiter rained lightning on the world outside. It was as if Rome were at the centre of a great storm, untouched, and yet always threatened.

Rufio found his way back to the steps of the temple of Antoninus and Faustina and sat down, his heart racing after his sprint out of the bowels of the Suburra. He searched for Peli's form beside him, but found the dog absent. Strangely enough, that made him feel all the more lonely, for he had grown accustomed to the canine's presence.

He buried his face in his hands, unsure more than ever as to what he should do. He was torn, well and truly. On the one hand, the realization of what had happened between Clara and Felix felt like such a betrayal. He had never felt an anger like that, for Felix had known for years what Clara meant to him. *And yet, as soon as I was out of the scene, they…*

Rufio could not bear to think of it. He balled his fists and pressed his knuckles painfully into the marble steps of the temple. *I spent all those years longing for her, wasted so much time, when really, she had given herself to Felix and married another man!*

On the other hand, he knew he was being unfair. Clara had told him of her late husband, and how it had been more of a father-daughter relationship. That had been a relief for Rufio, to know she had been treated kindly. *How lonely she must have been?*

He knew something about loneliness.

It was then, as his heart began to soften, that he remembered Clara's words. "She's right," he told himself as he sat there, alone on the temple steps. "I left them. I could have waited one day…just one! Then none of this would have happened."

It was no use. He could not plead with the Gods to turn time back on itself. He was not a god, or a hero. He was just a peasant who had mistakenly grown up with dreams that had been too big for himself.

"Clara was right. I was scared. That's the real reason I left without saying anything." He felt like weeping, but he was too angry with himself to do so. He could see Clara's distraught face and her crying eyes, and it was like a pugio to his chest. *She had said she loved me!* "I'm the one who broke *her* heart! She said so!"

And then there was Felix…

Rufio felt his hand still throbbing from when he had punched his friend, like a mad man hitting an oak door, knowing too late that he would lose that fight, but unable to stop himself. Felix, he knew, had only ever been himself. He had tried to help all three of them make their dream come true, and Rufio had turned his back on him. "Only, he had the courage to see it through, and I didn't." Rufio said, drawing strange looks from a group of passing citizens who spied the lone man sitting on the temple steps, the distant lightning flashing on his face. "Piss off!" Rufio growled, and they hurried away.

Though he had found it hard to shake the thought of Felix and Clara together, he knew now that it had happened because he had let them both down. He had betrayed the two people who had meant the whole of the world to him. Besides, it was much harder to get rid of the thought of those thugs setting upon Felix, maybe even killing him, when he could have done something about it.

"Ach!" Rufio growled to himself.

Something clawed at his back then, and he jumped down a few steps with a squeal.

There was a bark, and Rufio turned to see Peli staring down at him from the temple steps. "Where have *you* been?"

Peli barked again and descended the steps to sit before Rufio. Another bark.

"What? You too? You agree with Meretrix and Astarte?"

Bark.

Rufio sighed. He knew what he had to do, and the realization brought with it mixed feelings of calm certainty and excruciating terror.

"Come on then," he said and Peli stood and came to his side. "We need a place to spend the night. Then, we need to help our friends!"

Peli barked one last time and took off into the nearly deserted lanes of the Forum Romanum with Rufio running after him.

XIX

THE PLAY

Thunder had rumbled throughout the night, and when day finally arrived, it carried with it an uncomfortable finality, as if Phaethon himself were mounting his father's chariot for his doomed and fiery arc across the daytime sky. One had only to wait for the time and place where Jupiter would hurl his bolt.

Felix had barely slept that night, his normally confident facade giving way to uncharacteristic panic, rage, and fear. He stood to lose everything he had spent years building in the space of a few hours. Though the sun had risen, and the rest of the company was already awake and eating at the long table in the warehouse, Felix had yet to emerge from his cubiculum to commit fully to the day and whatever it and the Fates had in store.

Electra sat across from him, her hair already done, her jewels about her long, olive neck. Her dark eyes bored into Felix where he sat.

"Snap out of it!" she commanded before standing and going before him. "Stand up!"

Without a word, Felix obeyed, his shoulders slumped, his face a wreck of exhaustion and worry.

She slapped him hard across the face, once, then a second time, and when his raging eyes focussed on her, she kissed him hard upon the mouth. "Where is the man I know? The man I love?" she demanded. "Today, of all the days of this life, I need you. Your company needs you! You are our captain, Felix! Our leader! Would you bend over and accept defeat, and the loss of your company, of your hard-won dreams - of me! - to some lowly thug?"

"Of course not!" Felix finally said.

"Then, by Apollo, and the goddess who brought us all to this place and time, do not give up now! Lead us to the victory that is rightfully ours!"

"You are not Andromache," he said, his voice low, "and I, most certainly, am not Hector."

"No!" she said, her voice quavering, her eyes like newly-kindled, twin fires. "I don't want to be a Trojan woman, pining after the dead. I am your Penelope, Felix Modestus. Fight for me as I would fight for you!"

Felix felt a chill run up and down his spine and his limbs, and tickle the crown of his head. It was as if the Gods were guiding Electra then, urging him to take up his arms and skill, and march out. He shook his head and stretched his shoulders. A deep breath filled his lungs. He took Electra by the shoulders and kissed her. "Hector dreamed his death," he said, "but I dreamed of death, *and* of victory."

"It is for you to decide," she said.

They hugged tightly then, and Electra pulled back to look up at him again. "We can do this, Felix, with or without Silas or Rufio. But, if this is to be our last performance, we *must* make it the performance of a lifetime no matter what has happened!"

"The Gods blessed me when they gave me you," he said, kissing her once more before rising to his full height. "Come. Let us to our troops!"

Felix marched out of their cubiculum, and Electra hung

back for a moment, wiping her eye with a shaky hand. "Goddess…please let this not be the end."

After a few more heartbeats, she followed Felix out.

"Felix, there you are!" Clara said the moment she saw him emerge from behind the curtains. "I need to speak with you. It's important. I know why Rufio-"

"Not now, Clara," Felix said, his hand up, his mind determined to address his players. "The day is wearing on quickly and I need to speak to the company." He passed her by and strode directly to the table of dejected and fearful faces. Felix paused, his hands gripping the edge of the table for a moment before he stood tall and smiled at them.

"I know this seems like the most insurmountable challenge we have ever had to face. And I know that I have put you all in a terrible position."

They were silent as they stared back at him, having had far too much time to mull over the consequences of failure.

Felix pressed on. "I am sorry…truly…my friends. Do not worry about what will happen to you, for I have made arrangements to keep you safe if things go ill. But I know…*I know*… that the Gods are on our side. The goddess who brought us here would not have done so just to have me slain and all of you clapped in chains. Not when we bring so much joy to this world. And we do! Each one of you does!"

They were all looking squarely at him now, their features softened, their eyes beginning to see the sun beyond the mist that had engulfed them.

"I know that Silas and…" he caught himself, "…and Rufio…" *Breathe Felix. You don't need them!* "They are gone, and probably will not return. That is fine, because we are The Etrurian Players! And we can perform anything anywhere. How many times have we gone on while one of you was sick? Or injured?"

They nodded at that.

"How many times has Damon played his flute from the wings because he could not walk properly?"

"If only he would stop trying to play his flute with his arse!" Castor teased.

Everyone laughed properly at that, and Damon twirled a few notes on said flute.

"You see! We have been here before!" Felix reiterated. "We can do this!"

"Yes!" Julius roared, slapping the table. "Felix is right!"

"Of course I am!" Felix bellowed. "Now! Let's get to the theatre of Pompey and prepare to give Rome the greatest show of these games!"

Everyone was on their feet, slapping the table, clapping, and gathering their things.

Soon enough, The Etrurian Players were marching toward the warehouse doors and out into the summer sunlight.

Clara was the last to leave, her request to speak with Felix clearly forgotten. She missed Rufio acutely in that moment, but she also felt a great sense of betrayal at what he had done, anger at what he had said. "Maybe it's for the best. Nothing need be said now about the past…" She began to walk toward the light when Electra's form entered.

"Are you coming, Clara?" she asked.

"Yes."

Electra approached her, stopped before her, and then, to Clara's surprise, hugged her. "I am sorry about Rufio."

"I just can't believe he's done it again."

"I know. But right now, we all need you. Felix needs you. The play needs you." Electra's eyes were wide and dark and stared into Clara's without a trace of reticence. "You are a wonderful actress, Clara, and it is an honour to share the stage with you."

Clara was both shocked and pleasantly surprised, as much as if she had been propositioned by a Vestal Virgin.

"Let's walk to the theatre together."

Clara nodded. "Yes," she said. "Let's go."

They walked out into the light and joined the train of their fellow players as they went to their work.

THEY ARRIVED AT THE THEATRE WITH JUST ENOUGH TIME TO arrange the set pieces and stage to perfection, for shortly after, the eager audience of Rome began to file into the theatre of Pompey like a swarm of oncoming bees, through the gardens of the quadriporticus and into the theatre to claim any seat that had not been reserved for the elite of Roman society.

Behind the scaena frons, within the stage house, The Etrurian Players were putting the final touches on their costumes and makeup, checking each other before presenting themselves before their commander.

Felix stood before them, resplendent in his deep blue tunica with the golden meander borders. The leather of his black cingulum and sandals creaked satisfyingly, and his dark hair was like the main of a Numidian lion. He looked upon each of them and nodded, the buzz of the gathering crowd loud in his ears.

"Are you all ready?" he asked them, his eyes meeting each of theirs as though he were Alexander before the battle of Gaugamela. "I believe in each of you, and your skills. You all know this play back to front. We are well-prepared."

"We're ready, Dominus," Julius said.

"Absolutely!" Clara echoed.

Felix looked to her and smiled. It was the same smile he used to have when they were young, acting upon their makeshift forest stage. It gave her courage, and though Rufio was not with them, it gave her joy.

"Here is how we will begin," he said. "The aedile has three cornicens ready to sound their horns when the emperor and empress arrive. Once they are seated, the aedile will introduce us from the orchestra before taking his seat beside the emperor. Castor and Pollux, you will lower the aulaeum at my signal. Damon, you will be in position on the docks playing the sound of the gulls upon your flute for a few moments before everyone joins in the opening song. Just as we have rehearsed a hundred times."

Damon nodded, already armed with his flute.

"All of your voices will join in the first song before I come on to perform the prologus. When that is done," he turned to Julius, who looked strange now dressed as a slave, "Peniculus will come on stage, to sit upon the edge of the fountain - lazy one that he is! - and set off on his opening monologue."

Julius turned to Felix with Peniculus' disdainful look.

"Just so!" Felix laughed. "Now. Time to warm up, all of you! May the goddess bless us this day!"

While the members of the company began to warm up with their individual vocal exercises and ululations, Clara approached Felix as he was about to make his way up to the stage.

Felix stopped before her and took both her hands and kissed them. "Thank you for being here with me, Clara. I couldn't have done this without you."

"Yes. You could have, Felix. You are a marvel at what you do." She smiled, but a little sadly. "But I am happy to help."

They were both silent for a moment, both feeling the sting of Rufio's departure.

"What was it you wanted to tell me earlier?" he asked. "I'm sorry I was distracted before."

Clara thought about telling him, but then, shaking her head, she decided against it. "Nothing. Just that I know we can do this."

The spark in Felix's eyes told her that she was right to leave it alone now, for she would not have doused that light for anything in that moment. She would not rob him of his strength before that curtain revealed them to the people of Rome.

"Come," he said. "Let's take a look. I always allow myself one peek at the audience before going on."

Together, they went to the doorway that was Erotium's and looked out at the crowded auditorium.

"Gods," Clara gulped, but Felix's arm about her put her at ease.

"What a magnificent sight!" he whispered. "See how excited the people are? You can feel their energy, their antic-ipation."

"There isn't an empty seat in the entire theatre," Clara marvelled as her eyes strayed up the long aisles of the cavia fanning out to either side of the temple of Venus at the top.

"Over twenty-two thousand Romans have come to see us perform, Clara."

"Not sure I want to know that."

Felix turned her to face him. "You will light up this stage, Clara. Just as you have lit up my life since we were young."

He spoke with such certainty, such feeling, that she could not help but believe him and feel a calm wash over her. *Rufio is not here, but we must go on.* "We are meant to be here."

Felix smiled and his face brightened considerably. "Yes. We are."

Clara placed her hand upon his shoulder. "I should warm up," she said.

Felix watched her leave, and turned to look back at the crowd, his eyes searching the seats toward the front for any faces he recognized among the murmuring throng.

There were several.

Beyond the two throne-like seats reserved for the emperor and empress, and those now occupied by three Vestal Virgins and a gathering of togate senators, Felix spotted Longus' dishevelled head of red hair, his brilliant eyes searching the stage.

He spotted Felix and waved, but quickly put his hand down, smiling the breadth of his face in anticipation of the performance, just as the rest of the audience was.

Farther up the auditorium, he spied Philemon and his daughter from the Taberna Macedonica, and some of the other patrons he passed in and out of those welcoming doors.

Other faces he might have recognized from his dealings with suppliers. There appeared to be the actors from other theatre troupes who had come to the city for the games. One could pick them out for the way they pointed at and observed what was visible of the set and stage pieces, their eyes wide at the expense of the production. Unfortunately, Titus Gallicus was there too, with members of The Messenian Masters.

"Futuo!" Felix cursed under his breath when he saw them.

"What is wrong?" said a panicked voice behind him. "Is everything all right? Please say it is!"

Felix turned to see the sweaty visage of the aedile, Sextus Annius Sabinus. He wore a neatly-pressed toga with a dark, broad stripe around the hems. His hair was newly-cut and oiled, and his face was red from being recently shaved. "You should calm down, Aedile. All is well," Felix lied.

"Are you sure?" the aedile said, wiping his brow with a cloth he grasped for just that purpose. "I was just speaking with the rest of the company, wishing them luck, and noticed that two of your main players are not there? What happened to Menaechmus Sosicles and Peniculus?"

"We have had to make a last-minute change to the casting," Felix said, not really noticing that he was gripping the aedile's shoulders tightly as if to steady himself. "It is in hand."

"What? Oh, what was it?" His eyes shut tightly in panic, as if doing so would make it all go away.

"Artistic differences, that is all," Felix lied again. "Sextus," he said more softly. "Listen to me."

The aedile opened his eyes and stood a bit straighter. He nodded.

"This will be the greatest play Rome has ever seen. Trust me."

"I do. That is why I have poured so much of my budget for the games into this one production. It has to work, Felix Modestus. It must! Or else I am done for in Rome."

"As will we all be," Felix said darkly. He then turned the aedile to look beyond the doorway to the audience gathered there. "Look at those faces. They already adore us. They have heard about us…caught glimpses of us. The set pieces they can see beyond the aulaeum are already mesmerizing them. They have truly loved these games which you are responsible for putting on."

"They have gone well," Sextus Annius Sabinus said, more to reassure himself.

"They have!" Felix confirmed. "I have heard people saying so everywhere I have gone in Rome since the games began. You have already won them over."

The aedile looked to the space beside the two thrones set up, where his wife sat waiting for him to join her. She appeared nervous too, anticipating the imperial arrival.

"When you introduce the play," Felix continued, "you will be doing so to an audience - to an emperor and empress - who are already grateful for the work you have done. And then, this performance will be the final seal upon your written success."

"You really think so, Felix Modestus?"

"I do. Now, go. Join your wife, and wait for the emperor and empress."

"Thank you," the aedile said nodding vigorously, forcing himself to calm his breath. "Yes. This is a good day."

"It is a magnificent day," Felix added with a smile. "Enjoy the show, Aedile."

With a final smile, Sextus Annius Sabinus went down the stairs to the side and walked slowly across the orchestra to join his wife, nodding to the senators who watched him cross the smooth surface of the floor. As soon as he sat down, however, the sound of cornui blared, and the emperor and empress emerged onto the orchestra floor from the other side, flanked by a few Praetorians.

The aedile rose up from his seat quickly, as though someone had placed a pine cone upon his chair. His wife, stood also, followed by all of the senators, Vestals, and most of the audience present, all the way up to the velaria that provided shade from the early evening sun.

Felix, and the rest of the company crowded behind him, watched as the aedile and his wife greeted Emperor Severus and Empress Julia Domna graciously, applause for the imperial couple ringing out from the seats above.

"Great beard!" Felix said as he looked upon the emperor.

"I've never seen them up close," Clara said.

"I hear the empress knows everything about theatre," Castor added.

"Look at her hair!" Beatrice said, trying to see between the others. "So simple and elegant!"

"All right everyone," Felix said, seeing the severe look in Electra's eyes. "This is no time to panic. We are ready for this, right?"

"Yes, Dominus!" they said.

"I am very proud of all of you," Felix told them, looking at each of them. "We can do this. We *will* do this, and do it well."

They smiled at that, and he saw it, that light of certainty that kicked in before every performance.

He smiled. "Now, take up your positions. You know what to do."

They dispersed, including Clara, who tried to ignore the loneliness that seemed to be hampering her.

Felix took Electra's hand then and kissed it. "Bona Fortuna."

"Tyche," she replied as she backed away to take up her position and wait.

Felix turned back to see the emperor and empress settle into their seats and the aedile move slowly to the centre of the orchestra floor to address the crowd.

Felix looked up at the temple hovering above the theatre, and for a moment he thought he could see the shimmering outline of a goddess standing on the temple steps. His heart pounded in his chest and he shut his eyes. It was not Venus, of that he was sure, for he recognized the goddess who was responsible for the entirety of the journey that had led him to that place and time. *Oh, divine Goddess…let this performance surprise and delight everyone here. Let it save us.*

A hush fell over the entire audience then as Sextus Annius Sabinus cleared his throat and spread his arms to address the crowd. He felt like a lone man, standing upon a beach as a titanic wave rushed toward him, the audience high above, looming, staring down at him. He bowed to the emperor and empress.

For a moment, Felix feared he would panic or faint as he did so, but then the aedile's voice rang loud and clear for all to hear.

"Most victorious Emperor Severus," he began. "Glorious Empress Julia Domna… Fellow senators and citizens of Rome. I welcome you to this, the final performance of the Ludi Apollinares, which it has been my sacred honour to sponsor this year. I have travelled the length and breadth of our divine empire. I have seen the performances of myriad theatre companies in some of the greatest theatres and odea in the world, but this…" he looked around the theatre of

Pompey, slowly, dramatically, "…this first theatre of Rome… this place built by Pompey Magnus in honour of Venus Victrix…this is perhaps the greatest of all settings." He looked back down at the audience, trying not to be shaken by the imperial eyes focussed so sharply upon him. "And that is fitting, for I have been able to secure this performance by the greatest theatrical company I have ever been fortunate enough to see perform."

Felix smiled at that, and chuckled when he saw the disgruntled look on Titus Gallicus' face.

"It is my honour to bring to you…for the very first time in Rome…The Etrurian Players!"

Applause erupted at the announcement of the company's name, for Rome had been hearing about them, catching tantalizing glimpses of them, for a long time. And now, it was happening. The time had come.

"And so," the aedile said, more loudly, his arms kindly asking for quiet. "And so… Before we all bear witness to the greatest performance Rome has ever seen…it is left to me to call on our divine patrons that they too may bear witness to what is about to happen upon this sacred stage."

Sextus Annius Sabinus raised his arms to the sky and closed his eyes. He felt the warmth of the setting summer sun upon his face, illuminating it in orange and red hues as he did so. And then, he spoke to invoke the Gods…

"Oh Goddess Venus…Oh, Far-Shooting Apollo…Divine Muses… We honour you, Children of Jupiter… We offer to you this wondrous performance, and ask for you to bless our emperor and empress, and the people of the Tiber who are gathered here. May the words of immortal Plautus touch our hearts and move our souls this day…and always… We offer our thanks for the art and creativity that touches and enriches all of our lives."

Sextus Annius Sabinus bowed once more to the emperor

and empress, and then, as the audience applauded, he made his way to his seat beside Emperor Severus.

"Well done, Sextus," Felix said as he stood before the central doorway that led onto the stage. He looked to his left and to his right to see the faces of his company, his friends, and, despite the fleeting sadness at not seeing Rufio there, he smiled at them and nodded. He waited for Damon's flute to pipe up, to send the gulls soaring into the air about the auditorium.

The audience gasped at the skill of such playing, and did so again as the aulaeum was lowered into its pit in the floor before the stage by a hidden Castor and Pollux.

The port and city streets of Epidamnus appeared before the audience as if by some sleight of the Gods' hands. A ship sat at berth to the right where a lone dock slave played a flute as he leaned upon a sack of grain in the midday sun. In the centre of the street, a fountain trickled with a sound that gently roused the ear. The stage was set, glinting in gold and marble, a place any should like to live in.

Goddess guide me, Felix asked as he took his usual deep breath, and then walked through the central doorway onto the stage.

All eyes were upon him as he walked to the front of the pulpitum, his glorious presence filling the street of Epidamnus. Some men in the audience looked upon Felix with a hint of jealousy, and some with admiration. Several women sighed, and others clenched their fists to assuage the sudden hunger that tickled their senses. Others waited, anticipating the first words that would emerge from the actor's mouth.

Felix observed them for a moment, his gaze never lingering on any one person. And then, as the gulls from Damon's flute quieted, he spoke…

"In the first place now, spectators, at the commencement, do I wish health and happiness to myself, and to you." He bowed, mainly toward the emperor and empress, but most of the audience felt that it was meant for each of them.

"I bring you Plautus, with my tongue, not with my hand. I beg that you will receive him with favouring ears. Now learn the argument, and give your attention; in as few words as possible will I be brief. And in fact, this subject is a Greek one; still, it is not an Attic, but a Sicilian one. But in their comedies the poets do this; they feign that all the business takes place at Athens, in order that it may appear the more Greek to you."

Felix turned to look to one side of the theatre as he spoke, his hands accentuating the words and meaning perfectly, as if he were a mage mesmerizing his audience, lulling them into the world of which he spoke.

"I will not tell you that this matter happened anywhere except where it is said to have happened. This has been my preference to the subject of this play. Now I will give the subject, meted out to you in a measure, nor yet in a threefold measure, but in the granary itself. So great is my heartiness in telling you the plot."

As was customary, Felix then outlined the plot for the audience. Though many Romans who loved theatre knew Plautus' work as though he were their very own grandfather whose stories they had heard over and over, they listened with eager ears.

"This is the city of Epidamnus," Felix said, as he reached the end of his prologus, "while this play is acting. When another shall be acted, it will become another town, just as our companies too, are wont to be shifted about. The same person now acts the procurer, now the youth, now the old man, the pauper, the beggar, the king, the parasite, the soothsayer…"

Felix bowed graciously to the audience and backed away before turning and going back out through the central door.

A song of soft chatter floated on the air then, a chorus unseen and unheard as the company set off on the first melody.

It was a tune to lull the audience and lift their spirits in accordance with Plautus' immortal will to please. Damon's gulls then were loosed aloft, and as the song faded out, that most hateful parasite, Peniculus, skulked onto the stage as if he were up to some mischief or other.

Julius, who hid behind the facade of that naughty slave, marvelled at the sight of that packed theatre, and he was taken back to the lost days of his youth when he would regularly see such sights. It was marvellous to him, and as the audience looked upon him most suspiciously, he wrinkled his face at them before he spoke from his lazy perch on the edge of the fountain.

"The young men have given me the name of Peniculus, for this reason, because when I eat, I wipe the tables clean."

The audience laughed at that, and some jeered.

"The persons who bind captives with chains, and who put fetters upon runaway slaves, act very foolishly, in my opinion at least. For if bad usage is added to his misfortune for a wretched man, the greater is his inclination to run away and to do amiss…"

Felix and Electra watched and listened to Julius' cunning performance with awe, almost as rapt as the audience by the veteran's performance, but for the fact that they had to be ready to play their own parts in the story.

"I can't believe he's done it," Electra whispered. "And without much in the way of rehearsal."

"He's amazing!" Felix hissed, observing the constellation of faces fanned out on the other side of the orchestra. He looked to his right and smiled at Clara who stood behind the door of Erotium's domus, and then to his left to see Fausto and Castor whose Messenio and Menaechmus Sosicles stood at the ready.

Castor, Felix noted with not a little worry, seemed poised with fraught silence, Fausto whispering to him that all would be well.

Don't think on it! Felix chided himself as his mind drifted to Rufio. *He's gone. Leave it alone, and focus!*

"Are you ready?" Electra asked him as Peniculus neared the end of his parasitical opening.

Felix nodded, took his breath, and then his Menaechmus of Epidamnus came to life as he scowled at his jealous wife.

Electra scowled back, ready to unleash her frustrated growl such that it burst forth from the doorway onto the audience itself.

Now!

Menaechmus of Epidamnus burst out of the door of his home onto the street, clearly frustrated as he turned to the door of his own home, yelling at his jealous wife.

"Unless you were worthless, unless you were foolish, unless you were stark wild and an idiot, that which you see is disagreeable to your husband, you would deem to be so to yourself as well…"

Rufio Pagano had spent the better part of the morning combing the stinking streets of Rome for any sign of Silas, too embarrassed to go back to the warehouse, and yet too worried not to attempt anything to stop the man's betrayal of the entire company.

The irony of the situation was not lost on him, and he felt uncomfortably close to the parasite that Silas had been enacting for so many months. He did not want to be such a person as that, so hateful, betraying and selfish.

And yet, *that's just what I've done!* he chided himself as he ran, sweaty-faced and stinking, through the streets of Rome.

The previous night, he had been fortunate enough to find Meretrix again, her hospitality toward him as open as ever. However, the price he had had to pay was to listen to a long, well-meaning lecture, laced with not a little guilt, that took the better part of the night.

The lupa had, for better or worse, convinced him of the decency and need with which Felix and Clara had comforted each other at a time of loss and betrayal, and that Rufio, as the author of that betrayal, was more or less bound to forgive them and to make right the wrong he had done them so long ago.

"You can't repeat the mistake that has haunted all of you for so long!" Meretrix said, her bangles jingling as she wagged a finger at him while she dressed.

"They won't want to see me now!" Rufio complained.

"Rufio Pagano, wake up! You can make this right. You cannot leave your friends to this...this parasite...Piles...or Pilas, or whatever his name is!"

"Silas," Rufio added.

"Whatever! Now. I am leaving to pick up Astarte, and then we will eat something before going to the theatre."

"You're just going to leave?" Rufio complained.

Meretrix stepped toward him and held his face in her hands. "Yes. I am leaving you. I am pushing you out of the nest so that you may fly, little bird."

"Little bird?" Rufio shook his head free of her scented hands.

"I suggest you go to the baths and wash, for you stink of all manner of things. Then, get yourself to the theatre to help your friends!"

After she had left, Rufio spent some time pacing in Meretrix's apartment, listening to the increasingly busy hubbub in the streets below.

"She's right! Gods! Why do you play with me so?" he demanded.

As if on divine cue, there was a bark in the street below, and Rufio looked out of the window to see Peli standing there, looking up at him.

"What are you waiting for?" Rufio asked.

Then Peli barked back and sat staring up at him, an accusatory glint in his strange eyes.

"Ohhh....all right!" Rufio cried, finally giving in to the idea. He quit the happy lupa's den, and rushed clumsily down the stairs, so quickly, in fact, that he tripped the last few and came falling out of the front door to roll through a pile of horse droppings that had been laid by the early morning carters. "Ahh!"

Pedestrians laughed and pointed as they passed, happy to start their day with a bit of humour.

Rufio was anything but amused, however, and as Peli rushed over to him, he pat the dog and pushed himself to his feet. "I need a bath!" he said as if the hound understood him.

"You sure do!" someone yelled as they walked past.

Rufio ignored them and started off at a jog for the baths of Titus.

After the baths, with a bit more clarity in his muddled and panicked brain, he decided that perhaps the best thing was to try and find Silas and stop him before he even got to the theatre.

But it was no use. The parasite was well-hidden, as were the thugs whom he had seen the previous night. It was probably better, he knew all too well, that he did not find them, for they would have made him pay for his grand escape from the taberna.

Breathless and hungry now, Rufio stopped his search and went back to the warehouse to check one last time.

It was empty there, quite empty, though he checked every square inch of the place. There were no letters or notes for him, no signs of Silas. Nothing. He stood in the cubiculum which Felix had built for him, so generous with all of the scrolls, and the painted scene that reminded him of their youth.

Rufio Pagano felt his heart clench then, and it hurt, deep down, in a place he had refused to visit in over eight years, the well of love and friendship from which everything sprang for him, was dangerously close to drying out because he had let it do so. It was his fault.

He thought of Felix and Clara, of the rest of the company whom he had, against his own stubbornness, come to admire. He even considered them friends, all except Silas, that is.

The thought of Silas made Rufio angry then. He shook his head. "I won't let him do this to my friends!" he shouted, his voice a lone echo in the almost empty warehouse. "Come on, Peli!" he said to the dog as he ran out. "Let's get to the theatre!"

The sun was going down when Rufio approached the perimeter of the theatre of Pompey, and he could already hear the sounds of joyous laughter rising up to the sky as he approached.

"It's started!" he said as he stumbled into the quadriporticus and sprinted across the gravel of the gardens toward the stage house. *Gods, please let me not be too late!*

He raced past the statue of Plautus, head bowed in guilt, but determined not to disappoint the master's shade, and burst sweaty and panting into the stage house just in time to trip and roll to a stop at Electra's feet.

The company looked down at him in shock.

Electra, resplendent in her burnt orange and black stola, stared down at him, a great anger in her eyes.

Rufio thought she might kick him, but then the anger leached away from her face and she smiled.

"A professional actor never arrives after the play has started!" she reached down to pull him up, just as Fausto and Castor came bounding up.

"I'm a shit farmer, not an actor," Rufio replied.

"What happened?" Beatrice asked, her eyes bulging at the scene before her.

"There's no time to explain," Rufio said quickly before turning to Castor who, he could see, was in costume to play his role. "Do you still want to play Sosicles? I won't take it away from you if you do."

Castor looked supremely relieved. "Please do it, Rufio!"

Fausto laughed nervously. "He's been puking the whole morning!"

Rufio looked Castor over. "Where did you get the other tunic?"

Beatrice helped Castor pull the identical costume up over his head as Rufio removed his own. "Dominus asked me to make two," she said, turning to Rufio and straightening the new one properly on him. She smiled. "He said you were clumsy."

"He's right."

Beatrice began applying some makeup to Rufio's face, around his eyes.

"Felix, Julius and Clara are almost finished with the first act!" Castor said. "Rufio?"

Beatrice finished her hasty dressing of the newly-arrived cast member.

"Come on, Rufio!" Fausto said as he rushed to the doorway for their entrance.

"Quickly!" Rufio hissed to the group. "Don't tell Felix or Clara, but Silas is planning on sabotaging the play somehow and hurting Felix. We have to be on the lookout for him and some of Leno's goons."

"When?" Electra said, panic in her voice. "Where?"

"I don't know!" Rufio said as he jumped up onto the stage to join Fausto, no time to think, no time to breathe.

They watched him go, their eyes wide, just as Menaechmus

of Epidamnus and Peniculus emerged backstage at the far end, and Erotium and Cylindrus could be heard at the entrance of Erotium's domus.

"I've now told you the guests," Erotium said. "Do you take care of the rest."

"Very well," Cylindrus replied with an exasperated bow of his head to his domina. "It's cooked already; bid them go and take their places."

"Make haste back."

"I'll be here directly," Cylindrus rushed off stage, while Erotium went in at the door of her domus, a vision of bright silk and hugging ribbon.

Rufio caught a glimpse of her as he stepped out onto the stage behind the ship that was their transport, and with that, Menaechmus Sosicles and his loyal Messenio appeared to the crowd, just having disembarked from their long voyage.

Rufio froze for a moment, for he had not glimpsed the enormity of the audience filling the theatre like so many amphorae jammed into the hull of a titanic transport ship.

"Dominus?" Messenio urged his pausing master.

Line, Rufio! he yelled at himself. *Line! It's just like you've rehearsed a hundred times before!*

And then it clicked like the key in an iron lock.

"There's no greater pleasure to voyagers, in my notion, Messenio, than at the moment when from sea they espy the land afar."

Messenio sighed under his breath and plunged into the dialogue with relief. "There is a greater, I'll say it without subterfuge - if on your arrival you see the land that is your own."

A few members of the audience nodded and laughed at that.

"But, prithee, why are we now come to Epidamnus? Why, like the sea, are we going round all the islands?"

"To seek my own twin brother born!" Menaechmus Sosicles said, clearly annoyed with his servant's constant pecking.

"Why, what end is there to be of searching for him?" This is the sixth year that we've devoted our attention to this business…"

"CASTOR?" FELIX FELT SHEER PANIC STRIKE THROUGH HIM AS though he had been struck by lightning. "What in Hades are you doing?"

"Don't worry, Felix!" Electra said, rushing to him. "He's returned!"

"Who?" Clara asked, trying to dampen her own panic.

And then they heard the loud, clear and certain voice of the man upon the stage.

"For that reason I am looking for a person to give me that information for certain, who can say that he knows that he really is dead. After that, I shall never take any trouble in seeking further," Menaechmus Sosicles said as he strolled with Messenio about the fountain in the street.

"Rufio?" Felix said to Electra who nodded.

Felix and Clara listened, as did the others, and a thrill of hope spread through the group.

"He came back!" Clara said to Felix, squeezing his arm tightly.

"But otherwise I shall never, while I'm alive, desist; I know how dear he is to my heart," Menaechmus Sosicles continued.

"You are seeking a knot in a bulrush. Why don't we return homeward hence, unless we are to write a history?" Messenio said, catching a glimpse of the smile upon the empress' lips in the front row.

"Have done with your witty sayings, and be on your guard against a mischief."

"Why's he yelling that line so much?" Felix hissed into Clara's ear.

"Don't you be troublesome; this matter shan't be done at your bidding," Menaechmus Sosicles chided his servant.

Clara laughed. "I don't know, but he's brilliant. Do you hear it in his voice, Felix?"

"Yes!" Felix replied. "Rufio's back!" He turned and looked at the others. "All right, everyone. Rufio is back in his role. Carry on as we were." He turned to Clara. "Get Pollux and get ready to go out. And Don't forget the mantle!"

Clara nodded. "It'll be fine."

"Of course it will!" Felix said, continuing to watch Rufio and Fausto and the smiling faces in the audience. "I know it will."

"I'VE CATERED WELL, AND TO MY MIND," CYLINDRUS DECLARED to the audience as he walked with a large basket full of food. "I'll set a good breakfast before the breakfasters. But see, I perceive Menaechmus. Woe to my back; the guests are now already walking before the door, before I've returned with the provisions. I'll go and accost him. Save you, Menaechmus!"

Menaechmus Sosicles and Messenio turned to face the servant who, in that moment, was rushing breathless toward them. "The Gods bless you, whoever you are…" Menaechmus Sosicles said, backing away, a wary eye upon the Epidamnian servant.

"Who I am?" Cylindrus asked.

"I'faith, not I, indeed," Messenio muttered, already having won over the crowd, loyal servant that he was.

"Where are the other guests?" the cook asked.

"What guests are you enquiring about?"

"Your parasite."

Menaechmus Sosicles observed the angry expression upon

his servant's features. "My parasite?" He turned to Messenio. "Surely this fellow's deranged."

To the amusement of the audience, they argued in the street, back and forth, each trying to ascertain the madness hidden within the other, for that is how confounding the entire conversation was, Cylindrus claiming to have known the man before him well, having served him on several occasions, but the former firmly denying any of it, even as he was shown the house of Erotium, tucked neatly beside what was supposed to be his own domus.

"May the Gods send to perdition those that live there!" Menaechmus Sosicles said.

"Surely," Cylindrus muttered, "this fellow's mad. Who is thus uttering curses against his own self. Do you hear, Menaechmus?"

"They love it!" Felix said from his hidden vantage. He looked back and saw that Electra was speaking with Julius, Beatrice, Castor and Damon in a huddle. "Hey, what are you all jabbering about?" Felix hissed. "Get ready to sing!"

Electra waved to him and leaned in. "Don't tell Felix or Clara. They don't need the distraction. But we need to keep a watch!" she said, her face as stern as an Amazon general.

Clara had been standing at the ready, in the frame of Erotium's domus door, with Beatrice behind her. They had been watching Rufio, Fausto and Pollux, trying themselves not to laugh as Plautus' masterful dialogue was lobbed back and forth like rotten fruit in a marketplace.

"Almost time," Clara said to Beatrice.

"Be silent for a moment, then, for the door makes a noise.

Let's see who's coming out from there." Menaechmus Sosicles turned toward Erotium's door.

"Meanwhile," Messenio said, relieved to be rid of the cook, "I'll lay this down." He jingled a purse heavy with coin and set their satchels upon the street. "Do you keep watch upon these things, if you please, you sailors."

It was at that moment that Erotium opened her door fully, her body turned to the interior of her domus as she addressed her servants.

"Leave the door ajar thus. Begone. I don't want it shut; prepare, attend, and provide within, what is requisite. Let it be done. Lay down couches, burn the perfumes; neatness, that is the charm for the minds of lovers."

Menaechmus Sosicles, or rather Rufio, was mesmerized by the sight of Erotium as she emerged onto the street of that crazed and untrustworthy city.

She spied him, the man she thought was her lover Menaechmus of Epidamnus, but who was, in fact, Menaechmus Sosicles. "My dear life, it seems wonderful to me that you are standing here out of doors, for whom the door is wide open, more so than your own house, inasmuch as this house is at your service."

Menaechmus Sosicles looked around the street, confused, wary, but intrigued by the beautiful woman shining before him. He put his hand upon his chest.

"Everything's ready as you requested and as you desired; nor have you now any delay in-doors. The breakfast is ordered, is prepared here; when you please, you may go and take your place."

The audience laughed and willed the reluctant young man to the doors into which he was invited. They laughed at the way Erotium reeled him in like a fisherwoman pulling in a net by the sea.

Menaechmus Sosicles edged closer and closer, tantalizing the audience, his eyes wider, his face redder as he went.

"Didn't I say that these things are in the habit of occurring here?" Messenio warned. "The leaves are falling now, in comparison with this; if we shall be here for three days, the trees will be tumbling upon you…"

But the servant's warnings were of no avail, for his master Menaechmus was too drawn in, handing him the purse for safekeeping as he leaned more and more to following Erotium into her loving lair. She pressed him about the mantle he was supposed to have stolen from his wife that very morning, and he feigned ignorance of it at first. But then the mention of his late father's true name, of Moschus of Syracusae, gripped him more and led him to believe she could not be denied.

"I shall assent to the woman, whatever, she shall say," Menaechmus told Messenio, "if I can get some entertainment. Just now, madam," he addressed Erotium, "I contradicted you not undesignedly. I was afraid of that fellow." He pointed at Messenio. "Lest he might carry word to my wife about the mantle and breakfast." A wink to Messenio, followed by laughter in the auditorium. "Now, when you please, let's go indoors."

After a last, unsuccessful attempt to disuade Menaechmus Sosicles from following Erotium, Messenio was left alone in the street with the group of sailors there to carry their luggage.

"I'm undone. Are you going away then?" He stared at Erotium's door. "He is certainly ruined. The piratical craft is now leading the boat straight to destruction. But I'm an unreasonable fellow to wish to rule my master. He bought me to obey his orders, not to be his commander." He turned to the sailors. "Follow me, that, as I'm ordered, I may come in good time to meet my master."

.   .   .

THE ENTIRE COMPANY BROKE INTO SONG AT THE END OF THE second act, Damon's flute leading the melody, flitting about, flirting with the audience's ears for a minute before the start of the third act when Peniculus wandered out to whine about his misfortune and ill-treatment at the hands of his master.

Backstage, there wasn't much time, but just as Erotium led Menaechmus Sosicles through her doorway, Clara threw her arms about Rufio and hugged him tightly.

"Thank you for coming back," she said into his ear.

"You were right, Clara," Rufio said. "I was afraid. I'm so sorry."

"What matters is that you're here now, and you're amazing!"

"Rufio!" Felix said as he bounded up the stairs to take him in a great hug. "I knew you'd come back!"

Rufio raised an eyebrow. "Really?"

"Well, no. But I'm so glad you did!"

Rufio looked beyond Felix and Clara to the darker corners of the stage house. "Are you all right?" he asked Felix.

"Of course! And so much the better now." Felix tilted his head to listen to Julius' lines. "It's almost time for you to go back on."

"Here," Clara said, raising the bejewelled mantle and putting it over Rufio's shoulders.

"Just be careful," Rufio said quickly.

"Rufio… Please. I know my lines better than anyone," Felix said before he pushed Rufio toward Erotium's door.

Rufio smiled at them, and then Menaechmus Sosicles strode out with a most satisfied look upon his face, the mantle draped over his shoulders to dazzle the crowd with its richness.

Upon the stage, Peniculus was speaking the final lines before he accosted Menaechmus Sosicles whom he took to be his own Menaechmus. "By my troth, I'm not the person that I am, if I don't handsomely avenge this injury and myself... I'll give something."

THE THIRD ACT TWISTED THE DAGGER OF HILARITY IN THE GUT of every person in the audience that night, even of Leno who, with his scarred face had been wishing only failure upon the cast of that most astonishing performance. In his own mind, he now thought about all the ways in which he could make chests full of coin with every performance, even touring this single play over and over across the empire. His harsh laugh rained over the massive audience such that the Praetorians on the fringes of the theatre noted his presence.

Higher up, toward the base of Venus' temple, Meretrix and Astarte watched with intermittent laughter and worry, for Rufio had told Meretrix what Silas was about the night before. The lupa's eyes scanned the stage from right to left constantly, wondering if something grave was happening behind the scaena frons on which everyone's eyes were locked.

"Maybe this Silas has given up on his plan?" Astarte wondered, as she pulled at the uncomfortable stola which she had donned for the occasion, unused as she was to such fulsome clothing. "My breasts are itchy," she complained.

"Shhh!" someone above barked at her. "I can't hear Menaechmus!"

She turned to her accuser. "Which Menaechmus are you speaking of?" she retorted.

"The funny one! Now shut up!" the man spat.

"You're the funny one!" Astarte bit back before leaning in close to Meretrix. "Rufio is funny, isn't he?"

Meretrix smiled. "He is. They all are. I've never seen anything like it." Her smile faded. "I just hope they make it all the way to the end without any problems."

The third act delighted the audience even more and the

confusion mounted without end, beginning with Peniculus accusing the wrong Menaechmus of leaving him behind when he went to Erotium's, and then telling him he would reveal his actions to his jealous wife.

Menaechmus Sosicles was further enriched when Erotium's maid rushed from the domus to hand him a golden bangle, also taken by the other Menaechmus from his wife, so that he could take it to the goldsmith to be repaired. Of course, Menaechmus Sosicles claimed never to have stolen such a thing but then, catching on less than quickly, he remembered that yes, indeed, he did take a golden bangle from said wife.

In the front row, to the left of Emperor Severus, Sextus Annius Sabinus was supremely relieved to hear the emperor and empress laughing along with the people behind them. It may not have been the hearty, taberna-worthy bellowing of the common citizens, but with a subtle glance to his right, the aedile could see the emperor and empress' faces creased with smiles that told him a world of good news to that point. He felt his wife squeeze his hand and they gave each other knowing smiles as the Vestals and gathered senators of Rome, who were also present, joined in the mirthful atmosphere. He relaxed into his seat and decided he could enjoy the rest of the performance without worry.

Music and song struck up again as the applause following the third act quietened and the fourth act of that most joyous, smile-inducing, face-hurting production commenced. People leaned forward in their seats to watch what would come next, and even cheered when the dark and beautiful wife of Menaechmus strode onto the stage, followed by the parasite, Peniculus, who tried to kiss her robed buttocks as they walked down the street.

"And shall I allow myself to remain in wedlock here, when my husband secretly pilfers whatever's in the house, and carries it thence off to his mistress?" the wife asked of the air and the audience.

"Why don't you hold your peace?" her Peniculus said from behind her, squinting with displeasure as he tried to plant another kiss on her behind. "I'll let you now catch him in the fact…"

When Menaechmus of Epidamnus walked onto the street, muttering to himself about the good and bad clients who had harried him that day as he went about his work, some audience member even yelled out in warning to him.

"Look out, Menaechmus!"

Menaechmus of Epidamnus added a cock of the ear, as though someone had called him in the street, but proceeded on his way.

Backstage, while Julius, Felix and Electra enacted the most accusatory scene between Peniculus, Menaechmus of Epidamnus and his jealous wife, all accompanied by the song of Damon's flute, Rufio searched every corner of the stage house for any sign of the truant Silas, with Beatrice, Castor, Pollux, and Fausto lending their own eyes to the endeavour.

"Rufio, what is going on?" Clara demanded as she waited for Erotium's entrance near the end of the act.

"Just don't worry," Rufio whispered back. "Not yet, anyway."

"Rufio! No more secrets!" she demanded. "Tell me what is going on!"

He approached her, making sure not to be seen through the doorway. "Last night, I came across some thugs in a taberna. They said they were coming here with Silas during the performance to try and ruin the play and harm Felix."

Clara's face whitened visibly, even through the layers of

makeup which Beatrice had so deftly applied to her face. "No…no…. This can't be happening. We can't allow it!"

"That's why we're searching. So that we can stop them before anything happens."

"We have to tell Felix! We have to stop the play!"

"We can't do *that*!" Rufio said, a bit too loudly, clapping his own hand over his mouth. "If we stop the play, all is ruined and everyone will be taken by that Leno bastard. And…"

"What? There's more?" Clara demanded.

Rufio shook his head. "No." It did not bear thinking about what the thugs had said about the women. "We just need to keep a lookout for anything suspicious."

Clara nodded and leaned in to kiss his cheek. "You came back to help us?"

Rufio shrugged.

She shook her head. "You're full of surprises, Rufio."

Then, it was Erotium's turn to answer her door at the persistent knocking of her lover on cue.

"Open here," a desperate and wife-berated Menaechmus of Epidamnus called out, "and some one of you call Erotium before the door."

Erotium strode out into the street. "Who's enquiring for me here?" she asked, looking everywhere but at the bedraggled husband before her.

"One that's more of an enemy to his own self than to yourself."

"My dear Menaechmus? Why are you standing before the house? Do follow me in-doors."

"Stop," Menaechmus replied. "Do you know why it is that I'm come to you?"

"I know well; that you may amuse yourself with me," she said in a most sultry and cheeky way, her lashes batting for the audience.

· · ·

THE LAUGHTER REACHED INTO THE BOWELS OF THE STAGE house, at odds with the frantic search that was still going on, now joined by Electra and Julius who was only just told of what possible wrong-doings were lurking in the shadows.

As Menaechmus of Epidamnus denied being in possession of either the mantle or the bangle which Erotium claimed to have given him for repairs, Rufio, Electra and the others met in the middle of the floor behind the scaena to deliberate.

"We just have to press on with the performance," Electra said. "If we stop the play, we're ruined!"

Rufio could see that she was losing her composure, so dreadful of the possibility of Felix's harm, and of her enslavement to Leno. He took her hands and squeezed hard so that she took notice of him. "Nothing is going to happen. Do you hear me?"

Electra nodded and found her strength again. "If that little malaka shows up, I'll beat him senseless."

"Not if I get to him first!" Fausto said.

"We'll all keep a watch," Pollux added, patting his brother on the back.

At that moment, Erotium stormed back through her door, slamming it behind her.

Clara rushed over to the group of players. "Any sign of them?"

Rufio shook his head, and they all heard Felix speak the final lines of the fourth act.

"She has gone indoors, and shut the house. Now I'm regularly barred out; I have neither any credit at home now, nor with my mistress. I'll go and consult my friends on this matter, as to what they think should be done."

The applause was uproarious, and the company lifted their voices in song to play out the scene.

· · ·

THE SMELL OF THE FOUR MEN HE SAT WITH WAS ALMOST TOO much for Silas. As he sat at the far end of the quadriporticus, he held a cloth dipped in rosewater to his nose to try and mask the tang of sweat, garlic and, he could swear, faeces, that wafted off of them. *They are a necessary evil to endure,* he kept telling himself.

In fact, he had been telling himself that the whole of the previous night as he had slept in the slave quarters of Leno's domus on the Aventine hill. He had wondered at the bedraggled state of the servants - men, women and boys - who slept like the dead all around him, paying him no heed as they fell exhausted on their pallets. His thoughts had been whirling since he had stormed from the theatre and left the company, and all he could think of was his anger with Felix. *So many years of loyal service, of wondrous performances I gave, and he just pushes me aside? Now, it's my turn!* He told himself it was too late to go back, that Leno would make good on his promise to allow Silas to run the company as he saw fit when it was all over.

All Silas had to do was ruin Felix.

He had thought it would be easy at first - a small disturbance, or something else to ruin the cast's concentration - but the more he had thought about it, the more difficult it had all seemed. It was during the night at Leno's that he had lit upon the idea.

The brawl between Menaechmus of Epidamnus and the servants brought by the jealous wife's father and the medicus to accost him. That was the moment.

Felix had wanted that brawl to be when the entire cast was on stage in a chaotic and hilarious fracas all about the city street of Epidamnus.

It was the perfect time for Silas and Leno's men to sneak in, bring ruin to everything, and for one of Leno's men to take care of Felix once and for all.

Silas eyed the man with the pugio, sitting in the shadows of the quadriporticus, picking dirt out of his nails with the tip of the blade.

"Is it almost time?" asked another of the men. "I'm getting hungry!"

They all turned to Silas.

"Almost," Silas replied, standing and cocking his head to hear. "There it is," he muttered.

"What?" asked the stinkiest of the group.

"Applause," Silas nodded. "The end of the fourth act."

"Then let's go!" said the leader. "I'm tired of waiting."

"Not yet," Silas growled at him. "We have to wait until the ideal moment when the entire cast is on stage."

"This isn't one of your plays, slave!" barked another.

Silas was about to shout at the man, but the snarling look upon the man's face terrified him. They would have no compunction about turning on him. He felt as though he were holding four slavering mastiffs on thin leashes, waiting to set them upon someone. They could just as easily turn on him. *Just a little longer,* he reassured himself. *Then, I'll be free!*

Music rang out then, as the fifth and final act began.

"It's almost time," Silas said to them. "We can move close to hear better, but let's be quiet so no one hears us."

The four men stood and followed him along the shadowed wall of the quadriporticus, sneaking the length of it toward the looming stage building ahead.

Silas felt his heart beating wildly in his chest the closer they got, straining to hear above the blood pounding in his ears. *Almost time…*

BACKSTAGE THE OTHER MEMBERS OF THE CAST CROWDED AT the doorways and wings to watch Electra and Rufio launch them into the last act with such energy and timing that they nearly forgot to keep an eye out for Silas. However, such was the banter between the jealous wife and Menaechmus Sosicles that they and the audience were tickled to no end.

Menaechmus Sosicles, proudly wearing the lavish mantle upon his shoulders, walked along the city street, a glittering sight to see, wondering where his Messenio had got to, when the jealous wife who was not his wife, accosted him.

"Are you not ashamed to come forward in my presence, you disgraceful man, in that garb?" the wife accused.

"What's the matter?" Menaechmus Sosicles replied, never having seen the woman before. "What thing is troubling you, woman?"

"Do you dare, you shameless fellow, to utter even a single word, or to speak to me?"

"Pray, what wrong have I committed, that I shouldn't dare to speak to you?"

"Do you ask me?" she screeched. "O dear, the impudent audacity of the fellow!" she said to the vast and laughing audience.

"Castor?" Felix hissed backstage, waving him over. "It's almost time for the old father to enter. Get your walking stick and bend your back!"

"Y…yes, Dominus," Castor replied, his eyes scanning the stage house carefully as he picked up his prop.

"What is wrong?" Felix demanded, going over to him.

"Dominus…" Castor could not help it. He had never kept anything from Felix. Too much was at stake. "We need to stay alert."

"Of course we do! We're in the middle of the greatest performance of our careers!"

"No. That's not it. Rufio… He overheard some men last night saying that they, and Silas, were going to come during the play…to ruin it and harm you!"

"What?" Felix said, a little too loudly, shaking his head.

"There's no way. Silas wouldn't dare. He's too much of a coward for such a thing. Rufio must have misheard."

Castor shrugged. "That's what he said. I hope it's not true, but if it is, we need to be ready."

Felix looked around the stage house quickly, spotted Peli lying in the middle of the floor, the members of his cast looking behind them but also drawn to the action beyond the scaena frons. "It will be fine, Castor. Thank you for telling me. Just go, and do you utmost. Quickly!"

With a pat on his back from his brother, Castor took up the walking stick, bent his back, and went to stage right for the aged father's entrance.

"Do you deny you know me?" the wife asked of Menaechmus Sosicles' confused and increasingly frustrated face. "Do you deny that you know my father?"

"Troth, I shall say the same thing, if you choose to bring your grandfather."

"I' faith, you do this and other things just in like fashion."

At that moment, the wife's aged father hobbled onto the stage, bent and tired, looking awkwardly up at his daughter and the man he believed was his son-in-law, walking down the street, most warily, toward his obviously defeated daughter. He mumbled to himself of his age, his daughter, and the repetitive, argumentative nature of her marriage. "By my troth," he said, "my daughter never sends for her father to come to her except when either something has been done wrong, or there is a cause for quarrelling. But whatever it is, I shall now know. And see, I perceive her before the house, and her husband in a pensive mood. 'Tis the same as I suspected. I'll accost her."

Near to tears, the wife greeted her father, the latter receiving her, but at the same time pointing at the mantle-clad Menaechmus.

"Why does he in anger stand apart from you?"

The wife paced the street listing all of her complaints about her very husband, pointing at the man who was not he, but unaware of the fact.

The complicit audience howled at her confusion, few pitying the frustration of her shrew-like character.

"How often have I told you to be compliant to your husband? Don't be watching what he does, where he goes, or what matter he's about."

The audience howled at that, many an elbow laid into many a husband's ribs in the seats.

"Why, but he's in love with a courtesan here close by," she complained, pointing at the door of Erotium's domus.

"He is exceedingly wise: for this painstaking of yours, I would even have him love her the more."

"He drinks there too."

"And will he really drink the less for you, whether it shall please him to do so there or anywhere else?"

Backstage, Felix could not help but watch Electra set the fire alight within the jealous wife, her rage and despair growing to such comedic heights as he had never seen her display. He felt his heart fill with love for her.

"She's wonderful!" Clara said beside him as they watched.

"Yes, she is," he replied as the father moved to approach and reproach Menaechmus Sosicles.

After some time of denial of either knowing his wife or purloining her things, and of living in the house that was supposed to be his, Menaechmus Sosicles confounded the father and daughter to no end, the audience to their spectacle laughing heartily at the growing confusion.

What Castor had revealed to Felix, however, started to weigh on the leader of the players, and when he saw Clara tear her eyes from the stage to search the stage house with Fausto and Julius, he took her aside.

"He's told you too?" Felix asked.

"We won't let him ruin the play, Felix."

"I told Castor, Silas wouldn't dare do anything. He's too much of a coward."

"Over the past weeks, I've seen anger grow in that little man. He may have loved you before, but that's grown to hate."

Felix shook his head as though bees were swarming him. "We can't think about that right now, Clara. We have to make this work! Too much depends on our success."

"You're right. Let's focus," she said. *We'll keep a watch.*

For the next while, Menaechmus Sosicles, wishing to be rid of the wife and her aged watcher, played up his madness, dancing about the street as if in his personal Bacchanal, mumbling and speaking of their false accusations of his person.

When the father threatened to get the servants to bundle off his mad son-in-law, Menaechmus Sosicles chased his so-called wife who, to his great relief, ran away into her domus.

As Menaechmus Sosicles and the aged father threatened each other upon the stage, the audience members hooted for a fight, many recognizing the edgy relations they in turn had with their own fathers-in-law.

Backstage the players prepared for the onward slog of their production.

RUFIO CAME RUSHING BACK.

Felix and Clara smiled at him.

"Get ready everyone!" Felix directed, checking them all as though they were gladiators about to walk onto the sands. "Pollux," Felix said. "Get ready to join your brother."

The bulky brother, hoisted his long medicus tunica, and made his way to the far end of the stage so that the doctor could approach the aged father from down the street.

"Go!" Felix directed.

"What did you say was this disorder?" the medicus said as he approached the tired and panicked father of the jealous wife. "Tell me respected sir. Is he harassed by sprites, or is he frenzied? Let me know. Is it lethargy, or is it dropsy, that possesses him…"

"Rufio, Castor told me what is happening," Felix said quickly to his friend as he prepared to go out.

"I didn't want to worry you about it. We have to be careful!" Rufio said.

"It'll be fine," Felix said with a wink before he strode onto the stage.

As the two older men watched, Menaechmus of Epidamnus entered, wondering at the courtesan and parasite who had caused him no end of confusion and ills in the streets of Epidamnus.

The medicus tried to reason with Menaechmus of Epidamnus, but to no avail, only to threats of perdition and violence.

Clara and Rufio watched Felix upon the stage and thought how wonderfully he brought his character to life, more so than in any rehearsal before. He endured the medicus' questions with growing frustration and confusion when it came to his drinking, his eyes, and his bowels until, having no more of it, Menaechmus of Epidamnus turned accuser on his father-in-law.

The medicus and aged father went their separate ways, seeking help with the increasingly annoyed, seemingly mad, Menaechmus of Epidamnus, leaving him alone upon the streets of that fevered city.

"Well done!" Fausto said to Castor and Pollux when they came backstage, feeling the thrill of their mutual performance.

"Any sign of Silas?" Pollux asked quickly.

"Shhh!" Electra put her finger to her mouth where she stood inside the central doorway with Clara.

The players gathered round, ready for their various entrances, Fausto foremost among them. They listened to Felix then, his Menaechmus of Epidamnus standing at the front of the pulpitum to address the auditorium.

"MY FATHER-IN-LAW IS GONE, THE DOCTOR IS GOING; I'M alone. O Jupiter! Why is it that these people say I'm mad? Why, in fact, since I was born, I have never for a single day been ill. I'm neither mad, nor do I commence strikes or quarrels. In health myself, I see others well; I know people, I address them. Is it that they who falsely say I'm mad, are mad themselves? What shall I do now? I wish to go home, but my wife doesn't allow me. And here," he said, pointing at Erotium's domus, "no one admits me. Most unfortunately this has fallen out. Here will I remain; at night at least, I shall be let into the house, I trust."

Menaechmus of Epidamnus went to stand near his own domus doorway.

From the tavern door then, near the moored ship, Messenio emerged onto the scene.

RUFIO STOOD NEAR TO WHERE PELI WAS DOZING, HIS EYES reaching up to the rafters and stairs that mounted to the upper levels of the stage house. But for the laughter of the audience, and Felix's Menaechmus, there was not a sound.

"Anything?" Electra asked him, she perhaps more worried than any of the others. "I wouldn't put anything past Silas!" she hissed. "He hates all of us."

"I won't let anything happen," Rufio said. "Go now. You're

all supposed to be on stage soon." Out of the corner of his eye he saw Pollux, Damon and Beatrice changing hurriedly into their servant costumes to be led by the aged father onto the streets of Epidamnus.

"I wish he hadn't arranged such a large brawl scene," Electra said, now regretting her agreement with Felix's direction. "I must go. Be careful!"

Rufio nodded and watched as Peniculus, the jealous wife, her father, and the three servants went to stage right.

"Be careful, Rufio," Clara said beside him as Erotium prepared to go to her doorway and bear witness to the coming chaos. She looked around the stage house. "We're almost there," she said, before kissing him on the cheek and rushing to her perfumed post.

"By Gods and men," said the wife's father as he led the servants down the street, the sight of them making the audience tense and clench, "I tell you prudently to pay regard to my commands, as to what I have commanded and do command. Take care that this person is carried at once upon your shoulders to the surgery, unless, indeed, you set no value upon your legs or your sides…"

Rufio felt very lonely backstage as he watched and listened, robbed of his enjoyment of the play's experience, but also angry at the outcome he was waiting for, as if for the appearance of an angry lar in a haunted domus.

"I'm undone!" Menaechmus of Epidamnus shouted to the witness audience as if to marketers during a mugging. "What business is this? Why are these men running toward me, pray? What do you want?"

AS THE SERVANTS SURROUNDED MENAECHMUS OF EPIDAMNUS IN the streets of that same city, Peli lifted his head quickly, his lips curling, and a growl, so deep and suspicious, emanated from his canine gullet.

Rufio turned and went to the dog's side. "What is it, boy?" he asked.

Peli did not wait to give an indication, but rather, he bolted for the doors leading to the gardens beyond.

"Peli!" Rufio called, his voice covered by the growing hubbub upon the stage.

There was a sudden squeal in the darkness outside and the barking ceased.

Rufio took up a small wooden club prop and ran in the direction of the garden, his heart racing, but as soon as he broke free of the stage house, a cudgel reached out in the darkness to take him in the back of the head, sending him spinning so that he landed upon his back on the gravel path beside Peli's still form.

"Come-on!" Silas waved to the four men with whom he had been waiting for the precise moment. "Now's the time! Quickly!"

"Why don't you let me go?" Menaechmus of Epidamnus shouted in the street as the audience looked on, he surrounded by servants, the aged father urging them to his capture as if they were venatores out to capture a lion.

In that moment, Messenio arrived, running toward the group surrounding his master who was not his master. "O ye immortal Gods, I beseech you, what do I behold with my eyes..."

"Who is it that ventures to bring me aid?" Menaechmus called out.

"I, master, and right boldly," Messenio declared, squaring up against the enemy servants. "O shameful and scandalous deed, citizens of Epidamnus, for my master, here in a town enjoying peace to be carried off, in daylight, in the street, who came to you a free man. Let him go!"

"Prithee, whoever you are, do lend me your aid, and don't suffer so great an outrage to be signally committed against me!" Menaechmus of Epidamnus said to the brave stranger who thought him his master.

"Aye, I'll give you my aid, and I'll defend you, and zealously succour you…"

As if on cue, Silas and the four men burst onto the stage from the left to further enhance the threat about Menaechmus and Messenio.

The cast froze, and Felix, spying Silas and those others, heard the audible gasp of the entire audience, so much so that even Emperor Severus leaned forward in his seat to watch the coming commotion.

Felix raised his strong fists then, and eyed his players' characters.

Without missing another beat, Messenio spoke his defiant words as rehearsed. "I'll make a sowing on the faces of these fellows, and there I'll plant my fists! I' faith, you're carrying this person off this day at your own extreme hazard. Let him go!"

In that moment, all parties, real and imagined, clashed upon the staged street of Epidamnus.

Fausto went directly for Silas, chasing him about, while Castor, Pollux, Damon and Felix laid their fists into Leno's men, no fit players to be there.

In the audience, Leno strained to make sure that his men did their job correctly, but could not help laughing himself when one of the female servants clubbed his man from behind, sending him to his knees and face down into the fountain.

Even Erotium burst from her doorway to defend her Menaechmus in a turn of events Plautus could not have imagined.

The battle ranged all over the street, upon the docks and

ship, one party giving chase one way, the other retaliating the other.

People applauded the realism of the fight, the use of the blood bursting from the mouths, and the squeals of the goggly-eyed servant whom Messenio chased and threatened with such brave fury.

"OHHH," RUFIO GROANED WHERE HE LAY UPON THE GROUND. It was then he felt the strange sense of wet upon his face and opened his eyes to the sighing licks of Peli beside him. "My head," he groaned to the dog, his hearing coming in and out in muted waves.

Peli was on his feet then, pulling at Rufio's tunica and growling.

Rufio shook his head and pushed himself up, dizzy, but managing to stay upon his feet.

Then, he heard it. The sounds of battle and the gasps and shouts of the enormous audience.

Rufio reached down and picked up the club he had been carrying. "Come-on Peli!" he yelled before running back into the stage house, as eager as a Fury with the sinner in her sights.

"YOU RASCALS! YOU VILLAINS! YOU ROBBERS!" MESSENIO shouted, Fausto panting as he squared up again, pulling Julius to his feet.

The audience looked this way and that, confused as to the method of all that madness as the fighting raged on. They were on their feet then as Menaechmus of Epidamnus, his wife held fast by one brute, was knocked down by another with a dagger poised over him.

In the audience, the aedile, Sextus Annius Sabinus, leaned

over to his wife and whispered. "He said they had made some changes, but this seems rather drastic!"

"It's fantastic!" she hissed back at him, leaning forward with everyone else.

At that moment, Menaechmus Sosicles came to the rescue of his own servant, bursting onto the stage from Erotium's doorway, a snarling hound at his ankles, and clubbed the dagger-wielding brute who was hovering over the other Menaechmus, sending the man head over heels over the edge of the stage and into the pit of the aulaeum.

"OH!" The auditorium rang with the sound of people's shock.

The man from the fountain was dragged by Erotium's cook and sent into that same abyss to more applause.

A third was hit with a gladiatorial fist in the mouth by Menaechmus of Epidamnus such that his teeth burst forth onto the city street as though he had been gnashing a mouth full of beans. He spun and fell with a thud.

The fourth brute ran for his life, down the street and off the stage, pursued to the fringes by the baying hound that had joined in the fray.

The commotion was not yet done, however, for Menaechmus Sosicles struggled with the goggle-eyed servant who had led the others into battle. They clawed and slapped at each other in a most comical and loud fashion, snarling and spitting.

For a moment, all thought it was over as Menaechmus Sosicles lost his footing over a rope from the destroyed ship's rigging. The servant then turned and bore down on Menaechmus of Epidamnus with a discarded pugio, but in that heart-palpitating moment, as Erotium screamed for her lover, Menaechmus Sosicles rushed in with the loyal hound.

Just as the blade was about to rob Menaechmus of Epidamnus of his life, the hound clapped onto the attacker's groin with such force and ferocity that a crunch could be heard throughout the theatre. The man turned, screaming, his eyes positively popping from his head, only to see Menaechmus Sosicles before him, a daring smile upon his bearded face before he laid his fist full force into his visage.

The servant crumpled, and with unimaginable speed, Menaechmus Sosicles fell to his knees and tied him swiftly with the rope he had been wielding as if the servant were an escaped hog. The servant thus trussed, Menaechmus Sosicles then kicked the human swine into the pit of the aulaeum with the others that he may cause no further harm.

To add further insult to the parasite, Peli, as if trained to it, crept to the edge of the pulpitum, lifted his leg, and sent a golden stream down to the ground upon the disappeared bundle.

The crowd howled with laughter, which was good, for it gave breathing space to the characters.

An instant later, Menaechmus Sosicles and the dog were off the stage, and Menaechmus of Epidamnus and Messenio stood in the street breathing hard from their victory, the servants, the wife, the aged father, and Erotium all breathless after the brawl, their eyes wide and confused.

Messenio stepped forward. "Right well have I...marked his face, and quite to my liking." The audience laughed with great relief at that. "Troth, now, master, I really did come to your help just now in the nick of time."

Menaechmus of Epidamnus breathed in and out, most heavily, exhausted from the battle, but he found the words to speak aloud to the strange rescuer who claimed to be his servant. "And may the Gods, young man, whoever you are, ever bless you... For had it not been for you, I should never have survived this day until sunset."

"By my troth, then, master, if you do right, you will give me my freedom."

"I, give you your freedom?"

Messenio stood taller, more confident, as if his chains were already melted from his limbs. "Doubtless, since, master, I have saved you!"

Rufio leaned upon the inner doorway of Erotium's domus, Peli panting at his side as the two of them watched the story unfold. It was a great relief to him that no audience member frowned, none departed in frustration, but all eyes remained fixed on the scene, post-battle, wondering how on earth so much excitement could have unfolded in such a short period of time.

He could see Clara glance his way, her stola askew, slightly ripped from the fighting, but none of it taking away from the aura of her beauty in his eyes.

Her smile told him all was well, that the story was yet intact.

The cast listened as Menaechmus of Epidamnus and Messenio debated the knowing of each other, that the one owned the other, that freedom was truly granted, and that Messenio's loyalty to him knew no bounds, for though free, he would remain with him in his employ.

When Messenio returned to the inn to gather his master's belongings, Rufio rushed over to Fausto.

"Are you all right?"

Fausto bent over and puked upon the floor, nodding as he finished. "I'm fine. Did we save the play?"

"We'll see," Rufio said. "I can't tell whether the audience believes it or not." He looked as Menaechmus of Epidamnus and Erotium went back into her domus and the servants in the street dispersed, singing the final song as they did so, melting back into the setting.

Damon went back to his post by the ship, to doze against

the sacks of grain and play his flute so that the gulls could be heard once more by the seaside.

"Ready?" Rufio asked Fausto.

"Ready."

Messenio and his master, Menaechmus Sosicles, walked out of the inn and into the street, giving voice to the debate about the so-called saving of his life and the given freedom of which Menaechmus Sosicles had no recollection.

"I, bade you go away a free man?"

"Certainly," Messenio answered.

"Why, on the contrary, 'tis most certain that I myself would rather become a slave than ever give you your freedom."

In that moment, Menaechmus of Epidamnus emerged from Erotium's, accusing her of lying when she claimed to have given him a bracelet and mantle until he stood before the two men already in discourse in the street outside.

"Immortal Gods," Messenio exclaimed. "What do I see?"

"What do you see?" Menaechmus Sosicles asked.

The audience was silent as a necropolis at night, listening to every utterance of the characters as the main revelation was about to come to light.

"Your resemblance in a mirror," Messenio said, his voice hoarse.

"What's the matter?"

"'Tis your image; 'tis as like as possible."

Menaechmus Sosicles turned then to see the other, his voice slow and incredulous. "Troth, it really is not unlike, so far as I know my own form."

Menaechmus of Epidamnus strode over to Messenio in that moment, his arms wide in gratitude. "O young man, save you, you who preserved me, whoever you are."

Messenio looked from one to the other of the men before

him, his eyes wide. "…tell me your name, unless it's disagreeable."

Menaechmus of Epidamnus walked closer, though hesitantly still. "My name is Menaechmus."

At that point, his face brightening like a pale tree when the dawn first touches it, Menaechmus Sosicles too moved closer. "Why, by my troth, so is mine."

"I am a Sicilian, of Syracusae," the first Menaechmus said.

"The same is my native country."

"What is it I hear of you?"

"That which is fact," Menaechmus Sosicles said, his voice wavering, but loud enough for the entire audience to feel the full force of his emerging emotion.

BACKSTAGE, THE BATTERED PLAYERS LOOKED ON KEENLY, NO longer afraid of the gorgon at their backs. Rather, they were rapt by the revelations being played out on the other side of the scaena. It did not matter that they had rehearsed all of this, seen it a hundred times and more over the last months.

It was different now, before the people of Rome, before the emperor and empress, when the stakes were supremely high and their lives nearly forfeit.

Clara and Electra leaned upon each other, their eyes blurry with tears as the end of the play neared, as they watched their two Menaechmi and Messenio put the pieces of their once-shattered lives back together.

Beatrice went from one to the other of them, fixing their costumes with shaking, scratched hands, adjusting Clara and Electra's hair, dabbing the blood from Castor and Pollux's faces.

"It's all right, Beatrice," Julius said to her as she stood before him, near to weeping. "We've done our very best under the circumstances. Trust that the Gods will have taken notice. Be calm for the final scene. Enjoy it."

Beatrice nodded silently and let Julius bring her to the rest of the players where they were gathered to go out, for Felix wanted them all upon the stage, together for the final scene, as pedestrians.

"Ready everyone?" Electra whispered as she looked back at them.

They nodded and dispersed to the various doorways.

Electra smiled at Clara one last time and walked out, the others following.

"Immortal Gods," Messenio was saying as people began to fill the street, a low hum from their throats, "what unhoped for hope do you bestow on me, as I suspect. For unless my mind misleads me, these are the two twin-brothers; for they mention alike their native country and their father. I'll call my master aside - Menaechmus."

"What do you want?" both Menaechmi answered at once.

As the servant took his true master aside to discuss the situation and discern the true identity of the mirror image standing not far off, the people in the street sang a more hopeful tune and the sound of the gulls overhead grew louder as though it were the beautiful setting of the sun at the end of a long, dark day.

After six years of searching for his lost brother, Menaechmus Sosicles and Messenio plied Menaechmus of Epidamnus with questions. He of Epidamnus related the story of how, long ago, he went with the father, Moschus, and was lost to him, and that he was ever more separated from his twin who had stayed behind.

"I recognize the proofs!" Menaechmus Sosicles exclaimed, his eyes wet with relief and joyous tears. "I cannot refrain from embracing him. My own twin-brother, blessings on you. I am Sosicles!"

"O welcome, unhoped-for brother, whom after many years I now behold!"

"And you, whom with many and anxious labours I have ever been seeking up to this time, and whom I rejoice at being found!"

The brothers hugged tightly, a sight most satisfying to the audience before them, the auditorium accented with sniffles and sighs. The onlookers laughed as the mysteries of the erotic breakfast, the mantle and the golden bracelet, still glinting before their eyes, were at last unravelled.

The movement about the stage slowed and all eyes turned to Messenio and the Menaechmi standing before the fountain.

"Do you make any objection that I should be free as you commanded?" Messenio asked.

Menaechmus of Epidamnus, his hand upon the loyal servant's shoulder turned to his brother. "He asks, brother, what's very fair and very just. Do it for my sake."

Menaechmus Sosicles laid his hand upon Messenio's other shoulder and smiled. "Be thou a *free* man."

With Menaechmus of Epidamnus' declaration that he would return to his native land with his new-found brother, all that was left was for him to auction off all of his possessions, including his parasitical slave who skulked in the background.

It was decided then that Messenio, at his own request, would be the auctioneer, a request of his own devising.

And with the brothers arm-in-arm, and the people of that story singing in the street, Messenio walked to the front of the stage to address the audience.

"An auction of the property of Menaechmus will certainly take place on the morning of the seventh day hence. His slaves..." He looked to Peniculus. "...furniture, house, and farms..." He looked to the doorway directly behind. "...will all be sold. All will go for whatever they'll fetch at ready money prices. His wife, too, will be sold as well, if any purchaser shall come!"

The jealous wife wagged her finger at her husband, as she always did, but this time, he took no notice of her, and she fell to pulling at her hair.

"I think," Messenio continued, "that by the entire sale, Menaechmus will hardly get fifty hundred thousand sesterces."

He leaned down then, a conspiratorial glint in his eye, meant only for the constellation of faces, high and low, before him. "Now, Spectators, fare you well...and give us loud applause."

The silence that followed stretched on for an age in the ears of the players standing upon the stage, but as Messenio backed away from the edge of the pulpitum, as if ready to run for his life, the entire auditorium exploded with applause and joyful words bursting from red and glistening faces!

The players sighed beneath their collective breath and set off into their final, joyous song as they lined up before the people of Rome.

Flowers soared in beautiful arcs to land at their feet and upon their sweaty crowns as they bowed once, twice, three times.

The aedile could not help but join the masses upon his feet, clapping and smiling at Felix, for he was keenly aware of the imperial couple to his right, also clapping and smiling, and joining in the general joy of the moment which they shared with their subjects.

Rufio turned then to look back at the central doorway, and there he saw Peli standing, highly alert, tongue lolling, tail wagging. He whistled to the dog. "Come on then!"

Peli shot out onto the pulpitum to spin circles before the bowing players, and the crowd grew even louder at his appearance for, as everyone knows, a bit with a dog is the highlight of many a play. After a couple of spins, and a chorus of loud barking, Peli shot off again.

Rufio looked out into the crowd and there he saw both Astarte and Meretrix clapping and shouting, waving to him. He smiled back, his grin broad beneath his beard.

Felix too looked out over the audience and, pushed forward by Electra, Clara and Rufio, bowed to his adoring fans. To his relief, Leno was clapping too, for he knew he would get his money back, and that was all he cared for. Longus howled and applauded for his fellow artists.

All were happy, content, fulfilled by the healing drama that the company had performed for them. For a time, they had each forgotten the ills of their individual lives, their toils and stresses, having journeyed together, alongside their emperor and empress. It was an evening none would forget.

Felix spread his arms wide and bowed, and then turned to applaud his players, like a wounded band of warriors after a hard-fought battle, and in that moment, even the emperor and empress rose to their feet to applaud them.

The aedile was almost hopping on the spot, trying with all of his might - most unsuccessfully - to exercise restraint before his senatorial peers who, to his delight, also hooted and applauded.

It was then that the cornu sounded and the Praetorians, who had been standing like sentry statues to the sides, stepped forward to accompany the emperor and empress not out of the theatre, but onto the pulpitum itself.

The wind went out of the audience's sails at once as the entirety of The Etrurian Players bowed before the purple-draped imperials, Felix Modestus foremost among them.

"Rise," Emperor Severus said. "Rise..." He waited for complete silence before he spoke again. "Where is Aedile Sabinus?"

"I am here, sire!" Sextus Annius Sabinus said as he

emerged from behind the wall of Praetorians behind the emperor and empress. He bowed before them.

The emperor smiled, the curls of his long beard shuddering as he did so. "Aedile…"

"Yes, imperial majesty…"

"We would like to thank you publicly for presenting us with such wonderful games, and for bringing The Etrurian Players here to delight us with their magnificent performance!"

The crowd, all of which was standing now, applauded at that.

"Thank you, sire," the aedile bowed again. "It was my honour to be able to organize the Ludi Apollinares."

"You did well," the emperor said.

"Very well, indeed," the empress echoed, making a mental note to invite the aedile to her next intellectual symposium.

"And Felix Modestus!" Severus said loudly then for all to hear. "I am not usually one for comedy, but…"

Felix and the rest of the company held their breath.

"…this was one of the greatest productions I have ever seen!"

More applause resounded, for the audience had been won over by Felix and his company, and they now wished him all the very best.

"I thank you, sire," Felix said, bowing low, his action echoed by Electra, Rufio, Clara and the rest of the company.

"You have made us all feel alive and joyous," Severus said. "That is no small feat, for it is often easier for mortals to wallow in sadness and fear. You…you have lifted our spirits and filled us with hope, as should be the goal of any great leader."

At that moment, the empress turned to one of her retainers who held out a purple cushion upon which rested a golden corona of laurel leaves. She took it with her long, slender, olive fingers and handed it with much grace to her husband.

There were whispers in the crowd at the glinting gold, and people wondered whether it was the emperor or the empress who had decided to honour Felix Modestus, for the latter was well-known to be a patron of many artists and intellects.

Severus accepted the corona from Julia Domna, and turned back to Felix. "Kneel, Felix Modestus."

Felix felt his heart beat wildly as he knelt before the emperor, and nearly felt faint when the weight of the corona was laid gently upon his head.

"We present to you, and your company, this corona of artistic excellence. May it be a mark of our high regard for you, your skill, and your vision."

"Thank you, sire," Felix said, his hand upon his heart.

"Rise, and be presented to the people of Rome," the empress said, smiling down at Felix, the pearls hanging from her ears swaying, her smile showing genuine appreciation for what he had done.

Felix rose, stepped forward to face the audience, and spread his arms wide as he bowed, careful not to bend so much that the corona would fall.

He savoured the moment as the crowd cheered him to deafening heights, their smiling faces rising from the senators and Vestal Virgins, all the way up to the temple at the very top of Pompey's theatre. It was with immense relief that he saw the fleeting glimpse of that goddess before the temple, her expression one of purest joy.

He had never had such a feeling of utter relief in all of his life, and he bowed again, this time, only for that immortal goddess, whoever she was, who had brought him there.

Felix turned back to the emperor and empress, and bowed again. "Thank you, imperial majesties."

"It is we who thank you for such an evening," Severus said before taking a couple of steps closer to whisper to Felix. "You thought well on your feet, Felix Modestus, for I suspect there were a few…unaccounted for interruptions."

Felix froze. *He knows!* He could not help the sheepish look upon his face.

"The empress knows her Plautus," Severus said, looking back at Julia Domna. But then, he smiled. "You would be a good optio or centurion in my legions, Modestus. You can think on your feet." He looked at the players behind them. "What say you?"

Felix bowed his head. "Alas sire, I am but a humble entertainer. My players are my troops."

Septimius Severus smiled and chuckled to himself. "And a good cohort they are!" he nodded to the company, all of whom bowed to him. "Perhaps then, I can entice you to Leptis Magna and the newly renovated theatre there?"

"It would be an honour, sire," Felix replied, bowing again.

"I will send word," Severus said, before he turned, took the empress' hand, and led her off the stage where the Praetorians formed a perimeter and led them out of the theatre. The people of Rome applauded and cheered for them as they departed.

When they were gone, Felix turned to the company of grinning players and motioned for them to step to the front of the stage for one more bow.

"Take it in, my friends. This is the greatest feeling in the world!"

The crowd cheered in riotous fashion as the crowned players stood before them, even as Leno's men and the bundled Silas stared up awkwardly from the pit below.

"We did it, Rufio!" Clara said as they bowed one last time, the world all about them smiling and joyful.

Rufio did not answer.

XX

NICELY DONE!

A beautiful hum filled the entirety of the theatre of Pompey after the emperor and empress were gone, the sound of people raving about the performance, the individual players, and the great success of the production as a whole. They talked in their seats, in the orchestra, and filled the gardens of the quadriporticus beyond where tables of wine and food had been set out. This was a surprise addition, courtesy of the aedile who had had a small army of servants waiting with wagons under guard in the street outside until the end of the play.

A crowd of admirers had gathered in the orchestra in order to meet the members of The Etrurian Players, including Clara and Rufio who were a little overwhelmed by the attention, unused as they were to such glories.

Rufio watched as Meretrix and Astarte walked up to him with Peli.

"I knew you could do it, Rufio!" Meretrix said, turning to Astarte. "Didn't I say so?"

"As did I!" Astarte added, her face rosy from hours of laughter.

Rufio found it odd to look upon her fully clothed for once, for she was not in the garb of a street priestess, but rather a bright, pink stola.

"You were both right," Rufio told them. "Thank you."

"Are you happy with the performance?" Meretrix asked.

"Yes," Rufio answered, unsmiling as his eye caught sight of Clara speaking with the aedile and his wife.

"You don't seem very happy," Meretrix said, turning to see the source of Rufio's distraction. "You need to speak with her. Make things right."

He shook his head. "I nearly betrayed them again."

"But you didn't!" Astarte said. "You came back."

"None of this," Meretrix waved at the stage, "would have been possible if you had not come back to help. Talk to Felix. Speak with your Clara," she said.

Clara heard her name and looked in their direction, eyeing the two women with Rufio.

"And do let her know we have not been intimate," Meretrix added. "Much as I would have liked to. I know the look she is now displaying."

"Meretrix," Astarte said, tugging at her friend's stola. "Let's see what's on offer in the gardens."

Both women leaned in to kiss Rufio on his bearded cheek, and then departed in a flurry of strongly-scented wool and silk, and jingling jewellery.

Rufio then caught sight of Leno standing by his three remaining men.

They were battered and bruised, standing beside their master, arms crossed, fury etched deeply onto their ugly features.

Leno looked in Felix's direction. "Modestus! I would speak with you," he growled.

Felix finished speaking with a small group of spectators, thanked them for attending, and then turned to look into the pit of the aulaeum behind him where Silas was staring up at him like a harpy from the depths of Hades. "Castor, Pollux!" he called, nodding into the pit. "Get him out of there!"

The brothers descended into the pit and pulled the angry bundle up with some difficulty. "Ach! You stink Silas!" Castor said.

"Rufio, can we talk?" Clara said to him a few feet away.

But when Rufio saw Leno and his men approaching, he shook his head. "Not now, Clara. There's going to be trouble." He walked up to stand beside Felix, as did the rest of the players as Castor and Pollux deposited Silas on the ground between them and the angry Suburrans.

"Untie him," Felix said, and Castor and Pollux did so.

Silas jumped to his feet with ready vitriol for Felix, but the latter's hand lashed out to slap him across the face, making him squeal.

"How dare you!" Silas hissed.

"How dare I?" Felix said. "How dare you, you ungrateful wretch. After all I've done for you! You betrayed us! You would have seen everyone here enslaved."

"Yes," Leno said, stepping up to Felix, ignoring Silas as he did so. His men were close behind. "About that. I still have not been paid, Felix Modestus. So, it seems to me that your entire company now belongs to me." He smiled, his eyes lingering on Electra and Clara who stood nearby.

Rufio stepped up at that. "No way in Hades, you shit!"

"Oi!" said one of Leno's men. "I know you! You scammed us last night!" The man lunged for Rufio, but Leno's arm shot out to stop him.

"Calm yourself!" Leno barked. "You three failed as well." He turned back to Felix. "I don't have my money, Modestus. You owe me now. A deal's a deal."

Felix looked at Leno and the thugs behind him. He knew he did not have the funds yet, and that the deal was what it was - payment at the end of the play. He just did not think Leno would come for his money immediately. There were no funds from receipts since the play had been sponsored by the aedile.

Felix had thought to borrow more money from wealthy patrons to repay Leno, after the play's success. But now, there was no way Felix was going to hand anything or anyone over to Leno. He removed the corona from his head and turned to hand it to Electra. "Hold this," he said to her, before kissing her.

"Don't, Felix," she whispered, seeing the anger in his eyes, the potential of real violence that so rarely made an appearance.

"No choice, my love," he said before turning.

"Erm… Perhaps I can be of assistance here?"

Felix stopped suddenly, his fists still clenched, even as Leno's men squared up.

The aedile, Sextus Annius Sabinus, stepped up to the group to stand beside Felix and face Leno. "I believe this is the amount which Felix Modestus owes you." The aedile held up a large leather pouch full of coin.

Leno grabbed the pouch, undid the drawstring, and peered inside. His eyes widened and he nodded, though his lips were pursed. "How did you come to know of this, Aedile?"

"That is none of your affair, sir. Now, if you wouldn't mind, The Etrurian Players have an adoring public to mingle with." Sextus Annius Sabinus stood tall and sophisticated before Leno and his men, unafraid, his perfectly wrapped toga like impenetrable armour over his body.

Leno smiled and nodded. "It's been nice doing business with you, Modestus."

The company relaxed at that.

"After tonight," Leno continued, "I'm thinking about investing in the theatre. How about I invest in your next production?"

"Piss off," Felix said, rising to his full height and towering over the man.

"You heard him, sir," the aedile said. "Unless you wish me

to call the Praetorians back here and tell them how you sought to commit murder in front of the emperor?"

Leno took a step back. "There's no need for that, Aedile. We'll be leaving." The group of them began to walk away.

"Leno, wait!" Felix said. He eyed Silas who stood there with purest hate in his eyes. It was then that Felix knew with absolute certainty that he was not fit to be a part of The Etrurian Players any longer. He had almost brought them all to great harm, and for that he could never be forgiven.

"What is it?" Leno asked impatiently.

"I'll sweeten the deal for you. You can have this slave, Silas, for free. He's a bit disloyal, and eats more than his fair share, but he can manage a theatre company if you're thinking of starting your own."

Silas shook his head and fell upon the ground before Felix. "No, Dominus. Please, no!"

Leno thought about it for a moment as he looked upon the begging slave, his hair matted from the dog's urine. He shook his head. "No thanks, Modestus." He hefted the pouch of coins. "I've got all I need." With that, he and his men left the theatre.

"Please, Felix. Don't send me away. Don't sell me!" Silas begged before everyone there.

"You betrayed us, Silas," Felix said. "I can't forgive that."

"I only did it out of love for you!" Silas replied, bending over to kiss Felix's foot.

Felix shook his head in disgust. "Oh, my Peniculus…how can I ever trust you again? You as well as any know art imitates life. Only, I am not auctioning you off. I give you your freedom, such as it is. If you can convince Leno to keep you, you're welcome to do so. Maybe he will give you the opportunity to lead your own company."

"That's not what I meant!" Silas yelled. "I'm sorry! I didn't mean any of it!" he cried, looking at all of the faces of his former company members.

Everyone was unmoved by his pleas, even as he looked to each of them for aid.

"Goodbye, Silas," Felix said evenly.

Silas began to back away, but not before casting a last, hateful glance at Rufio and Clara. "Amateurs!" he spat, before panic set in and he turned to run. "Leno! Wait for me!"

Everyone sighed with long-held relief as Silas left them for good, Fausto foremost among them as they gathered round to talk at last of the performance.

Felix turned to Sextus Annius Sabinus and his wife who had joined them with Clara, Rufio and Electra. "How did you know about my debts to Leno?"

The aedile smiled. "I never invest so heavily unless I have my people look into everything. I didn't have enough funds to give you for such a lavish production, but I also didn't want you to skimp. I knew you had gone to Leno, but I also knew that you could pull it off, Felix Modestus. And you did! By Apollo, you did!"

Felix smiled. "I'm in your debt, Aedile."

Sextus Annius Sabinus shook his head and smiled. "No. You are not. This night was more of a success than I could possibly have imagined." He looked at the entire company. "I thank you all, with a full heart. And I congratulate you! We shall never forget it," he said, taking his wife's arm in his. He turned back to Felix. "If you are amenable, Felix Modestus, I should like to be your company's permanent patron, wherever you perform across the empire. I foresee that we could do great things together."

"It would cost a fortune to do this all of the time!" Felix exclaimed, unable to hide his shock.

The aedile shrugged. "Bread and circuses pay well when it comes to votes, but theatre inspires the wealthy to dig deep into their purses! And my fellow senators have seen how popular you are. They have already offered funds to invest in your future. Well, *our* future, if you'll agree."

Felix's eyes widened and he looked back at his excited actors behind him. "I agree wholeheartedly, Aedile."

"Please, call me Sextus," the aedile said. "Now, if you don't mind, I think I'll join the party in the gardens. We'll speak of our plans the day after next when you come to our home."

"I look forward to it!" Felix said.

"Bring the entire company," the aedile said. "We can also see how to spruce up the gardens with Beatrice' wonderful paintings!"

The aedile and his wife left the theatre to join the party in the quadriporticus which was in full vigour by that time.

Felix turned to face the company, his eyes glossy with the relief and gratitude which he felt. "I'm so very proud of all of you," he said. "Nicely done, my friends. Nicely done!"

"Is the aedile really going to fund us from now on?" Fausto asked.

Felix nodded. "Seems that way, Fausto. No more dealings with the likes of Leno ever again. The Etrurian Players are going to take the Middle Sea by storm, and now, legitimately!"

Everyone cheered and clapped, their relief now fully expressed.

"Now, go! Eat as much cheese as you like! Drink as much wine as you can! Enjoy the adulation of the crowd, and sleep with whichever admirers you choose!"

Castor and Pollux hooted and led the way as Damon trilled his flute, followed by Fausto, Beatrice and lastly, Julius who looked back at Felix one more time.

"Well done, Julius," Felix said. "You were a wonder!"

"As were you, Felix. As were you all," the veteran said with a broad smile on his aged face, going after his fellow performers to enjoy the rest of the night.

They watched Julius disappear into the scaena frons and the sounds of revelry and cheering in the enormous gardens beyond where The Etrurian Players were welcomed by the throng of spectators who had witnessed their grand production.

Felix smiled when he heard his company welcomed, his back still to Electra, Clara and Rufio. He looked down at his hands which had, only just then, begun to shake. His eyes burned, and his heart shook more wildly than an Egyptian sistrum.

"Felix?" Electra went to him and wrapped her arms about his thick shoulders. "It's finished now. It was a success. We're saved." She clung to him tightly and with such gratitude that Clara began to feel awkward.

Felix did not say anything, but nodded silently, focussed on the feeling of Electra's body, the sound of her words as he tried to gather himself.

A great sadness came over Clara then, for now that the performance was finished, her part played, she was uncertain of the role left to her. She had thought, before coming to Rome, that she had known what she wanted to do, the new life she had wanted to create for herself. But the last months had changed much. She turned to Rufio, and saw only his back as he gazed up at the temple of Venus, now silent at the top of the auditorium.

Rufio stood there, staring up in silence at the temple, the empty seats which had, only a short time ago, been filled to capacity with the denizen faces of theatre goers. He had at last performed the role that had, for so long, eluded him, or rather, that he had eluded. Now that it was finished, success achieved, and his friends saved from Leno and his men, Rufio's mind wandered back to the sad truths he had learned the previous day.

His thoughts turned dark once again, and all he wanted in

that moment was to run back to his sad farm and wallow in anger and regret, for that is what he was used to, the state of being he was familiar with.

Felix, his tears dried, his breathing steady once again, turned to face Electra and his friends. A broad smile spread across his bearded face and in a burst of sudden relief, he howled into the auditorium with his arms spread wide. "Wooo! We did it!" he shouted, the delicate golden branches of the corona which Electra had put back upon his head bouncing slightly with his victorious movements.

Rufio turned from his dark reverie, startled by the sudden outburst.

"You two!" Felix said, walking slowly toward Rufio and Clara like a prowling lion before he grabbed them both up in a great hug, his arms crushing them together. "Thank you, my friends! Thank you!"

They said nothing, but allowed Felix to express his gratitude, no matter how much it hurt. Finally, Felix put them down and took a step back to look at them. "It's just as we had always dreamed! Better! Did you see how the audience laughed? Even those stuffy old senators! Even the emperor and empress!!!" He grinned, his eyes closing briefly as if to recapture the sight of it all, the myriad feelings the night had brought. Felix's eyes locked onto both of them. "The goddess was right! You *did* save my life." His eyes glistened with the threat of tears again, but his joyful smile overwhelmed them. "It's unbelievable in a way…"

"What is?" Clara asked, finding it hard not to smile along with Felix.

"Since we were in Rome all those years ago, I wondered what it would have been like to do this together. And now that we have…well…there are no words." He rushed in and hugged Rufio and Clara again. "Well done, my friends! Well done!"

Rufio pushed off of Felix's bulk, his face red and contorted. "Nicely done?" he shouted. "Nicely done? It was anything but that!"

Felix, Clara and Electra stared at Rufio who stood before them with his back to the gaping auditorium.

Rufio stood there, his breathing rapid, his fists clenched. "You almost got everyone enslaved with your antics, Felix!"

"Me?" Felix said, his smile now a flat line beneath his beard. "What are you talking about?"

"Do you even remember what happened with Leno and his men?"

"Of course I do," Felix said. "But it all worked out in the end, didn't it?" he tapped the corona on his head.

"Oh really?" Rufio bit back. "You've moved on already? Another conquest for Felix Modestus?"

"Another victory, Rufio! And you were a part of it!"

"Those men were out to murder you on the stage!" Clara and Electra were silent as they watched the two men staring at each other.

"You're just excited, Rufio," Felix said, his hands up. "Calm down. Have a few glasses of wine."

"Shut up!" Rufio paced now, trying to gather his raging thoughts. His recent proximity to a grisly death was now harrying his mind, and he could feel himself spinning out of control. "The things I heard Leno's men say… Do you even know what they would have done to Clara and Electra, or Beatrice and Fausto for that matter? Everything was almost ruined. And I mean everything!" He glanced quickly at Clara, then back to Felix.

"But it wasn't, Rufio!" Felix said. "The performance was a success! You came back to us! You saved it!"

Rufio shook his head. "I didn't come back to save your stupid play. I came back to save your miserable life!"

Felix had no response now as his eyes narrowed and his arms crossed.

"Believe me, I wanted to leave you. All of you!" Rufio snapped. "I was ready to, until I overheard Leno's men in the Suburra, talking about Silas and what they were going to do."

"But you see? You didn't leave! You wanted to be a part of this!" Felix presented the victorious stage. "You wanted to perform with us just as the goddess had shown me! You wanted to do what was left undone all those years ago."

Rufio rubbed his jaw, and then walked up to Felix and pushed him hard so that he stumbled backward and landed on the edge of the fountain behind. "Do you even know why I left yesterday?"

"Because you were afraid of performing again." Felix waved it off. "Don't worry, Rufio! Every performer has a process. Some empty their guts before going on stage, some shit for days. You like to pretend to run away."

"You're a supreme idiot!" Rufio hissed. "The first time, I left because my mother died."

"We both know that's not entirely true, Rufio," Felix said. "You were afraid."

"The second time... - Last night! - I left because of what you and Clara did to me all those years ago."

Felix stood up from the fountain. "What we *did* to you? I'm sorry, Rufio, but we didn't *do* anything to you. You left us, remember? You left without a word. You abandoned us! Had you told us about your mother, we would have helped you, been there for you. But you just took off like a coward!"

"And wasn't that nice for you?"

"What are you talking about?" Felix demanded.

Clara stepped up, her face red with the growing shame she felt. "Felix...I told him."

But Felix put up his hand to stop her.

"You both betrayed me!" Rufio shouted. "After I left, you

got stinking drunk and slept with each other the whole of the night!"

"What?" Felix said.

"I knew it!" Electra burst out, the first words she had spoken in some time.

Felix turned to her. "Wait! No!"

"Do you deny it?" Rufio demanded. "Silas told me all about it a while ago, but I didn't quite grasp what he was saying."

"Silas. Really? You believed that shit?"

"Do you deny it?" Rufio asked again.

"No," Clara said.

"I hate you!" Electra yelled.

"What?" Felix looked quickly to Clara and then back at Rufio. "We did get drunk, yes!"

"And then you spent the night together, now that Rufio was out of the way. Stupid Rufio! Idiot Rufio!" Rufio pointed at Clara. "I loved her for the whole of my life, only to be played a fool!"

Peli, who had just come running onto the stage, spun around on the spot and barked loudly at each of them.

"No!" Felix said to the dog. "Stop or I'll cook you!"

Peli promptly plopped himself down, head on the ground.

"Rufio, I said I was sorry. Please!" Clara pleaded. She had felt such joy at seeing him return to them that night, at hearing him upon the stage. And now, like a recurring night-mare, she was losing him again, and the feeling was breaking her heart.

"Yes?" Rufio turned on Clara. "What do you have to say? What could possibly have changed?"

"Nothing. I told you Rufio, I'm sorry. Yes, we did sleep together. But we were heartbroken that you had left us. You betrayed our pact when you left us in Rome. Felix comforted me! I was so upset, and so was he!"

"What?" Felix said, only to have Electra's hand slap him hard across the face.

Clara grabbed Rufio's hands tightly, refusing to let him go, even as he tried to pull away from her. "I tried to tell you last night. I'm sorry, Rufio. What we did to you has haunted me for years since because, ever since we were children... I've...I've loved you, Rufio. And I know that you love me!"

"How can you say that you love me when you jumped into Felix's bed as soon as I was not there? How could you both do that to me?" Rufio shouted.

Electra made to slap Felix again, but he caught her wrist in his hand. "Stop hitting me, woman!"

Clara looked down at the floor, tears streaming from her eyes then.

"We didn't do anything!" Felix roared, his voice pushing the three others a pace back. "Gods, how you three are ruining tonight! Can I not enjoy this moment?" He turned to Electra. "I told you this!"

"You're a natural liar!" Electra hissed.

Felix shook his head, and turned to Rufio. "You have it all wrong, you silly farmer!"

"Silly farmer?" Rufio shouted. "Well, you're a backstabbing shit! At least I tell the truth!"

"Do you?" Felix demanded. "You know, Rufio, I think the reason you're so bitter all the time is that you regret having left us all those years ago."

"Oh really?"

"Yes! You didn't need to leave us hanging like that. You were just afraid. But the truth is that, tonight, you enjoyed performing. You loved it! You were amazing at it!"

"And you tried to take Clara from me!"

Felix was still, looking evenly at his friend. "You're so absorbed in your anger and guilt, that you didn't even hear me before. I said we didn't do anything."

"It's no use, Felix," Clara said, wiping her eyes, taking a step away from Electra, who looked like she was about to tear her hair out. "We might as well tell him the truth."

"The truth?" Felix asked.

"That's the reason I came to Rome. I wanted to speak to you about it, about what we did. I need to move on."

"All right, all of you listen to me right now!" Felix shouted again, and then turned to Clara. "I told you, we didn't do anything."

"I don't understand. I remember it!" Clara protested.

Felix shook his head. "You remember us getting drunk."

"Yes," she confirmed.

"And we did get drunk!" He turned to Rufio. "We *were* deeply upset that you left, Rufio. All of our dreams seemed to go up in smoke. BUT!" Felix eyed the three of them. "Clara then passed out. I tucked her into her bed, and stayed up the whole of the night to make sure she was all right. If you remember, we didn't have a lot of coin then, and the apartment we had rented was in a terrible tenement. The door didn't even lock! We slept in the same room, but not in the same bed. It was while I was watching over her that I came up with the idea to form my own company."

There was an awkward silence. It was deeply uncomfortable.

Rufio found he could not look at Clara or Felix, the one with her eyes wide and confused, the other his arms crossed, looking down with a grave face at all of them.

Rufio turned to look up at the temple of Venus, and wondered if the goddess was playing him for a fool, as he always believed she had done. *I can't be here anymore!* He was about to walk away when he felt someone pulling at his tunic, stopping him in his tracks.

"Don't you dare walk away!" Felix said as he dragged Rufio back to the centre of the stage. "You three, listen to me!" he said. "I have always been truthful with you, honest. Except for the dealings with Leno, but that was to protect you." He looked at Rufio and Clara who now stood beside each other. "I love you both more than I can say. You are my best friends…my family. And I mean that most sincerely."

"For all these years," Clara said, "I've thought that…that we…"

"I know I'm a fine specimen," Felix smiled, "but no, Clara, we did not. I would never do that to either of you. Do you count me such a low friend that I would have taken advantage of you? You're like a sister to me." He turned to Electra. "I'm not a monster."

Electra stared at him, her lips, her eyes, her brow unmoving as though she were a sphinx trying to stare into the heart of a passing hero.

Rufio turned to Clara. "Why didn't you go away to act in Felix's company?"

Felix put up his hand. "How could she, Rufio, when the one she truly loved was gone? Her heart was never in acting again. She went home and her father married her off."

"I didn't know what else to do." Clara buried her face in her hands, failing in her determination not to cry.

Felix stepped closer to the two of them, and put his hands on their shoulders. "I've always known you two loved each other. You just wouldn't admit it to yourselves. But the goddess brought us together again."

Rufio turned to Clara and reached up to pull her hands away from her face. "Is this true?"

She looked at him, the makeup around her eyes running in her tears, giving her a beautiful and tragic grace. She nodded.

Felix smiled to himself and took a step back.

Rufio sought Clara's pale eyes, brushing the escaped strands of her blonde hair away from her wet face.

"What is taking you all so long?" Castor asked suddenly

from the back of the stage where he and the other members of the company had just appeared. "It's not the same without you!"

"Shhh!" Electra hissed at them, freezing them to the spot as though she were Medusa herself. She turned back to look at Rufio and Clara.

So many wasted years, so much guilt... Clara thought, her heart straining as she looked upon Rufio, his round face, his pale hair and beard, and those confused eyes. She shut hers tightly, and more frustrated tears fell. "I'm so sorry Rufio," she muttered, as his hands held her face most gently.

When Clara dared to open her eyes again to look upon the man she had always loved but never dared to tell, she did not see the oddly confused look in his eyes to which she was accustomed.

Rather, Rufio Pagano was quietly determined, like a warrior returned from battle to his sweetheart.

Without another word, Rufio pulled Clara close and kissed her gently upon the lips.

And she kissed him back, not to play the part of an actor in a scene, but for her...for them.

It was as if a lifetime of mutual, silenced love cried out at last with joy at the advent of that single, lingering kiss.

It was the most honest and heartfelt action of their lives.

Felix, Electra and the rest of The Etrurian Players broke into hoots and cheers and a round of applause to which Rufio and Clara were deaf, for they only saw and felt each other until their lips parted and they smiled and laughed together, hugging each other tightly, as though they would never let go.

Felix, his chest puffed out proudly for his friends, then reached down to take Electra's hand in his, but she quickly pulled it away. He looked at her.

She scowled at him and shook her head. "I've always been an outsider."

"What are you talking about?" Felix asked.

Electra brushed back her long, dark hair and stood tall to face him. "Your friends have always dominated your thoughts after your own selfish needs. I've only ever been your slave, something to use."

"Electra, stop…"

"No!" she shouted, and the sound threatened to dampen the joy kindled between Rufio and Clara, and the celebratory leanings of the rest of the company. "I'm through!" Electra stated. "I'll not have it anymore!" she declared before turning, and setting off at a march.

"Woman, STOP!" Felix roared, and it was as though the entire theatre shook with his command.

Electra stopped and turned, but she did not approach, for she was fuming, red-cheeked and enraged, despite the pale makeup which Beatrice had applied.

Without turning, Felix held out his hand. "Clara, may I have the bracelet you are wearing?"

Clara unclasped her hand from Rufio's, and looked down at the richly-bejewelled, golden bracelet about her wrist. She had forgotten she was wearing it, but she quickly removed it, smiled to Rufio, and went to place it in Felix's hand.

Felix, his eyes never leaving Electra's, walked over to her as though he were slowly approaching a lioness. She was beautiful, strong-willed, and raging. Vibrant and full of life. He smiled a little, but her outside demeanour did not crack. Holding her eyes in his, he spoke. "My friends may have dominated my thoughts all of these years," he said.

Electra crossed her arms. *I knew it! I'll leave and never come back!* she told herself.

Felix continued. "But you…you insane, beautiful, magnificent woman…" Felix shook his head and smiled at the same time. "You have dominated my heart."

"Don't play with me," Electra growled.

Felix shook his head. "You always have…and you always will."

The rest of the company looked on, smiling and grasping each other as the scene unfolded, as what seemed impossible to them finally came to pass.

"What are you doing?" Electra demanded.

"What I have wanted to do for some time," Felix replied as he pried her right hand away from her body and slid the bracelet onto her wrist. "I intended this to be a gift for you. Clara was only keeping it safe."

"It was for the play," Electra said, looking at the rubies and emeralds upon the bracelet's surface.

"It was for you all along, Electra."

"For what reason?"

"A present," Felix stated as he took both her hands in his.

"For what?"

Felix smiled at her and in that moment, as the rest of the company gasped, like a chorus that had been waiting for the right moment, he knelt before Electra. "A wedding present."

Then, like the constant showman he was, Felix reached down to a hidden pocket on the back of his cingulum and produced a band of purest gold which he placed upon Electra's finger on her left hand, the finger that connected directly to her heart.

"This is for you, Electra…" he looked up at her wide, dark eyes, "…the woman I want to be my wife."

Electra was silent for a stunned moment, but then her dark features broke into a wide smile. She fell to her knees with Felix and kissed him such that their audience blushed and smiled and cried for all that they felt in that wonderful moment.

Rufio looked at them and then turned to Clara who was still staring at him, smiling as though she were a young girl once more. They embraced tightly and kissed again too.

Damon's flute burst into a wildly happy tune and the rest

of The Etrurian Players clapped and danced and sang with full hearts for love and for victory and the new world each of them envisioned.

Felix helped Electra up and immediately, she was embraced by Clara and Rufio who welcomed her with open arms.

Electra returned the affection for all she felt in that wonderful moment.

The days of their respective lives to that point had not been wasted after all.

Felix took a moment to look up at the temple at the top of the theatre, grateful that love had blessed him and his friends, and that they were alive to see it. But then, he spied another smiling, tender form in the dim light at the top of the auditorium, looking down on him. He smiled at her, for he now recognized the goddess from his dream.

"Thank you, Sincerity," he said beneath his breath, his heart filled with gratitude.

The goddess smiled in the one moment, and was gone the next.

Electra turned to Felix, a frown upon her face. "Who is Sincerity?" she demanded.

Felix froze for a moment, as did the others, but then Electra laughed and rushed into his arms to kiss him once again.

Though the company could not see them, or even divine their intentions, the Gods were indeed pleased as they looked down upon that singular space in the heart of Rome.

XXI

THE GODS LOVE YOU

The three days after the performance blurred into one riotous, extended victory celebration, perhaps greater than any had by a returning general of Rome.

Invitations to one party after another for the entire company were delivered constantly by smiling servants grateful for a glimpse of the players about whom everyone was speaking.

The aedile, Sextus Annius Sabinus, was thrilled to play host to The Etrurian Players and his new business partner, Felix Modestus, for they were a lively bunch of the sort that brightened his and his wife, Martia Annia's, hearts. The future did indeed look wondrous for their partnerships, for ever since the day following that grand performance at the end of the Ludi Apollinares, invitations for the company to perform had been flooding in.

Together, Felix, Electra, Sextus, and Martia went over the letters begging for The Etrurian Players to come to this city or that island to perform. They laughed and drank, and planned for a dramatic future that looked very bright indeed.

The first performance to bless their partnership was, of course, to be in Leptis Magna, the jewel of Africa Proconsularis, the home of their emperor.

"The emperor and empress will be leaving for Leptis

Magna soon, so you will have to put something together quickly," the aedile said as they sat beneath the loggia in his villa's gardens. "I've already arranged for quarters for you and the company there. Near the renovated theatre."

"Worry not, Sextus," Felix said, leaning over and patting his patron on the shoulder. "It will all work out."

"I know it will," the aedile said, smiling and kissing his wife's hand. "And I think it a good sign that all of your players have decided to stay, even after you have freed them of all obligations to you."

Felix nodded. "I never had any doubts. They are consummate professionals." *I just hope they're sober enough to finish packing!* He chuckled to himself, and Electra squeezed his hand, for she knew what he was thinking.

"Once all of the celebrations and wine, and heady toasts wear off," the aedile said, "I'm sure they'll be up for anything. I've never seen such an admirable bunch!"

Felix nodded. "That they are. Truly."

"It's a new beginning for everyone," Electra added, her adoring eyes turned to Felix.

He returned to look, and kissed her hand most tenderly.

"And what of the two who only recently joined your company?" Martia Annia asked.

"Yes, Rufio and Clara," Felix confirmed.

"Do you think they will remain? You seemed unsure about their plans."

Felix sighed. "I do not know. That will be up to them."

Electra pat Felix's shoulder tenderly. "We've learned not to question the Gods' plans," she said.

Felix nodded and smiled, if not a little sadly.

THE NEXT DAY, BACK AT THE WAREHOUSE, THE GOLDEN LIGHT of a new day poured in at every window and doorway. Here and there, members of the company rolled in inebriated sleep, having been blessed by Bacchus the previous night.

There were no more rolls of fabric, or piles of wood shavings among timbers. The scent of paint and dyes no longer lingered in the air, and the sound of hammering or cutting had been silenced. Everything was packed in crates, many of which were already upon the barge bound for Ostia from where The Etrurian Players would journey to Leptis Magna, ahead of the imperial family. It had all come together rather quickly, but as the emperor had asked for their presence there, in the city of his birth, refusing was not really an option.

"Besides!" Felix said to the company at their last banquet in the warehouse the night before. "What would our fans think if we did not show up? Half of Rome is going to Africa Proconsularis with the emperor!"

Together with his proud new patron, Felix had decided that on such short notice, they should perform something they already knew. Terence, the playwright from Carthage, would be the one they would honour, and the play, *Andria*.

"Another comedy?" Electra said, a little exasperated, but unable to hide the constant joy she felt at Felix's side.

"We're on a roll, my love!" Felix replied. "We need to keep the momentum!"

"What if we're not as funny without Rufio and Clara?" Pollux asked from down the laden table.

"And Peli!" Castor added, still laughing at the dog's final showing upon the stage and how he had clapped down on Silas's figs as if on cue.

"We'll be fine," Felix told them. "Wherever we go, whatever we perform! We're the best company in the empire, remember? For now, the Gods love us!"

They all raised their cups and drank to that, and the night thereafter was filled with revelry and joyous reminiscences.

· · ·

As Dawn's light spread through the streets of Rome the next morning, however, all was quiet. There was a peace in the air, but even more so in the hearts of the three friends who had, so long ago, made an attempt at a shared dream in that eternal city.

Felix Modestus continually thanked the goddess who had brought him there, for he had reached such heights of joy as he had never dared to imagine before, for the company, for his daring art and, most of all, for himself and the woman who was now his wife, lying next to him in the early light.

Felix watched as Electra seemed to smile in her sleep, and though the day ahead was going to be unimaginably chaotic, he took the time to thank that mysterious goddess yet again as he leaned on his elbow to watch his wife doze. He smiled to himself, for her, for how things had turned out, and for Rufio and Clara, his best friends, who had finally come back to each other.

Though he knew he had a hand in their reunion, Felix did not dare claim the victory of the heart that had occurred between them. The goddess was owed her dues for all that she had done.

They'll be all right, Felix told himself, and he leaned down to kiss his wife.

In Rufio's cubiculum, the morning light angled in from one of the high windows to warm the bed where he and Clara lay on their sides in a soft pool of sunlight, staring at each other. They had not stopped smiling for the last three days, it seemed, had not stopped holding onto each other as if afraid they would be torn apart at any moment.

The room which Felix had built for Rufio was now dismantled, as was Clara's. The pigeon hole shelf was empty, the scrolls all carefully packed, as were the furnishings from both rooms. The clothing, the bronzes, even the blank papyrus scrolls. Everything. The panels of painted scenes were dismantled too, those images of the settings of their youthful dreams.

And all of it, from both cubicula, was packed onto two wagons which Felix had rented for them to return to Etruria together.

"Please!" Felix had said. "Accept it all as a present from me!"

He would not take 'no' for an answer.

"Are you sure we shouldn't go with them?" Clara asked Rufio one last time as they lay there, a tangle of naked legs beneath the thin sheet of the bed. "We always said we wanted to act. This might be our chance."

Rufio looked at her and smiled sadly. "I won't lie. I don't want to see him go. It feels good to all be together again."

"It does," Clara agreed. "We could travel the empire, see so many new places, and be together."

"True. But, I don't know that I ever *really* wanted to be a player."

"Really?"

"I don't know. What I do know, is that I only ever wanted to be around you. I love you, Clara. I always have!" He leaned in to kiss her and hold her close, and to his great joy, she clasped him as tightly as he did her.

I still can't believe this is happening! he thought.

There was a bark from the floor nearby, and they both laughed as they turned in the bed to look down at Peli.

"He's a good boy after all, isn't he?" Clara asked.

"He certainly is." Rufio smiled at Peli who sat up and stared at the pair of them. "We're not getting up yet," Rufio told him, and Peli sat back down.

Clara was quiet for a moment, thoughtful, for things had happened quickly, and she did not want to leave anything unsaid before they left Rome. She reached out to touch Rufio's face. "I'm sorry for not being there for you when your mother died. I was too ashamed of what I thought had happened."

"And I'm sorry I left," he added. "But I never stopped loving you, Clara, even though I wouldn't admit it to myself."

"We're together now. That's what matters." She sighed and settled into the crook of his arm to squeeze a few more joyful moments from that morning calm before that big day of change.

Soon, the entire company was up and making final preparations to load the remainder of their possessions onto the barge that bobbed at its berth on the Tiber outside the warehouse. Time, it seemed, was working against them, for they could not miss the ship out of Ostia.

Felix's parade ground voice echoed loudly in the empty warehouse as he rallied his troops for the voyage.

Everyone in the company was laughing, and smiling, and excited about the new day and the new life that awaited them. They were still players, but somehow, each of them felt different, freer, more open to what lay ahead.

"To the docks everyone!" Felix said as he gripped Electra's hand tightly in his.

He had not spoken much with Rufio and Clara yet that morning, for the thought of leaving them behind stung too much. After so much joy, how could he bid them farewell again. *Gods, how I've loved seeing them!*

But he knew that, for all the joy of their reunion, for all the thrill of their victorious stage appearance, he had to say goodbye once more. When they were down at the docks, the blue waters of the Tiber flowing quickly by, Electra and Felix watched as the rest of the company took it in turns to embrace the two honorary members of their troupe.

Despite the joy all felt, there were a few tearful, heartfelt farewells as Beatrice, Fausto, and Julius, Castor, Pollux, and Damon hugged Rufio and Clara one last time before walking up the gang plank to settle themselves among the piles of secured supplies of their small, theatrical force.

Gulls circled overhead in the sunshine as Felix looked up and wondered how many farewells had occurred on that quayside over time.

"Felix," Electra said softly. "It's time, my love."

"Early this morning," he said, "I saw a young tribune bidding farewell to his woman on these very docks." Felix sighed. "I wondered how long they would be apart. I was so sad for them."

Electra kissed his cheek and held him close as they walked toward Rufio and Clara. "People in love should never be separated."

"That is why I will never let you from my side. I almost lost you." He shook his head. "That will never happen again."

She squeezed him tightly then, even as they came to a stop before Rufio and Clara.

There was a sad silence in the air between them, little left to say but for the truth.

"Well, my friends. It's time to go." Felix's eyes were glassy as he spoke, his voice a little shaky. "Are you sure you won't come with us?" He had to try one last time. "We're a better company with both of you in it."

Rufio shook his head and took Felix by his thick shoulders. "The player's life is not for me, but..."

"But what?" Felix said quickly, a hopeful look in his eyes.

Rufio smiled. "You are blessed, my friend. Keep the dream alive for all of us. And... Thank you for writing to me."

Felix grabbed Rufio and squeezed him tightly. "Thank you for coming back, Rufio. You saved us all."

Rufio could feel the shuddering in Felix's chest as he

hugged him, as if a great spring were about to burst forth from the rocky ground.

But Felix kept the tremors at bay, sighed, coughed, and released him. "Thank you."

"Let us know when you are near. Write to us often," Clara said, as she stepped up to hug Felix.

"Oh, I will!" he said before swooping her up. "And take care of this one!" He nodded toward Rufio who was giving Electra an awkward hug. "He needs you."

"I will," Clara said. She grew silent for a moment as she looked into Felix's eyes. "I...I didn't know. I feel such a fool, having thought that for so long."

Felix winked and presented himself. "It's only natural to think of that when *I'm* around!" he laughed.

Clara shook her head and laughed along with him. "Well, thank you for watching over me that night."

"You're welcome."

"You're a committed man now." Clara leaned in to whisper to him as they watched Electra kiss Rufio on both of his reddening cheeks. "She's a wonder! Don't let her go."

"Never," he said, with a sparkle in his dark eyes.

"Dominus!" Fausto called from the deck of the barge. "We need to depart!"

"Worry not, Fausto!" Felix called back. "The tides shall wait for me!" He turned back to Rufio and Clara. "You're both going back to Etruria then?"

They looked at each other, smiled, and nodded. "Yes," they said in unison.

"Make an offering to the forest nymphs for me in the place where it all started."

"We will," Rufio said. He was feeling his eyes burn then. "You had better go."

"Yes. We should go." Felix nodded. "I'll write, worry not!"

"I'll make sure he does!" Electra added, giving them each a

last hug before turning and going up the gangplank to the barge.

"Farewell," Felix said one last time, his voice shaking in his muscular frame before he turned and followed Electra.

The barge set off at once, being carried away by the flow of the Tiber as the captain and his crew pushed off the quayside with long poles to steer out into the current.

"I'm happy for you both!" Felix shouted and waved to Rufio and Clara, and at the same time, the rest of the company stood up and waved and sang to the sound of Damon's flute as The Etrurian Players departed Rome.

Along the banks of the Tiber, many citizens applauded the company as the barge sailed away, Felix Modestus and his company waving to all of them as they passed, lauded and praised for what they had given to Rome.

Rufio and Clara watched them go, silent for a time, both of them unleashing a few stray tears, for they did not know how long it would be before they saw Felix again. Indeed, they would miss all of them.

"Are you sad we're not going with them?" Clara asked.

Rufio wiped his eyes and turned to her, a great smile upon his face. "How could I be sad when we're together?"

She kissed him then, in that golden morning light, and their hearts swelled with love and gratitude.

"We should finish packing," Rufio said.

"Yes. I'm good with Rome now. I can't wait to see Etruria again!" she said excitedly. "The hills, the forest, the vines…all of it!"

As they turned to walk back to the warehouse, Peli trotting silently at their heels, Rufio began to worry about something. He had been so taken up with actually being with Clara that he had forgotten where he was taking her to!

"There's something I have to tell you, Clara."

She stopped and turned to him. "What is it?"

Her voice was soft, melodic and sincere. He looked at her, so beautiful in that morning light, the same as when they were young and running in golden fields.

"Clara, I'm not a wealthy man."

"I know, Rufio. I don't care."

"Wait. Let me finish. I'm not the best farmer either. All I have is an old, grumpy servant, a donkey, a hog, and a horse that kicks me. Actually, I don't know if I still have the horse." He shook his head. "The only dwelling I have is a tiny villa rustica with a leaky roof."

Peli whined then and placed his paw on Rufio's leg.

"Let me speak, you," he said to the dog, before turning back to Clara. "I don't have much, but I can offer you a home and my heart, which has always been yours."

Clara was silent for a moment as she looked upon him, her face, to Rufio, terrifyingly thoughtful.

He wondered for a split second if she was going to decline, but then a broad smile spanned her lovely face. "It sounds perfect!"

He felt great relief and joy at that, more than he could ever describe in all the words of all the plays he had ever read. Without another thought, he knelt before her - with Peli sitting beside him - and grasped both her hands. "Will you marry me, Clara Probita? For I have always loved you, and I want to spend all of my days with you whatever may come to pass."

Clara looked down at Rufio, unable to hide her smile at the sight of him and Peli looking up at her, most hopeful, most sincere. Then, she knelt too and wrapped her arms around him. "Yes, Rufio! I would not have it any other way!"

They laughed for all the happiness they felt, and kissed each other, unable to stop Peli from licking their faces with so much excitement as they did so. They pat the dog, stood, wiped their faces and started off again toward the warehouse, past the loaded carts which Felix had rented for them.

"I think I have just about enough money for some food for the road," Rufio mused, feeling the weight of the small purse hanging from his cingulum.

As they continued into the dark and silent warehouse, Clara put her arm through Rufio's.

"I need to visit the Capitoline hill before we leave," she said.

"Really? Why?"

She smiled. "There's something I haven't told you about my financial situation…"

EPILOGUS

The Gods bore witness to many things since the day of that theatrical success in Rome, a time when there had been more laughter and song than at any other moment in recent memory.

The Gods, such as they were, could not help but be pleased at the outcome, their divine applause led by Venus and Apollo, as well as by She who had set the events in motion. Some say the Gods do not really have a hand in the everyday lives of mortals, that they cannot be bothered. But what occurred in Rome betwixt those three friends had been a series of events worth watching from their Olympian heights.

Time, such as it was to immortals, passed. The sun rose and fell, and the moon shimmered and shone in its shifting cycles.

Every once in a while, that goddess who had played such a crucial role in the lives of those three simple mortals, strolled to the edge of Olympus to gaze down the long pathways of the sky at the lives of her favoured few.

She could not help but smile…

ANOTHER SPRING MORNING DAWNED IN ETRURIA, REPLETE WITH birdsong among the olive trees and cypresses. Tiny spheres of dew glinted upon the grass and the petals of poppies splashed across the fields. The deep, rich furrows of the farm steamed, and the sound of the cock crowing from the peak of the new outbuilding roused the rest of the livestock.

With his eyes open, and gazing out of the window of the cubiculum on the upper storey of the villa, Rufio Pagano lay in bed smiling to himself. He loved those first moments of a new day, so filled with life and possibility. It was difficult to remember how things had been before, so devoid of hope and even the smallest of joys. But he reminded himself that the Gods had blessed him, every moment of every day. At least he endeavoured to do so, to be utterly grateful lest it be taken from him.

He turned over to look at the source of all his joy and there, with her golden head upon the feather pillow beside him, tangled in soft sheets and blankets, lay Clara. He looked at her lips with an urge to kiss them, at her shoulder wanting to caress it, but decided not to. She was so peaceful and still, he could not bring himself to rouse her.

Slowly, and as quietly as possible, Rufio slipped from the bed and walked across the smooth, tiled floor to the other side where their newborn daughter lay sleeping in her tiny crib. She did not always sleep soundly, but of late, she had settled into her new life with the two of them. "You're beautiful like your mother," he whispered, fighting the urge to kiss her soft head. Rufio stepped back and went to an olive wood stool nearby to put his favourite indigo tunica over his head. He then took up his sandals, and went out of the cubiculum as quietly as possible.

On the lower level, he spotted Errol through the door of his own cubiculum, snoring away. Rufio smiled to himself and let the old man be. He had earned his time over the years, and while Rufio had been in Rome, he had not burned the place down or eaten the animals. There was something to be said for that. *The other workers can start the day's work without him*, Rufio thought. He then turned to look down the hallway to the back door. "Peli, you coming?"

Peli lifted his head from where he was sleeping, keeping watch as he always did by one of the doors. He looked at Rufio, then tilted his mismatched eyes up toward the ceiling.

"Fine then. Wait until they're awake." Rufio laughed. "I'll be outside."

Peli put his head back down, his eyes watching Rufio pick up a small pitcher from a shelf and walk quietly out into the misty light.

Ever since his time in Rome, Rufio felt immense gratitude for all that he had, for the land he worked, for the home he owned, for the familia that surrounded him, as small as it was. And every morning, he walked out of the newly rebuilt villa to observe his tiny kingdom. It was not a lot, but it was his and Clara's, and it was thriving and peaceful.

The olive and fruit groves were healthy and free of pests, and the vines had survived yet another winter and showed much promise for the coming season. The vegetable crops also promised a good yield, with even the artichokes safe from the army of moles that had once hampered them, thanks in large part to the cats Errol had obtained while he had been away. Even his horse had stopped kicking and biting Rufio as it once had.

As the sun spread its warm blanket over that dewy landscape, it was as if the Gods were smiling upon all of it, blessing it.

Rufio could hear the clip clop of Stella's hooves as she roused herself from inside the barn and ran out to join him in the early morning light.

"Good morning!" he said to his loyal donkey as she nuzzled his hip and he rubbed her furry ears. "Another beautiful day!"

Stella settled into a walk beside him as he went down the sloping hill to the spot beneath the flowering apple tree. He looked down at the two flower-covered graves and the recently commissioned grave stelae with his parents' names upon them.

"Mater… Pater… All is well. You needn't worry any more. I hope your shades are resting easily in Elysium." Rufio looked up at the sun-dappled tree and breathed deeply of the scented blooms. He then poured his daily libation of wine over the graves before lifting it to his lips and drinking some himself.

"You did your best, I know. And I shall do mine." He began to walk away, but then, with a wry smile upon his lips, he turned back to that place of shades. "You should have heard the applause though!" He couldn't help but smile. "It was wondrous!"

Rufio cocked his head to listen for any muffled and mocking laughter or clapping from within the earth, but all he heard was the gentle song of that beautiful spring morning. He turned to make his way back to the villa only to see Clara coming down the pathway holding their daughter in her arms.

Stella ran ahead to greet them and Peli, with whom she ran in circles about the field.

"Good morning, my love," Rufio said as he walked up to Clara and kissed her. "Did you sleep well?"

"She's finally sleeping through the night."

"Thank the Gods!" Rufio laughed. "For a while, I doubted it would ever happen." He reached out to accept his daughter from Clara, cradling her in his arms. "Felicia, thank you for sleeping," he said, admiring the soft, beautiful round face and blue eyes that stared up at him from beneath that downy crown of blonde. "She looks more and more like you every day," he said.

"Oh, I don't know..." Clara smiled. "Her hair might redden yet."

"As long as she doesn't have my beard!"

They laughed as they walked.

"Going to be a busy day today," Rufio mused, looking forward to the labour in a way he had never imagined. "Shall we eat?" he looked at Felicia with a wide-eyed silly face that made her little lips smile.

"Oh, she's already done that!" Clara said. "She's always hungry!"

"Then you sit, my love, and I will serve you." Rufio handed the baby back to Clara and kissed her again. They turned to go back to the villa when the distant echo of galloping reached their ears.

They turned to see a courier riding up the path toward them.

"What's this about?" Rufio wondered, standing before Clara and Felicia.

The rider came to a skidding halt, his horse rearing before he dropped to the ground.

Peli rushed in to stand beside Rufio, barking at the newcomer.

"Easy, Peli!" Rufio said, and the dog stopped immediately. "Can I help you?"

The courier reached into his leather satchel and pulled out a leather tube. "Are you Rufio Pagano?"

"Yes, I am."

"This is for you!" the man replied, stepping forward to hand Rufio the leather tube.

Rufio accepted it and tipped out a sealed papyrus scroll.

"I have urgent orders to travel back with a response before the ship leaves Pisae in three days."

"Where did the ship come from?" Clara asked.

"From Ephesus, lady. The sender spared no expense to get this to you," the man replied. "What the?" he looked down and kicked his leg as Peli lifted his own to urinate on him.

"Don't worry about him," Rufio said. "It means he likes you." He continued reading. "It's from Felix and Electra!"

"Really?" Clara came to stand beside Rufio and read along. "She's had a baby! A son!"

"Felix will be happy of that!" Rufio added with a big smile. "He kind of glosses over that...strange..."

"What's he-"

"I don't know, he-"

"What?" Clara stood back.

Rufio looked up at her. "He wants us to join him and the

rest of the company in Athenae for a performance at this year's Panathenaea!" He sighed. "He says it's a matter of life and death."

"Do you have a reply?" the messenger asked.

Rufio and Clara looked at each other.

THE END

Thank you for reading!

Did you enjoy *Sincerity is a Goddess*? Here is what you can do next.

If you enjoyed this dramatic, romantic comedy of ancient Rome, and if you have a minute to spare, please post a short review on the web page where you purchased the book, or on the Eagles and Dragons Publishing website.

Reviews are a wonderful way for new readers to find this book and your help in spreading the word is greatly appreciated.

More Eagles and Dragons Publishing novels will be coming out soon, so be sure to sign-up for e-mail updates at:

https://eaglesanddragonspublishing.com/newsletter-join-the-legions/

Newsletter subscribers get a FREE BOOK, and first access to new releases, special offers, and much more!

To read more about the history, people and places featured in this book, check out *The World of Sincerity is a Goddess* blog series at the following link:

https://eaglesanddragonspublishing.com/the-world-of-sincerity-is-a-goddess/

Become a Patron of Eagles and Dragons Publishing!

If you enjoy the books that Eagles and Dragons Publishing puts out, our blogs about history, mythology, and archaeology, our video tours of historic sites and more, then you should consider becoming an official patron.

We love our regular visitors to the website, and of course our wonderful newsletter subscribers, but we want to offer more to our 'super fans', those readers and history-lovers who enjoy everything we do and create.

You can become a patron for as little as $1 per month. For your support, you can also get fantastic rewards as tokens of our appreciation.

If you are interested, just visit the website below to watch the introductory video and check out the patronage levels and exciting rewards.

https://www.patreon.com/EaglesandDragonsPublishing

Join us for an exciting future as we bring the past to life!

AUTHOR'S NOTE

Sincerity is a Goddess is not like any other book that I have written before. It was, truth be told, quite difficult, as the setting and themes are far outside my usual realm of battles, death, and tragedy. For that same reason, however, it was crucial that I write it.

It was important to me that I change pace and write something more lighthearted, somewhat funny, yet no less dramatic and moving. At least, I've done my best to do so.

The genesis of this book goes back a few years, however. On one of our family trips to Greece, before the modern plague, I slept through the entirety of one night, an occurrence that is very rare for this sometime insomniac. During that calm, hot Mediterranean night, I dreamed this book from start to finish, the characters, the plot, and even some of the comic episodes. That had never happened before, or since. There were even real life actors in the roles of Rufio and Clara (thank you Simon Pegg and Rosamund Pike!). When I awoke, I spent the first two hours of my day hurriedly writing everything down, my in-laws looking on as if I had finally cracked.

But I hadn't cracked, thankfully. I was inspired.

I've spoken of the Muse before, and my belief that when it comes to creative pursuits, there are times when we get help from something, someone, beyond our understanding. Was it one of the Muses who gave me this story? Was it Apollo who inspired me as I slept beneath a full summer moon somewhere in the Argolid peninsula? As I've said before, I'm not a religious person in the traditional sense of the word, but when it comes to creativity, I'm certainly a man of belief in something greater. This experience cemented my beliefs.

I knew that I was meant to write this book.

I first envisioned this story as a kind of Oscar Wilde in

ancient Rome story. Something along the lines of *An Ideal Husband* crossed with *A Funny Thing Happened on the Way to the Forum* which, as it turns out, also made use of Plautus' plays and characters. Also, I have always loved the idea of stories-within-stories, or the play-within-a-play, and so Shakespeare (*Hamlet*) and the modern playwright, Tom Stoppard (*Shakespeare in Love*, and *Rosencrantz and Guildenstern are Dead*), had some influence over how this book developed.

The only thing that was really missing from my dream was the actual play the characters were going to perform.

Of course, I knew I wanted it to be a Roman play, and so there were really two classic, comic options to choose from: Plautus and Terence.

After a bit of research and reading, I went with Plautus' *Menaechmi* not just because it had the right number of characters to fit my dream, but because it is an eminently funny work, with just the right amount of nuanced misunderstanding. *Menaechmi* was, and is, believed to be Plautus' greatest work, so much so that it influenced and inspired later works, including Shakespeare's *The Comedy of Errors* and *Twelfth Night*.

Menaechmi has all of the stock Roman comedic characters, and those fit nicely with the characters in the story that I wanted to write, including the braggart, the courtesan, the parasite, the comic servant and the domineering wife. It all seemed to fall into place.

In researching and writing *Sincerity is a Goddess*, I discovered the genius of comedy, as well as the healing nature of it. With everything going on in the world, it seemed like the perfect time for this book.

Then came the research. The world of the theatre in ancient Rome is vastly different to that of the legions on the edges of the Roman Empire. I won't go into all the details about the history of theatre in ancient Rome here. That is explored in the blog series *The World of Sincerity is a Goddess*.

Briefly, however, theatre companies in ancient Rome were mostly comprised of male actors. There were female actors, some of whom became *archimima*, leading ladies, but it was quite rare, and actors in general were, like gladiators, more akin to slaves, or among the lowest social class.

For Felix's theatrical company, The Etrurian Players, I decided to include female actors, not just because it is more interesting, but also because it did happen on occasion. Where I might have strayed more from the theatrical norms of the time is in having Felix and his company of players speak their lines. Normally, in comedic performances such as pantomimes and mimes, the lines would have been sung, kind of like musical productions today. Also, masks would have been worn.

I did not use songs or masks for the performance of *Menaechmi* in the book because I wanted Felix Modestus' production to be something that Rome had not seen before. In Felix's production, there are a few female actors, the lines are spoken, and the audience can see the actors' faces. The songs come between scenes.

When it comes to the reign of Septimius Severus and the world of ancient Rome during the early third century C.E., I am in familiar territory. Fans of the *Eagles and Dragons* series may have recognized a few familiar places and faces, with surprise references or 'Easter eggs' related to that series. This was mainly a bit of fun on my part, but it also allowed me to view the period after the triumph of Severus, as well as the Ludi Apollinares, from a different, funnier angle, as opposed to the time of deception and intrigue as experienced by the *Eagles and Dragons* protagonist, Lucius Metellus Anguis. For fans of that series, I hope you enjoyed those aspects of this book.

Some readers may see some passages as too crude or bawdy but, it must be stated, the ancient Roman sense of humour could be quite crass and rude with many a reference to body parts and functions, sexual acts, and more to make us blush today. I have tried to include some of these for authenticity's sake but to not take things too far.

The incident with the dog beneath the table, however, is taken from real life. I'll leave it at that.

I am undecided as to whether or not I shall write a sequel to *Sincerity is a Goddess*. I probably will as I did very much enjoy developing these characters, the world of the theatre, and exploring the more humorous side of ancient Rome. I will always return to a world of battles, gods, goddesses and heroes, but the temptation to return to the comic side of ancient Rome is very tempting.

One thing is certain, if Felix Modestus had ignored the dream the goddess sent him, the lives of everyone in the story would not have been the same.

I'm so happy that I didn't ignore my own dream.

Thank you for reading.

Adam Alexander Haviaras
Stratford, Ontario
September 2022

GLOSSARY

adyton – the innermost sanctuary or shrine in
     the cella of a Greek or Roman temple
aedes – a temple; sometimes a room
aedile – an elected Roman official responsible
     for public buildings and public festivals
aedituus – a keeper of a temple
aestivus – relating to summer; a summer camp
     or pasture
agora – Greek word for the central gathering
     place of a city or settlement
amita – an aunt
amphitheatre – an oval or round arena where
     people enjoyed gladiatorial combat and
     other spectacles
apodyterium – the changing room of a bath
     house
ara – an altar
archimima – a rare 'leading lady' of the ancient
     theatre world
argentarius – (plur. argentarii) a banker, usually
     for the wealthy
assarius – (also as) lower denomination bronze
     coin, later minted in copper
augur – a priest who observes natural occur-
     rences to determine if omens are good or
     bad; a soothsayer
aulaeum - the curtain that was raised out of the
     floor before the stage of a Roman theatre
aureus – a Roman gold coin; worth twenty-five
     silver denarii
auriga – a charioteer

avia – grandmother
avus – grandfather

bireme – a galley with two banks of oars on
    either side
bracae – knee or full-length breeches originally
    worn by barbarians but adopted by the
    Romans

caldarium – the 'hot' room of a bath house;
    from the Latin calidus
caligae – military shoes or boots with or without
    hobnail soles
cardo – a hinge-point or central, north-south
    thoroughfare in a fort or settlement, the
    cardo maximus
cavia – the seating in the auditorium of a
    Roman theatre
cella – the inner chamber of a Greek or Roman
    temple
cena – the principal, afternoon meal of the
    Romans
cetus – (plur. ceti) a whale
chiton – a long woollen tunic of Greek
    fashion
chryselephantine – ancient Greek sculptural
    medium using gold and ivory; used for cult
    statues
cinaedus – (plur. cinaedi) the 'receiver' in a
    homoerotic relationship
civica – relating to 'civic'; the civic crown was
    awarded to one who saved a Roman citizen
    in war
civitas – a settlement or commonwealth; an

administrative centre in tribal areas of the empire

clepsydra – a water clock

cognomen – the surname of a Roman which distinguished the branch of a gens

collegia – an association or guild; e.g. collegium pontificum means 'college of priests'

colonia – a colony; also used for a farm or estate

consul – an honorary position in the Empire; during the Republic they presided over the Senate

corbita – a large, Roman merchant ship capable of carrying very large cargoes

cornicen – the horn blower in a legion

cornu – a curved military horn

cornucopia – the horn of plenty

corona – a crown; often used as a military decoration

cubiculum – a bedchamber

curule – refers to the chair upon which Roman magistrates would sit (e.g. curule aedile)

cythara – ancient harp used by Apollo

decumanus – refers to the tenth; the decumanus maximus ran east to west in a Roman fort or city

dediticii – a class of persons who were neither slaves, Latin allies, or Roman citizens

depositum – the deposit of a very large sum of money, usually with an argentarius

denarius – A Roman silver coin; worth one hundred brass sestertii

dignitas – a Roman's worth, honour and reputation

domus – a home or house

dupondius – bronze Roman coin worth two
    asses

eques – a horseman or rider

equites – cavalry; of the order of knights in
    ancient Rome

fabrica – a workshop

fabula – an untrue or mythical story; a play or
    drama

falcata – curved, single-edged blade capable of
    delivering extremely heavy blows

familia – a Roman's household, including slaves

flammeum – a flame-coloured bridal veil

forum – an open square or marketplace; also a
    place of public business (e.g. the Forum
    Romanum)

frigidarium – the 'cold room' of a bath house; a
    cold plunge pool

fullo – a launderer

funeraticia – from funereus for funeral; the
    collegia funeraticia assured all received
    decent burial

futuere – literally 'get fucked!'

garum – a fish sauce that was very popular in
    the Roman world

gladius – a Roman short sword

gorgon – a terrifying visage of a woman with
    snakes for hair; also known as Medusa

greaves – armoured shin and knee guards worn
    by high-ranking officers

groma – a surveying instrument; used for accu-

rately marking out towns, marching camps
and forts etc.

hasta – a spear or javelin
horreum – a granary
hydraulis – a water organ
hypocaust – area beneath a floor in a home or
    bath house that is heated by a furnace

ientaculum – breakfast in ancient Rome, which
    was a small meal often consisting of puls
    (porridge), or bread dipped in honey or
    olive oil
imperator – a commander or leader; comman-
    der-in-chief
insula – a block of flats leased to the poor
itinere – a road or itinerary; the journey
invictus – unconquerable

lanista – a gladiator trainer
landica – literally 'clitoris', a very big insult in
    Latin
lares – (singular lar) guardian spirits or deities in
    Roman religion
lararium – the household shrine to the lares and
    other gods
latifundium – (plur. latifundia) a large agricul-
    tural estate, typically worked by slaves
lemure – a ghost
lena – (masc. leno) a madam or pimp
libellus – a little book or diary
lituus – the curved staff or wand of an augur;
    also a cavalry trumpet
lorica – body armour; can be made of mail,

scales or metal strips; can also refer to a cuirass

lotium – literally 'urine', sometimes used as an insult

lupa – a prostitute (literally a 'she-wolf')

lustratio – a ritual purification, usually involving a sacrifice

manica – handcuffs; also refers to the long sleeves of a tunic

marita – wife

maritus – husband

matertera – a maternal aunt

mati - the 'evil eye'

maximus – meaning great or 'of greatness'

mortarium – wide Roman kitchen vessel used for grounding, mixing and pounding food

mundus stercoris – literally 'a universe of shit' as a curse

murmillo – a heavily armed gladiator with a helmet, shield and sword

nomen – the gens of a family (as opposed to cognomen which was the specific branch of a wider gens)

nones – the fifth day of every month in the Roman calendar

novendialis – refers to the ninth day

nutrix – a wet-nurse or foster mother

nymphaeum – a pool, fountain or other monument dedicated to the nymphs

officium – an official employment; also a sense of duty or respect onager – a powerful catapult used by the Romans; named after a wild ass because of its kick

paganus – meaning 'peasant', or also referring to a 'pagan'

palaestra – the open space of a gymnasium where wrestling, boxing and other such events were practiced

palliatus – indicating someone clad in a pallium, a cloak

parentalis – of parents or ancestors; (e.g. Parentalia was a festival in honour of the dead)

pater – a father

pax – peace; a state of peace as opposed to war

peregrinus – a strange or foreign person or thing

peristylum – a peristyle; a colonnade around a building; can be inside or outside of a building or home

plebeius – of the plebeian class or the people

pompa funebris – a funeral procession

pontifex – a Roman high priest

popa – a junior priest or temple servant

posca – watered vinegar (poor man's wine)

pronaos – the porch or entrance to a building such as a temple

protome – an adornment on a work of art, usually a frontal view of an animal

pugio – a dagger

pulpitum – the raised stage or dais on which actors performed quadriga – a four-horse chariot

quadrans – smallest coin denomination used
until c. A.D. 301

quinqueremis – a ship with five banks of oars

retiarius – a gladiator who fights with a net and
trident

rosemarinus – the herb rosemary

rusticus – of the country; e.g. a villa rustica was
a country villa

sacrum – sacred or holy; e.g. the via sacra or
'sacred way'

scaena frons - the stage background of an
ancient theatre

schola – a place of learning and learned
discussion

sestertius – a Roman silver coin worth a quarter
denarius

sica – a type of dagger

sistrum – (plur. sistra) instrument made up of a
handle with metal discs that one shook

skene – the theatrical backdrop of an ancient
Greek theatre

spina – the ornamented, central median in
stadiums such as the Circus Maximus in Rome

stadium – a measure of length approximately
607 feet; also refers to a race course

stibium – antimony, which was used for dyeing
eyebrows by women in the ancient world

stoa – a columned, public walkway or portico
for public use; often used by merchants to
sell their wares

stola – a long outer garment worn by Roman women

strigilis – a curved scraper used at the baths to remove oil and grime from the skin

taberna – (plur. tabernae) an inn or tavern

tabula – a Roman board game similar to backgammon; also a writing-tablet for keeping records

tabulae – the books or codices in which an argentarius would record the details of transactions

tepidarium – the 'warm room' of a bath house

tessera – a piece of mosaic paving; a die for playing; also a small wooden plaque

thermae – public baths

thymele – altar to Dionysus set in the middle of the orchestra of a Greek odeon

titulus – a title of honour or honourable designation

torques – also 'torc'; a neck band worn by Celtic peoples and adopted by Rome as a military decoration

trepidatio – trepidation, anxiety or alarm

tribunus – a senior officer in an imperial legion; there were six per legion, each commanding a cohort

triclinium – a dining room

tunica – a sleeved garment worn by both men and women

ustrinum – the site of a funeral pyre

vallum – an earthen wall or rampart with a
     palisade

velarium – (plur. velaria) awnings that extended
     over the seats of a theatre or amphitheatre
     to provide shade for spectators

venator – (plur. venatores) a hunter

veterinarius – a veterinary surgeon in the
     Roman army

vicus – a settlement of civilians living outside a
     Roman fort

vigiles – Roman firemen; literally 'watchmen'

vitis – the twisted 'vinerod' of a Roman centu-
     rion; a centurion's emblem of office

vittae – a ribbon or band

vomitorium - (plur. vomitoria) passageways in
     and out of a theatre, circus, or amphitheatre
     to ease the flow of pedestrian traffic

ACKNOWLEDGMENTS

It is almost impossible to thank all of the people who have had a positive impact on the creation of *Sincerity is a Goddess.* Though I may forget to acknowledge some, I will do my utmost to mention as many as I can remember from over the years.

Firstly, after the gods who inspired my creativity, I should acknowledge the shade of the English translator, lexicographer, and antiquarian, Henry Thomas Riley whose translation of Plautus' *Menaechmi* (c. 1878) I have made use of. Wherever he is in the Afterlife, I'm sure he's surrounded by ancient texts!

Among the living, I would like to acknowledge the work of Professor Mary Beard in the Classics Department at the University of Cambridge. Many people will be familiar with Professor Beard from her myriad books and documentaries about ancient Rome. In particular, I wanted to mention her book *Laughter in Ancient Rome: On Joking, Tickling and Cracking Up* which has helped me to gain some much needed insight into the world of Roman humour which, it has to be said, can be very different from our own ideas of what is funny. Thank you for the fascinating book, Professor Beard!

I would also like to thank Professor Edith Hall, in the Department of Classics and Ancient History at Durham University, for all the work she has done on ancient drama. I am very grateful to her for her kindness in sharing her works on ancient theatre with me during the research phase of this novel, specifically her books *Greek and Roman Actors*, and *New Directions in Ancient Pantomime*. Much gratitude to her for making her books freely accessible (www.edithhall.co.uk/books). Those of you who are interested in ancient Greek and Roman theatre and drama should check out her website.

As ever, thank you to my fellow historians and

Romanophiles in various Facebook groups who have provided some helpful direction along the way. I would like to acknowledge the group Classics International in particular for the professionalism of its members, for all the inspiration that it provides, and the kind and enriching atmosphere it maintains.

It is no secret that artists, writers included, need support from different sources, and so I would like to thank all my wonderful Eagles and Dragons Publishing patrons who support the work I do and the books I try to get out into the world. As always, I am extremely grateful for your support, and I appreciate you all. Special thanks to my patrons at the time of publication: John DeTore, Dig it With Raven, Edwin K. Gwaltney, Greg Hancock, Kathleen Larson, Bonnie Miller, and Tchavdar Tchouchev.

I would be remiss if I did not thank, as ever, my wonderful editors J.M. Dagger and, of course, A. Diassiti at Beautiful Ink Editing who always works hard to make every novel of mine that much better. I can't imagine launching a book without her!

To my good friend, David Hogan, a wonderful actor, director and producer at the Victoria Playhouse in Petrolia, Ontario, I want to give special thanks. Over the years, David has shared his enthusiasm for theatre and given me many a sneak-peek behind-the-scenes of that world in all its glory. His enthusiasm and always-optimistic attitude have long been an inspiration, so much so that much of it has, no doubt, infused the character of Felix Modestus in this story.

If I am not a stranger to the world of theatre and the arts, it is in large part due to my mother, Jeanette Dagger. As a theatre scholar, actress, singer, dialect coach, director, and producer, she made sure that I was constantly exposed to all aspects of the arts as a child. She introduced me to the theatre at a very young age and brought me to performances in different cities over the years. I was very fortunate to be exposed to so much live performance growing up. She also introduced me to the varied cast of characters that were her students and colleagues who would, inevitably, be invited to holiday dinners where impromptu performances always took place. It was sometimes terrifying for the young introvert that I was, but it seems that I was merely assimilating all of the stimuli which informed the writing of this book years later. Her input into this book during the editorial process was also extremely helpful.

As ever, I have to thank my daughters, Alexandra and Athena, for putting up with me, my mad writing habits, and the numerous history lessons I tend to give at the dinner table. This time, I also want to thank them for giving me some much-needed input when it came to the jokes I was trying to pull off as part of this process, in fiction and in life. Thank you, girls, for helping me to avoid a plethora of 'Dad jokes'!

Lastly, I want to thank my wife, Angelina, to whom this book is dedicated. She has always been there for me when at my best, and worst, and no matter what, she has been ready with words of encouragement or chastisement, depending on what was required to put me back on track. Most of all, her love and friendship are unwavering. She is my inspiration in all things, and as much as to any god or goddess, I am grateful to her.

Adam Alexander Haviaras
Stratford, Ontario
September 2022

ABOUT THE AUTHOR

Adam Alexander Haviaras is an author and historian who has studied ancient and medieval history and archaeology in Canada and the United Kingdom. He currently resides in Stratford, Ontario with his wife and children where he is continuing his research and writing other works of historical fiction.

Historical Fiction/Fantasy Titles

The Eagles and Dragons Series
The Dragon: Genesis (Prequel)
A Dragon among the Eagles (Prequel)
Children of Apollo (Book I)
Killing the Hydra (Book II)
Warriors of Epona (Book III)
Isle of the Blessed (Book IV)
The Stolen Throne (Book V)
The Blood Road (Book VI)
The Eagles and Dragons Legionary Box Set (Books 0-I-II)
The Eagles and Dragons Tribune Box Set (Books III-IV-V)

The Carpathian Interlude Series
The Carpathian Interlude - Complete Trilogy Box Set
Immortui (Part I)
Lykoi (Part II)
Thanatos (Part III)

The Mythologia Series
Chariot of the Son: The Story of Phaethon

Wheels of Fate: The Story of Pelops and Hippodameia
A Song for the Underworld: The Story of Orpheus and Eurydice
The Reluctant Hero: The Story of Bellerophon and the Chimera

Heart of Fire: A Novel of the Ancient Olympics

Saturnalia: A Tale of Wickedness and Redemption in Ancient Rome

The Etrurian Players
Sincerity is a Goddess (Book I)

Titles in the Historia Non-fiction Series
Historia I: Celtic Literary Archetypes in *The Mabinogion*: A Study of the Ancient Tale of *Pwyll, Lord of Dyved*
Historia II: Arthurian Romance and the Knightly Ideal: A study of Medieval Romantic Literature and its Effect upon Warrior Culture in Europe
Historia III: *Y Gododdin*: The Last Stand of Three Hundred Britons - Understanding People and Events during Britain's Heroic Age
Historia IV: Camelot: The Historical, Archaeological and Toponymic Considerations for South Cadbury Castle as King Arthur's Capital

Eagles and Dragons Publishing Guides
Writing the Past: The Eagles and Dragons Publishing Guide to Researching, Writing, Publishing and Marketing Historical Fiction and Historical Fantasy

Stay Connected

To connect with Adam and learn more about the ancient world visit www.eaglesanddragonspublishing.com

Sign up for the Eagles and Dragons Publishing Newsletter at www.eaglesanddragonspublishing.com/newsletter-join-the-legions/ to receive a FREE BOOK, first access to new releases and posts on ancient history, special offers, and much more!

Readers can also connect with Adam on Twitter @Adam-Haviaras and Instagram @ adam_haviaras

On Facebook you can 'Like' the Eagles and Dragons page to get regular updates on new historical fiction and non-fiction from Eagles and Dragons Publishing.

To watch Eagles and Dragons Publishing's mini documentaries and other fun videos, be sure to follow us on TikTok and subscribe to our YouTube channel.

www.ingramcontent.com/pod-product-compliance
Lightning Source LLC
Chambersburg PA
CBHW051305190726
48290CB00001B/20